AN AMERICAN GOTHIC

By

Alice K. Arenz

DEDICATION

For Dolphie—it took a while, but here it is..

ALICE K. ARENZ

ACKNOWLEDGMENTS

A big thank you to friend and fellow author, Bonnie Engstrom, for encouragement and, yes, even pushing me at times. But especially for bringing Cynthia Hickey and *Forget Me Not Romances*, a division of *Winged Publications*, together. THANK YOU, Cynthia, for taking a chance on me!
Finally, I want to thank all the members of my family for believing that my "story" wasn't over just because my health has thrown me a curve ball. God's provided the opening, who am I to disagree?.

PROLOGUE

February 20, 1998

"What's your response to the allegations that you're responsible for Amy Webster's death?"

"No comment." I shoved at the microphone and averted my face as another journalist snapped a photo. They followed me from the steps outside the apartment building all the way to my car, bombarding me with the same questions they'd asked over the last two weeks. Tears burned my eyes as I tossed a canvas tote onto the passenger seat, aware that every move I made, every expression, or lack thereof, was fodder for these bottom feeders.

A barrage of questions and accusations were hurled at me, multiple voices converging into an impossible melee of noise.

As I climbed into the driver's seat, one of the sharks

grabbed the car door.

"How did it feel to supply the little girl with the drugs that killed her?"

Heaven help me.

After a slight tug-of-war, and more than a few dirty looks, I slammed the door in their faces.

I took my time getting to my grandmother's house, going out of the way in the hope of leaving the entourage behind. It was useless, of course; they already knew everything there was to know about me.

The smell wafting out of the house took me back to memories of a childhood that hadn't always been easy. Grandmother had done her best, I knew that deep in my heart, but it didn't soften the hurt and rejection I'd often felt. I'd loved her in spite of it all and eventually learned to cope with the deaths of my parents even while she continued to grieve. Now, she was gone, and it was up to me to close the final chapter of her life.

After depositing the tote in my old bedroom, I walked through the five-room house in a daze. Where to begin?

I unloaded boxes from my car and carted them into the house, relieved not to see any reporters outside. With luck, they were off on a new assignment.

The rest of the morning was spent making stacks—things to save, things to throw, and things to donate to her church's rummage sale. Searching through my grandmother's belongings was a painstaking ordeal best done on autopilot, the emotion attached to most items almost too much to bear.

When my stomach growled, a look in the fridge was enough to make me lose my appetite. The food was in such advanced state of decay it was hard to recognize items through the mold and fuzz that clung to everything.

I slammed the door, reached for my bottle of cool water, and tried to silence the grumbling in my gut. Another half hour went by, the protests continued accompanied by some lightheadedness, convincing me of the need to eat before my blood sugar dropped any lower. Would it be possible to get to McDonalds and back without anyone hounding me?

I'd just grabbed my purse to make a run for it when there was a knock on the back door. Part of me said to ignore it, while my forever curious side decided to check it out.

"It's me, Lyssie," came the muffled voice.

I opened the door to my boss and mentor, Dr. Angela Hadley, director of Langston Children's Center.

"It appears your retinue is gone," she reported, scooting into the kitchen. "Mine, however, were hot on my trail. I'd no idea this city had so many reporters!" She held up two bags with the McDonalds logo. "Had a feeling I'd find you here, so I took the initiative and brought you some food."

I tried to clear some space on the table so we could use it for lunch. A copy of *Time* on top of a stack of newspapers fell to the floor, revealing an envelope with my name scrawled across it. Taken aback, I returned the papers to the table and sank onto a nearby chair, staring at the envelope.

Dr. Hadley placed a salad and packets of dressing in front of me. "Water?"

I nodded toward the counter where I'd set a cooler filled with bottles. Not wanting to do so, but feeling compelled at the same time, I lifted the envelope off the stack. Beneath it, the headlines on the top newspaper screamed—*LOCAL INTERVENTION WORKER ACCUSED IN CHILD'S DEATH*. A picture of me being led away by a police officer accompanied the article.

I hurled the paper across the room, barely missing Dr. Hadley as she returned with our water bottles. Without a word, she set them down and tried to appear nonchalant as she folded the next newspaper and placed it beneath the table. She hadn't been quick enough—*LYSETTE DANIELS IMPLICATED IN CHILD'S DEATH* burned into my retinas.

"Lyssie?" Angela Hadley held out her hands, her compassionate expression making it difficult not to respond.

I put my hands in hers, bowing my head as her clear voice rang out in the stillness of the house.

I shouldn't have, but I tuned out her prayer. When she was finished, I withdrew from her grasp, my attention returning to the envelope. After a deep breath, I pulled open the flap. I read the enclosed note then gazed up at my boss in amazement.

"What?" she asked, holding her hand out for the small slip of paper. "*I will turn darkness into light before them, and make crooked ways straight,*" she read aloud. "Um, that's Isaiah, I think."

I removed my fork from the plastic wrap and opened the lid on the salad.

"This is going to be over before you know it and you'll be back at work—"

"I'm not going back."

"The kids miss—"

"I'll never work with children again. I'm going to

take a long vacation, stay at Tan-Tar-A down at Lake of the Ozarks. My inheritance will allow me to do that." I poked at the salad, wondering if I'd actually be able to eat it without getting sick.

"A sabbatical will help get your head together." Taking a bite of her own salad, Dr. Hadley watched me with concern. "So, you got the house sold. Is it a thirty-day escrow?"

I nodded but refused to depart from the original topic. "I won't return to Langston."

"Lyssie—"

Tears burned in the corners of my eyes. "It's always been my dream to write. A mystery, suspense, maybe an old fashioned gothic. Give me a mystery filled with clues to solve and I'm happy. It's a lot better than being the headliner in real life."

"Elizabeth Webster is throwing up a diversion—"

"I'll sit in the sun at Ha Ha Tonka and write, then sleep and dream without being afraid. Maybe even fall in love at first sight and live happily ever after!"

"You always were a romantic," Dr. Hadley came over and took me into her arms. "You'll get through this. We all will."

While I cleaned up after lunch, Dr. Hadley shuffled through the stacks of newspapers remaining on the table.

"Isn't this the family of the girl you roomed with in college?"

I looked at the headline she indicated— *FOXXE/COURTNEY FAMILIES SUFFER ANOTHER TRAGEDY.*

"Must be another report on the death of Pier's father last month. There's been talk it wasn't an accident." I dried my hands on a towel. "I've been meaning to send her a card."

Later, after Dr. Hadley had gone, I returned to the kitchen and picked up the newspaper with the story on the Foxxe family. As I read the article, a strange tingling sensation etched its way up my spine.

"Edward Foxxe, CEO of Foxxe Industries, died just two weeks ago when the car he was driving missed the Mull's Hill turn south of Bristol and plummeted into the valley below. Ryan Foxxe, his son, was gravely injured in what is now being considered a possible deliberate act by a person or persons unknown.

"On the heels of this tragedy, Dylan Courtney, model and inspiration of FoxCo Toys' Dylan Doll series, has been reported missing by family members. Miss Courtney was last seen leaving the corporate offices of Foxxe Industries approximately two weeks ago, just days before the mysterious traffic accident that killed her stepfather, Edward Foxxe. Miss Courtney is also a "person of interest" in regard to the arson of Garrett Law Offices, attorneys for Foxxe Industries. While there is no apparent connection linking the two incidents, police indicated that they will be looking into Miss Courtney's activities prior to her disappearance . . ."

Chapter 1

She fled in the darkness, thankful for its cover and praying the moon would remain hidden behind the scattering clouds. She dared not stop even for the moment it would take to catch her breath or get a sense of her bearings, for she could sense the danger as clearly as one could feel the electricity in an oncoming storm. And like that storm, the torrent about to strike out at her was equally as frightening . .

.

"Not again!" I looked up to find several people staring in my direction, their expressions instantly bringing heat to my cheeks. Embarrassed, I held up my mechanical pencil, showing them the reason for my sudden outburst. My awkward smile did little to assure them of my sanity.

After digging in my backpack for the packet of lead I'd been going through all morning, I remembered using the last of it about an hour ago. And the pen I discovered at the bottom of the bag proved to be as dry as the proverbial bone. Though I may not be able to write, it didn't mean I couldn't get comfortable and soak in the view of one of my favorite vacation haunts: Missouri's Ha Ha Tonka State Park.

The skeletal remains of Robert Snyder's 'dream' castle had fascinated me many years ago with its scorched and burned timbers and the charred walls where the fire had tried to burn through the stones themselves.

Looking down into the ruins of the 60 room mansion always gave me a chill—and an overpowering urge to create, to rebuild the magnificence of the place if only on paper.

I imagined the site as Snyder had seen it in the early 1900s and sensed the power of his dream to turn the area into an American version of a European estate complete with a castle. How excited he must have been when construction had begun, and how sad he had not lived to see its completion.

I remembered the faded, water-pocked photographs that had once been on display at the site. The grandeur of the completed mansion was surely everything Snyder had dreamed—his son would have seen to that. What a tragedy that it was all destroyed twenty years later when stray sparks from a fireplace set off an inferno.

I stretched my legs out before me and gazed up at the towering sandstone walls that were not only stark and forlorn but also beautiful and possessed of a strange and compelling magic. Writing had always been a passion of mine, and this place added to that desire in a way nowhere else ever had.

"Why aren't you writing?"

I winced at the sound of the voice, then gazed up into the petulant face of Pier Foxxe.

"Are you enjoying yourself?" I asked, deliberately ignoring her question.

She plopped down onto the bench next to me. "It's hot, and I'm thirsty."

I pulled the last bottle of Aquafina from my bag and handed it to her. I could have reminded her that it hadn't been necessary for her to come with me today but held my tongue. When I'd made the same suggestion the night before, it seemed to upset her. Her reaction hadn't made sense to me. I simply accepted it as one of Pier's many quirks.

"You wouldn't have to sit here mooning over this burned out shell if you'd come home with me," she said after chugging the water. "Oh, I, know, it's the romance of the thing, the inspiration. But honestly, Lyssie, what you really need is Foxxemoor."

I'd come here to get away from everything and everybody. So, when Pier walked up to my table as I was eating dinner two nights before, it hadn't been the most pleasant surprise. I'd last seen her at our college graduation a little over three years ago and couldn't believe the coincidence that brought us to the same resort. It's not that I wasn't happy to see her again, just that I hadn't wanted *any* company.

"Let's walk around a bit." My suggestion was greeted by an exaggerated sigh. I looked up to find her grinning at me. She grabbed my bag then made a gesture for me to lead the way.

I drank in the scenery as we wandered over the pathways, lingering at each site and dreaming of the way it must have been. Though the estate had been built in the 1920's, I placed it further back in time, back to an age of dark, foreboding mansions, young, impressionable governesses, handsome, brooding lords of the manor, and the threat of danger which was forever present and waiting to descend—the traditional setting for a Gothic, romantic suspense novel, my particular passion.

Pier's tolerance was wearing thin, and rather than force the issue, I decided to forgo investigating the caves, sinkholes, and natural bridge. Besides, I was getting hungry and knew that Pier was likely to be as well. I suggested she start for the car then turned back for a final look at the ruins.

As I gazed up into the clear, azure expanse, I spied two hawks circling high above me. They soared through the air, their wings outspread, their small heads bent down, their eyes, I was certain, alert to the movement of prey. I watched as they dipped and crossed one another's paths, their graceful beauty as awe-inspiring as the ruins of Snyder's castle. I sighed in deep contentment.

"I didn't mean to rush you," Pier said as I climbed into my car.

"You didn't." Our joined laughter eliminated the awkwardness of a moment before.

On the drive back to the Tan-Tar-A Resort, Pier once again plied me with reasons why I should accompany her home to Foxxemoor.

"What you need is the real thing—the old house, rambling estate, and enough angst to carry you through several novels. Foxxemoor is a sprawling mansion well over a hundred years old. Even better, it's half empty.

You'd have all kinds of places to explore, dank, dark staircases, and mysteries waiting to be imagined and solved. Not only is it the perfect setting, but you would be staying as my guest. You can't beat free room and board with the right atmosphere thrown in as a bonus. It's an offer you can't refuse."

"Pier, we've been over this."

"Not really. Whenever I mention it, you change the subject." She twisted around in her seat to look at me. "I know something's going on that you don't want to talk about. I get it and promise not to pry. But let's be honest here. I've seen your expression every time you talk about going home. It's obvious you're not ready for that, and there's no way you can continue to stay at Tan-Tar-A. You said you're on sabbatical, right?"

"Um, sort of." I kept my eyes on the road, wishing I could see her face. Even then it was doubtful I'd be able to read what was going on inside her head. She'd always been adept at hiding her emotions.

"Langston's not expecting you back." She pressed on.

I drew in a deep breath and nodded. Langston Children's Center was the last place I wanted to go. Not after what happened with Amy . . .

"And we've already established that you're not ready to return home."

"With everything that's going on with your family, I'm the last thing they need."

"Maybe. But you're exactly what *I* need. Since my father's death, there hasn't been a moment's peace. My stepmother is a handful, and my brothers . . . There's no one for me, Lyssie, and there hasn't been since Mother died three years ago. Running into you is the best thing that's happened to me since, well, forever." Her voice broke on the last statement, and my heart went out to her.

Yet how could I go someplace I was sure to feel uncomfortable? In the old days, I'd pray for guidance. But that was before . . .

"You've no idea what it's been like, Lyssie."

Pier's tight voice brought me back to the present.

"The papers, tabloids, news people in general," she gulped. "All the innuendo and nasty conjectures plastered on local and national news. There's been no consideration for my family, for our loss, for Ryan's injury. Foxxe Industries and FoxCo Toys are traded on Wall Street, so I guess that means the founding families have no right to privacy."

Keeping face had always been important to Pier, so I knew how difficult this must be for her. I also knew when to keep quiet.

When we'd been paired as roommates our freshman year at college, we hadn't gotten along very well. The beautiful daughter of a famous industrialist forced into living with a plain, ordinary person wasn't what she'd had in mind. But by the end of that first semester, we were friends and ended up rooming together all four years. After graduation, we'd kept in touch on a fairly regular basis until this last year. There had been fewer and fewer notes, dwindling down to nothing as our lives became more and more complicated.

"I know it must all sound bizarre and totally unreal." From the corner of my eye, I saw her reach out to the dashboard as if to steady herself. "Then, in the middle of all the craziness, Dylan pulled a disappearing act. Can you imagine? Like we didn't have enough to worry about!"

I nodded but didn't comment.

Dylan Courtney was the daughter of the Foxxe's partner in FoxCo Toys, the raven-haired girl whose beauty had been the model and inspiration for their famous Dylan Doll series. Dylan's lovely face had been among the family photos that had graced our dorm walls. Always there in the background, surrounded by Pier and her twin older brothers, Dylan had become an enigma to me. Pier chose to reveal nothing about her— nothing except the catch in her voice whenever Dylan was mentioned.

As we pulled up to the check-in booth at the resort's entrance, a family walked in front of the car, a little girl trailing behind.

"She's about Dee's age." Pier's comment was little more than a whisper.

I was about to ask who Dee was when a horn sounded behind me, making me realize I was holding up the line.

The silence in the car was palpable as I hunted for a parking place. Pulling into a spot on the upper level beneath the main building, I heard Pier release her seatbelt before I'd shut off the car. I turned to find her gray-green eyes studying me.

"What?"

"You're writing a romantic suspense, a Gothic with a spooky house and the poor heroine facing mysteries and danger around every corner."

"Y—yes."

"You've a hero that's as dashing as he is dangerous, full of angst with a capital 'A'. Right?"

"You seem to have the genre down pretty well." I

agreed with reluctance.

Pier caught hold of my hand.

"When we were roomies, did I ever steer you wrong? Ever treat you in any way other than with respect?"

"Pier, I don't—"

"Answer the question, please," she winked.

"Ok," I sighed. "Um, there was that one time with Hank Morgan—"

She released my hands, laughing. "Hank Morgan! The one time I didn't screen a guy to see if he met your religious requirements! Ok, now. Seriously, Lysette Daniels, answer my question." Her expression was more sober than I'd ever witnessed before.

"Alright," I said slowly. "Through all the wackiness, all those blind dates you arranged, no, you never steered me wrong. Except for Morgan," I added with a mischievous grin.

"Then believe in me now, Lyssie. Come to Foxxemoor. It'll be great. You'll have time to write, night or day, completely free of cares. When you want a break, we can go riding on those horses Gray lives for, or we'll walk the trails, or take a swim in our pool. Foxxemoor has it all, the atmosphere for your book and a friend who is dying to give you a break." She looked at me anxiously. "Sure, I've selfish motives for wanting you there, but you can't deny it would be the ideal location and situation for you as well."

As we got out of the car and headed for the restaurant, I agreed to think about her invitation.

But as we sat down to dinner, I had the feeling that no matter what I might want to say or do, I would be going to Foxxemoor.

Chapter 2

Diana found herself by the edge of the lake just as the fog rolled in to surround her, confusing her sense of direction and making her escape doubtful. She reached her hands out before her, her eyes straining to pierce through the shroud that threatened to entrap her . . .

The moment I agreed to go home with her, Pier began painting a picture of Foxxemoor and the town where she grew up. It wasn't long before I felt the peace and serenity of Bristol, the people who lived there, and how supportive they'd been through the series of misfortunes that struck her family. Her description of Bristol was oddly reminiscent of my fictional village of Craven, and I was intrigued by the similarities. As for the estate of Foxxemoor, I filed away every detail for future reference, altering reality to fit my purposes.

Foxxemoor lay in the heart of the rolling hills of Missouri, nestled in a valley surrounded by a generous expanse of woods, rich farmland, and lush grazing plains. The small town of Bristol, site of the original FoxCo Toys factory, was less than twenty miles from the entrance gates to the Foxxe estate. Because of the generosity and patronage of more than four generations of Foxxes, the town contained most of the amenities of a larger city—two shopping centers, a Super WalMart, a multiplex movie theater, a community pool, and a parks and recreation department which organized activities for the area year round.

"My great-great grandfather started it all," Pier told me with pride. "It was one of the few estates to not only withstand the ravages of the Civil War, but to grow in the process."

She led me down the avenue of oaks which lined the half mile drive from the main highway to where Foxxemoor stood triumphantly at its end. The final approach to the mansion was a large driveway which encircled a rock garden with a stone and marble fountain at its center. To the right of the drive was the old carriage house, now a four car garage, and on the left, a short lane which led to the stables. At the top of the circle sat the front third of the great house, with a wing going off at an angle on either side.

"People say the house looks like a giant, prehistoric bird," Pier laughed, her grey-green eyes twinkling with mischief. "Ryan christened it 'Bird of Prey' after the Klingon warships from the old *Star Trek* TV series."

The front portion of Foxxemoor was the original building, both wings having been added in the latter part of the 1800's. The top floor of the three-storied mansion, originally designed as servants' quarters, was now used for storage. The second floor contained apartment-sized suites for the family, each consisting of a bedroom, dressing/sitting room, and its own bathroom.

The main floor was filled with large, airy rooms designed for both beauty and comfort. The original part of the house held a library, den, and a modern living room complete with the latest in electronic equipment. The north wing consisted of the kitchen areas and family dining room, and the south held a formal dining room and ballroom which were rarely used.

"I don't expect you to memorize the layout, Lyssie," Pier had told me as we ate ice cream on Tan-Tar-A's Arrowhead Deck, which overlooked the Lake of the Ozarks. "But it'll give you food for thought."

The vastness of the house boggled the mind. I'd read about such mansions but never actually stayed in one. Now here I was, following Pier's hot red Mustang convertible, on my way to what I would liken to a castle. Maybe Pier was right; why leave it to imagination when the real thing was available to inspire my creative juices?

Realizing I'd left my tape recorder running while my mind strayed, I reached over to press rewind. As I kept my eyes on the road, I listened to the few minutes of manuscript I'd dictated.

The nuance and threat of danger was there, but something was missing. I replayed the piece, trying to catch the omission to correct it, but again found my mind wandering.

The Foxxe household was quite large. Both her brothers lived at home, and, of course, there was her stepmother, Margaret Courtney Foxxe. In addition to a live-in housekeeper and her husband, the gardener, there was a cook and a maid who came in from town each day. Then, finally, there was Dee.

Deidre Courtney, Dylan's six-year-old daughter, had been Pier's responsibility for the last five months—the reason Pier had been so desperately in need of a vacation. Pier stated that since Dylan's disappearance, the child had run wild.

"Skittish as an untamed colt is how Gray describes her," Pier smirked. "She's always been a bit precocious, but the most loving little kid I've ever known. Then Margaret decided that we needed to stop 'coddling' Dee," she stated with derision.

When local authorities ceased their active investigation into Dylan's disappearance six weeks earlier, Margaret Courtney Foxxe also pulled her team of private investigators from the case. A week later, without consulting the rest of the family, Margaret arranged a memorial for her daughter and erected a stone for Dylan in the Foxxe family cemetery.

"She said it was to help Dee, that after nearly five months and no word—" Pier's voice caught, making it obvious the memory was painful. "Then out of the blue, Margaret hired a nanny and sent me off to Tan-Tar-A. Not that I didn't need the vacation, I just wasn't sure about leaving Dee."

Pier felt that as Dee's grandmother, Margaret should have been responsible for caring for the child all along.

"But it's obvious she isn't the best example for an impressionable little girl. Just look how Dylan turned out!"

Concerned for Dee's welfare, Pier stepped in, moved Dee into her suite, and tried to give the little girl the love she so badly needed. Dee reached out to her 'Aunt Pier' at first, but gradually, rebellion had taken over to the point that not even Pier could reach her.

I wondered about Dee's father, who he might be, and where he was, but I didn't ask. I knew that if it was something Pier thought I should know, she would eventually get around to telling me. So I waited, my curiosity and imagination running as wild as she'd said the child had become.

As for her brothers, Pier spoke very little about them. She mentioned how Ryan's spine had been injured in the car accident that killed their father. He could walk a little, but, because of the pain it caused, he preferred to remain in a wheelchair for the time being.

Ryan, she said, was the brains, Gray the brawn. When I'd asked what she meant, she explained that Ryan was involved in the inner workings of Foxxe Industries and that Gray was content with running the home farms and working with the horses.

"There's more to it," she said with a shrug, "But I've never really known what all it entails."

For Pier, happiness and contentment lay in ignorance of the day to day operations of the family business. The fortune was there, and her future was secure because of trust funds established at her birth. These wise investments gave her the freedom to live without the necessity of having to support herself.

"I would've left Foxxemoor a long time ago if . . . ." She tossed her long brunette hair and shrugged again. "For a little word, 'if' holds so many connotations. Ah, well," she sighed. "Things will be so much better with you there, Lyssie!"

While Pier always possessed an enormous ego and had a high opinion of herself, she'd also been a kind and generous companion during our college years. Now, a completely different picture was forming of my old roommate. I was beginning to see her more as a trapped and desperate individual—much like the heroine of my story. There was one big difference between them: Diana wanted to solve the mysteries of *Craven* and live to tell about them; Pier wanted to escape.

The whirring sound of the tape at the end of the roll brought me back to the present. I switched the machine off, reprimanding myself for daydreaming rather than staying on task.

I noticed Pier's left turn signal and realized we must be nearing the final stage of our journey. Sure enough, a sign confirmed that Bristol was straight ahead.

I took the turn off the highway onto the blacktop that led into town and eventually to Foxxemoor Lane. Watching the scenery slide past, I noted that the majority of farms and houses were well cared for and looked quite prosperous. The fields had a fresh, spring green look, the young plants of corn, soy beans, and others I didn't recognize, looked fresh and healthy under the beautiful June sky.

We drove on through the center of Bristol, past churches, supermarkets, a McDonalds, Applebee's, several gas stations, a handful of homes, and were once again in the country. I took particular note of a beautiful, old-fashioned church on the outskirts of town and filed away service times listed on the message board that sat near the side of the road.

I felt a thrill of excitement building as miles went by. How could I have taken so long to accept Pier's invitation? Every new piece of information about the estate had intrigued me to the point that, by the time of my acceptance, I'd become a Foxxemoor trivia junkie. Like an addict hooked on the latest drug, I'd determined that nothing should be withheld to hinder my addiction.

Not even Pier's strange behavior following the call to her family had affected my decision. Her comment that it was better as a *fait accompli* had been a little disturbing, but I refused to look at it as some sort of omen or silent warning. I didn't stop to pray or ask God for guidance as I might have done once. And since there were no alarms sounding, I figured going with Pier was a safe choice.

We traveled down the blacktop road at sixty miles per hour, a good clip on such a narrow road. I slowed down around the curves and near the tops of the hills, afraid I might come upon a tractor or other slow moving vehicle. Pier, in contrast, seemed unaware of the possible danger. In fact, she appeared to speed up. I lost sight of her a couple times but wasn't worried. I knew from her descriptions that the lane into the Foxxemoor estate was well-marked, and I was unlikely to miss it.

About ten to fifteen minutes after we'd left Bristol, we rounded a bend in the road that led steeply up the side of a hill. I knew from Pier's description that at the crest of the hill the road took a sharp right then plunged steeply down into the valley. It was somewhere near this area that her father lost control of his car. Keeping this in mind, I once again reduced my speed and watched in alarm as the fiery red Mustang kicked into passing gear and sped off at breakneck speed.

I steered my car carefully around the curve as I drank in the breathtaking view from atop the hill. The vibrant shades of green pastures, golden wheat fields, and lush wooded areas took my mind off Pier's recklessness and reminded me of the reasons I'd decided to follow her to Foxxemoor. Here my imagination could run free; here was a place I could build my world of rich green valleys, tranquil lakes, and a house called Craven where dangers lurked around every corner. This was inspiration, where reality lent itself to the world of make-believe, taking a little from each to create and mold into whatever I desired. Here I would create lives on paper and try to forget the reality and devastation I had left behind.

Pier waited for me at the entrance to the Foxxemoor estate. She stood leaning against her car, her head thrown back, her face to the sun. As I pulled beside her, she turned to look at me, shielding her eyes from the glare reflecting off the cars.

"What took you so long?"

Rather than comment on what I thought of her driving, I said that I'd been enjoying the view.

"It's beautiful, isn't it? This part of the state has the best there is to offer by way of scenery. I'm not immune to it, you know, just used to it. You find passion in the scenery; mine comes from the road itself. There's nothing more exhilarating than taking the hills and curves at a fast clip, and this baby handles it all so smoothly." She patted the hood of her car as she grinned mischievously. "It's even better when the top's down."

"A little dangerous, though."

She laughed. "Depends on your perception. Besides, facing danger can make life more exciting. It's why amusement parks do so well. They offer an element of danger from the roller coasters rocketing over tracks that seem to bend and sway under the weight of the cars. It's the rush that keeps people going back for more. They may be terrified, but they can't get enough of it."

"Perhaps. I've heard the same thing in relation to abusing drugs, the danger and rush, but it doesn't lessen the insanity of putting your life on the line. I figure there's no reason to invite disaster."

"I'll bet you never ride roller coasters, do you?"

Her tone was derisive, but I chose not to take it seriously. "I don't like heights." I answered simply.

"Pity." Pier sighed then gazed down the oak-lined lane before us. "I suppose we should get to the house. Mrs. Merrick will wonder what's keeping us. And if Margaret's back, she'll be impatiently waiting to play hostess. I could care less about her, but Mrs. Merrick's a dear, and I don't want to worry her." She started to climb back into the Mustang, changed her mind, and came over to my car. She bent close to the window and peered in at me.

"Remember that whatever happens, whatever might be said, first and foremost you're my friend and guest. I know this sounds odd, but I can't explain right now. Just keep in mind that Foxxemoor's a third mine." She sauntered back to her car, climbed inside, and gunned the engine. The Mustang leaped through the open wrought iron gates in response, reminding me of the horse for which it was named.

The lane was exactly as I'd imagined it, the ancient

oak trees towering above on either side to form a kind of dome high above us. The sun played a game of peek-a-boo, appearing now and again in the break of entwined limbs then darting out of sight to leave the lane in cool shadows.

As we neared the end of the drive, my breath caught in my throat. Neither Pier's description of Foxxemoor, nor my imagination had been accurate. Somehow, I had gotten the impression of a dark, brooding mansion whose true grandeur was from a bygone era. Instead, I found myself looking at a manor home befitting a large southern plantation, its clean white paint gleaming in the summer sun. Even the pale bricks that fronted the main portion of the house looked freshly scrubbed, and the chain that held the porch swing sparkled in the sunlight.

I pulled up to the garage beside Pier, and looking in the rearview mirror, could see how the house had a vague resemblance to a bird. Recalling her brother's nickname for their home, 'Bird of Prey,' I laughed.

"Glad to see you're in better humor." Pier stood close to my car door. "What do you think so far?"

"It's—magnificent." I climbed out of the car and turned to stare at the mansion. "Completely overwhelming."

Pier smiled, obviously satisfied with my reaction. "I warned you that mere words couldn't do Foxxemoor justice. Wait till you see inside."

I followed her up the drive, paused for a moment to gaze in wonder at the profusion of color in the rock garden and marvel at the beauty of the fountain, the stone cupids laughing up at the trickle of water cascading over them. The sound of the dancing water, birdsong and far-off hum of a tractor filled the afternoon air, lending a magical quality to our approach to the house. My senses were filled to bursting, my fingers itching to take pen in hand and write down all that my eyes could see and imagination could build. I just hoped my brain wouldn't overload and lose everything before I had the opportunity to get it on paper.

On the porch, I ran my hand up the smooth chain links that held the bench swing. The chain was new and cool to my touch, the swing recently painted a cobalt blue to match the shutters which hung on every window facing the drive.

We entered the overlarge doorway through a modern screen door. The main door was pushed against an inside wall of a vast entryway and opened onto a wide hallway that appeared to stretch from the front to the back of the house. Large windows with sheer curtains allowed for plenty of natural lighting even with the numerous shade trees which practically surrounded Foxxemoor. The curtains moved gently back and forth with the light breeze coming in through the opened windows. The fresh air and spaciousness added to the enchantment and dream-like sensation I'd felt since first seeing the mansion.

The floor was made up of black and white tiles, squares geometrically forming a diamond pattern which caught your eye upon entering and forced it to follow the rows as far back as you could see. The cream-colored walls held mirror-backed sconces with fragrant candlesticks whose delicate scent drifted on the breeze from the windows. Scenic paintings separated each set of sconces with views of different parts of the estate, each showing intricate detail and attention to even the most minute object. My eyes wandered over the paintings, studying them and realizing they were from another age.

"A distant relative painted them sometime in the late 1800's. They *are* interesting, Lyssie, but if you give so much attention to everything you see, we'll never get out of the foyer!" Pier placed a gentle hand on my arm and pulled me along the hallway. "First thing to do is let people know we're here, give them advanced warning to be on their best behavior."

I was entranced by the beauty of the marble staircase that was located several feet to the right of the front door. The banister was highly polished oak with a scrolled pattern which followed the curving staircase to the second floor landing and hall, curved again, then continued its journey to the next floor.

I felt as if I'd entered an enchanted world where everything beautiful converged in a feast for the eyes and senses. I'd never been to such a place as this in reality—TV, movies, and books had given me images of such things, but my imagination could never have come up with anything like this.

"It's unbelievable." I spoke in a half whisper, totally awed.

"Some things are as they always were, others, well, Margaret's additions can be a little gauche. She won't be criticized, however, and refuses to allow Foxxemoor to retain its dignity and integrity. I'm not against change, of course, modernizing is great, but Mar—" Pier stopped in mid-sentence as a striking, older woman appeared from a room to our left. Her pale blue eyes and rich black hair told me immediately that this was

Dylan Courtney's mother, Pier's stepmother, Margaret Courtney Foxxe.

"I thought I heard voices." Margaret's cool smile lit briefly on Pier then was directed at me. "And you must be Lysette Daniels, Pier's old friend from college. What a marvelous coincidence that you two chose the same vacation spot."

She held her hand out to me, and I took it. The warmth of her hand belied the coolness of her smile, and I gazed deeply into Margaret Courtney Foxxe's pale blue eyes where I saw hesitation and a hint of the friendship she really wished to convey.

I noted the flecks of silver in her short, black hair, the fine lines around her eyes and lips and realized that while still a beautiful woman, Margaret was a good deal older than she first appeared. At approximately five-ten, slim and healthy looking, I'd guessed her to be in her early fifties when I'd first seen her; now I realized I was several years off target.

"I'm glad Pier informed us you were a writer, my dear, else I'd be wondering if you were always this—"

"Rude?" Pier offered flippantly.

I felt the heat of embarrassment stain my cheeks as I withdrew my hand from hers. "I was staring, wasn't I? I'm sorry, I, uh—"

Margaret laughed. "Please, don't apologize. I'm sure you meant nothing by it. I simply felt a little awkward under your scrutiny." She waved us into the room and motioned for us to sit down.

I sat on a nearby couch, sinking so far back into the depth of cushions it felt as if I was being swallowed. Conscious of her eyes upon me, I didn't indulge in my usual tendency of studying my surroundings. Instead, I turned my attention to my hostess while I carefully sought Pier's whereabouts from the corner of my eye.

"We haven't had real company at Foxxemoor in quite some time, so this shall be a treat for us. We entertain clients and investors, but one can hardly term them as friends. I believe it's time we start reclaiming old friendships and begin living again," Margaret smiled as she seated herself in a warm blue, brocade chair opposite me. She daintily crossed her legs, pulling the hem of her black skirt level with the top of her knees. "How was your drive?"

"Long." Pier's tone remained flippant and, as she came into view, I could see that her body language matched the tone.

"It might be a long trip, but well worth it," I quickly interjected. "The scenery is magnificent."

Margaret's eyes left her stepdaughter and returned to me, the look of reproach for Pier's behavior finely drawn on her features. "We have some lovely country here, and I believe you'll find that our estate embodies the very best there is to offer. We're quite proud of our holdings—"

A "harrumph" from Pier received a quick, sidelong glance.

"I hope you will take advantage of our hospitality and explore to your heart's content. We'll make our house and grounds open to your discerning eye, Miss Daniels—or may I call you Lysette? Good," she nodded, "and you shall call me Margaret. No need for formalities." She looked at the gold watch on her arm and shook her head. "I'd no idea it was this late. I'm sure you're both exhausted and would like time to rest and freshen up, so I'll excuse myself." She rose and looked over to where Pier stood before a marble fireplace mantel. "We've made up the suite next to yours, Pier. I figured you'd both feel more comfortable knowing the other was nearby." The look exchanged between the two of them hinted at some deeper, hidden meaning behind the words, but I was at a loss to guess what it might be.

At the door to the room, Margaret turned back around. "Oh, and Deidre's been established in her own suite."

Pier didn't answer, just watched the older woman leave. The antagonism she felt for her stepmother was apparent. It was obvious she did little, if anything, to hide it. In contrast, Margaret appeared completely unaware of Pier's feelings, she was coolly polite, nothing to hint at the underlying currents between them. I had to admire Margaret's reserve and wondered about the cause of Pier's open hostility.

"I'm sure you think I'm one of the rudest people you've ever met." Pier's voice broke in on my thoughts. "Don't look so surprised, Lyssie; your face reads like an open book. Do yourself a favor, my friend, and stay away from poker. Trust me on this."

I blushed, ashamed my thoughts were so readily apparent. I'd never been adept at concealing my feelings but hadn't realized just how transparent my face could be. I made a mental note to work on the fine art of deception—or at least acquiring some form of 'poker face' to avoid being so readable.

I watched as Pier fidgeted before the fireplace. She looked at me a couple of times like she was about to say something, then quickly glanced away the moment our eyes met. This added to my growing discomfort, and again I wondered if I should find some excuse to cut my visit short. I certainly didn't feel up to becoming embroiled in a family feud, and it was painfully obvious that's what it was between Pier and her stepmother. I'd no any idea what brought about the thinly veiled hostility between the two women, nor did I want to know. While I thought my presence here at Foxxemoor might be a mistake, I was selfish enough to wish that peace could be maintained long enough for me to get a sense of the place for my manuscript.

"I suppose we'd better go up to our rooms. Margaret was right about our needing the chance to rest; you look positively bushed, my friend, so up you go."

I followed Pier from the room and up the first rise of the staircase. On the second floor landing, Pier turned to the right, leading me down the hall to the south wing. We passed through a kind of doorway, the connecting passage from the old house into the newer section, then up two steps. We stopped before a closed door on the immediate right.

"This is my suite." She opened the door and looked inside as if expecting to see someone. Even though the room appeared empty, she peered around the back of the door.

"Dee?" She called the name softly, and when no one answered, shrugged and turned back to me. "Thought the little imp might be hiding. Anyway, these are my rooms; your suite is just down the hall." As she gave the room one last perusal, I gave it a quick study.

Pastel colors met my eyes: pale pinks, mauve, and lavender. The 'sitting room' was more like an apartment-sized living room containing a love seat, a couple of overstuffed chairs, an entertainment center, and a desk. Long windows with delicate sheers allowed the sunshine to fill the room and add to its charm and gentle beauty.

"It's a beautiful room, Pier."

"Thanks! As I designed it, I'll take that as a personal compliment." She shut the door and smiled at me, the tight lines that had formed around her eyes and mouth since seeing Margaret gone. "I used to have one of the suites in the main section of the house, but when I turned thirteen, I decided to strike out on my own. These rooms weren't exactly run down, but it had been a while since they'd been occupied. Mama allowed me to choose what I wanted and saw to it that my wishes were granted. We had such a wonderful time redecorating my suite that we did the others in this wing as well."

This time, the door was on the left, and when opened revealed a lovely room done in various shades of blue. The room mirrored Pier's, from the chairs and couch, to the desk and TV set-up. Once again I was made aware of the opulence that was Foxxemoor.

"I see someone brought up your laptop and backpack. If you give me the key, I'll see that the rest of your bags are delivered in a flash."

"Oh, Pier, I'm quite capable—"

"Relax, and enjoy the opportunity to be pampered. We've more than enough help around here, not to mention my brothers—er, rather, Gray." As she shook her head, her dark hair fell over her face, temporarily hiding it from view. "I keep forgetting about Ryan's poor legs. He was always so athletic," her large eyes peered up at me for understanding. "It's hard to see him in that awful chair. The thought of him not being able to walk or run . . . So, we just won't think about it!" She pushed her hair back from her face, regarding me intently. "You're probably wondering what kind of household I've brought you to, aren't you?" She grabbed my hands and held them tightly. "I'm really glad you're here, Lyssie. Really glad. Whatever happens, please remember that, and just hang in there."

She left me abruptly, only to return a moment later for my car keys. After she'd gone, I stood in the center of that beautiful room and did, indeed, wonder what in heaven I'd gotten myself into.

Chapter 2

Diana found herself by the edge of the lake just as the fog rolled in to surround her, confusing her sense of direction and making her escape doubtful. She reached her hands out before her, her eyes straining to pierce through the shroud that threatened to entrap her ...

The moment I agreed to go home with her, Pier began painting a picture of Foxxemoor and the town where she grew up. It wasn't long before I felt the peace and serenity of Bristol, the people who lived there, and how supportive they'd been through the series of misfortunes that struck her family. Her description of Bristol was oddly reminiscent of my fictional village of Craven, and I was intrigued by the similarities. As for the estate of Foxxemoor, I filed away every detail for future reference, altering reality to fit my purposes.

Foxxemoor lay in the heart of the rolling hills of Missouri, nestled in a valley surrounded by a generous expanse of woods, rich farmland, and lush grazing plains. The small town of Bristol, site of the original FoxCo Toys factory, was less than twenty miles from the entrance gates to the Foxxe estate. Because of the generosity and patronage of more than four generations of Foxxes, the town contained most of the amenities of a larger city—two shopping centers, a Super WalMart, a multiplex movie theater, a community pool, and a parks and recreation department which organized activities for the area year round.

"My great-great grandfather started it all," Pier told me with pride. "It was one of the few estates to not only withstand the ravages of the Civil War, but to grow in the process."

She led me down the avenue of oaks which lined the half mile drive from the main highway to where Foxxemoor stood triumphantly at its end. The final approach to the mansion was a large driveway which encircled a rock garden with a stone and marble fountain at its center. To the right of the drive was the old carriage house, now a four car garage, and on the left, a short lane which led to the stables. At the top of the circle sat the front third of the great house, with a wing going off at an angle on either side.

"People say the house looks like a giant, prehistoric bird," Pier laughed, her grey-green eyes twinkling with mischief. "Ryan christened it 'Bird of Prey' after the Klingon warships from the old *Star Trek* TV series."

The front portion of Foxxemoor was the original building, both wings having been added in the latter part of the 1800's. The top floor of the three-storied mansion, originally designed as servants' quarters, was now used for storage. The second floor contained apartment-sized suites for the family, each consisting of a bedroom, dressing/sitting room, and its own bathroom.

The main floor was filled with large, airy rooms designed for both beauty and comfort. The original part of the house held a library, den, and a modern living room complete with the latest in electronic equipment. The north wing consisted of the kitchen areas and family dining room, and the south held a formal dining room and ballroom which were rarely used.

"I don't expect you to memorize the layout, Lyssie," Pier had told me as we ate ice cream on Tan-Tar-A's Arrowhead Deck, which overlooked the Lake of the Ozarks. "But it'll give you food for thought."

The vastness of the house boggled the mind. I'd read about such mansions but never actually stayed in one. Now here I was, following Pier's hot red Mustang convertible, on my way to what I would liken to a castle. Maybe Pier was right; why leave it to imagination when the real thing was available to inspire my creative juices?

Realizing I'd left my tape recorder running while my mind strayed, I reached over to press rewind. As I kept my eyes on the road, I listened to the few minutes of manuscript I'd dictated.

The nuance and threat of danger was there, but something was missing. I replayed the piece, trying to catch the omission to correct it, but again found my mind wandering.

The Foxxe household was quite large. Both her brothers lived at home, and, of course, there was her stepmother, Margaret Courtney Foxxe. In addition to a live-in housekeeper and her husband, the gardener, there was a cook and a maid who came in from town each day. Then, finally, there was Dee.

Deidre Courtney, Dylan's six-year-old daughter, had been Pier's responsibility for the last five months—the reason Pier had been so desperately in need of a vacation. Pier stated that since Dylan's disappearance, the child had run wild.

"Skittish as an untamed colt is how Gray describes her," Pier smirked. "She's always been a bit precocious, but the most loving little kid I've ever known. Then Margaret decided that we needed to stop 'coddling' Dee," she stated with derision.

When local authorities ceased their active investigation into Dylan's disappearance six weeks earlier, Margaret Courtney Foxxe also pulled her team of private investigators from the case. A week later, without consulting the rest of the family, Margaret arranged a memorial for her daughter and erected a stone for Dylan in the Foxxe family cemetery.

"She said it was to help Dee, that after nearly five months and no word—" Pier's voice caught, making it obvious the memory was painful. "Then out of the blue, Margaret hired a nanny and sent me off to Tan-Tar-A. Not that I didn't need the vacation, I just wasn't sure about leaving Dee."

Pier felt that as Dee's grandmother, Margaret should have been responsible for caring for the child all along.

"But it's obvious she isn't the best example for an impressionable little girl. Just look how Dylan turned out!"

Concerned for Dee's welfare, Pier stepped in, moved Dee into her suite, and tried to give the little girl the love she so badly needed. Dee reached out to her 'Aunt Pier' at first, but gradually, rebellion had taken over to the point that not even Pier could reach her.

I wondered about Dee's father, who he might be, and where he was, but I didn't ask. I knew that if it was something Pier thought I should know, she would eventually get around to telling me. So I waited, my curiosity and imagination running as wild as she'd said the child had become.

As for her brothers, Pier spoke very little about them. She mentioned how Ryan's spine had been injured in the car accident that killed their father. He could walk a little, but, because of the pain it caused, he preferred to remain in a wheelchair for the time being.

Ryan, she said, was the brains, Gray the brawn. When I'd asked what she meant, she explained that Ryan was involved in the inner workings of Foxxe Industries and that Gray was content with running the home farms and working with the horses.

"There's more to it," she said with a shrug, "But I've never really known what all it entails."

For Pier, happiness and contentment lay in ignorance of the day to day operations of the family business. The fortune was there, and her future was secure because of trust funds established at her birth. These wise investments gave her the freedom to live without the necessity of having to support herself.

"I would've left Foxxemoor a long time ago if . . ." She tossed her long brunette hair and shrugged again. "For a little word, 'if' holds so many connotations. Ah, well," she sighed. "Things will be so much better with you there, Lyssie!"

While Pier always possessed an enormous ego and had a high opinion of herself, she'd also been a kind and generous companion during our college years. Now, a completely different picture was forming of my old roommate. I was beginning to see her more as a trapped and desperate individual—much like the heroine of my story. There was one big difference between them: Diana wanted to solve the mysteries of *Craven* and live to tell about them; Pier wanted to escape.

The whirring sound of the tape at the end of the roll brought me back to the present. I switched the machine off, reprimanding myself for daydreaming rather than staying on task.

I noticed Pier's left turn signal and realized we must be nearing the final stage of our journey. Sure enough, a sign confirmed that Bristol was straight ahead.

I took the turn off the highway onto the blacktop that led into town and eventually to Foxxemoor Lane. Watching the scenery slide past, I noted that the majority of farms and houses were well cared for and looked quite prosperous. The fields had a fresh, spring green look, the young plants of corn, soy beans, and others I didn't recognize, looked fresh and healthy under the beautiful June sky.

We drove on through the center of Bristol, past churches, supermarkets, a McDonalds, Applebee's, several gas stations, a handful of homes, and were once again in the country. I took particular note of a beautiful, old-fashioned church on the outskirts of town and filed away service times listed on the message board that sat near the side of the road.

I felt a thrill of excitement building as miles went by. How could I have taken so long to accept Pier's invitation? Every new piece of information about the estate had intrigued me to the point that, by the time of my acceptance, I'd become a Foxxemoor trivia junkie. Like an addict hooked on the latest drug, I'd determined that nothing should be withheld to hinder my addiction.

Not even Pier's strange behavior following the call to her family had affected my decision. Her comment that it was better as a *fait accompli* had been a little disturbing, but I refused to look at it as some sort of omen or silent warning. I didn't stop to pray or ask God for guidance as I might have done once. And since there were no alarms sounding, I figured going with Pier was a safe choice.

We traveled down the blacktop road at sixty miles per hour, a good clip on such a narrow road. I slowed down around the curves and near the tops of the hills, afraid I might come upon a tractor or other slow moving vehicle. Pier, in contrast, seemed unaware of the possible danger. In fact, she appeared to speed up. I lost sight of her a couple times but wasn't worried. I knew from her descriptions that the lane into the Foxxemoor estate was well-marked, and I was unlikely to miss it.

About ten to fifteen minutes after we'd left Bristol, we rounded a bend in the road that led steeply up the side of a hill. I knew from Pier's description that at the crest of the hill the road took a sharp right then plunged steeply down into the valley. It was somewhere near this area that her father lost control of his car. Keeping this in mind, I once again reduced my speed and watched in alarm as the fiery red Mustang kicked into passing gear and sped off at breakneck speed.

I steered my car carefully around the curve as I drank in the breathtaking view from atop the hill. The vibrant shades of green pastures, golden wheat fields, and lush wooded areas took my mind off Pier's recklessness and reminded me of the reasons I'd decided to follow her to Foxxemoor. Here my imagination could run free; here was a place I could build my world of rich green valleys, tranquil lakes, and a house called Craven where dangers lurked around every corner. This was inspiration, where reality lent itself to the world of make-believe, taking a little from each to create and mold into whatever I desired. Here I would create lives on paper and try to forget the reality and devastation I had left behind.

Pier waited for me at the entrance to the Foxxemoor estate. She stood leaning against her car, her head thrown back, her face to the sun. As I pulled beside her, she turned to look at me, shielding her eyes from the glare reflecting off the cars.

"What took you so long?"

Rather than comment on what I thought of her driving, I said that I'd been enjoying the view.

"It's beautiful, isn't it? This part of the state has the best there is to offer by way of scenery. I'm not immune to it, you know, just used to it. You find passion in the scenery; mine comes from the road itself. There's nothing more exhilarating than taking the hills and curves at a fast clip, and this baby handles it all so smoothly." She patted the hood of her car as she grinned mischievously. "It's even better when the top's down."

"A little dangerous, though."

She laughed. "Depends on your perception. Besides, facing danger can make life more exciting. It's why amusement parks do so well. They offer an element of danger from the roller coasters rocketing over tracks that seem to bend and sway under the weight of the cars. It's the rush that keeps people going back for more. They may be terrified, but they can't get enough of it."

"Perhaps. I've heard the same thing in relation to abusing drugs, the danger and rush, but it doesn't lessen the insanity of putting your life on the line. I figure there's no reason to invite disaster."

"I'll bet you never ride roller coasters, do you?"

Her tone was derisive, but I chose not to take it seriously. "I don't like heights." I answered simply.

"Pity." Pier sighed then gazed down the oak-lined lane before us. "I suppose we should get to the house. Mrs. Merrick will wonder what's keeping us. And if Margaret's back, she'll be impatiently waiting to play hostess. I could care less about her, but Mrs. Merrick's a dear, and I don't want to worry her." She started to climb back into the Mustang, changed her mind, and came over to my car. She bent close to the window and peered in at me.

"Remember that whatever happens, whatever might be said, first and foremost you're my friend and guest. I know this sounds odd, but I can't explain right now. Just keep in mind that Foxxemoor's a third mine." She sauntered back to her car, climbed inside, and gunned the engine. The Mustang leaped through the open wrought iron gates in response, reminding me of the horse for which it was named.

The lane was exactly as I'd imagined it, the ancient oak trees towering above on either side to form a kind of dome high above us. The sun played a game of peek-a-boo, appearing now and again in the break of entwined limbs then darting out of sight to leave the lane in cool shadows.

As we neared the end of the drive, my breath caught in my throat. Neither Pier's description of Foxxemoor, nor my imagination had been accurate. Somehow, I had gotten the impression of a dark, brooding mansion whose true grandeur was from a bygone era. Instead, I found myself looking at a manor home befitting a large southern plantation, its clean white paint gleaming in the summer sun. Even the pale bricks that fronted the main portion of the house looked freshly scrubbed, and the chain that held the porch swing sparkled in the sunlight.

I pulled up to the garage beside Pier, and looking in the rearview mirror, could see how the house had a vague resemblance to a bird. Recalling her brother's nickname for their home, 'Bird of Prey,' I laughed.

"Glad to see you're in better humor." Pier stood close to my car door. "What do you think so far?"

"It's—magnificent." I climbed out of the car and turned to stare at the mansion. "Completely overwhelming."

Pier smiled, obviously satisfied with my reaction. "I warned you that mere words couldn't do Foxxemoor justice. Wait till you see inside."

I followed her up the drive, paused for a moment to gaze in wonder at the profusion of color in the rock garden and marvel at the beauty of the fountain, the stone cupids laughing up at the trickle of water cascading over them. The sound of the dancing water, birdsong and far-off hum of a tractor filled the afternoon air, lending a magical quality to our approach to the house. My senses were filled to bursting, my fingers itching to take pen in hand and write down all that my eyes could see and imagination could build. I just hoped my brain wouldn't overload and lose everything before I had the opportunity to get it on paper.

On the porch, I ran my hand up the smooth chain links that held the bench swing. The chain was new and cool to my touch, the swing recently painted a cobalt blue to match the shutters which hung on every window facing the drive.

We entered the overlarge doorway through a modern screen door. The main door was pushed against an inside wall of a vast entryway and opened onto a wide hallway that appeared to stretch from the front to the back of the house. Large windows with sheer curtains allowed for plenty of natural lighting even with the numerous shade trees which practically surrounded Foxxemoor. The curtains moved gently back and forth with the light breeze coming in through the opened windows. The fresh air and spaciousness added to the enchantment and dream-like sensation I'd felt since first seeing the mansion.

The floor was made up of black and white tiles, squares geometrically forming a diamond pattern which caught your eye upon entering and forced it to follow the rows as far back as you could see. The cream-colored walls held mirror-backed sconces with fragrant candlesticks whose delicate scent drifted on the breeze from the windows. Scenic paintings separated each set of sconces with views of different parts of the estate, each showing intricate detail and attention to even the most minute object. My eyes wandered over the paintings, studying them and realizing they were from another age.

"A distant relative painted them sometime in the late 1800's. They *are* interesting, Lyssie, but if you give so much attention to everything you see, we'll never get out of the foyer!" Pier placed a gentle hand on my arm and pulled me along the hallway. "First thing to do is let people know we're here, give them advanced warning to be on their best behavior."

I was entranced by the beauty of the marble staircase that was located several feet to the right of the front door. The banister was highly polished oak with a scrolled pattern which followed the curving staircase to the second floor landing and hall, curved again, then continued its journey to the next floor.

I felt as if I'd entered an enchanted world where everything beautiful converged in a feast for the eyes and senses. I'd never been to such a place as this in reality—TV, movies, and books had given me images of such things, but my imagination could never have come up with anything like this.

"It's unbelievable." I spoke in a half whisper, totally awed.

"Some things are as they always were, others, well, Margaret's additions can be a little gauche. She won't be criticized, however, and refuses to allow Foxxemoor to retain its dignity and integrity. I'm not against change, of course, modernizing is great, but Mar—" Pier stopped in mid-sentence as a striking, older woman appeared from a room to our left. Her pale blue eyes and rich black hair told me immediately that this was Dylan Courtney's mother, Pier's stepmother, Margaret Courtney Foxxe.

"I thought I heard voices." Margaret's cool smile lit briefly on Pier then was directed at me. "And you must be Lysette Daniels, Pier's old friend from college. What a marvelous coincidence that you two chose the same vacation spot."

She held her hand out to me, and I took it. The warmth of her hand belied the coolness of her smile, and I gazed deeply into Margaret Courtney Foxxe's pale blue eyes where I saw hesitation and a hint of the friendship she really wished to convey.

I noted the flecks of silver in her short, black hair, the fine lines around her eyes and lips and realized that while still a beautiful woman, Margaret was a good deal older than she first appeared. At approximately five-ten, slim and healthy looking, I'd guessed her to be in her early fifties when I'd first seen her; now I realized I was several years off target.

"I'm glad Pier informed us you were a writer, my dear, else I'd be wondering if you were always this—"

"Rude?" Pier offered flippantly.

I felt the heat of embarrassment stain my cheeks as I withdrew my hand from hers. "I was staring, wasn't I? I'm sorry, I, uh—"

Margaret laughed. "Please, don't apologize. I'm sure you meant nothing by it. I simply felt a little awkward under your scrutiny." She waved us into the room and motioned for us to sit down.

I sat on a nearby couch, sinking so far back into the depth of cushions it felt as if I was being swallowed. Conscious of her eyes upon me, I didn't indulge in my usual tendency of studying my surroundings. Instead, I turned my attention to my hostess while I carefully sought Pier's whereabouts from the corner of my eye.

"We haven't had real company at Foxxemoor in quite some time, so this shall be a treat for us. We entertain clients and investors, but one can hardly term them as friends. I believe it's time we start reclaiming old friendships and begin living again," Margaret smiled as she seated herself in a warm blue, brocade chair opposite me. She daintily crossed her legs, pulling the hem of her black skirt level with the top of her knees. "How was your drive?"

"Long." Pier's tone remained flippant and, as she came into view, I could see that her body language matched the tone.

"It might be a long trip, but well worth it," I quickly interjected. "The scenery is magnificent."

Margaret's eyes left her stepdaughter and returned to me, the look of reproach for Pier's behavior finely drawn on her features. "We have some lovely country here, and I believe you'll find that our estate embodies the very best there is to offer. We're quite proud of our holdings—"

A "harrumph" from Pier received a quick, sidelong glance.

"I hope you will take advantage of our hospitality and explore to your heart's content. We'll make our house and grounds open to your discerning eye, Miss Daniels—or may I call you Lysette? Good," she nodded, "and you shall call me Margaret. No need for formalities." She looked at the gold watch on her arm and shook her head. "I'd no idea it was this late. I'm sure you're both exhausted and would like time to rest and freshen up, so I'll excuse myself." She rose and looked over to where Pier stood before a marble fireplace mantel. "We've made up the suite next to yours, Pier. I figured you'd both feel more comfortable knowing the other was nearby." The look exchanged between the two of them hinted at some deeper, hidden meaning behind the words, but I was at a loss to guess what it might be.

At the door to the room, Margaret turned back around. "Oh, and Deidre's been established in her own suite."

Pier didn't answer, just watched the older woman leave. The antagonism she felt for her stepmother was apparent. It was obvious she did little, if anything, to hide it. In contrast, Margaret appeared completely unaware of Pier's feelings, she was coolly polite, nothing to hint at the underlying currents between them. I had to admire Margaret's reserve and wondered about the cause of Pier's open hostility.

"I'm sure you think I'm one of the rudest people you've ever met." Pier's voice broke in on my thoughts. "Don't look so surprised, Lyssie; your face reads like an open book. Do yourself a favor, my friend, and stay away from poker. Trust me on this."

I blushed, ashamed my thoughts were so readily apparent. I'd never been adept at concealing my feelings but hadn't realized just how transparent my face could be. I made a mental note to work on the fine art of deception—or at least acquiring some form of 'poker face' to avoid being so readable.

I watched as Pier fidgeted before the fireplace. She looked at me a couple of times like she was about to say something, then quickly glanced away the moment our eyes met. This added to my growing discomfort, and again I wondered if I should find some excuse to cut my visit short. I certainly didn't feel up to becoming embroiled in a family feud, and it was painfully obvious that's what it was between Pier and her stepmother. I'd no any idea what brought about the thinly veiled hostility between the two women, nor did I want to know. While I thought my presence here at

Foxxemoor might be a mistake, I was selfish enough to wish that peace could be maintained long enough for me to get a sense of the place for my manuscript.

"I suppose we'd better go up to our rooms. Margaret was right about our needing the chance to rest; you look positively bushed, my friend, so up you go."

I followed Pier from the room and up the first rise of the staircase. On the second floor landing, Pier turned to the right, leading me down the hall to the south wing. We passed through a kind of doorway, the connecting passage from the old house into the newer section, then up two steps. We stopped before a closed door on the immediate right.

"This is my suite." She opened the door and looked inside as if expecting to see someone. Even though the room appeared empty, she peered around the back of the door.

"Dee?" She called the name softly, and when no one answered, shrugged and turned back to me. "Thought the little imp might be hiding. Anyway, these are my rooms; your suite is just down the hall." As she gave the room one last perusal, I gave it a quick study.

Pastel colors met my eyes: pale pinks, mauve, and lavender. The 'sitting room' was more like an apartment-sized living room containing a love seat, a couple of overstuffed chairs, an entertainment center, and a desk. Long windows with delicate sheers allowed the sunshine to fill the room and add to its charm and gentle beauty.

"It's a beautiful room, Pier."

"Thanks! As I designed it, I'll take that as a personal compliment." She shut the door and smiled at me, the tight lines that had formed around her eyes and mouth since seeing Margaret gone. "I used to have one of the suites in the main section of the house, but when I turned thirteen, I decided to strike out on my own. These rooms weren't exactly run down, but it had been a while since they'd been occupied. Mama allowed me to choose what I wanted and saw to it that my wishes were granted. We had such a wonderful time redecorating my suite that we did the others in this wing as well."

This time, the door was on the left, and when opened revealed a lovely room done in various shades of blue. The room mirrored Pier's, from the chairs and couch, to the desk and TV set-up. Once again I was made aware of the opulence that was Foxxemoor.

"I see someone brought up your laptop and backpack. If you give me the key, I'll see that the rest of your bags are delivered in a flash."

"Oh, Pier, I'm quite capable—"

"Relax, and enjoy the opportunity to be pampered. We've more than enough help around here, not to mention my brothers—er, rather, Gray." As she shook her head, her dark hair fell over her face, temporarily hiding it from view. "I keep forgetting about Ryan's poor legs. He was always so athletic," her large eyes peered up at me for understanding. "It's hard to see him in that awful chair. The thought of him not being able to walk or run . . . So, we just won't think about it!" She pushed her hair back from her face, regarding me intently. "You're probably wondering what kind of household I've brought you to, aren't you?" She grabbed my hands and held them tightly. "I'm really glad you're here, Lyssie. Really glad. Whatever happens, please remember that, and just hang in there."

She left me abruptly, only to return a moment later for my car keys. After she'd gone, I stood in the center of that beautiful room and did, indeed, wonder what in heaven I'd gotten myself into.

Chapter 4

Diana awakened with a start, her head aching, her limbs icy and leaden. She looked about in horror, shivering with the memory of how she had come to be here.

With immense effort, she pulled herself up from the stone floor where she'd fallen and dragged herself over to the window. She pushed at the sash, forcing the aged wooden structure up with a moan of protest. But the sound was nothing in comparison to the cry that came from the very depths of her being at what was before her: iron bars blocked the window eliminating any chance for escape . . .

I'd written more in the last four days than I had in months. Words never came so easily, the flow so even. Sometimes, I stopped to read what I'd written, the thoughts having come so quickly that I'd no recollection of actually having *written* them. But there it was, plot and story coming together without conscious effort.

It was the same with my adjustment into life at Foxxemoor. Despite the rather rocky beginning, I no longer felt my presence was unwanted. Margaret and Ryan had gone out of their way to make me feel comfortable, as had Pier. I hadn't seen Gray since the first evening and from what I'd learned from Pier, this was completely in character for him.

As I'd guessed, the twins didn't get along, and while Pier would not go into detail, I got the impression it had something to do with an age-old struggle for their own identity. Being identical in every way but one, the birth defect that caused Gray's slight limp, had caused them problems throughout their lives. And according to Pier, Gray's way of coping was staying to himself. It hadn't always been that way, she'd said with a far-away look in her eyes. Things changed when her mother died. And when Margaret married their father, the break in the family dynamic fractured even more.

Problems getting along with other members of your family was something I could relate to. But it did make me curious about what was really behind the rift between the twins.

While Gray had been absent, the same could not be said about Ryan. In the beginning, I thought it was coincidence that the two of us met so often. Now I wondered if it was deliberate. Those times we 'bumped' into one another were pleasant, and although we never did more than exchange comments on the weather, it was a nice diversion. Gone was the irritation and anger I'd witnessed that first evening, and the cloak of bitterness that seemed so much a part of him on our initial encounter was nowhere in evidence. I didn't totally believe in his change of heart and acceptance of my being here. I figured he'd simply resigned himself of the fact and decided to make the best of the situation.

Each time I saw Ryan, I was amazed at the progress he'd made recovering from his accident. He still relied heavily on his cane, but it appeared that the stiffness and limp were lessening, as was his self-consciousness about his infirmity.

I saw little of Margaret, which Pier said I should consider a blessing. When she was present, she held herself in quiet reserve, something that I believed, was for the sake of peace between her and Pier. Margaret always had a welcoming smile for me, and I often got the impression she would like the opportunity to talk with me. About what, I'd no idea. It was just a feeling I got.

After that first evening, mealtimes were very informal, always set out buffet-style in the dining room for everyone to come and go as they pleased. Pier and I had our meals together, and once or twice during the week Margaret or Ryan joined us for a while. Little was said during those occasions, but after the interminable silences of that first night, these were a breeze. I wondered if this was the norm for the Foxxe's but not enough to ask Pier about it.

What I considered most peculiar about this household was the absence of Dee. If I hadn't known about her, I'd never have guessed of the girl's existence! There was nothing to hint at her presence; no swing set in the yard or solitary swing hanging from a tree, no toys or any of the usual paraphernalia that speaks of a child in the house. Nothing. It was odd, almost eerie in the sense that she was here and yet not. But then, I was finding so much about Foxxemoor that embodied this same feeling.

While I may not see Dee, I often felt her. I would be sitting in the back garden and get the overwhelming impression I was being watched. Though I would see no one, the feeling of being observed remained. On guard, my senses heightened for the slightest hint of movement or sound, I'd eventually be rewarded with a glimpse of Dee's pale hair, or a fleeting look at her retreating figure. I'd thought about asking Pier about this strange behavior, but knew they had enough to contend with as far as Dee was concerned, and I didn't care to add to it. I came to expect that Dee would come to silently watch as I enjoyed the peace of the garden.

I took full advantage of Pier's offer to use Foxxemoor's 'atmosphere' to spur my imagination. As a result, it limited the time Pier and I spent with one another, which made me feel a little guilty. After all, she was my hostess, and I wanted her to know how grateful I was for this wonderful opportunity. But as excited as I was about my productivity, I'd spent so much time at my computer, I was getting stir crazy. It was time to get away for more than the ten or fifteen minutes I ordinarily allotted myself. I was ready, anxious, to explore the estate.

By mid-morning, I'd decided on a new way to spend my days. Mornings would be spent at the computer, afternoons were for friends and exploration, and the evenings were open for anything that might come up. I took a break to share my plans with Pier and hoped it wouldn't be too late to spend the rest of the day together.

We met one another on the staircase.

"I was just coming to see you." Her dark hair had been pulled back into a ponytail and perspiration dotted her furrowed brow.

"Same here. I thought we could go riding or do something else together. I've been so preoccupied since we got here that I haven't really thanked you for everything. I hope you don't feel I've taken advantage of you."

"Not a problem. The idea was to help with your writing; if it has, that's great." She smiled a little, but the grim look on her face made me wonder what crisis I had stumbled onto now. "You reach a stopping point and I'm unable to join you!" She sank onto one of the marble stairs. "The woman who's been taking care of Dee has reached her breaking point. She's decided that Dee is incorrigible and has turned in her notice. Effective immediately. Unfortunately, I'm the only one available to take her to the bus station."

I sat next to Pier and took her hand in mine. "Is that all that's bothering you?" I looked into her grey-green eyes in an attempt to read what was there. Her free hand brushed back tears that threatened to fall.

"I'm so tired of living like this, always waiting for the other shoe to drop. And when it does, wondering how it's going to affect me this time?"

"Then this is a perfect time for me to ask the next question." I squeezed her hand. "I think we could both use a little divine intervention, and since tomorrow's Sunday—" I felt her hand stiffen in mine.

"I don't do church, Lyssie, but there's a nice little Baptist church just outside Bristol where you turn to come out to Foxxemoor." She patted my hand and drew back her shoulders. "I refuse to let this get me down." She stood and gave me a weak smile. "Since there's no bus stop in Bristol I have to drive her over to Linden. If everything goes all right, I should be back by late afternoon. How about a swim before dinner?"

"Sounds great. I'll just go back—"

"You were going to take a break, so take it. Besides, you don't need me to go riding. Just go on down to the stables whenever you're ready. I'll call Gray so he knows to expect you."

"I don't know—"

"Come on, Lyssie. It will do you a world of good to get out for more than an hour or two. You'll have a wonderful time, and I'll feel better knowing that at least one of us is enjoying this beautiful day."

"I could go with you."

She shook her head. "I'd thought about that, but I've some errands to run for Ryan and Margaret, and I don't want to ruin your free day. You stay here and enjoy yourself. Gray can point out the trails and open pastureland where you can ride. Trust me. It's a lot better than being cooped up in a car with a crotchety old biddy—or young one, for that matter," she laughed, offering me a hand up. "Your time here is unlimited—"

"Now, I—"

"Ok then, limited to whatever you choose. If you don't tire of us too soon, we'll have plenty of time together." She looked down at her watch. "Oh, good Lord, I'd no idea it was getting so late. If I don't get going, I'll have to sit and wait with Miss Allen until the afternoon bus arrives!"

At the bottom of the stairs, she waved up to me then

disappeared from sight. I turned to go back up to my suite, but there was a part of me that didn't want to be confined to the room any longer. Wrestling with the other part, the one that urged me back to my laptop, I stood on the stairs, trying to decide what to do. I wasn't there more than a couple minutes when Ryan came into view at the bottom of the staircase. He looked up at me questioningly.

"Up or down?"

I shrugged. "That's what I'm trying to decide."

He laughed, his handsome face lighting up with amusement. "So the workaholic is struggling with whether or not to take a break or slave on."

A horn sounded from outside. He turned carefully with the use of his cane and headed for the door. "I'd like to stay and help you make your decision, but duty calls," he said, opening the door. "But if I were you, I'd opt for playtime. I think you've earned it."

"Thanks." He was gone before the word was out of my mouth.

I walked slowly down the stairs with no conscious thought of what to do. It was too early for lunch, too late to go to the stables for a ride and then be back in time for lunch. I could return to my suite and write, and the pull to do just that was very strong. If I did, however, I would likely spend the entire day wrapped up in the world of *Craven* instead of exploring Foxxemoor and its surroundings.

I wandered aimlessly through the foyer and hallway, studying the paintings. It wasn't long till I found myself at the entrance to the living room. Going in, I was taken once more by how beautiful it was. There were two large picture windows that looked out upon part of the garden at the back of the house. From the slant of this portion of Foxxemoor, you were just able to see the corresponding section on the other side before it spread out into the south wing, thus enclosing the garden on three sides.

Inside, the living room contained a fully equipped bar at the rear of the room, several chairs of all types and sizes, the 'man-eating' sofa, a beautiful marble fireplace with polished brass fixtures, and cozy window seats with plush cushions and pillows. The walls were filled with photographs of both the Foxxe and Courtney families. Most of the pictures had been taken years before when Pier's parents were alive, and all of them showed a happy, loving family. There were the twins playing ball, laughing up at the camera as they toppled over each other; beautiful Dylan Courtney smiled out as she stood between the brothers, their hands clasped, their shoulders touching; and there was Pier, not more than twelve, surrounded by her brothers and Dylan as they wrestled a dog back into an outdoor tub.

The adults were there too. Photographs of the Foxxe's and Courtney's on an outing without the children, others containing group shots of both children and adults—none of them even hinting at the antagonism and dislike apparent today.

I wondered what had happened. Had it been Margaret's marrying Edward Foxxe so soon after their spouse's deaths, or had the problems always been there under the surface, hidden to the outside world—and to each other?

There were magazines on one of the coffee tables, and I grabbed one up and carried it over to a window seat. I'd just become involved in their fiction special when I heard a sound in the hallway.

"Miss Daniels?" The housekeeper, Edna Merrick, came just inside the doorway and stood looking at me apologetically. She held an old-fashioned apron in her hands, drying them. Her soft brown eyes were hesitant as she looked at me. "I really hate to disturb you, but I was wondering if I might ask a favor?"

"No problem." I tossed the magazine onto a nearby table.

"My husband hasn't been feeling very good the last couple of days, and I was finally able to talk him into seeing the doctor. If I leave now, we can make it before the office closes for lunch. I was wondering—"

Seeing her continued hesitation, I broke in, "If you're worried about my lunch, don't be. I can get it myself. Please, go take care of your husband."

"I really appreciate that, Miss Daniels. With the cook off today, things are a bit crazy. I wouldn't think of leaving if it wasn't for Henry. I," she smiled slightly, looking down at the floor then back up at me. "I thought you'd understand, so I took the liberty of preparing a picnic for you. I hope you don't think it too forward of me. It's in the little ice chest by the front door, along with Gray's and little Dee's lunch. If you could take theirs down with you when you go to the stables I'd be extremely grateful."

After reassuring her it wasn't a problem, she was on her way. I sat back on the window seat and marveled at the kind of servitude Mrs. Merrick displayed. Though she didn't look as I would picture the typical 'housekeeper,' recalling Mrs. Danvers in *Rebecca* and Ellen Dean of *Wuthering Heights*, she'd definitely been trained to please and to serve. I'd have thought this type of domestic help disappeared long ago, and wondered about the Merricks' loyalty and peculiar subjectiveness to the Foxxe family.

I checked out the lunch, discovering a Thermos of lemonade, several ham and cheese sandwiches, a small container of potato salad, baked beans, and three generous slices of strawberry pie. Just seeing the food made my mouth water, and after running upstairs to put on a pair of jeans and change my shoes, I grabbed the ice chest and left for the stables.

It was the first time I'd been out for the day and was delighted to find the air lighter, not as hot and humid as it had been the last several days. The gentle north breeze was refreshing and, when surrounded by the trees on the pathway to the stables, almost chilly. It was a temporary illusion, but after the heat permeating the rooms in Foxxemoor, a welcome one.

I don't know what I expected, perhaps several barns and a paddock full of Arabians, but it certainly wasn't the small stable I saw before me. It was less than half the size of the stables at the Tan-Tar-A resort, tall and whitewashed with huge doors and large bales of hay piled nearby.

"I see you found us all right. And bless you, you've brought lunch."

Gray took the chest from me before I was able to assimilate his presence, coming upon me so quietly I hadn't heard him.

"Mrs. Merrick—"

"I know, she called a while ago. I hadn't expected you so soon. You must have sensed I was starving." He grinned and indicated for me to follow him.

"I was hungry and didn't see any reason to eat alone

when this feast was prepared for three to share."

We went through a side door I hadn't noticed and entered a thoroughly modern office—computer, desk, work table, filing cabinets, everything spotless and organized.

"Three?" He turned to me as he placed the chest upon the work table. "I guess that means Dee is expected to join us." He said something under his breath, cursed, then looked back at me. "You didn't happen to see her on your way down here?"

I shook my head. "Sorry. To be honest, I haven't actually seen her since my first day here. I don't think she cares much for me."

Gray peered at me curiously, but didn't say anything. He opened the chest and began to unload its contents. As he set the things on the table, I attempted to lay out the plates, silverware, and napkins in normal place-settings before the chairs.

"What makes you think Dee doesn't like you?" He asked finally, not looking up as he continued to fuss with the food.

I related the incident of the butterfly and went on to tell him about the way she watched me whenever I was in the garden. He listened attentively, his deep blue eyes studying me.

"So you've come to the conclusion that Deidre doesn't like you because she spies on you?" He laughed, the sound more sarcasm than humor. "Do you consider yourself a good judge of character, Miss Daniels?"

"I—yes, I do. And I don't appreciate your tone, Mr. Foxxe. I wasn't implying Dee hates me or anything, just that she doesn't appear to want to meet me. She's curious, but that's all." I was annoyed he was making so much out of my simple observance. If I hadn't been so hungry, I'd have walked off. Instead, I stood facing him, full of righteous indignation, and ready for anything he might throw at me.

"Calm down, will you? You didn't imply, but I did infer." He pulled out one of the chairs and gallantly offered it to me. "Mind if I call you Lysette? All this formality makes me cringe. Look, let's call a truce and have some of this wonderful food. I apologize for ruffling your feathers. I seem to have a knack for that."

I accepted his apology as graciously as possible, my curiosity about him and his relationship to the rest of his family increasing. I wanted to ask if we should wait for Dee but wasn't certain bringing up that subject again was a good idea. As it turned out, I didn't have to wonder for long.

"She's around somewhere," Gray said as if reading my thoughts. "As a matter of fact, she's probably hiding out and watching us right now. And yes, she seems to size people and situations up before deciding to join in. You were very astute to realize that and to notice she's been watching you on the sly." He handed me a sandwich, then took one for himself. "As young as she is, Dee has an uncanny way of judging people. She knew from the beginning that Miss Allen wouldn't make it here. And believe me it had nothing to do with Dee's being incorrigible."

I gazed out the large window we were facing and into the pasture beyond. "Perhaps the woman didn't like being spied on," I suggested quietly.

Gray laughed. "Probably not. But then, dear Miss Allen had a reason for that; she was a drinker. Dee discovered this the day of the woman's arrival. She told me, and I warned Margaret. Unfortunately, it wasn't until some booze came up missing that Margaret decided it was time to take our word for it." His laughter was oddly sardonic. "Her dismissal would have come sooner, but with Pier on vacation, we were forced to keep the woman here. She'd promised to stay on the wagon until Pier's return. At any rate, I imagine the first thing she'll do once safely away is grab the nearest bottle of Scotch available."

"I take it you didn't like her any more than Dee did."

"The woman had absolutely no idea how to handle a child, let alone one with emotional problems! She came here hoping to be waited on hand and foot and under the impression that Dee would simply take care of herself. And that's exactly what happened. I doubt she ever knew where Dee was or what she was doing from one minute till the next, let alone from day to day. Her disinterest is likely why she and Margaret got along so well at the interview." His vehemence made me glad it wasn't directed at me.

I was at a loss for words and decided it would be best to tackle my lunch. Gray's dislike and disapproval of his stepmother and her choice of nanny for Dee seemed just another in a long line of differences between him and the rest of the household. Whether his accusations against the former nanny were true or not, I didn't know. Pier hadn't indicated problems with the woman, only issues Miss Allen had with the child. But then, Pier had also been away several weeks. From what I knew about my friend, she would be more concerned with how she might be affected by what might happen than about Dee's welfare. She'd said as much earlier, and it hadn't been the first time I'd seen this in her.

I peered at Gray, the fall of my hair shielding my eyes. My heart caught in my throat as I reaffirmed his strong resemblance to my character Leo Craven. He must have felt me watching him, for he looked up suddenly and stared frankly into my eyes.

"Are you all right? Not choking or anything?"

I shook my head. "I'm fine. It's just," I laughed, embarrassed. "This is so weird," I felt myself biting my lower lip, a habit I had whenever I was nervous. "You're almost the spitting image of the character in my book," I blurted with no forethought.

Gray laughed good-naturedly and grinned, a mischievous twinkle in his eyes. "Is that all? Here I thought I must have mustard on my chin or something equally embarrassing." He laughed again. "So, Lyssie Daniels, what kind of books do you write? Sizzling romances designed to titillate the common housewife?" He leaned close to me as his hand covered mine.

"No," I withdrew my hand and before he had a chance to recover it, grabbed my tumbler of lemonade. "And this is my first book. It's a Gothic. The genre is basically a mystery/suspense—"

"I know the kind. So it *is* a romance. Hard to imagine someone like me in the role of a romantic hero."

"Well, to be honest, the character's more devil than divine."

Again the hearty laughter. "Then perhaps you've already made my acquaintance in a previous lifetime, Lyssie, because that is the precise description my family has given me."

A noise in the stable area brought his attention back to our earlier subject.

"Sounds like Dee will be joining us sooner than I'd expected." He left the table and went to a different door than the one we'd entered. From its location, I guessed it led into the stable area. He listened at the door for a moment and then rejoined me at the table.

"Won't be long now," he commented, helping himself to another sandwich.

Within a matter of seconds, the little wraith of a child slipped almost soundlessly through the door—the gentle creaking of the object the only sound accompanying her entrance. Dee's large, dark eyes regarded me solemnly as she walked past, watchful and clearly ready to flee at the slightest hint of what she might perceive as danger.

I didn't speak, hardly even breathed as I continued to watch the child before me. She seemed smaller than her six years, short and petite in stature, her long, stringy hair uncombed, perhaps even in the same tangles as on our first encounter. Her small oval face was pale in contrast to the tanned hands that reached toward the stack of sandwiches on the table. The only thing to brighten the little face was a tinge of sunburn beginning to bloom in her cheeks.

She was dressed in cut-off jean shorts and a summer top that looked a size too small—obviously one left over from last year and not discarded. Dee's elbows were almost black with the exception of a small area on the left one where the skin had been peeled back in an abrasion. This, too, was unclean, as were her skinny legs and bare feet.

Deidre Courtney seated herself at the table close to Gray, disregarding the place setting I'd put between us. Her dark eyes looked up at Gray expectantly and, without a word, he picked up the plate, silver, and tumbler and set them before her.

I didn't know whether or not to acknowledge her presence. In all my dealings with emotionally disturbed children at the Langston Center, I'd never felt such overwhelming confusion, and thanked my lucky stars not to be responsible for aiding in her 'recovery.'

"So, my little bug, what have you been up to today?" Gray poked her playfully in the ribs. "No good, I'll bet. Good Lord, look at you! When was the last time you've seen the inside of a tub?"

Dee giggled as she smiled up at him. "I seen it today, Gray, but there wasn't any water in it." Her voice had a sweet, melodic ring, completely feminine and perfectly delightful.

"Well, if you want to go swimming later today, honey, you'd better get acquainted with that water, or the pool will be off limits to you."

"Why—y?" Her eyes darted quickly over to me then back to Gray. "Is she gonna ride my mamma's horse?" She'd lowered her voice to a whisper, but, as with most children her age, it was more of a stage whisper than the real thing.

"In answer to your first question, you're too dirty. And," he glanced at me then turned back to Dee, "That all depends on how much of a horsewoman she is. If she hasn't much experience, then Heathers it will be."

The news did not seem to sit very well with her. She put her sandwich down, missing the plate, and sat back in her chair, her arms folded and a pout on her tiny face.

"I haven't ridden that often, but surely you could find another—"

Gray answered without turning to me. "Heathers is the gentlest we have at present, and she hasn't had nearly enough exercise these last few months. Dee will just have to get used to the idea."

A single tear rolled down the child's right cheek which had reddened at Gray's statement. She stared down at the table, then quickly grabbed the remainder of her sandwich, jumped up, and ran out the side door.

Even though I knew I shouldn't interfere, I got up, prepared to follow her. Gray's hand on my arm stayed me.

"Let her go." His voice was quiet, but I could discern the tension behind it.

"Surely someone should go after her; she was crying." Our eyes met briefly, his the first to turn away.

"Perhaps, Miss Daniels, but let me assure you that you're not the right one to do it. And right now, neither am I." He leaned heavily back in his chair. "We wouldn't be able to get within a foot of her without her running away, so it's best to leave her to herself."

"It appears there has been too much of that already." I'd spoken more harshly than I'd intended but meant every word.

"You're right. I'd be the first to agree with you. All you have to do is look at Dee and see she's being neglected. Miss Allen had no desire to exert herself, Pier's been preoccupied with you, and Margaret has no idea what to do or where to start. As a result, Dee goes off on her own, managing the best she can. Under the circumstances, I'd say she's done pretty well."

"You call that doing 'pretty well?' I'd like to know

what you consider a cry for help, Mr. Foxxe. Obviously we see things quite differently." I shook off his hand and headed for the door.

"And you think that you, a complete stranger, might offer that help?" His laugh was filled with sarcasm. "Right now she sees you as the person who stole her mother's room and is about to take her horse as well."

"Stole—Dylan's room?" I grabbed the back of a nearby chair to steady myself. "I'd no idea."

"Of course you didn't, but Dee doesn't know that. All she knows is that one day Dylan's things were there, the next, you were. Of all the fool things Margaret's done, that tops it!"

"But why? I mean, there's so much space—"

Gray left the table to pace the length of the office. "I wouldn't even hazard a guess. I imagine the excuse was for you to be near Pier. I'm sure Margaret has her reasons, but I doubt any of them are good enough to have usurped Dylan's place in the house the way she has—whether she's dead or not."

"I don't understand."

He stopped pacing to stare at me in disbelief. "I can't believe Pier didn't tell you all about Dylan's disappearance. I thought it would be her opening topic of discussion." The disgust in his voice surprised me.

"She mentioned it, of course, but didn't go into any details. From what I understood, she was presumed dead."

"*Presumed.* With no evidence to suggest she's dead, you'd think her own mother would allow the benefit of doubt. But maybe Margaret knows something the rest of us don't." The latter statement was made half under his breath and was obviously not meant for my ears.

"I'll ask to be moved—"

"What good would that do now? The damage has already been done, and there's no going back. It has nothing to do with you," his eyes lost some of their anger when he turned back to me. "You shouldn't have come here." His voice was flat, emotionless.

"I'm here because Pier invited me."

He came very close to me then, towering over me and making me feel small and insignificant. "Haven't you wondered about the coincidence of you and Pier showing up at the same resort at the same time?"

"You alluded to that before, my first night here. If you have something to say, I wish you'd just spit it out."

He was so near I could feel his hot breath on my cheeks.

"Perhaps you should use some of your writer's curiosity and investigate on your own." He stalked out of the room and into the main part of the stable.

I stood there for a moment, breathing deeply and trying to put together exactly what had just happened. My brain felt like mush and no matter how hard I tried, I couldn't organize my thoughts.

I went out into the stable proper, glanced up and down the open-ended building, listening for any sound that might tell me where Gray had gone. Hearing nothing but the occasional snort of a horse, or the stamping of hooves, I walked the length of the building in search of the man. Unable to find him, I decided that meant my ride had been called off. Disappointed and confused, I started back for the house.

Chapter 5

A noise came from just beyond the door. Diana drew back, shrinking against the far corner of the room and wishing she could somehow avoid his piercing eyes and certain wrath. In her mind, she realized how futile this was, but within her heart, hope remained.

With a suddenness that sent a chill through her very soul, the door flew open, and he stood there regarding her from beneath furrowed brows.

"You should not have run away, Diana. You should have known I would never allow you to go . . ."

Within the coolness of the shaded pathway, my heart finally settled to a normal beat, and my mind began to relax along with it. A fallen tree at the side of the path beckoned me, and I gratefully answered its call.

I sat thinking about the encounter with Gray and Dee, trying to assimilate the information into some form that made sense. I'd gone down to share that wonderful luncheon, hoping for the chance to get to know Gray better, and maybe get more than a passing glimpse of Dee. Things started out fine, not great, but there'd been no indication it would end as it had. True, it got a little sticky when the conversation led to Dee, but . . .

Face it, I told myself sternly. It was a disaster from the beginning. The moment Gray discovered Dee was expected to eat with us, his attitude changed. What actually set him off, I couldn't say. But I didn't believe it had anything to do with not wanting the child's company. I guessed it had more to do with the knowledge that Dee had virtually been left alone. It was obvious he knew everyone else had gone, and from his reaction, this wasn't the first time something like this had happened. While I agreed it was no way to treat a six-year-old child, I did feel that Gray had overreacted to my 'part' in it.

And what was all that about Pier and I meeting at Tan-Tar-A?

I shook my head, and stretching my legs out in front of me, allowed the cool breeze to flow over me like a refreshing wash.

"I thought you was gonna ride." The voice came from close behind me, the words spoken with the slightest touch of hesitation.

"I decided against it," I said without turning.

"Were you too scared of Heathers, 'cause if you were, you don't have to be."

I realized now that Dee was somewhere above me,

and I peered up from the corner of my eye to see if I could locate her. It didn't take much effort—she was a little to my left and about eight to ten feet up in a lone maple among the path of oaks.

"I wasn't afraid," I assured her. "Your, uh, uncle and I just had a little misunderstand—"

"You fought!" She laughed with unbridled glee. "He's got a horrible temper. Worse'n me."

"Really?" I couldn't keep the sarcasm from my voice. Dee, however, didn't seem to notice.

If I hadn't been watching, I wouldn't have seen her nod of assent.

"Gray don't like a lot of people. He says they get on his nerves. All I know is that he has an awful lot of fights an' is always gettin' in trouble. That's what I've heard Aunt Pier say, anyway." She swung down over the branch, her knees crossed, holding her to it while her small arms reached toward the ground.

"Do you like to climb trees?" She asked with the perfect innocence of a child.

"I used to very much. I'm afraid it's been a long time since I've done it, though."

"Would you like to now?"

I couldn't help but laugh as I finally turned around to get a good look at her. "I don't think I'd be very good at it."

"Not as good as me?"

Her pale blond hair swept the ground below her as she pushed her body forward to start swinging.

"Definitely not as good as you. If I did what you're doing now, especially after just having eaten, I'm afraid I'd be sick."

She giggled again, delighted with her discovery.

"You couldn't do this?" She made her body move faster, the back and forth motion causing the small branch she was sitting on to move dangerously with her.

"You'd better be careful, Dee, or you, and the branch you're holding, are both going to tumble to the ground."

She swung a bit faster for a moment, then stopped and stared at me. She pushed the hair from her forehead, her dark eyes becoming serious. "Would I die?"

The question reverberated in my ears, one I'd heard asked many times in the years I worked at Langston—one that was never easy to answer. My heart seemed to skip a beat from the sudden memory of Amy Webster intruding in my brain. It took a moment to catch my breath.

"I don't think so," I spoke with far more calm than I felt. "You might be hurt badly enough that you wouldn't be able to climb trees for a long time."

She wrinkled her nose. "I wouldn't like that very much."

With a practiced grace, she righted herself on the limb, then stretched out on it, belly down, her bottom snug against the base of the trunk.

"Why are you cryin'?"

How observant she was! I'd thought I managed to brush away the tears as she was pulling herself back upon the branch.

"Did I do somethin' to make you sad?"

"No, of course not."

"It wasn't 'cause I said that about Heathers?" She seemed really worried now; her little face watched me with a most serious expression, her dark eyes reflecting their concern.

"No, Dee, it has nothing to do with the horse or what you said. It, um, it's just a memory." I turned away, wishing there was some way I could leave and not hurt her feelings. I had no desire to delve into this with anyone—let alone a six-year-old child.

"I know about sad memories." Her voice took on a grown-up, confidential tone. "Lots of bad things have happened to people around me. Both Pa Pa and Grampa died, Uncle Ryan got hurt real bad, and," she paused for a moment, her voice catching in her throat. "And then my mamma went away."

I sat there not knowing what to do, what to say. There was something very strange and touching about her attempt to comfort me when up until a few moments ago she hadn't deemed me worth talking to.

I felt her small hand upon my shoulder and looked up to find her standing next to me.

"When somethin' bad happens, it's hard not to feel sad. So, it's ok if you wanna cry. I won't laugh or nothin', I promise."

"Thank you." I smiled up at her and took a grubby little hand in mine. "You're being very nice to me, Dee. I appreciate that."

She shrugged and withdrew her hand from mine. "Why are you sad?"

I could see the offer of friendship was conditional. She'd given something, telling me about her family's problems, now I was expected to give in return.

"I was remembering a little girl just a few years older than you."

"And that made you sad?" She asked, amazed.

"Yes. You see, she—she died, and that makes me very sad." Please God, please have her leave it at that.

"O—oh." Deidre Courtney sat on the log next to me, placed her small hands on my knees, and peered up into my face. "What was her name?"

"Amy." Saying her name aloud made the vision of rich brown hair and dark brown eyes become a reality. I could see eleven-year-old Amy Webster before me as easily as I could see Dee. Not even closing my eyes could block out the picture or take away the sudden onslaught of pain.

Tears once again formed in my eyes, too many to brush away and keep hidden from the child in front of me. I'd thought I was done with the tears, with the pain and all that went with it, but being here with Dee brought it vividly back.

"Was she your little girl?" Dee's voice was soft and considerate. It was obvious this child was used to seeing grown-ups cry and had taken it upon herself to try and ease the sorrow whether she understood it or not.

"No. She was someone I was trying to help. By the time I got to her, it was already too late, the damage had been done." The words were the same Dr. Hadley spoke to me upon Amy's death. And while I knew in reality it might be true, the theory that I had based my work upon insisted they had to be false.

"Did you love her?"

I pushed at the fog that threatened to engulf my brain and looked at Dee thoughtfully. "I—I didn't know her very well."

Dee appeared confused by this information. A line formed between her brows as she squinted her eyes at me. "Then she must have been someone awful special for you to cry when you think about her." She sat back on the log and crossed her arms in front of her. "You wanna know what?"

I smiled, relieved the conversation seemed about to change subjects and directions. "What?"

"There's a robin's nest up there in the tree I was in. It has three babies in it now, but there used to be four. Right after they came outta their shells, one of them fell or somethin', 'cause he wasn't there the next day. I think the mamma bird was pretty unhappy 'cause I heard her makin' a lot of noise. She was sittin' over there on the ground, squawkin' an' carryin' on somethin' terrible. But then, she just flew away an' when she came back a while later, I saw her sittin' up there feedin' her other babies. That was kinda gross, so I didn't watch for very long."

"I see." And I did. In her own way, Dee was trying to tell me that life had to go on in spite of the death and sadness we might experience. "You know," I patted her on the knee. "You're one very smart cookie."

"I know."

I stood and brushed off my jeans. "I'm headed back to the house to find something more to eat. Want to come with me?"

She shrugged her narrow shoulders. "Maybe a little way. I'm not really hungry, but maybe Ole Edna's still got some of those chocolate chip cookies around. You sayin' I was a cookie made me think of 'em."

"I see."

She nodded and grinned. "Can I call you Lyssie?" She waltzed up next to me and took my hand.

"I don't see why not."

"My grandmother would make me call you Miss Daniels, I think."

Surprised by the sudden formal tone, I glanced down at her. "Well, I'm not your grandmother, and I think after our conversation just now that your using my first name is far more appropriate."

It was obvious she liked this news very much. Her smile widened, and she gave my hand a gentle squeeze. We turned to start down the lane and had taken just a few steps when I felt a slight tug on my hand.

Dee had ceased walking and stood with her head hanging upon her chest, a sudden, serious expression on her face.

"What did you do with the butterfly?" Her voice was so soft I barely heard her.

"After admiring how pretty it was, I let him go." I kneeled down in front of her. "Why did you throw him at me, Dee?"

"I only threw him 'cause it was you." She dropped my hand and backed slightly away from me, the change in her demeanor mirroring the attitude she'd had toward me back at the stables.

"The curtains were drawn back and the windows were open, and—and I—" Tears filled her eyes. "I thought you were Mamma." She flung the words at me in much the same way she had the Monarch. Before I had the opportunity to say anything, she'd run off.

"Brilliant, Lysette!" I muttered aloud. How could I have been so stupid? After all this, I'd pushed too hard too soon and blown it. Big time.

I got off my knees, and with a heart even heavier than it had been earlier, started back for Foxxemoor. I was no longer in the mood for company, neither did I want to sit in my suite and write. I felt antsy, and I had no idea what to do to dispel the feeling.

I must have been more than three-fourths of the way back to the house when I decided I'd had enough. I'd looked forward to riding all morning, and that's what I was going to do. If Gray wasn't around to saddle up for me, I would ride bareback if I had to.

The mere thought of it made me laugh, and the laughter did more than anything else to lighten my spirits.

I reminded myself that I was a guest here at Foxxemoor. I could, and would, engage in friendly conversation with the family but refused to get involved in the myriad of problems existing among the members of the household. I was Pier's friend, her guest, invited to keep her company and help my writing. That was it. Period.

Looking at my watch, I was surprised to find it only a little after one. With everything that had happened, I couldn't believe only ninety minutes passed since I'd first left for the stables. I picked up my pace with a renewed determination, and within a few minutes, walked into the stable office.

The food we'd left on the work table had been cleared away, the table wiped clean, and the ice chest placed on the floor near the desk. Other than a stray napkin that had drifted to the floor beneath the table, there was no sign of our 'attempted' meal.

The door to the stable was open, and hoping I would find Gray or an assistant with the horses, I went through it.

Most of the stalls were empty and looked as though they had been that way for some time. Of the four that were currently occupied, only one of them contained its boarder—a beige and white Shetland who was being brushed by Gray. I stood and watched him for a moment, the gentle strokes with the brush, the reassuring caresses of his hand, and the whispered words that I was unable to make out, all putting the pony at ease throughout these ministrations.

It would have been easy to be taken in by the tenderness he displayed toward the animal if I hadn't been so irritated by his earlier behavior. Instead, I shook myself mentally, cleared my throat loudly enough for him to hear me, and waited. He looked up, patted the horse on the neck, then came over to the gate.

"If you've come back for your ride, it's too late. I've set the others loose in the pasture." His voice was flat.

I refused to allow his attitude to irritate me. "I suppose that's it, then. I'll just have to make it another time. Would tomorrow around two be convenient for you and the horses?"

"Fine." He started back toward the pony, the slight limp I'd noticed before seeming more pronounced than usual. He was almost to the far wall when he turned back around to face me. "Look, I'm not very good at this, but I'm sorry about the way things went earlier. I'm not the most tactful person in the world, but that's no excuse. You just wanted to help Dee, and I made a mountain out of a molehill. I'd no right to lay it on you the way I did."

"Since I'm here as your sister's guest and have no desire to ruin my vacation by making enemies, I'll accept your apology." I remained cool, reserved, matching tone for tone. Inside, however, I felt my soul soar with foolish hope. "I'm here to write, relax, and have a little fun along the way. I've neither the time nor the energy to get involved with your family's problems. Nor do I have the right to criticize Dee's care or your behavior. For that, *I* apologize." I started to leave before I lost the cool I had affected.

"Wait, Miss—Lysette." I turned to find Gray wiping his hands on a heavily soiled cloth as he walked toward me. "I don't want to alienate you. And I truly appreciate your concern about Dee." He flung the rag aside and continued to wipe his hands on his jeans. "You know, a person can never have too many friends. Truce?" He held his hand out to me.

I started to take it then hesitated. "The last time you said that we immediately had an, er, a disagreement."

"True. But couldn't you take the chance anyway?" His mischievous grin made my heart catch in my throat yet again.

I took his hand, and he gave it a firm squeeze. "Tomorrow at two, then."

As I watched him return to the stall, I got the strangest feeling of *déjà vu*. A tingling along the base of my spine sent an involuntary shiver throughout my body. Turning around to make the trek back to Foxxemoor, I couldn't help but wonder what would happen next.

Chapter 6

Craven stood over her, making her feel smaller and more insignificant than ever before. His dark eyes bore into her, and she felt the charge of tension in the air as his thunderous voice echoed in the small room. If she answered his question, spoke the truth regarding her flight into the darkness, what would he do to her? How much more could he harm her?

Diana cringed in the knowledge that, within these walls, Craven was lord and master of all. Whatever diabolical plan he came up with would be carried out without question by his underlings. None of them would help her; none would come to her defense. She was
doomed . . .

Sunday morning was delightfully cool, and the drive to the church Pier had suggested was relaxing. It turned out to be the beautiful, old-fashioned church I'd noticed outside of Bristol. From the moment I walked into the sanctuary, the warmth it exuded felt like a much needed hug.

There was a combination of traditional and modern songs that filled the church to the rafters with praise. During the 'meet and greet,' my hand was shaken so many times it started to swell. If this wasn't enough to tell me I had come to the right place, the reading of Psalm 86:5 would have confirmed it.

As I contemplated David's words, *"For You, Lord, are good, and ready to forgive, And abundant in mercy to all those who call upon You,"* a young man came to stand behind the pulpit. I was surprised to find him so self-effacing in speech, when the air that surrounded him was sure and confident. He spoke as one used to standing before a crowd, his easy mannerisms and ready smile drew everyone's attention to what he insisted was not a sermon but a 'lesson.'

"For those of you who don't know me," he said, looking over the top of his small, wire-frame glasses. "I'm Gerald MacKay, the pinch-hitter for Pastor Hollings, who is ill today. When Evan called late last night, all I wanted to do was make an excuse as to why I couldn't help out. But, as you can see, I'm here." He grinned as laughter filled the sanctuary. "At least it gave me a subject for today: forgiveness."

Goosebumps covered my skin as I listened to Bible verses about the infinite forgiveness of God.

"If God could forgive his chosen people when they continually turned away from Him, He can certainly forgive you." Gerald MacKay smiled out at the congregation. "Funny thing, this. We know God will forgive us when we come to Him and ask. So, why is it that we find it so hard to forgive ourselves?"

It was all I could do to keep from breaking down. I sat in the pew, my back aching with the effort of keeping it so straight. At the end of the service, I smiled at all those who greeted me and was relieved when I finally got to the church door.

As Gerald MacKay shook my hand, I gazed up into his kind, grey eyes, thanked him for the message, and made my escape. Clutching the church bulletin tightly, I forced myself not to run to my car.

It *had* been a wonderful service with a timeless and timely message. But right now I wasn't ready to contemplate his words.

Back at Foxxemoor, I changed my clothes and grabbed a bite to eat without seeing a soul. At one-thirty, I went down to the stables to find a groom waiting to help me into the saddle of Dylan Courtney's horse, Heathers.

The mare began an easy cantor, her head held high in an almost regal manner, which made me wonder if she'd ever been entered in competition. With gentle prodding, she broke into a full and graceful gallop. I reveled in the feel of her powerful body and the wind whipping through my hair. The ride through the nearby pasture was pleasant, Heathers's character and responsiveness perfect for a novice like me. After an hour, I returned to the stables rejuvenated.

I didn't encounter Gray and, though it disappointed me in some ways, I was also relieved. We needed time to let both of us become more settled about what happened—at least, that's what I thought.

As for Dee, I hadn't seen her since she left me on the pathway the day before. I thought she might be in the maple tree, and as I walked past, checked to see. I even lingered at the fallen log for several minutes, thinking she might happen along. When she didn't show, I continued my walk back to the house alone.

Pier's humor had not improved with the defection of Miss Allen. She was more distracted and withdrawn than I'd ever seen her. When I tried to engage her in an activity, it was obvious she participated more from a sense of obligation than anything else. Her attitude did nothing to bolster my sagging spirits, and with this rather oppressive atmosphere, I found it more and more difficult to be creative. The well, or muse, had gone dry, and I was at a loss as to how to revive it.

I'd never experienced writer's block before. It always seemed I'd more ideas than the time to write them down. This was an opportunity to put myself to the ultimate test, see if I had what it took to complete a novel, and I was determined not to fail.

From the beginning, my imagination had carried me away, offering a world in which to escape from the reality I'd left behind at Langston. Tan-Tar-A and Ha Ha Tonka fed the flame, and coming to Foxxemoor had fueled it even more. I'd believed nothing could extinguish that flame until the final touches had been placed upon *Craven*. I hadn't counted on the turmoil and mixed emotions I'd experienced since meeting Gray and Dee.

No matter what I did, Dee was never far from my thoughts. The child was heartbroken over her mother's absence, and no one here at Foxxemoor seemed willing—or capable—of helping her. Except, perhaps, for Gray.

My head ached from the images whirling around

inside my brain. The intensity of the heat and humidity didn't help matters. Neither had the inability to get a good night's sleep.

The last two nights I'd awakened in a sweat, the perspiration running from my body as if I had been sleeping in a sauna. Whether it was the heat or the remnants of a nightmare that awakened me, I was uncertain. Whichever it was, I'd been unable to go back to sleep.

Tonight, exhaustion lulled me to sleep long before the sun set. But sleeping through the night was not to be. Within the darkness of the now familiar room, my ears strained for outside sounds. For a while, all I heard was the hoot of an owl somewhere nearby. Then, I thought I heard the sound of footsteps as they passed along the corridor outside my suite.

I could have sworn someone stopped before my door, thought I heard the door to the sitting room open and close quietly. As the hair on the back of my neck began to prickle, my heart pausing in the stillness, I heard the whisper of footsteps as they came across the thick carpeting in the other room.

The door connecting the bedroom and sitting room had been left open, and the moon coming in through the windows lent a hint of light to the rooms. I watched the area with great concentration, waiting and wondering if the intruder was of this world or the one occupied by ghosts and demons of the past.

I might not be able to write because of the block, but my imagination was still in full swing. The more intent my vigil, the more my imagination took flight. Finally, unable to stand the suspense any longer, I slid from my bed and tip-toed across the room to the doorway. While I weighed the pros and cons of confronting my nighttime visitor, the gentle whisper retreated back toward the door to the suite.

I rushed into the sitting room, ready to face whoever was there, entering in time to see the door leading to the corridor close silently. I ran across the room, grabbing at the door only to find it stuck—something that had never happened before!

I tugged at the door as the footsteps receded, heading farther down the corridor and into the south wing, an area I'd not yet ventured into. The echo could still be heard when I finally succeeded in pulling my door open. I stood there, exhausted from my struggle, shaking at the thought of the mysterious intrusion.

As I turned to go back into my room, I had the distinct feeling of being watched. Expecting to find Dee lurking in the dark hallway, I turned quickly around, ready to confront her. Instead, a sleepy, disheveled Pier stood by her door, her eyes looking past me into the darkness of the corridor beyond.

"Did you hear footsteps?" She whispered, still not looking at me.

I went to her, anxious to tell someone what happened. "I woke up from what I thought was a nightmare and heard someone in the hall. The next thing I knew, they were in my suite. Before I could catch them, they were back in the hallway." I touched Pier's arm, and she finally turned toward me. "The door was just closing on the hallway when I got to the sitting room. It shut quietly, like usual. But when I tried to open it just a few seconds later, it was stuck fast, immovable."

Pier gazed at me with frightened eyes. "It—it came

into my room first." Her voice shook as did the hands that reached out to me. "I couldn't get my door to open either, and I was terrified. I just stood there, not knowing what to do. When I heard you open your door, I tried mine again. It opened then, Lyssie, without a problem."

"I don't understand." I looked down the hallway into the darkness where the sound of the footsteps had gone. "Who do you think it was, and why would they do this?"

Pier shook her head, her large eyes reflecting the same fear I felt. "I don't know, but I'm locking both my doors, and in the morning, Mrs. Merrick and Margaret are going to get an earful. Now, I'm going back to bed, though I doubt I'll sleep. You should do the same."

I left her and returned to the entrance to my own suite. "Night," I whispered.

"Lock your doors." Was all she answered.

I did lock my doors and, to my surprise, I also went back to sleep. When I awoke the next morning, it was late, nearly ten o'clock, and the room was deep in shadow. Looking out the window, the overcast sky and thickness of the air told me we'd have a storm before the day was over.

My head felt heavy from the heat and the disturbed sleep from the night before. I was in no hurry to leave the sanctity of my suite, in spite of my curiosity about what Pier may have found out about the night's intrusion. I just wasn't in the mood for company or polite conversation.

I splashed cool water on my face and arms in an effort to dispel the sluggishness I felt, then slowly dressed in the lightest weight outfit I could find—a soft blue sun dress. Low-heeled sandals of the same shade with a matching ribbon in my ponytail finished my dressing. No make-up today; the heat would have it melting and running into my eyes within minutes of application.

Finished, I sat before my laptop and decided to send an email to Dr. Hadley. Connecting to the port Pier had shown me on the desk phone, I logged into my email account. I told Dr. Hadley about my trip to Tan-Tar-A and how I'd found Pier vacationing there as well. She was familiar with my background and my relationship to Pier, so I felt she'd approve of my change in plans and how things had progressed since coming to Foxxemoor.

I asked about a couple of the children who were at the Center when I'd left and also if she had heard anything further from Amy Webster's father. I included the Foxxe's phone number in case she needed to get in touch with me. She knew I wasn't great at keeping up with email, and since I'd never followed through on her suggestion of getting a cell phone, figured she would feel better knowing she had a direct line to me.

"Though I sometimes miss the work I did with the children, going away was the wisest choice for me at this time," I wrote. "I've become engrossed in my writing and am very pleased about what I have done so far."

"I'm not certain when I'll be coming home, or what my plans will be when I leave Foxxemoor. If I monitor my expenditures and am very careful, the inheritance from my grandmother should last quite some time. Then, of course, there's the trust from my parents that Grandmother had kept from me . . ."

With the email sent, I was ready to face the rest of the day. I stopped by the empty dining room and picked up a glass of iced tea on my way out to the gardens.

The heat was more oppressive than it had been for days, and the humidity was so heavy that the flower scents were overpowering. Still, you couldn't deny their beauty. There were rows upon rows of tiny tea roses in varying colors, geraniums, pinks, pansies, alyssum in both white and purple, and numerous varieties of colorful hot house plants and flowers I didn't recognize.

The garden was vast, taking up the equivalent of a city block as it stretched between the wings of the house then further back to be flanked by enormous evergreens. From the corner of the north and south wings, hedge rows 'fenced in' the garden on either side, giving it a secluded look, and separating it from the rest of the estate. Flowering bushes and shrubs dotted the landscape along with paved walkways, a goldfish pool, stone statues in Greek or Roman attire, and young shade trees with benches and chairs of both black and white wrought iron. Standing in the center of the garden was a gazebo-like structure with a large picnic table and cushioned seats around the outer circle of the little building. It was a beautiful place, and its peace and enchantment was exactly what I needed.

I went to my usual place beneath the shade of a young maple and sat back on the white iron bench. The glass of tea was sweating in my hands, and I put it to my forehead in an attempt to cool my weary brain. I wasn't there more than a couple of minutes when I heard someone approaching me from behind. I turned to see Ryan coming toward me, his progress slow and awkward as he leaned heavily upon his cane. Not wanting to embarrass him or make him self-conscious, I turned back around and, closing my eyes, leaned my head back.

"Hello," his deep voice, so much like his brother's, was friendly and completely lacking in any of his earlier hesitation and reluctance about my presence at Foxxemoor.

I opened my eyes and smiled up at him. "Are you taking a break from work as well?"

He laughed, grinning as he lowered himself onto the bench with care. "Being one of the bosses does have advantages at times. So, how's the book coming along?"

"Great. At least, it was till the last day or two. I'd been writing like crazy. Now, I'm blocked. I'm sure it won't last, but it *is* irritating."

"Ah, the inevitable writer's block. I've heard that happens to the best of them—though Stephen King may be the exception."

I couldn't help but laugh. "You're right; I doubt he's suffered from it a day in his life. If only the rest of us could be so lucky!"

He shifted around on the bench, using his hands to stretch his legs out before him. "There's a storm in the air; my legs have been stiff all day. I hope it comes before nightfall and gets it out of its system."

I nodded my agreement. "I'm not fond of night storms. Guess it's a hangover from childhood. They make me uncomfortable."

"Because you can't see what's coming. Things are always worse in the dark," he reflected.

"Maybe it has something to do with our primitive nature, going back to early man."

He laughed. "I'm not the philosophical type, Lyssie, so I wouldn't like to guess. As far as I'm concerned, it's just something I remember my mother saying. You know, like pain or a cold is always worse at night." He sighed. "She was right about the pain."

"I'm sorry, would you like more room?" Thinking it might be best to move to the bench across from this one, I started to get up, but his hand on my arm stopped me.

"It's ok."

"Would you like me to get a cushion from the gazebo to prop—"

"Relax, Lyssie, I'm fine. Really. It's thoughtful of you to think of it." He pushed his hair back from his damp forehead. "I shouldn't have said anything." He raised a hand to stop my protest. "I don't need your sympathy, no matter how well-intentioned. I'm coming along very well. The therapist seems pleased."

"That's wonderful." I swallowed hard, hoping not to put a foot in my mouth. "Pier told me about your accident. From the way she'd talked, I'd expected you to be in a wheelchair. You've made remarkable progress."

"Thank you." He took one of my hands into his and gave it a gentle squeeze. "I'm not afraid to discuss my infirmity, you know, it helps to ease the pain. Stop thinking you've said the wrong thing and offended me." His warm blue eyes smiled into mine. "Now, tell me, what kind of book are you writing?"

I told him that it was a Gothic and related a little about the *Craven's* storyline. As we talked, I couldn't help comparing Ryan to his brother. While they were identical twins, their characters were very different from one another, and, once again, I felt it would be easy to tell them apart. I recognized Leo Craven in Gray as much from his looks and voice as from his manner, yet saw nothing of the character in the man before me. Even the facial similarities were superficial and could be found in any man with similar coloring. Ryan bore no resemblance to Craven. In fact, when compared this way, even very little to his twin.

"I'd say Foxxemoor has been very good for you," he said when I finished my description. "Have you had the opportunity to explore the house?"

I shook my head. "I've been meaning to, but there's been such a pull to write that I haven't found the time."

"Then you need to make the time, Lyssie. If I could get around better, I'd give you the grand tour. At any rate, I believe it will be a nice supplement to your story." Again he gave my hand a gentle squeeze. "I would have enjoyed being your guide."

I felt myself blushing and was thankful when he released my hand. I didn't know what to say in response to his obvious come-on and was grateful for the interruption of Margaret's voice as it came to us across the garden.

"So there you are." Margaret hailed us from the patio before heading in our direction. "We've been wondering about you all morning, Lysette. No one had seen you, and we were beginning to get concerned." She sank onto the bench opposite us, taking out a pocket handkerchief to dab at her brow.

"I'm sorry; I didn't mean to cause problems. I slept in late, and with the heat and humidity, didn't feel like eating." Or having company, I left unsaid.

"Well, dear, after the night you had, it's quite

understandable. Are you feeling better now? No after effects, I hope."

"I'm fine, a little sluggish from the heat, perhaps, but fine." I took a sip of tea, the cool liquid refreshing as it slid down my throat.

"Oh yes, the heat will certainly do that. As a matter of fact, I'm feeling it a bit myself. I do wish the appliance man would get those parts in to fix the air conditioner. It's simply unbearable in that house!" She mopped her brow in a far more ladylike manner than I would have ever been able to imitate. "And with the storm coming . . ." Her voice trailed off as she got up and walked over to one of the fountains. She held her handkerchief beneath the flowing stream and then rubbed the water across her wrists.

"Have you heard the weather?" Ryan stirred beside me, lifting his legs carefully with his hands until each knee was bent with his feet firmly planted on the ground before our bench.

"A little while ago. There was a notice from the National Weather Service issuing a severe thunderstorm warning. It's about fifty miles west of us and heading this way fast. I've got Sarah and Edna shutting all the extra windows in the house, and Pier is hunting for Deidre." Margaret rejoined us to stand under the maple.

"Perhaps I could help Pier."

"I don't believe that's necessary, my dear. Pier knows all the child's favorite haunts, and I expect to hear from her momentarily. You just sit here and relax. Besides, I would like to hear your side of the disturbance last night. Pier was near hysteria at breakfast, making it quite difficult to understand. Something about an intruder in the house—which we all know is impossible." She returned to her seat, her pale blue eyes watching me intently.

"I'm not sure what woke me, the heat or a dream, but shortly after waking, I heard the sound of footsteps in the hallway."

"You're sure it wasn't just the old place settling?" Ryan's expression was filled with concern.

"The thought ran through my mind. But when they stopped outside my door, I was sure it was footsteps. I mean, a person walking by on the hardwood floor in the hallway has a pretty distinctive sound."

Margaret and Ryan exchanged a look I was unable to read.

"Then what happened?" Margaret urged me on.

I told them about hearing the door to my sitting room open followed by the sound of someone walking across the room.

"That's when I decided it was time to find out what was going on. I got out of bed and, as quietly as possible, went to the connecting door. With the moon shining into the room, I figured I'd be able to see whoever it was. I must have made enough noise for him to hear me because, as I entered the sitting room, I saw the door to the hall close." I paused for a moment to see what effect my story was having on my listeners. While they both appeared attentive, I could tell neither of them were concerned about what had occurred. Still, I continued. "The oddest thing about it was what happened when I tried to open the door into the hallway; it was stuck fast. I could hear the footsteps as they headed into the south wing, and it was wasn't until the last of them faded that I could get the door to open."

"That *is* very strange," Margaret said.

"Strange, but not uncommon in our old house." Ryan patted my knees. "With all the heat and humidity the doors will stick—swelling and all. As for your 'intruder,' I'm sure it's safe to say that was our own little poltergeist, Dee."

"Oh dear!" A hand flew to Margaret's cheek in what I thought was a rather over-dramatic gesture. "You don't think she's started roaming around again?"

"I'd count on it. Both you and Mrs. Merrick confirmed that all the outside doors were locked. There was no evidence of someone entering through a window, no loose or torn screens or anything?"

"None. If Dee is—"

"Excuse me," I interrupted. "I'm sorry, but I don't believe it was your granddaughter, unless she's gained a good deal of weight in the last few days. The footsteps were definitely those of an adult."

Both of them looked at me with amazement, and I got the feeling the conversation I'd just witnessed had been a set-up—planned and executed to shut me up and dispel my fears. My question was why, but I didn't ask it.

"I don't see how you can be so certain, my dear."

"You know how different things can sound in a silent house," Ryan smiled. "Echoes, a simple sound magnified by the silence around it." Again the reassuring pat on my knees. "In the middle of the night our imaginations run wild. Furniture can take the shape of a monster or something equally threatening. We were just talking about how different things seem at night. Storms are more terrifying because the darkness hides them. Even a gust of wind takes on a different aspect. It only stands to reason. Besides, Dee *has* done this sort of thing before." His voice was calm, his manner sincere, but I still didn't buy their explanation. It must have shown on my face.

"I've a confession to make, Lysette, and I hope it won't distress you too much." Margaret lowered her eyes for a moment, and when she raised them, they were filled with tears. "The suite you're occupying belonged to my daughter Dylan. She and Deidre shared it up until—until Dylan's disappearance. After Dee moved in with Pier, the suite was shut up. When we heard you were coming, we cleared Dylan's things out so we could put you next to Pier. I know this upset Dee, but it was for the best."

"So you believe Dee was looking for her mother last night?" The implication was clear, but the suggestion appeared to disturb both of them a good deal.

"Perhaps." Ryan spoke first, his voice maintaining the calm he had shown throughout the discussion.

"I do hope not." Margaret sat heavily against the bench. "I had hoped she would come to accept—"

"I can't find Dee anywhere!" Pier's anxious voice came to us from the patio. "The storm's expected to hit the Bristol area in minutes, and God only knows where that kid has gone. If you think I'm going out in it—" Pier reached our niche and stood staring down at us. "What's going on?"

"We were discussing last night's adventure." My voice was light in the hope it wouldn't alarm her or cause her more anxiety than was already reflected in her face.

"I suppose they explained about Dee, then." She breathed a sigh of relief. "If I ever get hold of the little urchin, I'm going to read her the riot act!"

"So, you believe it *was* Dee?" I couldn't help showing my amazement.

"Of course, it makes perfect sense. I should have realized it last night, but she'd awakened me from such a deep sleep, I wasn't thinking straight. She's done this before, Lyssie, when she was in our wing. Now that she's been moved next to Margaret, she'll likely wander all over the house. Anyway, I wish I knew where she was now."

The answer wasn't long in coming. From the corner of my eye, I could see Gray, the errant child upon his broad shoulders, coming through the hedge on the north side of the garden. The others spotted them the same time I did. Margaret went to meet them and helped Dee down from her perch. I watched the interchange between the two adults, could tell even from this distance it was not a pleasant one, and noticed how Dee clung to Gray's hand throughout. Margaret offered her hand to the child, smiling down at her, but Dee refused to budge from her refuge. Giving up, Margaret turned and headed back toward us. Gray, with Dee still clinging to his hand, followed closely behind. They reached us as the first raindrops fell, splattering in loud plops on the paved walkway.

Pier moved quickly to Ryan to assist him in standing, and the two of them started for the house. Margaret rushed by me, offering them her assistance, and when it was refused, continued to the shelter of the covered patio.

"You're not worried about getting wet?" Gray stopped before my bench, looking down at me amused.

By this time the rain was falling steadily, and in the

short period since it had begun, it had almost soaked me to the skin. I could feel my now limp ponytail wet against my back, and my bangs were plastered to my forehead. I pushed them to the side, feeling the rain water slide down my face, onto my neck, to eventually mark a trail running beneath my dress.

"I think it's the first time I've been cool in days!" I told him as I left the bench and joined them on the walkway.

"This is fun!" Dee released Gray's hand and ran a little ahead of us. She found a puddle at the side of the walk and jumped in it. Mud and water splashed up around her, covering her bare legs and the bottom of her shorts in a slimy goo. She grinned back at us and then went in search of the next puddle. A reproach called from the patio was naturally ignored as the child continued her search.

"She'll be in for it now," Gray's voice was full of amusement as he watched Dee. "What about you, do you think this is fun?"

"Ordinarily, no. But today it's perfect." I stopped on the walkway and raised my face up to the sky. The rain was cool and refreshing as it hit my face, and I relished the feel of it as it washed over me.

"So, these aren't ordinary circumstances? Maybe that's been our problem all along; we've been taking ourselves too seriously."

I couldn't be sure what he meant and, if truth be told, after my conversation with Ryan and Margaret, I wasn't interested in figuring it out. This was the first time since I'd awakened that I felt normal, and I wasn't going to banish the feeling by searching for hidden meanings behind his words. Instead, I walked past him to where Dee was standing knee deep in the run-off from the terraced walkway.

I don't know what prompted me to do it; it wasn't premeditated. I saw Dee splashing in the puddle as if it were a wading pool, her tiny, rain-streaked face looking up at me in glee. The next think I knew, I was in it with her—shoes and all!

Deidre Courtney grabbed my hands, and we danced around in the puddle like the best of friends.

Chapter 7

Cowering in a corner of the tower room where Craven held her, with the man looming over her in the dim light, was not Diana's idea of the woman she felt herself to be. Fear had pushed her into that corner, and it was the fear of losing an essential part of herself that made her rise up opposite him and look him in the eyes.

"I am not one of your hirelings, sir, to be looked upon with contempt and expected to do your bidding." Her voice gained strength as she spoke. She threw back her shoulders with a renewed sense of pride and determination.

Diana's dark brown eyes stared into Craven's, refusing to falter even as he took a menacing step toward her...

Dee was delighted with me—and the awkward position her family was in. After all, how could they admonish her for the romp in the puddle when I'd joined her?

True, I'd interfered and, in doing so, lost considerable favor in the eyes of my hosts—with the exception of Gray who applauded my actions. I believed he might've joined us if it hadn't begun to thunder and lightning at that moment. As Dee and I ran onto the patio, Pier grabbed my arm and pulled me off to the side.

"Have you lost your mind?" She whispered.

"Lighten up." Was all I said before retiring to a nearby deck chair to take off my wet sandals.

I noticed that Gray had removed his shirt and was using it to wipe the mud and water off Dee's feet. I couldn't help but admire his coolness in the face of adversity. I also admired his bronzed skin which stretched tautly across his muscular back. His arms were thick and powerful, his chest tight and dark with a fine layer of hair matching the color on his head, both glistening from the rain. When he turned suddenly in my direction, I averted my gaze, but not before he realized I'd been staring at him.

He left Dee to the ministrations of Sarah, the maid and assistant housekeeper, and came over to join me.

"Are you satisfied?" He handed me his shirt.

I took it gratefully and began to wipe away some of the mud.

"Shouldn't I be?" I challenged.

He chuckled into his hand. "That was quite a picture—not so much you and Dee as the rest of them. I think Margaret almost had a stroke!"

"Really?"

He patted my arm. "Not literally. Don't worry,

Lysette, it's all right."

Again, my face betrayed me. "I just—" How could I explain the sudden horror his words sent through me— or how ridiculous I felt for not taking it 'lightly' as he'd meant it? "They were all so fierce, yelling at her like that. I had to do something. She was just being what she is, a little kid."

"I doubt any of them could handle such a simplistic concept, so I suggest you don't even try to explain. As far as I'm concerned, it's not a big deal. It looked like a lot of fun to me."

I handed him back his shirt just as Sarah came by with a pan of water and some clean towels. I took them from her and renewed my effort to clean my feet and legs.

"I think you made Dee's day." Ryan joined us, looking down at me with approval. Considering his expression when Dee and I were playing in the puddle, this surprised me.

"I'm glad it made her happy." I grinned, pleased to have someone else on my, or rather, on Dee's side.

Gray took one of the towels that I'd laid on the nearby table and wiped his face. "I'm surprised you didn't join in, brother dear." His fixed stare was returned with equanimity.

"If not for my present condition, I would have," Ryan said through clenched teeth. "What about you, Gray, or is playing in a mud puddle not up your alley?"

Gray stood so quickly he almost knocked over the table. I grabbed for it, catching it before the towels and water tub slid onto the patio floor. The table was heavy, and with the tub sliding dangerously toward the edge, I knew there was no way to right it on my own. When I looked up to ask for help, it was to find the brothers looking at one another as if they would like to strangle the other.

"I could use a little help here."

Gray was the first to move, and because his handicap was not a new one and didn't require the use of a cane, he was far quicker on his feet. He righted the table and pushed the water tub back from the edge. The interruption was all that was needed to avert a possible volatile situation—at least for the moment.

Pier and Margaret moved in. Pier took Ryan's arm and urged him into the house. Margaret remained, watching the retreating figures, wringing her handkerchief between her hands. It was apparent she had something she wanted to say, and it appeared she wanted Ryan and Pier inside before she said it.

As soon as the screen door shut behind them, Margaret pulled up a nearby chair, her expression solemn.

"It's nice to see that Deidre has made a new friend in you, Lysette, but I do wish you hadn't encouraged her behavior just now." A smile attempted to soften the words. "We are having such a time with that child! I'm sure Pier has related some of the difficulties, and it just doesn't do to have anyone thwarting our attempts at discipline."

"For the love of—" The disgust in Gray's voice brought her up sharply. Margaret's back stiffened, and her chin thrust out in an unattractive manner as she stared up at him.

"They splashed around in a puddle. What's the problem?" The muscles across Gray's back became rigid, his jaw tightened. "Didn't you see the look on

Dee's face? That's the first time in months I've see the kid actually look happy, really happy. That alone should be worth something. And not one of your reprimands and lessons in proper etiquette. You need to remember you're dealing with a child, Margaret."

"And I suppose you know all about raising a child, Gray Foxxe." The woman's voice held a slight tremble as her cool, blue eyes burned into his.

"Not really. But the one thing I know is that the rules we have as an adult don't apply to a child. Maybe you should keep in mind the mistakes you made raising her mother!" Gray threw the towel he'd been using on the nearby table without taking his attention from Margaret.

"How dare you!" Margaret Courtney Foxxe stood, and within the blink of an eye, walked over and slapped Gray's cheek. "You stand there with that self-righteous look on your insolent face and dare to tell me my faults in raising Dylan when you won't even admit or accept responsibility for your own child! You have some nerve, Gray. Nerve, yes, courage, no."

Gray grabbed his shirt from the chair and, looking Margaret steadily in the eyes, loomed dangerously over her. "And you, my dear lady Margaret, are a witch." He turned on his heel and walked quickly to the door with direct access to the north wing. He limped badly, far worse than I'd ever seen before, probably a result of the emotional outburst I'd just witnessed.

When I turned back to Margaret, she was still shaking from the encounter with her stepson. She clutched the handkerchief against her chest, her face pale and rigid. Afraid she might be on the verge of a stroke or heart attack, I led the woman into the main section of the house where I helped her onto the couch in the living room. She never uttered a word, and worried for her, I went to search for someone to watch over her.

I found Pier coming out of the dining room, and without going into great detail, filled her in on Margaret's condition. A look of fear passed over Pier's face as she called for Ryan to come with us as quickly as he could manage. We returned to the living room and discovered Margaret still hadn't moved from the position I'd left her in, her pale blue eyes staring vacantly in front of her.

Pier knelt before her stepmother and, with a tenderness I hadn't expected, began talking softly to the woman, urging her to lie back on the couch and rest. Pier took one of Margaret's hands between hers and rubbed it, obviously an attempt to bring some warmth to them.

I got an afghan off one of the window seats and placed the blanket over Margaret as we eased her back onto the sofa. I watched, terrified; my part in what was going on may have been small, but . . .

"So, you've been awarded a show of my brother's true colors, Lyssie. Let that be a lesson to you; don't get too close to the grey fox." Ryan laughed, obviously amused by his own pun. He stood just inside the entrance to the room, leaning upon his cane, and watching his sister's ministrations to their stepmother.

"Perhaps we should call the doctor or an ambulance." I suggested, anxious they should do something to end the catatonic-like state Margaret was in.

Pier shook her head. "It's all right, Lyssie. We've

dealt with this before."

"Something like this has hap—"

"Another of our secrets out in the open." Ryan entered the room and gazed down at his stepmother. "She suffers from a disorder similar to epilepsy. I don't remember the term, but the gist of it is that emotional upsets, shock, violent arguments, etcetera, can set her off."

"Hasn't she medication to control it?"

"Of course she has," Pier flashed her brother a look that would wilt an ordinary man. "Did you ask Sarah to get it?"

Ryan nodded, taking a seat nearby. "Just as you ordered, sister dear. Relax, Pier. You know there's nothing you can do right now."

Pier appeared to take him at his word and sat on the floor in front of the sofa. Though her eyes remained on Margaret, I saw a definite change in the way she was watching her—from concern to a form of indifference in less than sixty seconds.

I stayed on the arm of the couch, my hand upon Margaret's forehead, gently stroking it in an effort to bring her around. It seemed to take forever for the medicine to arrive. The longer we waited, the more agitated I felt.

I hated the helplessness, the sense that no matter how hard you tried, you were incapable of doing anything to change the outcome. All the pent up emotion I'd had since Amy Webster's death began to boil inside me: the responsibility for not having done enough to prevent it from happening and the guilt I felt in spite of professional insistence that I was not to blame. These thoughts plagued me as I stared down into the face of the prostrate woman on the sofa.

A sound in the hallway signaled that help was on the way. We looked up to find Gray coming through the door with a bottle of medicine and a glass of water in his hands. Without a word, he came to the couch, handed Pier the glass, and with the same gentleness I'd seen him give Dee and his horses, he raised Margaret's head and slipped a capsule into her mouth. While he cradled her head in one arm, he administered a small amount of water and then stroked the woman's throat, encouraging her to swallow.

"Well done, well done," Ryan applauded. "First you dish out the poison, brother, then the cure. How appropriate."

It was clear from Gray's expression that he was trying to hold back his anger, but the redness creeping up his neck was a dead giveaway. As his fists clenched, Pier placed a calming hand on Gray's arm, surprising not only me, but him as well.

"Thanks for getting the pills. She'll be all right now." Pier glanced up at me and smiled. "It'll just be a few minutes for the drug to react, Lyssie."

I left my perch, detaching myself from them, and went over to one of the window seats. Sitting, I averted my attention from the others in the room and stared out into the rain-sodden garden.

My heart still beat a rapid staccato within my chest, and every breath I took seared my lungs in excruciating pain. I closed my eyes, shutting out Foxxemoor, and, in a flash, was back at Langston Children's Center.

When I tapped on Amy's door that morning and not gotten an answer, I'd thought she was still asleep. Opening the door, I called out to her.

"Amy? Amy, honey, if you don't get up you'll miss breakfast."

The moment I touched her I knew something was horribly wrong. I'd run to push the panic button near the door, then stood there waiting, my breath constricted as I stared at the still form on the bed. When they'd told me she was dead, I recalled her pleading voice, begging me not to let them send her back home to her mother—not even for one night. I'd reported her fear to Dr. Hadley who'd stepped in to calm the child and reassure her that this, too, was part of the healing process.

'The healing process,' how ironic it sounded in the end. We'd had it all mixed up, believed the wrong people: the lawyer, the judge, and the mother. How could we have known that the father wasn't the abuser, that it had been the mother all along. We'd allowed the mother's therapy to cloud our vision.

There were no bruises on Amy's little body, nothing to show what she may have endured during her twenty-four hours with her mother. Amy's silence when she'd returned to us had been taken as a sign that she'd not wanted to come back to the Center. Even when I had gone in to tell her good-night, she'd seemed fine. Her soft brown eyes had welcomed me, her little arms going around my neck as she told me she would see me in the morning.

But she hadn't seen me; she hadn't seen anyone. As near as the coroner could tell, the pills she'd used had been taken shortly after I'd left her the night before— pills stolen from her mother's medicine cabinet. Amy died in her sleep, quietly, just as she had lived. We didn't even have a note to let us know what pushed her over the edge.

Suddenly, I was back at Foxxemoor, rain and hail beat against the windows and roof, with thunder and lightning bursting in the sky overhead. Putting my hands to my face, I discovered I'd been crying. I wiped at the tears, pushing them away with the same fierceness that I pushed at the memory.

"You all right?" Pier stood nearby, and it was obvious from her expression that she'd been watching me for some time.

"Fine." I knew my voice and expression betrayed me, but, at the moment, I didn't care. "Margaret?"

"She's ok. She came around a little bit ago. Gray and Mr. Merrick helped her up to her suite. She'll be good as new by morning." Pier put an arm around my shoulders. "It's all right, Lyssie. You're not responsible for what happened. If anyone's to blame other than Margaret, it's Gray. If she'd taken her medicine, it wouldn't have gotten out of hand. But, like usual, she forgot."

"Forgot?" How could anyone forget to take medication that kept them from having a seizure? It didn't make sense to me.

Pier sat next to me. "She does it all the time, Lyssie. Most of the time it wouldn't make any difference, but after everything that's happened, our disturbance last night, the storm—she hates electrical storms—and the fight with Gray . . . Anyway, I think she 'forgets' because of the attention she receives when she has a fit. You'll see. Within a few hours, Margaret will be holding court in her room like a queen." She patted my knees. "It has nothing to do with you. Believe me. She may have been annoyed by your little game with Dee, but that's all it was. She wouldn't want you to be this upset. It's not in her plans."

"Plans? What plans?"

"N-nothing," Pier answered so fast that her disclaimer rang false. "Just a figure of speech." Again the reassuring pat on the knees. "Relax, quit worrying. Tell you what. How about I grab Ryan and we have a game of Scrabble? What could be better on a wet, dreary afternoon?"

I wasn't in the mood for a game but knew it would take my mind off Amy and what happened with Margaret. I knew better than to dwell on these things; my years at Langston had taught me that. If Amy's death hadn't still been so fresh, I wouldn't have been so vulnerable to Margaret's seizure. I would have taken it in stride, accepted it as part of her illness and nothing more. I was a strong-minded individual, maybe too sensitive for my own good, but far too determined to maintain my own mental health to fall into the traps I'd seen so many others step into.

Shaking myself both physically and mentally, I smiled up at my friend, determined to put the past where it belonged.

* * * * * * * * * * * * * * *

The Scrabble game was so enjoyable that Pier came out with more games. As the storm raged outside Foxxemoor, tempers were held in check inside. Gray joined us for a shortened version of Monopoly, managing to keep his cool when he went bankrupt to his brother. We laughed, teased, cajoled, and acted as if we were all the best of friends. It was a side of the family I hadn't seen. Even the attendance they gave Margaret throughout the day was more cordial, more caring than I would have imagined possible. The photos on the living room wall hinted at this bond between them; now I saw it in reality.

Dee joined us for awhile and left under protest when Mrs. Merrick came to hustle her off to bed. Gray left a short time later, saying he'd promised to tuck Dee in. As I watched him leave, I wondered if what Margaret had said was true; was he Dee's father? If he was, why hadn't he claimed the child?

By ten, Ryan and I were the only ones remaining in the living room. We'd withdrawn to read in different areas of the room—he on the sofa, me back on the window seat. The house was quiet but for the rain, which now tapped out a relaxing, rhythmic beat as it hit the windows.

I couldn't stay interested in the magazine, still too keyed up from the games to settle down. Instead, I gazed out the window, watching the lights in the garden cast eerie shadows among the plants and bushes, recalling *Craven* and my inability to get past the writer's block. Turning, I studied Ryan, who was fully engrossed in a Robin Cook medical thriller.

Before leaving, Pier helped her brother prop pillows beneath his legs to elevate his knees as he sat wedged in a corner of the sofa. The soft lighting in the room surrounded him, giving his rich, brown hair a golden glow. The lock of curls which fell across his forehead made him appear younger than his thirty years. As I watched, I had this sudden, overpowering urge to push back the hair and ease the lines etched between his brows.

The romantic in me was alive and well and needed to be held in check. It was one thing to acknowledge the attraction I felt for the twins; it was another to act on it.

In my musing, I hadn't realized *I* had now become the object of scrutiny. I was a little embarrassed to find Ryan's deep blue eyes studying me. But turnaround was fair play.

Our eyes met and locked; we both smiled, caught in our sly attempt to examine one another.

"See anything you like?" Ryan's voice was soft, melodic, as he gazed at me.

I laughed. "You look a lot like the character in my book." I lowered my legs and stretched.

"Pier told me. I'm flattered, though it's a bit misplaced since you began the story before we met." He began the business of moving his own legs from the sofa. I watched in admiration as he maneuvered on the 'man-eating' couch, a feat I could never hope to attain with such grace.

When his feet were on the floor, he turned back to me. "It's been a fun evening. I wish it didn't have to end, but I'm afraid I have an early morning."

I watched as he rose from the sofa with the use of the cane, the pain and difficulty it caused etched across his handsome face. I knew better than to rush to his aid or offer my assistance. Pier had told me how proud he was, how adamant to do things for himself. He would accept the help when necessary but didn't have to be happy about it.

I averted my eyes as he straightened up, not wishing to add to his discomfort.

"I'd offer to see you to your room, but the stairs still pose a problem. I'm not quite there yet. Perhaps you'd walk me to mine instead." He held out his arm, beckoning me with his beautiful, expressive eyes.

"How could I refuse such an offer?" I grinned as I took his arm.

"After the accident, Margaret and Mrs. Merrick converted part of the old ballroom into a bedroom for me. It's been very convenient, and they made it comfortable, too." He led me across the hall and into the south wing. We went past a set of large double doors, which he said led to the formal dining room, then on to a second set of doors. Opening these, he revealed a partitioned off area that was designed to resemble the suites upstairs.

"Very impressive, but then, I'd expect nothing less of Foxxemoor."

"They did an excellent job, didn't they?" He released my arm but retained hold of my hand. "I wasn't happy about your coming here, but now . . ."

I saw the unspoken words in his eyes, and unable to answer them, lowered mine.

"I've made you blush. You seem to do that frequently." He released my hand, and I felt his fingers dance across the bridge of my nose. "Did you know that it enhances the color of your freckles?" He kissed the tip of my nose, startling me.

I drew back. "G-good night, Ryan." I turned to leave, but, as I attempted to pass him, he reached out and caught my arm.

"You don't have to go, Lyssie." His voice was soft, sensual, and the intimation all too obvious.

"I didn't get a lot of sleep last night." My voice pleaded for him to release me, and I prayed he would do so.

Ryan Foxxe pulled me to him, and bracing himself, put his arms around me. "You're so small, so beautiful.

From the moment I met you, I've wanted to do this." His mouth came down hard on mine, the heat of his body calling for mine to answer. In spite of myself, I sank into the richness of his kiss, my arms going around his neck as I was lost in the romance of it all.

An alarm went off in my brain, and I disentangled myself. "I'm sorry, Ryan, I—" I shook my head for lack of words.

I turned and ran down the hallway. And continued to run past the living room where Henry Merrick was shutting off the lights, down the hall to the foyer, up the stairs. I shoved the door to my suite open and rushed inside.

Pier sat on the loveseat watching the evening news. The moment she turned to me, I knew she'd set me up.

"So Ryan made his pass."

"Pier, I—"

"Come on, Lyssie, give! Since the middle of the Monopoly game I knew what he had in mind. I'm pleased to see he followed through." She pulled me onto the loveseat and leaned in closely. "He's been so self-conscious because of his legs. All he does is work. Back and forth to the factory, day after day, how boring! But he's attracted to you. And I know you have to be attracted to him."

I shook my head and closed my eyes. "Pier—"

"Oh!" She clapped her hands together. "It's because they're twins, isn't it? You're not sure which—"

"Pier!"

"Don't be such a spoil sport!" She pushed playfully at my legs. "This could be very interesting."

"I find nothing amusing about it."

"You're just being silly. Relax. What's wrong with

a bit of romance with one of my brothers?"

The glowering look I threw her didn't faze her at all. "You're—incorrigible!"

"Runs in the family."

It took me a moment to realize what she meant. Remembering the nanny's remark about Dee soon had us both in stitches.

"I should have known better than to get involved with you again." I told her, holding my aching side.

"Ah, come on. We always had fun together."

"Either at my expense or the guy you set me up with."

"Maybe, but we had a lot of laughs."

"We did. This is different."

"Yeah, it's my brother. Now, are you going to tell me what happened or not?"

"Not." I said firmly.

Refusing to be deterred, she raised an expressive brow. "I'll tell you anything you want to know about either of them."

"A bribe?" I laughed. "Ok, I'll play. Is Gray Dee's father?"

Pier sighed, no longer smiling. "I did say anything. The answer is that no one knows. I mean, Dylan was always switching back and forth between them. She'd been engaged to both of them before getting pregnant."

"She never let on who—"

Pier shook her head. "Not as far as I know. She went off to Kansas City when she was about seven months along and didn't come back until Dee was a year old. Everyone went to see her, tried to get her to come home. Anyway, we accepted Dee was a Foxxe." She shrugged. "That was the sort of thing Dylan would do. She'd up and leave without telling anyone. So having a baby without being married, or even mentioning she was pregnant, that was so totally her. I'd never have lived it down, but Dylan . . ." The bitterness in her voice was apparent.

"So what happened?"

I could tell Pier regretted her offer to tell all. She shook her head as she rose from the loveseat.

"If she ever told the proud papa, I've no idea. When Margaret married my father, Dylan moved in here bag and baggage, dragging her daughter behind her. Next thing I know, it's back to playing the twins against one another. She was engaged to Gray when she disappeared."

My sharp intake of breath about choked me. I was glad Pier didn't notice.

"It never occurred to any of us that something might have happened to her. Like I said, she always ran off like that, leaving for days at a time, literally dropping of the face of the Earth. It was more than a week before Gray decided this wasn't normal, even for her. At the time, we were still so worried about Ryan and trying to deal with Daddy's death, that Dylan's disappearing act barely registered. I mean, there were cops and insurance investigators asking questions about the accident and suggesting foul play," a lone tear ran down her cheek. "How were we supposed to know what was going on with Dylan?"

"Foul play?" All that information and I latched onto the one thing that seemed to upset Pier the most.

"It was the same sort of trash that went around after Margaret and Daddy got married. You know, because it was so soon after her husband's death. Anyway, there was some crazy notion that the brake lines of the Caddy had been messed with or something. It was all dropped after Margaret told the insurance investigator that the company could keep their money. In the meantime, Gray was frantic. Margaret got the cops and some P.I.'s on the case, but the trail was already cold. The only thing they knew for sure was that Dylan had last been seen coming out of the factory in town.

"As much as everyone hated the idea, I know Margaret was only trying to be logical when she declared that Dylan was dead. She would never have stayed away from Dee this long. She loved that kid far too much to leave her behind like this."

I followed her to the door. "Pier, I'm sorry. I didn't mean—"

"Hey, it's my own fault." She took a deep breath, a sly smile forming at the corners of her mouth. "This was only a temporary reprieve, you know. Sooner or later you're going to tell me what happened between you and Ryan." After opening the door, she turned back to me. "I'm not sure how Gray's doing now, Lyssie. So, if you're looking to him for a little romance, keep in mind how difficult it will be to compete with Dylan Courtney's ghost. Stick with Ryan; he's safer in more ways than one."

I stood within the halo of light issuing from my open door and watched as Pier went to her own rooms. With a little wave, she disappeared inside, leaving me to ponder her last statement as the silence of the house settled around me.

Chapter 8

When she awoke, Craven was no longer in the room with her. It was dark, and the sounds of scratching within the walls terrified her with thoughts of rats and mice running rampant through the room.

Her head ached, and the tightness in her throat and ears told Diana that her adventure on the moors had led to the onset of a cold or worse. She grabbed at the tattered blanket on the cot, wrapping it about her in an effort to ease the chills that wracked her body. A fear of certainty stole over her as she pulled the blanket tightly around her.

He had left her here to die . . .

The sun shone even more brightly than usual after the storm, leaving Foxxemoor looking shiny and new in its wake. The air held a clarity that had not been there before; perhaps it was the lack of humidity and reduction in heat. The breeze flowing through the windows was light and cool, just what you would expect for June. It was a pleasant change from the stifling heat, a change which was sure to bring a renewed sense of energy.

I was up early the next morning, feeling more refreshed than I had for several days. After dressing in jeans and a T-shirt, with my honey-colored hair pulled into a ponytail, I went down to the dining room. There was no one about, so I took my glass of orange juice and a slice of toast out onto the patio.

The garden glistened in the sunlight, the dew and remaining raindrops sparkling like diamonds as the sun touched them. The odor of the flowers, mixed with the distinctive smell of wet earth, gave the air a pleasant, heady aroma. Birds were out in record numbers, all singing and chattering in full voice. Some splashed in a nearby birdbath; others filled the puddles along the walkway, while still others darted in and out of the goldfish pool. It was a beautiful morning, and I was determined to enjoy it.

My original plan to explore the house was put aside in favor of spending time outdoors. It would be the perfect day for riding, maybe even to explore the area beyond the pasture where I'd ridden in the past. I wondered if Pier might want to join me, but the sunshine made me too lazy to move from my perch to find her and ask. Instead, I sat watching the birds, enjoying the peace of the moment.

"You're up bright and early. Have a big day planned?"

I turned to find Gray standing nearby, noticing again the uncanny way he had of moving about with such stealth. This seemed quite an accomplishment for a man of his size and physical condition—just another reason for my foolish heart to admire him.

"The breeze coming in my bedroom window was too wonderful to ignore." I smiled up at him. "Care to join me?"

He brought his glass of juice to my table, brushed at the water on the chair, then sat down. "So, what's on the agenda today? I see there are a few puddles left, are you planning to take advantage of them?"

The teasing note in his voice made me laugh. "I think I've had enough of that for a while. Perhaps the next time it rains. As for my plans, I wondered if you'd have any objections to my taking Heathers off on a day-long adventure? I'd love to explore the estate a bit, ride the trails, see what's beyond the pasture."

"I hate to disappoint you, but after last night's downpour, the regular trails will be too muddy. Neither you, nor the horse, would like that much. I do have an alternate suggestion that might work out as well."

The curious expression on his face intrigued me. "I'm all ears."

"Great. I've been planning to check in with the tenants on some of the outlying properties. I've put it off because of the good weather—it's always a hassle to have to hunt them down when they're in the fields. Because of the storm, I'm more likely to find them closer to home." The way he cleared his throat gave me the impression he was nervous. "I ride to the closer holdings, and the way I go through the woods, means the ground would be firmer than on the more well-worn paths. It's a nice ride, plenty of scenery, and it will give you an idea about the vastness of the estate. If you'd like to come . . . "

"Sounds interesting."

"I'll be honest with you," he cleared his throat again. "Heathers isn't fond of storms and can sometimes be a bit skittish the following day or so. I'd feel a lot better about you riding if I'm there to keep an eye on the two of you."

My traitorous heart skipped a beat. "Sounds logical," I said, careful not to betray anything. "When do we leave?"

"Whenever you're ready. Meet me down at the stable."

"Can I come too?" Dee's voice rang out from somewhere close by. We both stood, looking around for her. She squeezed out from between two statues a few yards from the edge of the patio.

"It's 'may I.' Were you hiding there all this time?" Gray's attempt at sternness had the child in stitches.

"May I?" She mimicked through her laughter. She squealed in delight to his nod as she climbed the steps to join us. "An' I was only there a few minutes. I was watchin' the birds." She pointed out across the yard to where a bird feeder was crowded with a large variety of the creatures.

While her attention remained on the birds, I took in Dee's appearance with amazement. This was the first time I'd seen the child this early in the morning and was pleased to notice some care had been taken to see that she looked presentable. Her pale blonde hair was pulled back into a ponytail, the long, silky tresses hanging down her back in errant waves, while the shorter wisps framed her angelic face like a halo.

She'd been scrubbed clean. And it was obvious the clothes she wore had been clean when she'd put them on that morning. She was dressed in blue jeans, the knees a little scuffed and thin, but otherwise in good condition, and her lavender shirt looked new. She even had on shoes and socks.

Dee caught me staring at her, blushed and looked away. I could tell from the brief moment our eyes met that she was very aware of the change in herself.

"Ole Edna gave me a bath last night an' put these clothes out for me this mornin' when she came in. See how clean I am, Uncle Gray?" She turned around to model for him, her face showing how anxious she was for his approval.

"You look beautiful, honey." He grinned at her, taking her into his arms for a quick hug. As she pulled away from him, beaming from ear to ear, Gray winked at me. "What do you think, Miss Daniels?"

"You look terrific, Dee. That's a very pretty shirt you have on today. It makes the color of your eyes brighter." I smiled at her and was pleased to receive a grin in return.

"It itches, though." She wrinkled her nose, and, as if to prove the fact, squirmed around a bit. "My grandmother bought it for me the other day in Bristol, an' I got to cut the tags off myself." She told me with pride. She came over to my side and tugged on my arm until my head was level with hers. "Don't he know you well enough to call you Lyssie?" She asked in her peculiar stage whisper.

"Um . . . I think so." I glanced over to find Gray regarding us with amusement. "You think we should remind him?"

Dee nodded. "I'll do it, 'kay?" My nod of agreement sent her back to her uncle's side. "Gray, me and Lyssie think you know her enough to call her by her first name. It's Lyssie, 'member?" She was so serious as she gazed up at him that it was all I could do to keep from laughing.

"Lyssie? I seem to recall that, now you mention it, squirt. But as for knowing her well enough—"

"But you seen her a lot, Gray. An' yesterday, she was walkin' in the rain with us, an', well, you know. She seems like a nice person. Everybody else is callin' her that, so I think you should, too. Ok?"

He appeared to ponder the information she'd given him, weighing the pros and cons. "Ok," he said after awhile. "If you think it's all right with her."

"Oh, it is, 'cause I already asked. 'Sides, it's a lot nicer than sayin' Miss all the time."

"More friendly, huh?"

Dee nodded. "Uh huh. And I decided she's gonna be my friend just like she is Pier's." She came over to me and put her small hand into mine. "Would you like that, Lyssie?" The look she gave me could have melted my heart.

"I'd like to be your friend very much, Dee. You can never have too many friends." I looked to see if Gray recognized his words from the other day, but he was no longer paying attention. Ryan and Pier had come out onto the patio and were advancing in our direction.

Gray pushed back his chair, said a gruff good-morning to his siblings, then turned to Dee and me. "I'll ask Mrs. M to prepare us a picnic. You'll need to pick it up before you come down." On his way into the house, he turned back around. "Don't be too long. We wouldn't want to miss the best part of the morning." With that, he disappeared inside the house.

"What's that all about?" Ryan shot me a suspicious look, his words having a touch of sharpness to them.

"We're gonna go ridin' an' have a picnic." Dee answered before I had the chance to open my mouth. "Uncle Ryan, look at the shirt Grandmother bought me." Though she displayed it with pride, she appeared shyer with him than she had with Gray.

"It's pretty, Dee. And I see you finally got a bath. I'll bet by the time you were finished, the tub was as dirty as the puddles you were splashing in yesterday." He grabbed the child and pulled her against him for a hug. She put her small arms around his neck and hugged him closely. A poke in the ribs separated them with Dee pulling away giggling.

"Don't! That tickles, an' you know I don't like it." She rubbed the afflicted side, grinning up at him. "An' you're right. That water was awful dirty. Ole Edna said it was so bad that the tub was gonna need another good cleanin', an' it had just been scrubbed that mornin'! I hope Sarah's not too mad about it."

"As much as she hates cleaning your bathroom, kiddo, I think she'll be pleased to know it was for a good cause." Pier gave her a nod of approval. "I haven't seen you this clean in days, maybe even weeks!"

"Aw, Pier, you're just kiddin'. I get a bath most every night, you know that. I've just been playin' a lot lately." She turned back to me with a grin. "I'm gonna go get my boots. I'll meet you at the front door, 'kay?"

My nod sent her off and running. It did my heart good to see her responding like any normal child, and I wondered what could have happened to bring about the sudden change. I got up to follow her example, but as I passed Ryan, he took hold of my hand.

"Big plans this morning?" While his voice had lost some of its sharpness, his expression told me he wasn't happy about me spending the day with his brother.

"Gray's offered to show me around the estate," I told him.

"Checking up on the tenants, I'll bet," Pier interjected as she sat down at the table and placed their breakfast tray between her and Ryan. "Sounds like a boring day to me."

"I suppose you'll enjoy the ride. The picnic is a nice touch for Dee." Despite the lightness of his tone, I could tell Ryan still didn't approve.

"I'm looking forward to it. So is Dee." I turned to Pier. "You didn't have anything planned for us today, did you?"

"Nope. I figured you'd be writing all day. I think it's great you've decided to take the time off. You might be bored to tears, but at least you'll get a chance to see the estate." She took a bite of her toast and looked over at her brother. "Guess your plans to show her the factory this afternoon will have to be postponed. You should have mentioned it last night."

The gleam in her eyes told me she'd been prodding Ryan for information about what happened between us the night before.

I smiled down at Ryan, pulling my hand from his grasp. "Sorry. I'd no idea you had anything in mind."

"Of course you didn't. Not a problem," he patted my arm. Taking hold of my hand once again, he raised it to his lips for a kiss. "We'll make it another day."

"It's a date," I promised, reclaiming my hand.

I said my goodbyes, then made my escape into the house, realizing after I'd gotten inside that I'd forgotten to ask how Margaret was doing. I thought about going back out to ask Pier but decided against it. Mrs. Merrick was likely to know more than either Pier or Ryan.

Ryan's attitude confused me. His attention was flattering, but there was a hint of possessiveness that surprised me. I thought back over what happened between us last night and couldn't see any reason for this behavior.

In the kitchen, as I watched Mrs. Merrick and the cook put the finishing touches on our picnic, I asked after Margaret and discovered she was feeling much better. I thanked them for the lunch and picked up the basket. Putting Ryan out of my mind, I went off in search of Dee.

I hadn't far to look. The moment I reached the foyer, I heard her struggles on the lower step of the marble staircase. There she was, boot straps in hand, tugging on a cowboy boot that seemed to be fighting her all the way. She grunted and groaned, her cheeks growing redder by the second, till the boot finally slid on. She stood, stamped down hard, then jumped up to join me at the door.

"Having a little trouble there?"

"I think my foot musta growed." She opened the screen door and held it for me to go out before her. "I haven't wore them in a while. I usta all the time. Mamma said it was what you did when you went ridin'. When I go now, I just let Gray lead Shelly an' me 'round the pad'ock. I don't even use a saddle," she said the last with a show of pride. "Shelly's my very own pony. She isn't big like the other horses. She's special, little, for kids like me. Gray said her real name is Shetland, but I like Shelly better."

She danced ahead of me toward the path, catching me up in her energy and excitement.

"I saw your pony the other day," I called out to her. "I thought she was very pretty."

She answered me with a grin, continuing on her way, dancing a little jig and singing quietly to herself. I couldn't help being amazed at the transformation in her and again wondered what might have caused the change. I wasn't ridiculous enough to believe that our romp in the puddle could have anything to do with it. As odd as it sounded, I was a little concerned over the suddenness of the change. From everything I'd learned about Dee, it didn't seem like her to do a complete one eighty over night—which appeared to be what happened. Her lightheartedness had a sweet sincerity about it that I found disturbing, especially with the knowledge of how she'd reacted the last time she mentioned her mother. It just didn't seem in character for her. The emotional scars I'd witnessed went far deeper, too deep to have been wiped away in the last twenty-four hours.

"You're very happy today."

She grinned again and continued on her way without responding. I decided it was best to take her transformation at face value. After all, I reminded myself, I wasn't responsible for analyzing *this* child.

We were no more than two steps along the oak-lined pathway when I realized it was far too muddy to continue on. I called out to Dee, who was already ankle deep in mud, and asked if there was another way to the stables.

She wrinkled her nose as she regarded her once clean cowboy boots. Her unsuccessful attempt at scraping off the mud on a nearby log elicited a yelp of disgust.

"You can drive there, but that's kinda silly since it's not very far." She thought for a moment, then clapped her hands. "I know, we can go my secret way!"

"Your secret way?" I was almost afraid to ask, picturing myself climbing over logs, tree stumps, and heaven only knew what else.

Dee nodded as she plodded back to me, placing each foot along the path with exaggerated care in an attempt to keep any more mud from collecting on her 'cleaned' boots. "It's back that way an' through the woods. It's hardly ever muddy—least nothin' like this yucky stuff. You wanna try it?"

"Sure." I returned her grin, her infectious behavior leaving my worries behind.

She took my hand and led me out of the grove and into the sunshine. She pointed to where the line of oaks was flanked by a thick stand of evergreens and tugged at my hand.

"It's always kinda dark in there, but it's real pretty. When it snows, it's like you're standing in the middle of a buncha Christmas trees. That's what I think, anyway. My mamma said it was like some old forest in *Robin Hood*."

"You know the story?"

Dee nodded. "Mamma usta watch it. She liked that guy a lot."

"You mean the actor, Kevin Costner?"

"Nah, silly, Robin Hood." She let go of my hand and headed for the woods. I followed closely behind, trying hard to keep from laughing at the serious expression she'd flashed me.

"Do you like movies, Dee?"

"Kinda, I guess. We usta go sometimes, but I would fall asleep afore they got over. I like the Disney ones that I get for Christmas and my birthday. If I fall asleep, I get to start it all over when I wake up." She pushed aside some low hanging boughs and held them for me to pass.

"You like those a lot then."

"Yeah. They're pretty neat. I like the songs." Off she went in front of me, dancing and singing. I caught the words "under the sea," so I gathered it was something to do with *The Little Mermaid.*

While keeping her in sight, I looked around at the narrow path between the trees. Tall, majestic evergreens—blue spruce, Scotch pines, and various others—stood on either side of the little pathway. The branches blocked the sky and created a cool green environment, their thickness erasing the outside world, the luscious odor permeating the air. And just as Dee said, it reminded me of Christmas.

The ground was much firmer in here with very little mud. We walked on a thick carpet of needles, layer upon layer that crunched under our feet as we passed by.

"Whacha think?" Dee called back to me, standing on the path with her arms outstretched, her head thrown back to the non-existent sky.

"I think this was an excellent idea. It's beautiful." I put the basket of food down for a moment to give myself the opportunity to stretch a little. My arm felt strained by its surprising weight. There must be enough food in there to feed an army!

"Want me to carry that for a while?" Dee offered,

her eyes wide and darker than ever here in the woods.

I shook my head and told her to lead on. It took longer than the expected fifteen minutes to reach our destination, but in the end, I thought the additional few minutes had been worth it. Dee's secret path brought us out near the paddock, a few feet from where Gray had tied the horses—all saddled and ready to go.

As soon as we broke through the glade, Dee ran off toward the stables calling for Gray at the top of her lungs. He came out of the large barn door and caught her up in his arms.

"About time you got here, I was about to send out the troops." Putting Dee down, Gray came to take the basket from me. "They must've thought they were feeding a whole regiment!"

We followed him into his office where he began unloading the basket and repacking the food in a couple large saddlebags.

Dee climbed onto the work table next to him, eyeing him with suspicion.

"What're troops, and why were you gonna send them after us?"

Gray winked at me over her head. "Troops are a bunch of army guys, kiddo, and it wasn't intended for you to take literally."

"Huh?" Her dark eyes surveyed him, then she turned to me. "He doesn't make much sense sometimes," she explained in a tone far too serious for her years.

I laughed. "I think your uncle is trying to tell us that we took too long getting here."

"O-oh. Why didn't you say so?" Lowering her voice, she leaned in close to him. "We came by my secret path. The reg'lar way was too muddy. See." She held up one of her feet to show him the mud still clinging to her boots.

"Doesn't look like the secret way was much better."

"Oh, believe me, it was," I told him. "We'd never gotten here with dry feet, may have lost our shoes in the process. Dee's way was much better. How'd you get here this morning?"

"Truck." A shoulder pointed out the window to where a sturdy, four-wheel-drive pick-up sat in the graveled drive. "Ready to go?"

With Dee safely between us, we rode single file in a slow, easy cantor. Near the far end of the pasture, we went through a narrow opening in the trees, down a grassy slope, and across a beautiful stream that appeared to run the length of the pasture. The forty-five minutes it took to arrive at the first farmhouse had been filled with breathtaking scenery, already making the trip worthwhile.

We stopped before a barn, a modern steel building set upon a cement slab. Gray helped us down, nodding in the direction of the nearby house.

"This is the Morris's. While I look around for Kent, Dee can take you up to meet Gail. I shouldn't be long."

Taking my hand, Dee led me to the house, her excitement building as she told me about the Morris's two boys. After introducing me to the mother, the three children ran off to play.

"This is really nice." Gail Morris offered me a chair at her kitchen table. "It's been a long time since Dee's come around with Gray. She and her mother used to come every couple of months, and while the men were off discussing business, we'd get in a real nice visit."

After setting a glass of iced tea before me, she took a seat directly across the table from me.

"You've a beautiful home, Mrs. Morris." The rooms I'd seen were all good sized and decorated to make the most of the light and space. Warm, earthy tones were found throughout the living room, and the soft yellow, brown, and russet in the kitchen were pleasant to the eyes.

"Thank you. And please call me Gail. Every time I hear 'Mrs. Morris' I look around to see if my mother-in-law is somewhere nearby." She laughed at her joke and reached out to pat my hand. "So, you're visiting up at Foxxemoor. That's some place, isn't it? I've been there a time or two, and if I hadn't seen it with my own eyes, I'd never believed it. Makes me think of the books I read as a kid, big houses and such."

I smiled as I searched for something to say. "You said that Dee and Dylan used to come on these rounds of Gray's?" I grabbed at the only thing I could think of.

She nodded. "Especially the last year before, well, you know. It wasn't that she was interested in the farms, and she sure didn't like riding. I think she just liked getting away from Foxxemoor. And it gave the little girl a chance to make some friends as well."

I had difficulty placing Dylan anywhere other than among the grandness of Foxxemoor. I tried to picture her here in this homey kitchen, gossiping over a glass of tea. As good as my imagination was, I just couldn't see it.

"So, what do you do when you're not on vacation?"

"I work with children. Right now I'm on a sabbatical of sorts. Time off to pursue a writing career."

"How interesting! You couldn't ask for a better

setting than Foxxemoor."

"It's not the setting," I told her, explaining a bit about *Craven*. She listened attentively, a smile on her face.

"Remarkable. I just have to ask—how do you come up with your ideas?"

My answer that "stories just pop into my head," seemed to satisfy her. Before we could delve further into the subject, I managed to get her talking about her house and farm. They leased the surrounding land from the Foxxe's, but the house, barn, and connecting twenty acres belonged to them.

"There are six farms around the edge of the estate. We farm the land in a kind of cooperative. It's a very unique arrangement that works to our advantage— especially with things so tough on us farmers." Gail Morris laughed. "Goodness, I don't think I've ever talked so much to someone I just met. You've made it so easy. Not at all like Dylan Courtney. Hard as that girl tried, she was still the FoxCo darling. Pretty as a picture, and about as one dimensional as one!" She put a hand to her mouth, catching herself a little too late. "I shouldn't have said that, I know, but it *is* the truth." She leaned across the table and whispered. "Dylan tried. I know she did. I was in her class at school, and she worked very hard at being an ordinary person. But no matter what she did, the fact remained that the doll made her a celebrity. She didn't wear it well, poor girl, and couldn't get away from it no matter how old she got or how hard she tried."

As nice as Gail was, the gossip made me uncomfortable. She appeared on the verge to say something more when Gray and her husband came in.

She popped up from the table with a greeting, offered Gray a drink and a piece of pie, and seemed disappointed when he said we had to get moving.

The story was basically repeated at the next two farms. Dee would go off to amuse herself with the children, leaving me alone with the wife. Everyone was hospitable and all of them had nothing but good to say about Gray and the farming arrangements. Dylan was mentioned in passing, but I got the distinct impression that the country grapevine had been at work before our second stop. After the preliminaries were taken care of, there were polite questions about the Foxxe's, my relationship to them, and gentle prodding for gossip from the 'big' house. They seemed to steer away from the subject of Dylan Courtney—more intent on discovering new information rather than sharing the old. I was never much of a gossip, and since I didn't have anything to share, the conversations fell a little flat. It was a nice morning, though, and the roses that shone in Dee's cheeks by the time we stopped for our picnic made it all worthwhile.

We tethered our horses to the remains of an old farmhouse's foundation in the middle of a field of clover. High on a hillside, overlooking a valley of luscious green pasturelands, Gray led us to a patch of semi-dry ground where we spread a blanket for our feast.

Fried chicken, potato salad, carrots, and apples made up the picnic packed for us. Along with two small Thermos containers of iced tea, there was a bag with freshly baked chocolate chip cookies from the last farm we visited.

This time, there were no ill tempers to interfere with

our picnic. We talked and laughed, joked and teased. Anyone coming upon us would have thought we were a family from the way we acted. It was the closest I'd felt to anyone since my arrival at Foxxemoor. As I stretched out on the blanket, with Dee's head in my lap, I wished it could remain this way forever.

"Can I give the rest of my apple to Shelly?" Dee asked, looking up at me, her eyes hidden behind her windblown bangs.

I caught the nod from Gray out of the corner of my eye and gave her the go ahead. Dee jumped up and ran happily to her horse.

"Be careful over there, Dee," Gray warned. "Stay away from the foundation."

"I *will!*" She called back to him in such a way that told me she'd heard this warning before.

I gazed out across the hillside which was dotted with purple clover, sunflowers, daisies, and sprinkles of the occasional dandelion. There were peony bushes and roses intermingled with overgrown grasses and clover where the house once stood. The whole area was bursting with color and alive with the sound of busy insects and birds.

"It's beautiful up here." I knew it wasn't necessary to say it, but with Dee gone, I felt a little self-conscious with the silence.

Gray rolled over onto his side. "Are you absorbing it all for your book?" With my nod, he continued. "I can see it now, the ruins of the old house, sad and forlorn, with the untended garden flowers surrounding it. Against the backdrop is the crumbling chimney, sticking up from the ground like a tombstone." His grin was mischievous. "Am I close?"

"Um. Ever think of writing?"

He laughed. "I'm afraid I haven't much imagination." He rolled over onto his back and stuck the end of a weed in his mouth. Closing his eyes, he put an arm across them to shield them from the sun.

It was then that I noticed the long scar that extended from just below his elbow to the center of his bicep. It was a harsh white against the tanned skin, and from its appearance, I could tell it was from an old wound. I had an uncontrollable urge to trace its length, stopping at the bicep to feel the firmness and strength of his muscular arm. Holding myself in check, I watched his gentle breathing.

"By the way," he spoke without moving from his position. "I asked Dee about the butterfly incident the other day. There's a simple explanation for what happened."

"She told me that when she saw the room was open she thought I was her mother."

Gray nodded, removing the arm from across his eyes. "Right. I'd forgotten how much butterflies fascinated Dylan—something to do with the ability to transform from one form to another. I should have remembered. They used to come up here with jars. Dylan had this thing about bringing them back to the garden at the house. Something superstitious, I guess. She'd call it 'bringing back the magic.' I never understood what it was all about. Anyway," he rubbed his eyes with the back of his hand. "The Monarch was supposed to be a welcome home gift for Dylan. You know the rest."

"Have you noticed the change in Dee?" I drew my legs up and hugged them to me as I gazed out across the hillside to where Dee was dancing and singing among the wildflowers. "She's like a different person."

He raised himself on an elbow, and chewing on his weed, followed my gaze. "A lot like she used to be. And yes, I'd noticed. Perhaps it's something to do with you. Or, maybe she's come to accept that her mother isn't coming back." His tone was dry.

"Is that what you think, that Dylan's dead?"

His face didn't alter its expression, nor was his tone any less dry. "I didn't say she was dead, just that she wasn't coming back." He sat up and stretched, reaching his arms high above his head. "Now, you tell me something," he leaned in closer to me, his eyes meeting mine. "What do you think of my family?"

My laugh revealed how nervous his question made me. "That's some question." I hedged, searching for some way to change the subject. "Oh, how was Margaret this morning?" I asked, even though I already had the answer.

"Come on now, none of that. You're stalling." His warm blue eyes stared frankly into mine. It was as though he probed into my soul.

"No, really, I meant to ask about her earlier," I brushed some errant strands of hair from my face, tucking them under the band holding my ponytail. I watched as he shifted positions on the blanket, feeling he was trying to avoid the subject of Margaret as much as I wanted to keep from discussing my impressions of his family. I wondered if something else might have happened between them.

"I didn't see her." His voice was flat, without emotion. "I asked Mrs. M how she was doing and was told she'd eaten a hearty breakfast. If that's any indication, she should be back to normal by this time tomorrow." He cleared his throat in what I was beginning to recognize as a nervous habit of his. "I want to apologize for that scene yesterday. I shouldn't have lost my temper, I know, but Margaret has a way of provoking me."

"Um."

"What's that supposed to mean?" He must have realized how sharp his tone had been, because he drew back and offered a tenuous smile.

"You asked a moment ago what I thought of your family. If you really want to know," I paused, uncertain whether to continue. "I—I think the household is like a powder keg, all primed and ready to explode. All you need is a tiny flame and poof, up it goes." I nervously bit my lip. "I've never seen so many people with such short fuses."

His blank expression surprised me but not nearly as much as the hearty laughter that followed.

"You're a very astute young woman, Lysette Daniels." There was a hint of admiration behind the amusement. "Now you've found us out, are you ready to abandon us for more peaceful surroundings?"

"I'll admit to being tempted," I smiled. "Every time I start to tell your sister I'm ready to leave, I change my mind—or she changes it for me. She seems to want me to stay very badly. I just don't think I'll be able to oblige her much longer."

"I'm sure she'll be heartbroken." Again, I detected the note of dryness. "Don't mind me. I'm sure Pier will miss you, and the company has been good for her. It's nice to see her spending less time at Ryan's beck and call."

I, too, had noticed that Pier seemed to be constantly at Ryan's side. "They appear to have a very close bond. Was it always that way?"

He grunted, removed the weed from his mouth, and looked out across the meadow. "She rarely lets him out of her sight since the accident." He shrugged, turning to study my face. "You roomed with her four years, didn't she ever talk about us?"

I shook my head. "She had photographs she put up, the same ones every year. You were all in them, even Dylan. It's funny, but whenever I'd study those pictures, my attention was always brought back to her."

"You knew who she was?"

"Not at first, but later on. When Pier told me, it was like an afterthought. I don't think she would have mentioned it, but I had one of the teen dolls. When I saw how much it disturbed her, I took it back home."

Gray nodded. "She was always a little jealous of the dolls—especially the older she got. I don't think she realized how much Dylan hated being the model. Funny, isn't it? Pier wanting it so much and Dylan wishing it was anyone but her."

"It's sad. I asked Pier about it once, but all she said was that school was school and what existed at Foxxemoor couldn't touch her. I admired the way she handled it and wished I had some of that detachment in regards to my grandmother." The wistful quality in my voice made me sound weaker than I wanted to appear.

"That's right, Pier mentioned something about you being raised by your grandmother. Some mysterious tragedy in your background."

"Not so mysterious." I stretched out on the blanket and raised my face to the sun. "My mother was killed in a robbery when I was eight—a freak thing, being in the wrong place, etcetera. It destroyed my father and he died about a year later. Grandmother could never quite reconcile their deaths. It was very difficult for her."

"And for you." I opened my eyes to find Gray leaning over me. "How about you, Lysette? How have you weathered the tragedies in your life?"

"I was the lucky one." I smiled a little to myself. "My grandmother loved me enough to know she couldn't help me cope. Shortly after Daddy died, she took me to Langston Children's Center, a kind of halfway house for troubled children. There I met Dr. Angela Hadley, the founder and resident psychiatrist, and we became very close.

"I spent two years at Langston and learned to accept the deaths of my parents without shouldering the burden or blaming myself. Even after I was released from the program, I continued to attend sessions after school and helped out with the kids." I paused for a moment as Amy Webster's face flitted before my eyes. This time, however, I was able to handle the memory without the flood of pain and guilt. "I was working at Langston before my vacation. I guess you could say I've been there in one capacity or another since I was ten." I shielded my eyes from the sun and found him studying me.

"You've some very attractive freckles, Miss Daniels." With a gentle finger, he traced them across the bridge of my nose.

My heart beat so loudly I was certain he could hear it. I felt the heat of his body through the light touch of his finger, and closing my eyes, attempted to hide the emotion I was sure he could already see. I had a sense of his hovering over me, and imagined him lowering his head, his lips ready to meet mine. I gasped a little in anticipation. When the moment didn't happen, when the shadow he cast over me was no longer there, I reopened my eyes and found he had moved back to his side of the blanket.

I tried to hide my disappointment—chiding myself for allowing my imagination to get the better of me. I sat back up and made a great show of looking around for Dee. I'd half expected her to have joined us, wished it, in fact; it would have explained his withdrawal from me. But Dee was still among the wildflowers, knee deep with a sampling twisted around her little head like a crown.

"So, Pier didn't talk much about us." His voice seemed to come from a long way off. "Didn't that ever strike you as odd?"

"I suppose. But I learned that you couldn't press Pier about things. The best way to get along was for her to carry you in her own way. She taught me a lot about people, about myself." Feeling more than a little abashed from the moment before, I hesitated. "What about you, Gray? Now you know so much about me, how about sharing a little about yourself?"

He laughed. "Are you sure you want to delve into such a volatile subject?"

"I'll keep my matches extinguished. And since there's no one around to add fuel, I think it's a safe enough subject." He laughed again, his deep blue eyes crinkling up at the corners as he smiled up at me.

"Fire away—no pun intended."

"O—k." I readjusted myself on the blanket, so I was facing him. "Your name."

His burst of laughter widened his smile. "It's horrible, isn't it? Yeah, it's been a sore point between my father and me." He brushed at a fly that was annoying him. "The story is simple and odd. My mother told the nurse our names were to be Ryan and Gary. Ryan was to go to the oldest—by fifteen minutes. Either the poor woman was dyslexic or just couldn't spell because the placards read R-a-n and G-r-a-y. When my father saw them, he made them change Ryan's, but he decided mine was appropriate. I was grey at birth, not all pink and white, so the name suited me. Mother said that the idea of 'Gray Foxxe' suited my father's warped sense of humor." There was a sardonic cut to his words. "My father said it was a 'gift,' something to teach me to stand up for myself in spite of my shortcomings." He raised his arm and studied the scar. "I saw you looking at my arm—no, it's all right. Something happened before I was born, they never did explain it. Six operations on the sucker by the time I was ten and years of therapy afterward has made it pretty much like anyone else's. My leg was different. Some slight nerve damage causes the limp. I don't even notice it unless I'm more tired than usual." He sighed. It was obvious he felt self-conscious about all he'd revealed. "Ah, well. One perfect twin, one slightly damaged. At least it made it easy to tell us apart."

I studied his profile, the smooth, high forehead with a lock of curly brown hair tumbling across it. Beneath heavy brows, his deep blue eyes were as clear as a mountain lake. He had a straight nose, a full, generous mouth, and a firm, squared jaw line and chin that could be hard and unrelenting, or soft and gentle. It was true that Ryan and Gray *looked* identical upon first glance, but there was something about the eyes and mouth, some quality I could not readily identify, that should make confusing them a non-issue.

"I don't know about perfection," I told him quietly. "I mean, wouldn't that be boring, to be perfect?"

Our eyes met, and I could see the gleam of amusement shine from his. "Don't ever let on to my brother. If he thought he was anything less than perfect, it would destroy his ego."

"This is a ploy, isn't it? A way to hide what's really between you."

"It's said that twins, especially identical ones, share much more than just the genes that make them look alike." As he spoke it was as though his voice was trying to bridge a gap in time. "Emotions, everything are supposed to be similar. We were like that at one time. Our thoughts seemed to run in the same direction, and a glance was all we needed to know what the other was thinking." He shook his head. "Puberty, our teens, competition in sports, and girls intervened. I couldn't compete in the sports, but it was ok to sit back and take pride in his accomplishments. But there was one area where neither of us was able to stand back and let the other take over."

From the tone of his voice, it wasn't difficult to guess what he was referring to—Pier and Mrs. Morris had already given me the answer.

"Dylan Courtney."

He eyed me with respect. "Dylan." He agreed. "Despite having grown up around her, she remained an enigma." He shrugged. "She was a year older, but you'd never have known from the way she acted, the way she looked. She was beautiful, talented, witty, and flawed."

I was about to ask what he meant when Dee joined us. She rifled in the saddle bags for more cookies, and with a handful and a cup of tea, she went back to where she'd been playing to have her snack.

Gray looked at his watch and sighed. "It's been a good day, got a lot done and had a nice, relaxing picnic with two beautiful girls," he grinned. "What man could ask for more?"

"I'll thank you for the compliment on behalf of both Dee and myself. I've had a nice time. Thanks for bringing me along."

He reached out and caught a strand of my hair as it blew in the breeze. He let the tress slip between his fingers before he gently placed it behind my left ear. Again, I felt that bond, that draw toward him, and could have sworn he felt it too. His hand touched my shoulder, a light caress that sent a shiver throughout my body. I leaned closer, my eyes fastened on his. We were close, so close I could almost feel his lips as his breath touched my cheek. Then, just like the time before, he drew back to concentrate on packing the remains of our picnic into the saddle bags.

Hurt and confused, I helped him in silence. Once packed, Gray signaled to Dee that it was time to go. She returned from the field with reluctance and waited to be helped into her saddle.

When it was my turn, his arms lingered around my waist. I leaned back against his broad chest, resting my head against his shoulder before I received the boost needed to get into the saddle. As he handed me the reins, I saw a shadow of pain reflected in his eyes.

Pier had said that it would be safer for me to pursue

Ryan, that Dylan Courtney had no hold on him at the time of her disappearance. But you couldn't always help the direction your heart decided to take. From the first time I'd seen him, I felt an attraction to Gray that I'd never felt for another man. I'd tried to blame it on the resemblance he had to my protagonist in *Craven*, but I knew now that the fictional Leo Craven had nothing to do with how I felt.

Though I may not like to admit it, I was falling in love with Gray Foxxe—and falling hard. Somehow, some way, I had to find the key to erase Dylan Courtney from his mind forever.

Chapter 9

Tears filled Diana's eyes and fear gripped her heart when she heard the key turn in the lock of her prison. She shivered within the folds of the tattered blanket as she huddled against a far corner of the room.

Candlelight pierced the darkness, its gentle halo of light drawing the frightened girl out of her hiding place.

"Miss, Miss Diana?" A familiar voice called out to her, but the tightness of Diana's throat allowed no sound to escape. "It's all right, Miss. I've come to take you to your room." The older woman threw a shawl around the quivering shoulders and hugged the girl to her. "Master should be ashamed of himself for leaving you here like this . . .

Pier invited me for a swim shortly after we'd returned to Foxxemoor. At first, I thought she'd missed me, but it was soon evident that the invitation was a ruse: she wanted information.

She didn't believe that I had no juicy tidbits of gossip for her, and the more I insisted I hadn't heard anything worth repeating, the more petulant and cross she became. Sitting on the edge of the pool, Pier stared at me, a pout on her pretty face. With one leg dangling over the side, her foot sent ripples back and forth through the water.

"So, you didn't visit with the wives?" She asked, her acid tone and grey-green eyes reflecting suspicion.

"A little," I told her, trying hard not to lose my patience. She behaved as though she were more Dee's age than mine, and I was getting tired of the third degree. "I don't know what you expected me to learn, Pier. All the women were very nice, very hospitable. I'm a stranger, you know, and they weren't about to tell me their deepest, darkest secrets."

Pier shrugged but continued to pursue the matter. "I suppose they were curious why 'a stranger,' was accompanying Gray on his rounds. I mean, that's something Dylan did."

I sighed as I paddled about in the lukewarm water near her. "It was mentioned in passing." Not the whole truth, but I didn't think it was necessary to disclose what Gail Morris told me. "We talked about the weather and their farms, just as I told you. When they asked about my visit here, you know me," I stood in the water and looked up to where she sat, shielding my eyes against the afternoon sun. "Given the opening, I talked on and on about my writing."

I'd always been very reserved, introverted, throughout our college years. The comment was so off the wall that it succeeded in lifting the pout from Pier's face. She burst into laughter as she jumped into the water next to me.

"Which means you were so tongue-tied, they didn't know what to do with you." Pier giggled. "Dylan always came back with the best gossip." Sighing, she splashed me. "I'm bored, Lyssie. I'm tired of the country, tired of the birds, the flowers, the trees. I want some action!" Pier swam the length of the pool as though she were in a race. Back and forth, then back to where I stood at the edge. "How about you and I kick up our heels? I know this nice little tavern where we can have dinner, maybe find some good looking guys and go dancing. What do you say?"

The look in her eyes reminded me of our college days when she would suddenly decide it was time to crash a frat or sorority party. This was a Pier I knew only too well, one that wouldn't be satisfied with dancing and male companionship. When she was bored, she became more than a little dangerous.

I wasn't about to take on the challenge. "Sorry, but I promised to tuck Dee in with a bedtime story. I'd hate to let her down."

"Dee! You'd think she was the most important person in this stupid house!" She sloshed back through the water to the steps that led out of the pool. "If you think I'm going to stick around while you have your bedtime story with Deidre, you're wrong. You're supposed to be *my* company, Lyssie, remember?" She stomped out of the pool, grabbed her towel, and flinging it over her shoulder, headed back toward the house. I stood at the water's edge, watching her go, wondering what could have happened to make her so testy.

"Don't mind her." The voice startled me.

As my heart leaped from the sudden fright, Ryan appeared at the head of the pool. Leaning a little less on his cane than usual, he wound his way with care across the wet cement to a nearby cabana chair.

"She's been like that all day from catering to Margaret. It's nothing to do with you." He smiled down at me, making me self-conscious in my two-piece suit.

Lowering myself in the water, I moved my arms back and forth to warm up.

"I *have* neglected her," I said, his stare beginning to unnerve me.

"Don't be silly. She invited you here to help with your writing, not just for companionship. She can't expect you to be at her beck and call."

The turn of his head, the tone of his voice poignantly reminded me of his brother, which set the blood pulsating through my veins. Willing myself to relax, I began a slow, easy lap.

"How's the water?"

"Wonderful." I told him, righting myself.

I couldn't do this, couldn't carry on a conversation with him sitting up there while I was still in the pool. How did I look in my suit with my hair matted against my head? The thought made me uncomfortable. I waded over to the steps and pulled myself out of the pool, thankful that my terry wrap was on a nearby chair. After putting it on, I grabbed a towel and began patting my hair.

"I hope you didn't cut your swim short on my account." The thickness of his voice, and unmistakable sensuality of the look he gave me, did nothing to calm my nerves.

"I need to get back to the house to talk with Pier before she leaves." I slipped on my flip-flops and gathered the paraphernalia we'd brought to the pool.

"Are you going to give in to her, Lyssie, go to the bar and watch as she picks up a guy?"

"No." I was surprised to find Ryan already within a few steps of me. "I just don't want her to leave like that. She was so upset—"

Ryan took my chin and raised my head. "Let her go, Lyssie. You don't need that scene, the aggravation. All you need is right here." His lips came down hard on mine, bruising them as they pressed against my teeth. I couldn't believe his strength, the swiftness of the action. I was so overwhelmed, there was no time to think. As he attempted to part my lips, my senses returned, and I pushed him away so hard he almost lost his balance.

"I—I'm sorry." I reached out to steady him, then pulled my hand back when he attempted to take me into his arms. "Ryan, I—" what could I say? This was an impossible situation and I had nothing, no experience to draw on. Ryan was the spitting image of his brother, a man I'd wanted to kiss and hold me just a few hours earlier. They looked the same, sounded the same, and as much as I liked what I knew of Ryan . . .

"You can't keep running away from me, Lysette," Ryan's voice was thick with emotion. "We're attracted to one another. I know you feel it from the way you look at me."

"I won't deny there's an attraction." Lowering my eyes, I peered at him from behind my lashes. "It would be better to call it a fascination." I noted the way his lips thinned to the point of a sneer. "When I began writing *Craven*, some part of me must have remembered the photos Pier had on our dorm walls. I mean, that would explain why you and Gray resemble the character in my manuscript. So, I've stared, studied your movements, and the sound of your voices. I'm sorry—"

He advanced toward me, but seeing my hesitation, stopped a few steps in front of me. "I can give you what your fictional character can't, Lyssie. I'm the real thing." He turned slightly away from me. "I've never thrown myself at a woman, and I won't start now. I've had dozens of relationships, though none of them were serious—except one. Dylan Courtney was special, unique, but with one fatal flaw; she neither liked nor accepted herself. As a result, every relationship she had was doomed. Sooner or later Dylan found a way to destroy everything, and everyone, she touched." I'd seen the same pain in Gray's eyes when he discussed Dylan.

"I was the lucky one, Lyssie, I escaped from her clutches before she pulled this disappearing act. I was recovering from the damage she caused in my life when our car missed the turn on Mull's Hill and ended up in the valley below." He groped behind him for a chair and slowly lowered himself into it. "I awoke in the hospital to find my father was dead and the doctors uncertain about my future. I swore when I got out of there I wouldn't waste any more of my life chasing butterflies and dreams that would never come true. I'd been there, trailing after Dylan for more than ten years, waiting for the few tidbits she'd toss my way." His face grew hard with the memories. "You're looking down on this poor cripple and wondering why I'm telling you this."

"I don't look at you that way!"

"No?" He grimaced. "You're right, your heart's too soft for that. I'm sorry. It was a cruel thing to say." The color of his eyes seemed to darken with intensity as they studied me. "I'm pouring my heart out to you, Lysette Daniels. You're the type of woman I've searched for, that I want to make a future with. From the moment we met, you treated me as a whole man, showed me what I could be."

"Th-this is so sudden," I stuttered, feeling as if the fence surrounding the pool was closing in on me. I wanted to escape, longed for the shade of the giant poplars along the walkway to the house.

"It's too soon, I know, but I need you to know the truth. I'm falling in love with you, and if you allow yourself the chance, you'll realize you love me too." With considerable care, he rose to his feet. "You'd better go before you catch a chill." His tone was tender, solicitous. "I know you need time, Lyssie, and I'll give you all you need. Just think about what I've said. Promise?"

"I p-promise." He was right, I needed time to think, time to reconcile my thoughts and figure out what was happening.

The house was quiet and appeared empty. As I neared Pier's suite, the floor creaked and her door flew open. She'd changed to go out, and beneath a cloud of still wet curls, her face was pale in the dim light of the hallway.

"Did you see anyone else?" Her voice was strained to a high, unnatural pitch. "Just now, did you see anyone?" Pier asked again, her lower lip quivering.

"No, no. Are you all right? You're pale."

She pushed at my hand. "I'm fine." She shoved at a curl that dangled over one eye. "Just thought I heard someone out here by the door. You change your mind, want to come with me?"

I shook my head, wishing I could talk to her, tell her about what had just happened with Ryan and my general confusion where her brothers were concerned. But right now, all Pier could think about was herself. Until her urges were satisfied, her self-confidence and ego rebuilt, there would be no room for anyone else in her thoughts.

"Are you sure you wouldn't like to get a movie and some popcorn—"

With a roll of her eyes and a flick of her hand, she dismissed me and went back inside her suite.

This latest show of the Foxxe tempers added to the list of reasons why I should just leave Foxxemoor.

I kicked my flip-flops across the sitting room. If I hadn't promised Dee . . .

As I passed the floor-length mirror on the back of the bathroom door, I was drawn to it.

At a little less than 5'5", I was neither too thin nor too heavy for my frame. The sprinkling of freckles that dotted my nose were darker from sun exposure, adding a splash of color to my normally pale face. My eyes were wide, soft blue with a generous fringe of lashes— what I considered my one great feature. Strands of my long, honey-colored hair hung across my forehead, the rest was matted against my head and back giving me the look of a plaster statue.

It was a pleasant looking face, most of the time,

attractive by most standards. But no matter how hard I stared into the mirror, I couldn't find the answers to what bothered me. Why should it be so impossible for me to believe Ryan had fallen in love with me? He'd always been so sweet, so kind. Not at all like his brother.

"Then why are you falling for Gray?" I asked a reflection that only stared back with accusing eyes.

I wasn't a silly schoolgirl embarking on her first crush; I hadn't misread Gray. He *was* attracted to me; there was no way I could have imagined it. Something held him back, and I was pretty sure what, or rather, who it was: Dylan Courtney.

I recalled the beautiful girl in the pictures, the perfect features that launched the popular doll. Dylan Courtney, the raven-haired beauty, vibrant and alluring, her flashing, dark eyes capturing the hearts of thousands and enslaving two young men who seemed to have been pawns. Pier said Dylan played games with her brothers, going from one to the other as she grew tired or bored. Would the game have continued if she lived, or would she be married to Gray and living happily ever after?

Both men used the same words to describe Dylan, stating she was 'flawed.' Yet, the flaw hadn't kept them from falling in love with her. And it didn't keep Gray from missing her.

The phone on the nightstand rang in the peculiar tone that signaled it was a call from inside the house. Picking up, I found Mrs. Merrick on the other end.

"With Pier and the twins out, Miss Daniels, I wondered what you'd like to do for dinner. Mrs. Foxxe still isn't up for company, and Dee was going to take her meal here in the kitchen with my husband and me. Just a moment, please."

I heard her talking to someone, then she was back on the line. "Dee wants to know if you'd like to have dinner on the patio with her."

I smiled. Leave it to a child to make things simple.

"I'd love to, Mrs. Merrick." As I hung up, I said a little prayer. "Please, Father, just Dee and me tonight."

* * * * * * * * * * * * * * *

Dinner went smoothly with Dee such a chatterbox that I hardly said a word. She was full of the day's excitement, telling me all about her visits with the children. She'd even been allowed to curry Shelly for the first time, with Gray standing by to help if needed.

After dinner we went up to her room, and as this was my first time in this part of the house, Dee took me on a mini tour. As we passed the first door in this wing, Dee put a finger to her lips and mouthed "Grandmother's room." A little further down the hallway, she pointed to herself.

"This is mine," she whispered, throwing the door open and taking a quick peek inside. "They call this an island," she told me solemnly. "There are two sets of rooms in it. Mine an' Uncle Ryan's on the other side. If you wanna get there fast, there's a little hall down there. You just turn the corner an' you're there."

I asked about Gray and was told he had a suite in the north wing, one that mirrored the suite I now occupied in the south wing. The layout of the house was still confusing to me, but watching as Dee described it, made me see how much fun she must have exploring.

After the tour, we returned to Dee's rooms where

she engaged me in a marathon of games. Chutes and Ladders, Memory, Candy Land, and a couple hands of Crazy Eights filled the next three hours. Dee was good company, her laughter and high spirits a welcome change from the brooding I was sure to have indulged had I been left on my own.

At nine, Mrs. Merrick came in to remind Dee that it was bedtime.

"Will you stay while I get ready?" Dee asked. "You promised to read me a story, 'member?"

"Of course I do," I assured her with a wink at Mrs. Merrick as she hustled the child off to change for bed.

"I had a bath earlier, so it won't take too long." Dee peeked out around the bedroom door, her large, dark eyes dancing as they looked at me. "Ole Edna said I smelled like a horse." She giggled. "Didn't you?"

I didn't hear Mrs. Merrick's comment, but the giggling that followed, from both of them, told me how fond the two of them were of each other.

A few minutes later, Edna Merrick came out of the bedroom to wait for Dee in the sitting room with me.

"She's supposed to be brushing her teeth, but sometimes—" She shook her head and smiled at me. "She's been very happy today, Miss Daniels. I don't know if you realize how much of that is due to you."

As I started to protest, she raised a hand to stop me.

"No one has made this much of a difference, spent so much time with her. Not in a very long time. Henry and I try to, but with all of our other responsibilities, it doesn't always work. I know I shouldn't be talking like this, but I just wanted to thank you for what you've done."

"There's no need to thank me, Mrs. Merrick. Dee's

a sweet kid, and I've enjoyed spending time with her when she lets me. As a matter of fact, I'd be glad to take over from here—toothbrush inspection and all."

Dee peeked out a few moments later, and seeing we were alone, gave me a mischievous grin as she held out her toothbrush.

"I even got the back ones tonight!" She told me as she took my hand and led me into her bedroom. "Do you like my rooms?"

"They're very pretty," I told her as I looked around at the wallpaper adorned with pastel puppies and kittens. The theme was carried over in the bedspread and drapes, with the bedside lamps reflecting stenciled drawings on the walls. One wall contained a shelving unit that held her regular toys with a smaller unit divided off to display her collection of the FoxCo Dylan Doll series.

At her command, I closed my eyes and allowed her to lead me further into the room. With a sense of the dramatic, she told me to open my eyes, then stood and watched as I studied the Dylan collection.

I'd only seen photos of the earliest dolls and was fascinated as I looked into the faces of the babies before me. The first was designed as an infant, the next of a one year old, and from there, they skipped two or three ages at a time. If they were true reproductions of what her mother had looked like at each age, she had been a beauty since birth.

"My Grampas made these at the factory in town." Dee told me with pride. "They were made to look like my mamma. These used to belong to her, but she never liked them much, so they're mine now. I like them even though you can't really play with them 'cause they'll break."

"They're beautiful, Dee, and very special." She nodded her agreement. "You see this one," I pointed to the teenage doll in a lovely green velvet gown. "I was given one like that when I went away to college. I loved to look at it and imagine what it would be like to be as beautiful and glamorous as her."

"That's where you met Pier, huh?"

"That's right, kiddo." I gave her a playful poke in the ribs. "Now, unless you want Mrs. Merrick to get mad at both of us, you'd better climb into bed."

Giggling, she dashed for her bed and was between the sheets before I'd had a chance to leave the alcove. She held out a book for me to read, Disney's *Cinderella*, and leaned back upon her pillows.

The first order of business was Dee's prayers. As I sat on the edge of her bed, she folded her small hands together, closed her eyes, and began.

"An', dear God, thank you for my new friend, Lyssie, an' for having her like me enough to play with me an' read to me. An' bless my grandmother, Pier, an' my uncles Ryan an' Gray. Please say hello to both my Grampas, an' let my mamma know that I'm doin' fine. In Jesus' name, Amen." Rising from her pillows, she grimaced, then closed her eyes once again. "Oh yeah, I forgot to thank you for Shelly an' for lettin' me play with all the kids today. Amen." Dee readjusted herself on her pillows. "Do you think God gets mad when you stop talkin', you know, when you say 'Amen' an' then think of somethin' else to say?"

I couldn't help but smile at her serious expression. "I'm sure He doesn't."

"Whew, that's good, 'cause I'm always forgettin'

somethin'."

Dee settled back once more against her pillows and nodded for me to begin reading.

This was something I'd always enjoyed on the occasions I'd worked the late shift at Langston. I gave the story everything I had, changing my voice a dozen or so times, all to the delight of the little pixy in the bed before me. I drug the story out, watching Dee's face every step of the way. She appeared fascinated, but not very sleepy, and when we'd finished, her dark blue eyes were still wide open.

It was getting late, and even if Dee wasn't feeling exhausted, I was. I placed the book on her nightstand, hoping she wouldn't request another one. She'd been so good, so sweet, I knew I'd be unable to refuse her.

"That was really neat, Lyssie." Dee smiled through her first yawn of the evening. "I know I thanked God for you, but maybe I should thank you, too. I—" She lowered her eyes. "Um, I heard what Ole Edna said before she left, an' I just want you to know it was really nice that you played with me tonight. I know you would've had more fun goin' with Pier. She was upset 'cause you didn't go with her."

"I think you've been hiding out and listening in too much, little lady." From the way she hung her head, I knew I'd hit the mark. I had the feeling this habit of hers accounted for a lot of Dee's attitude and her grown up reaction to things. Now, she looked up at me from behind her dark lashes, contrite, and a little unsure of herself.

"You're not mad at me, are you?" Her voice was very small.

I took her hands in mine and gave them a reassuring

squeeze. "Of course not, silly. My grandmother always said that if you listen at doors, or eavesdrop, you shouldn't be surprised if you hear something bad about yourself."

She nodded. "Lyssie," she put her little hand on my chin, pulling my face down so that we were looking eye to eye. "Since my mamma went away, I do that, that eaves thing. I don't really mean to, but sometimes, I'm kinda hidin' an' people come around an' start talkin'. I know I've heard stuff I wasn't supposed to hear, but if I said somethin', they'd know my special places."

She released my chin, lowering her head, so I was unable to see her expression. "They think my mamma's dead. They thought it right away when she didn't come home on time. All 'cept Uncle Gray, an' he don't talk about it. The first time I heard 'em talkin' about it, they said they didn't want me to know, that 'we must keep this from Dee'," she altered her tone in a way that led me to believe she'd heard this phrase a lot in the last several months. "Anyway, I listen 'cause I wanna know about my mamma." Her dark eyes were bright with tears when they raised to mine. "But they don't know, Lyssie. They talk an' talk, but they don't really know."

The pleading look in her eyes, the tears and her soft, sweet voice wrenched at my heart. Gazing down into the angelic face, I couldn't keep myself from becoming involved. Taking her into my arms, I said, "If there's no proof—"

"That's it!" Dee sprang out of my arms. "That's what Uncle Gray says." She lowered her eyes for a moment. "*I've* got proof, Lyssie."

Something in her expression told me we should pursue this topic no matter how uncomfortable it made me. "And what's that, honey?"

"Can you keep a secret?" Her voice lowered into her squeaky stage whisper.

I nodded as she came to me, raised up to her knees, and whispered in my ear.

"Mamma came to see me last night." She drew back and watched for my reaction, her own face beaming with the news she'd just shared.

I swallowed hard, taking a deep breath. "Is that why you were so happy today?"

She grinned and nodded. "I wanted to tell Gray all day. Someone was always around, though. I knew no one else would believe me, so I just kept my secret."

My years of experience at Langston had taught me this was not a subject to be taken lightly. But at Langston, there was a staff of qualified child psychologists and therapists to take over where my meager knowledge and training left off. If Dee was having visions of her dead mother coming to her in the night, she needed professional counseling, not me and my inexpert advice and meddling.

She continued to sit there, her little face anxious, waiting for me to believe her story.

"You want to tell me what happened?" What else could I do under the circumstances? Right now, I would listen to what she wanted to tell me. Tomorrow, I would see about getting her the help she needed.

The story was simple, even classic in its style. Dee had been asleep and had 'awakened' with the feeling that someone was in her room. She hadn't been afraid, she told me.

"The moment I opened my eyes, I saw her; Mamma. She was standing right next to my bed." Dee pointed to the side nearest the window. "She was smilin' at me, an' told me to lay still an' be very quiet. Then she said that everythin' was gonna to be all right, that I was supposed to be good. I wanted her to stay, but she said she had to get back."

"Get back?"

Dee nodded. "Uh huh. I was awfully tired, Lyssie, an' just seein' her made me so happy! Before she left, she kissed me on the forehead just like she used to every night afore I went to sleep. That's how I knew it was real an' not just a dream."

"Because she kissed you?"

Again she nodded. "It was the way she did it. She pushed my bangs back, somethin' Mamma always did, an' then kissed me right here." She indicated a spot between her brows. "Mamma's the only one ever did that." She laid back against her pillows, obviously satisfied to have told me her story. "You do believe me, don't you?"

I bent over and kissed her cheek. "Yes, sweetheart, I believe you. I want you to relax now and get some sleep. Ok?"

She snuggled down into the bed. " 'Night, Lyssie."

I told her goodnight, shut off the lights, and leaving her suite, left the outer door ajar in case she should cry out in the night. With the way the rooms were divided in this house, I wasn't sure if anyone *could* hear her but thought it was for the best.

The hallway was dimly lit by a low wattage bulb in the ceiling—the one concession to the child as none of the other halls were lit this way. I stole past Margaret's rooms, wondered how she was feeling, then continued to my own suite.

Since I'd left long before nightfall, my rooms were dark when I entered. Rather than switch on a lamp, I made my way cautiously to the windows that looked out upon the back garden. The area was lit by a couple of small yard lamps that emitted just enough light to give the garden an eerie appearance.

As I stood beside the darkened window, I saw a figure emerge from the central portion of the house. When it stopped beneath one of the lampposts, I recognized it as being one of the twins. No evidence of a cane, so it must be Gray.

I watched him for a while, thought about going down to tell him about Dee's 'visit' from her mother then stopped myself just in time. Another figure was just visible in the gazebo, outside the range of the lamps. Before I turned away, the figure came out of the gazebo. While I could not see the person clearly, it was obvious it was a woman.

I went on into my bedroom to get ready for bed, thankful I'd not acted on impulse and made a mad dash outside. I would have made a fool of myself, maybe embarrassing all three of us. I was curious about the woman's identity and more than a little jealous.

"Like I've a right to be!" I scolded myself aloud, my voice echoing back to me in the silence.

I was tempted to return to the window, but after just telling Dee about the perils of eavesdropping, decided against it. If Gray Foxxe was meeting a woman in his own garden, it was no business of mine.

But what about this afternoon, what about . . .

Determined not to rehash the day, I grabbed a book and climbed into bed. I caught myself straining my ears once or twice to see if I could hear snatches of conversation carried in on the wind, but the only thing that drifted in on the breeze was the continuous song of the crickets.

I settled back on my pillows, determined to wait up for Pier so we could talk about what Dee had told me.

Exhaustion took over, and before I knew it, I awoke to find it past two in the morning, my lamp still burning. A noise down the hallway told me that Pier had made it safely home, but, by then, I was too tired to care. Instead, I switched off the lamp and snuggled back into the bed, relishing the cool breeze that blew in through the windows.

Sometime later, I awoke with a start, every hair on my body bristling, my heart thudding in my chest. A noise from somewhere nearby had my senses functioning at their peak.

The sound again, a slight rustling near the foot of the bed.

My eyes flew to the spot as I willed my leaden body to react. Barely discernible in the moonlight was a shadowy figure watching me with invisible eyes.

"Wh-who?"

The figure moved like lightning toward the open door to the sitting room.

I struggled to make my arms and legs obey, dragging myself out of the bed and forcing my uncooperative limbs across the room and into the next.

Although it seemed to take forever, I knew that, in reality, very little time had passed. Even so, by the time I got into the sitting room it was empty. . .

And so was the hallway.

Chapter 10

Mrs. Rhodes had been keeping house for the Craven family for more than forty years, long before Mr. Leo had been born. In all that time, she had never seen anything such as this.

Now, she led the poor little governess to a decent room in the great house, hoping it was not already too late. The child's body was wracked with shivers, and one could feel the fever right through her clothing—what was left of it, anyway.

The older lady shook her head and clicked her tongue in disapproval. What could have led Miss Diana out onto the moors on a night like that? Had the sickness already taken over, or was it the result of two days and nights within the garret?

"I saw him," Diana's weak voice broke through Mrs. Rhodes' musing.

"What's that, dearie?"

"You must do something to stop him before it's too

late." The young girl's eyes burned into the housekeeper's, imploring, insistent. "Must stop him before he murders again . . ."

Prayer got me through the night, helping me fall asleep in spite of the disturbance from my mysterious visitor. Even more surprising, I awoke bright and early the next morning, fresh and none the worse for the experience. I lay listening to the chatter of the birds outside my windows, the urge to be out among them pulling me from the bed.

There was still a cool breeze coming in, making the curtains dance back and forth with a gentle sway, so I grabbed up the jeans I'd worn last night and pulled out a clean T-shirt. A walk in the fresh air and early morning sunshine was just what I needed to chase away what was left of my 'nightmare.' And if luck was with me, I would be able to take that walk alone.

I picked up my sneakers, and on tiptoe, stepped into the hallway just as someone was coming out of Pier's suite. He was dressed in jeans and a denim shirt that looked as if he'd slept in them. When he turned, my surprise escaped me in a "yelp," and grimacing, he put a finger to his lips. I obliged, curious and more than a little alarmed. Pier had said she was going to town to find a man. The one she found couldn't have been more of a shock.

I followed closely behind him, his tall, lanky form cutting a comic figure as he tiptoed down the hallway in sock feet, his shoes in his hands.

He was sitting on the top step of the staircase by the time I got there. Slipping on his shoes, he gave me a hesitant smile.

"It's really not what you think."

I stared at the man, recalling how impressed I'd been with his sermon on forgiveness nearly a week before.

"Gerald MacKay, right?"

He blushed and held out his hand. "Mac. You must be Lyssie."

I shook his hand and nodded. "I enjoyed your sermon last Sunday."

Grey, intelligent eyes peered out at me from behind wire-framed glasses. "Not a sermon, just a conversation among a group of friends." He pointed at the stairs, and I followed him down. "Pier wasn't in any condition to drive herself home," he whispered, "so I brought her back. She was pretty well polluted, let me tell you." Turning back to me, he blushed again. "I'm just digging myself in deeper and deeper, huh?"

I placed a finger to my lips and mouthed, "We'll talk outside."

We managed to get the front door unlocked and opened with a minimum amount of noise. It closed behind us with a mild squeak. Mac grimaced, then indicated for me to join him on the swing.

"I've heard a lot about you," he told me with a smile.

"I wish I could say the same." Though it wasn't spoken as a question, I had a million of them behind the words. "You two old friends?"

"Sort of," he said, clearing his throat. "Let me explain—"

"It's really not necessary—"

"Oh, but I think it is. I wouldn't want you to think—"

"You don't owe me any explana—"

We stopped talking, looked at one another, and burst out laughing.

"We're both nervous about this, so why don't you just hear me out."

I nodded as I turned on the swing toward him.

"First, I want to clear up any misunderstanding—I spent the night on the couch in her sitting room. I didn't want to chance her getting back out in her car. She's already had a couple accidents when she's had too much to drink, and another one," he shook his head. "I didn't sleep with her, and I wasn't out drinking with her, either. A friend from Noah's Tavern called me when she started getting out of line."

"So, you went to rescue her?"

"What I'd like to do is *save* her, but she won't have any of it. Pier knows all the words, she holds the keys, but, right now, she doesn't buy into it. So, since I can't save her soul, I'll try to save her from herself."

"You're in love with her," I said, the realization bringing a smile to my lips. "She's not giving you an easy time of it, is she?"

"No, she's not." He sighed.

"So, Mac, what do you do when you're not having 'conversations' from the pulpit on Sundays?"

He pushed back a lock of brown hair from his forehead and smirked. "I teach at the college over in Linden."

"Drama?"

"Math." He grinned. "I'm sorry I startled you. I didn't expect anyone to be up."

"No problem. Have you known Pier long?"

"In one way or another, most of her life. I was in

her brothers' class in school, got along ok with them—not best friends or anything, but on speaking terms. Pier's five years younger, so we didn't see much of one another. Then, a few years ago, we ran into one another at the church—shocking, huh? She and her mom used to go on a fairly regular basis. Anyway, we met at a church supper and have been going out off and on since."

"I get the impression that you'd prefer it to be more on than off."

"You're right. After her mom died, her brothers tried to dissuade her from seeing me."

"Why?"

He rubbed a hand through his hair. "I made the mistake of trying to help Dylan out once—actually came riding to her rescue. The twins got the wrong idea, and I became *persona non grata*." He got up and walked the length of the porch to stare out across the yard.

"Rescue her in what way?"

"It happened shortly after Dylan came back into town with the little girl. I found her out on the highway, walking. She was barely coherent when I picked her up. I called her folks, and they must have told the twins. I was driving her home, and the next thing I know, they're pulling up beside me, ordering me to stop the car. When I got out to explain, one of them—Gray, I think—socked me in the jaw. By the time I got back up, they'd pulled away with Dylan in their car. I never did discover what it was all about."

I squirmed on the swing, the picture he'd just painted of the twins making me uncomfortable.

"You know, Lyssie, Pier was really glad you

decided to come visit. She's needed a diversion, someone sane to talk to."

I laughed. "Sane? Her words or yours?"

"Mine, I confess, but they're appropriate when considering this household. When she came in last week—"

Something clicked. "When she took Miss Allen to the bus station."

"Yeah. I know she blew you off, told you she had errands to run. She felt bad about that, but, well, she didn't want her brothers to find out, and we hadn't seen one another for a while—"

"Ah, I see. Now, tell me why you think I'm the only sane one here."

"That's easy. You haven't been around that long, and you never knew Dylan Courtney."

My eyes flew to his. "Why would you say that?"

"Because it's the truth. Somehow, some way, all the craziness that goes on out here is connected to her. At any rate, you're just what Pier—and the little girl, needs." He rubbed his face with the palms of his hands.

"You make it sound rather ominous." I studied his profile and could see why Pier was attracted to him. He had a handsome, open face, a caring, sensitive personality, and was just spiritual enough to intrigue Pier. It was obvious he cared very much for my friend.

"Look, after Pier's mother died, she was adrift. I thought she'd embrace the church as her mom did, but instead, she started drinking. When Phil Courtney died and her dad married the merry widow, I thought Pier would go over the edge. But she hung in there even when Dylan and her daughter moved in. The innuendo in the tabloids didn't seem to faze her. Pier stopped drinking, and we got really close. She was coming to church with me; we started making plans for the future. Am I boring you yet?"

I shook my head, amazed at what I was hearing.

"Then things really began to heat up. Dylan broke her engagement to Ryan and within a month, was engaged to Gray. The new Mrs. Foxxe was lording it over the entire household, and Pier was stuck in the middle. All within the year following her college graduation."

"I'd no idea."

"These last few months, Pier and I have had very little time together. I'd work all day, hoping to get together in the evening." He shook his head. "Dylan had other plans for Pier. She'd go off at night, leaving Dee to fend for herself. Pier hated that. She took that little girl under her wing and became the best aunt a little kid could have. Anyway, then Mr. Foxxe died and Dylan disappeared. Pier had been doing so well, Lyssie, hadn't been out drinking for a long time. I mean, she still wasn't coming to church, but she'd held it together. Until last night. I know something is bothering her, but she won't tell me what it is." He sat down on the steps leading off the porch.

"I'm sure she'll tell you." My words had an empty ring to them. Even I knew that when it came to Pier, you couldn't be sure about anything.

"You know, I was the one who talked Pier into asking for a vacation. She was wearing pretty thin, and I was worried about her. The family hemmed and hawed over the idea for six weeks, giving in only when it suited their own purpose. I'm sure your coming here made their day."

There seemed to be some hidden meaning behind his words. Not that *he* was hiding anything, but like there was something I should know and understand.

"I don't know that my being at Foxxemoor has made a lot of difference."

"Trust me when I say it has. Pier's glad you're here. She wasn't too happy with you last night, but by the time she gets up this morning, it'll be forgotten." He grinned. "You've got to remember that she was run ragged by Margaret yesterday. Between that, and all the extras she does for Ryan . . ."

I was getting another look at my friend, seeing a part of her that I hadn't realized was there. It was nice to hear about Pier's sensitive side, her devotion to Dee and her brother, and the responsibility she felt toward Margaret, in spite of not being fond of the woman. And after all the teasing I'd put up with because of my faith, it was nice to know she'd been seeking God even if she hadn't accepted Him yet.

"I'll make sure she takes it easy today." I got up and went to join him on the step. "What about you, Mac, where do you and Pier stand now?"

"The million dollar question." He looked thoughtful. "I love Pier, Lyssie, I have for a long time. I'd marry her in an instant. But—"

"She won't have you because of her brothers?"

"Something like that." He looked at his watch.

"Expecting someone?"

"Yeah, my sister. I phoned before I left Pier's room. Had to have a way into town since I'd driven Pier back here."

The sound of a car coming down the lane caught our attention.

"That will be the lady now." A Ford Bronco came screeching to a halt at the base of the gravel drive. "Walk with me?"

I joined him on the path, and he took my arm as if we were the best of friends. When we were just a few steps from the Bronco, he pulled up short, waved to his sister, then turned back to me.

"Do me a favor, Lyssie, and remember that sometimes the thing we're afraid of most is exactly what God is trying to get us to face. Call it a little twist of faith."

"I don't understand."

I walked him over to the Bronco, waiting for him to explain. As he climbed inside, he introduced me to his sister. Shutting the door, he reached out to touch my arm.

"Don't let them rope you into anything you don't feel you can handle, Lyssie. And remember to call on Him when you're not sure what to do."

"I really don't understand, Mac."

"You will," he promised. "You will."

I watched until they drove out of sight, pondering everything he'd told me. While it answered a lot of questions I'd had, it also created more.

I leaned my head back and looked up at the clear blue of the morning sky. There were a few fluffy, cumulus clouds in the west that appeared to be coming this way. It wasn't quite seven, but I knew that the Foxxe household would be starting the day. I still didn't feel inclined to face anyone so decided to go with my original plans and take a walk.

I took the path between the poplars that led to the pool, believing this would be one place where I was sure to be alone. I could sit outside the cabana in one of the lounge chairs and ease myself into the morning a little more calmly than I'd spent the last forty minutes. Besides, it would be an opportunity to digest what I'd learned as well as figure out what I should do about last night. It seemed obvious that someone was playing a rather sick game and needed to be stopped. Making me a victim was one thing, involving an innocent child was unacceptable.

The sun peeked through the poplars, catching the leaves and giving them a bright sheen as they danced in the breeze. The area was alive with sound: birds, insects, the far-off hum of a tractor, the rustle of the leaves, and the crunch of gravel under my feet. They were relaxing sounds, unhurried and non-threatening. It was the kind of morning I had dreamed about, longed for, when my mind seemed so full and ached with painful memories.

Thinking back over what Mac told me, I kept returning to the story regarding Dylan. He said she'd been walking along the highway and was incoherent. What happened to her, and why were the twins so angry about Mac trying to help?

I'd witnessed Gray's quick temper and cruelty, so it wasn't difficult to picture him slugging Mac. What I couldn't understand was why the twins had reacted so violently.

I gave myself a mental shake, wishing that I could erase the pictures from my mind as easily as the Etch-a-Sketch Dee had played with last evening.

The pool area was enclosed by a tall, chain-link fence with an outer barrier of trees on one side, the cabana/changing rooms blocking the front, and a meadow full of wildflowers and clover encompassing the view on the remaining two sides. The gate, which was usually latched, was open this morning. I heard the gentle swish of someone slicing gracefully through the water. I almost turned back, but as long as I was here . . .

He was just raising himself from the edge of the pool as I came upon the deck. He hadn't heard my approach and stood for a moment, gazing out across the meadow. I studied him, took in his tanned, muscular chest with its light covering of dark hair, and his thick, powerful legs. Even before he turned to find me standing there, I was already blushing.

"Good morning."

No smile, his voice flat, almost to the point of unwelcoming. The knowledge that he was aware I had been studying him was almost too much to bear.

"Hi." My voice squeaked past my vocal chords. "Beautiful morning. A little too cool for my taste—for swimming, I mean."

He looked over at the pool, watching the steam rise from the water. "Out here it's cool. In there, wonderful." He strode to a nearby lounger and grabbed up his towel, his slight limp barely noticeable. He rubbed the towel over his body, the motion brisk, leaving his head for last. His eyes met mine, his gaze steady, intense. Too intense. I lowered mine first.

"You're up early again this morning."

"The birds." I moved a lounger from the shade into the little spot of sunshine visible on the deck. "They were making such a racket I couldn't sleep. They must have a nest under the eaves." I couldn't believe my inept attempt at conversation.

"Mac get off all right."

I looked up at him in surprise, not sure how to answer. When in doubt . . .

"Yes, just a few minutes ago." I tried to discern what effect the news had on him, but his expression remained unreadable.

He nodded. "Good of him to see Pier got home safely."

He turned his back on me to sit on the edge of his lounger and pulled on a pair of tattered cutoffs.

"I never had a chance to thank you for yesterday," I spoke to his rigid back. "It was interesting and fun, and I appreciate your having taken the time for Dee and me. I'm a little sore this morning, since I'm not used to being in the saddle for so long, but I don't regret it."

"Good. I was glad for the company." Still no inflection.

I tried again. "It was all Dee could talk about last night. We had dinner together on the patio, then went up to her room and played games until bedtime. She's really a sweet kid."

Gray's dark eyes met mine and held them. "One of the best. Lyssie, I—" He stretched his neck around, rolling his head, then returned his gaze to my face. "I'm sorry. I'm not being very nice this morning. I came out here to see if I could get rid of a nasty headache but seem to have made it worse. Forgive me for not being better company?" He smiled a little, a movement of the mouth that failed to touch his eyes.

"Of course." I laid back in the lounger, determined not to bother him again. I didn't know what I might have done or said to have warranted his sudden coolness—I'd thought we'd gotten past that yesterday. I was getting weary of trying to figure out this family, walking around on eggshells and wondering which one was going to be foul-tempered this time.

My decision was made. Right there and then, I knew that no matter what protests Pier might make, I had to get away from Foxxemoor. As grateful as I was for the inspiration I'd had for *Craven*, I couldn't take the tension any longer. I was supposed to be on vacation, not becoming embroiled in the passions of the Foxxe brood. That had to be the cause of my sudden writer's block, as well as what had been eating at me the past several days.

Falling in love! How ridiculous could I be? I'd only been here a couple weeks, and to even believe I could fall in love with someone I didn't know was crazy. Gray and Ryan Foxxe resembled Leo Craven, and I was fascinated and intrigued by that resemblance. That's all it was, period.

A shadow passed over me, then returned to hover. I opened my eyes to find Gray standing there, blocking the sun. His shirt was open, the tails blowing in the breeze.

I swallowed hard, not wanting to look at him, but unable to keep from doing so.

Without a word, he leaned down and kissed me, his lips brushing mine tenderly. There was no bruising of the mouth like Ryan had done yesterday, only the soft pressure of his lips against mine. Just as quickly as it happened, he withdrew and stood, gazing down at me with a puzzled expression. I didn't know what to say, what reaction might be appropriate. Besides, at that moment, my heartbeat was so rapid I could feel it in my throat. I doubt I could have spoken had I tried.

A smile, a real one this time. "You're welcome." His voice was soft, as caressing as his lips had been. He touched my shoulder and then was gone.

I sat on the lounge chair, my fingers going to my lips. Closing my eyes, I relived the gentle kiss, as foolish as a schoolgirl.

And you insisted you weren't falling in love! My mind taunted me.

But another part, deep in my brain, ruled the morning. I'd still leave Foxxemoor. The sooner the better.

I left the pool and headed back to the house. It was time to let Pier in on my plans.

Chapter 11

Mrs. Rhodes bathed Diana's head with a mixture of water and alcohol, praying that the girl's temperature would go down. For three days, she had lain with a fever so high she was delirious and rambling most of the time. She didn't mind the talk so much for herself, but lately, Miss Ashleigh had been coming in to help watch over her governess. It wasn't enough that the poor child was terrified of the sickness, but then Diana would start mumbling about that murder she claimed the Master had committed. These words alarmed the twelve-year-old girl so much that she had angrily confronted her father about it. The scene that followed set the household in an uproar. Now they were at sixes and sevens night and day, walking around on tiptoe and hoping not to catch the Master's attention for fear of the wrath that might follow.

"No!" Diana cried out, rising from the bed, her

eyes wild as much from the fever as from whatever vision it had produced. "You mustn't come near me, please. Please, dear God, please save me. I don't want to die . . ."

It was obvious Pier had gotten out of bed to answer my rap on her door. She stared out at me with swollen, red-rimmed eyes so bloodshot they made me hurt just seeing her. Her gaze was apprehensive as I apologized for disturbing her. She allowed me to come in when I said we needed to talk, reluctantly moving aside so I could enter the sitting room. Mac had folded sheets, blankets, and pillows into a neat pile on the end of the loveseat. Pier's bedroom, in contrast, mirrored the disheveled state of its owner.

"I'm sorry for getting you up like this, but I didn't think this should wait." As determined as I was to follow through, I couldn't believe how nervous I'd become. "I've really enjoyed my time here, Pier, but I think I need to move on."

Pier's hand flew to her mouth, her look of apprehension changing to one I'd associate with fear. While this reaction wasn't at all what I'd anticipated, it just went to prove how complicated this family was.

"Look, this has been wonderful, Pier. I've loved our time together," though there hasn't been much of that, I thought. "I know you're not in the mood to discuss this now, but I wanted to warn you, tell you what I was thinking."

She grabbed at my arm, her expression frantic. "D-don't say anything yet, tell anyone until we've had the chance to talk. Please, Lyssie? If you still feel you need to go, I'll even help you pack."

I nodded my agreement, and before I could say anything more, Pier ushered me out of the room. I stood in the hallway, looking down into the dark reaches of the south wing, remembering the two late nights I'd searched those shadows for a sign of the person who had entered my room.

If I was staying another night at Foxxemoor, I was going to be prepared. Never again would I awaken to find someone watching me sleep, the darkness masking his or her identity. Fool me once, shame on you, fool me twice—not this lady.

Returning to my suite, I grabbed my purse and tape recorder then headed toward the marble staircase. I'd only gone down a couple steps when the sound of Dee's voice beckoned me from the central hallway. I turned to find her little face haggard, and wondered if she'd been disturbed by dreams of her mother again last night. Concerned, I went to her.

Her plaintive "Hi," was accompanied by an overall weariness. Rubbing her eyes, she said, "Ole Edna said I can't get up this mornin' 'cause I have a tummy ache. She thinks I have the flu."

"I see." I put my hand to her forehead and was relieved to find she didn't have a fever. "You feel pretty bad, huh?"

Dee leaned her head against my thigh. "Dizzy, I guess. I throwed up once, an' that kinda helped my tummy stop hurtin' for a little while. But I still feel funny."

I picked her up, surprised to find how light she was.

"Why don't I take you back to bed, honey. Maybe all you need is a bit more rest."

She pressed her little head into the curve of my

neck, and I carried her, without protest, back to bed. I laid her among the toys gathered there, pulling the sheet over her.

The room was stuffy with the windows closed, and after checking again to determine if she had a fever, I decided to open the far window a crack. The fresh air might do her some good, I told her, and if she got cold, she should just shut it.

"Lyssie," her weak voice called me back to her side. "Would you take that away? Just lookin' at it makes me wanna throw up again."

'That' was a glass of what appeared to be the remains of chocolate milk. I picked up the glass and looked at the filmy liquid with doubt.

"Ole Edna brought it in last night afore I went to sleep. She always does. I didn't want it, though, so I left it till this mornin'. I drank a little, but it tasted funny, so I just put it back on my night table." She screwed up her face. "I think it made me sick. Yuck!" She darted past me into the bathroom, and I could hear the sounds of her retching.

"Want me to get someone for you, honey?" I asked a few minutes later when she returned to crawl into bed.

Dee shook her head, her small face almost as pale as her hair. "I'm ok. Just tired." She closed her eyes, and within a short time, her breathing slowed as she drifted off to sleep.

As I left her rooms, I made sure the doors were wide open. In the hallway, I raised the glass of milk to my nose, then took it quickly away. Besides the distinct odor of chocolate, I detected something else, something with a faint, bitter smell that I didn't recognize. But not being a fan of milk, I was a very poor judge of the product.

I took the glass out to the kitchen where Mrs. Merrick was conferring with the cook. Placing it on the counter next to the sink, I waited near the door until they were finished speaking.

"I just wanted you to know that Dee was sick again," I told the housekeeper. "I stayed with her until she fell asleep. She said she was all right, but she's awfully pale."

"I'll look in on her in a bit. Poor little lamb. I've told Mrs. Foxxe, but since it's happened again, maybe I should say something else. The flu, no doubt." She gave me a weak smile, and I got the impression that Dee's illness would add even more of a burden to her shoulders.

I turned to go, then remembered what I'd wanted to tell her. "Did Dee say anything to you about the milk not tasting right? You think it might have soured left out like that?"

She laughed. "I'm sure it did taste odd to her. We've gone to using skim in the last few days, and that's quite a change from the two percent she's used to—trying to cut down on the fat and calories, you understand. As for it souring, I suppose it's possible. It was cool in her room last night, and I thought," she shrugged. "It's something her mother always did, and I just carried on the tradition. Maybe it's time to stop."

She followed me out into the main hallway where I told her my plans to go into town.

"I don't think I'll be too long. I just want to pick up a few things. Are there any errands you'd like me to run for you?"

She thanked me for my offer, assuring me she

would tell the rest of the family where I'd gone. As for needing anything, Sarah always brought things with her when she came every morning.

Satisfied, and glad to be on my own, I left the house and strolled to where my car was parked. Rolling down the front windows, I started the engine then sat for a few minutes to watch a cardinal that had flown across my line of vision and up to a nest in the eaves of the garage. The bird brought a smile to my lips as I recalled the story Dee told me about the birds in her maple tree. Our relationship had come a long way since that day, and I knew that I would miss her when I left Foxxemoor.

It was nearly ten when I got to Bristol, and I found the activity there a welcome change after the often oppressing atmosphere at the estate. WalMart was already filled with shoppers, so I wasted little time in finding the nightlights I was after. If I spent another night at Foxxemoor, I was determined to dispel the nighttime shadows that allowed intruders to hide. At the check-out counter, I included a mini flashlight and batteries for my security arsenal. If someone came into my room again, I'd be prepared, and intended on following the intruder.

Again? I'd just told Pier I'd be leaving soon, and here I was plotting a future that intimated more than the single night I'd had in mind. Talk about indecision! Still, it didn't hurt to be prepared—whether it was one night or more, better to err on the safe side.

After making my purchases, I took a driving tour of Bristol and of the nearby city of Linden. It didn't take long to find the college/university where Mac worked, and as I drove through the campus, I wondered if Mac was within one of the starkly modern structures or one of the older, more academic-looking ones. The thought of his standing before a classroom, acting the esteemed professor of mathematics, seemed a little incongruous, not fitting his appearance or demeanor.

The campus grounds were beautifully kept, and I enjoyed the quiet lanes. As the cool breeze drifted in through my windows, the gloom and pent-up emotions I'd felt melted away. Back in Bristol, just inside the city limits, I noticed a large, rambling building with a pretentious facade. A sign proclaimed it the community library, and without any conscious thought, I found myself pulling into a nearby parking lot.

The information desk provided me with direction, and I was soon pouring over a microfiche index of the *Bristol Gazette*.

I started with three years ago, searching through the index for listings regarding the Foxxe and Courtney families. I jotted down the fiche numbers for that year, found them, and took them to a nearby reader to scan the articles.

Using those machines tends to make me nauseous, so, after bumming change from an operator of a nearby machine, I copied the articles as I found them. It didn't take long to realize that I could go broke at this rate, and despite the risk of nausea, began to read the material once again.

Midway through that first year, I came across the obituary of Miranda Kelly Foxxe, Pier and the twins' mother. After what Mac said, I'm not sure what I expected, but it wasn't what I found. There was no mystery surrounding Mrs. Foxxe's death; she'd died after a "brief, but painful fight, with cancer," the obit stated, and would be missed by family and community alike. There was a long line of credits—an indication the lady had been very active in volunteer work throughout the area. A tiny picture showed me a face that was an older version of Pier's, with eyes very like her sons'. Sitting in the quiet audio-visual room, I studied the face for a long time, wondering what the lady would think about the state of her family today.

A hand on my shoulder stopped my musing, and startled, I looked up to discover its owner.

"Sorry if I scared you," the woman whispered as she leaned in closer to me. "I noticed what you were reading and realized you must be the young lady visiting at Foxxemoor."

Curious, I gazed up at the woman, amazed at her deductive ability.

She pulled up a nearby chair, smiled at me over a pair of glasses precariously perched on the tip of her nose, and sat down. Her silver hair was tucked neatly into a bun at the nape of her neck, and her appearance spoke of a woman who had tried to live up to everyone's image of the typical librarian.

She smiled again and nodded toward the screen. "Miranda was a lovely woman. She was English, you know, and brought her ways with her. She was never one to put on airs, always friendly and down to earth, considerate of others. Everyone loved her."

"Did you know her well?" My hoarse whisper seemed to echo in the little room, and I looked around to see if anyone noticed. It didn't appear as if they had, my neighbors too intent on the work in front of them to pay any attention to our quiet conversation.

"Oh, no, no." She shook her head. "I always felt

close to them, though. The Foxxe family has been my particular passion since I was a child. I've been a collector for almost as long as I can remember."

I raised my eyebrows in question.

"Articles," she laughed. "Everything I could get my hands on." She waved her hand at the screen. "It'll take you forever to go through the *Gazette* alone. I've got my own files and would gladly copy anything you'd like."

"I—thank you." I was rather at a loss.

"I'm sorry. I've gone about this badly." She held out a slender hand. "I'm Mary Dean, Sarah Williams' cousin."

I took her hand, nodding at the connection. No wonder she looked familiar and recognized me. The assistant housekeeper must have spoken of me.

"Thanks for the offer. It's very kind."

"Oh, think nothing of it. It's the least I could do." She scratched her head, her expression thoughtful. "With all you've got to contend with, well, as I said, it's no problem." Her eyes darted across the room, then returned to me. "Of course, you won't be wanting everything."

"No." There it was again, that elusive 'something' I was supposed to know, but didn't. "I'm most interested in the last three years." I told her, forced to hide my ignorance yet again.

She nodded. "They've been the most traumatic the family's had. You'll need things on the Courtney's as well." She glanced at her watch. "I've a tight schedule today, but I might be able to start the copying this afternoon. I'll have Sarah bring the items to you when I'm finished."

"Well, I—"

"It's no bother. Really. I'm happy to be of help. I'll even give you a break on the copy charges." She winked, giving me the odd feeling we were conspirator's in a crime.

"Great." There didn't seem any way to turn down her offer without seeming ungracious. I'd just have to delay my departure from Foxxemoor for a few more days. Knowing Pier, this would play right into her hands.

As Mary Dean got up to leave, she put her hand on my shoulder once again. "Pier's lucky to have a friend like you, Miss Daniels. As a matter of fact, the whole family's fortunate you're here." She patted my shoulder. "Take care of yourself now."

I watched as she went on to another patron, leaving me to ponder the hidden meanings behind her words. Maybe it was just my imagination. After all the inferences and innuendo thrown around at Foxxemoor, was it any wonder for me to hear something that wasn't there?

But there had been Gray's mysterious warning. And this morning, Mac said something—what was it? Oh yes, not to allow myself to be talked into anything I was unsure about. What did any of it mean?

I gathered the microfiche, shut off the machine, and put the packets in the return box.

I was tired of cryptic messages disguised as friendly advice. Why couldn't these people just be frank and open and stop all this beating about the bush?

I rubbed my temples. My head was pounding and going out into the sunshine didn't help. I got in my car, and once on the main drag, wondered what to do with myself. I wasn't ready to return to Foxxemoor. I didn't feel like facing the people or a blank computer screen. My stomach growled, giving me an excuse to put off my return to the estate for a while longer.

Fast food—a hamburger, fries, and a soft drink—and a quiet park to eat at. I sat in the car, watching a family picnic across the way, eating my greasy lunch and enjoying it far more than I should have.

Foxxemoor had seemed an idyll, its beautiful setting the source of my creative inspiration. I loved the house, the garden, all of it. Even the mood swings of its inhabitants had, at first, provided a source to tap for my creative juices, but now. . .

In my mind's eye I saw Gray. I could hear his laughter, the sound of teasing in his voice as it had been yesterday. Then, the tenderness of a few hours ago. He hadn't appeared to want my company, even acted a little annoyed by my arrival at the pool.

But he'd kissed me.

The memory of his mouth upon mine burned my lips. There'd been a tenderness to his kiss that had my heart racing. I wished I knew if it had done the same to him.

I pushed back the memory to have it replaced by Ryan's declaration of love. I'd felt his passion in his touch, seen it in the look of his eyes as they bore into mine. The power of it overwhelmed me, leaving me breathless. He seemed so sure of himself, of me—but my heart had chosen his brother. The irony of it all!

I sighed, took another swallow of Dr. Pepper, and gazed absently out the window.

Had that incurable romantic in me chosen Gray simply because of his unattainable status? Was there something inside me that instinctively knew he would be elusive?

"You're a dreamer, Lysette, always wanting something you can't have." My grandmother's voice came across the years to mock me. She'd been referring to my writing at the time, but the line was just as appropriate for the rest of my life. Hadn't I always wanted the boy who never looked in my direction? And the ones who seemed interested in me, I'd pushed to change to suit me.

Too many books and movies as influence with nothing in real life for a comparison.

No, that wasn't true. After all, it was my grandmother who pointed out that it wasn't illness that had taken my father's life. She swore he'd died of a broken heart. Was it any wonder that I looked for something as strong, as powerful as what my parents shared?

Romeo and Juliet, Antony and Cleopatra–Gray and Dylan.

The stories may be romantic, but they were morbid as well.

Yes, I could admit I wanted a great romance, to be swept off my feet. What woman wouldn't? But I'd seen firsthand the destruction, the devastation when one partner decided they were unable to live without the other. I didn't want anything so all-encompassing; it would be restricting, stifling, and entirely unhealthy.

Soul searching wasn't always easy, but it did have a way of planting your feet back on the ground where they belonged. My heart may leap at the sight of Gray Foxxe, but so did my fictional character's whenever she encountered Leo Craven. If I was falling in love, it was with the image, not the man.

Then why don't you feel the same about Ryan? My brain taunted me.

Ryan was sweet and kind, even heroic when you considered his fight to recover from his accident. He'd progressed so far in such a short time; you had to admire his determination and fortitude. In the few weeks I'd been at Foxxemoor, I'd seen his steps become surer, more confident. He was just as handsome, just as intriguing . . .

But he didn't have that haunted look in his eyes, or that brooding, mysterious air that enveloped Gray. Diana perceived that quality in Leo Craven, and I saw it in Gray.

The romantic in me recognized the image of the typical protagonist the moment Gray stepped into the living room that first evening. He'd held my attention so completely that I'd hardly been aware of the others in the room. Indeed, until someone had spoken, breaking the spell, it had been as though there were only the two of us. His gaze had riveted me, and I was certain he'd been well aware of its effect. He'd used it to his advantage, setting the others somewhat off balance while maintaining that extraordinary contact with me.

Had he manipulated me, or had I been the cause— my fascination and surprise making me stare to the point of rudeness? And the day I'd first gone to the stables, he'd run hot and cold, his anger seething just below the surface till it finally boiled over and onto me. Yes, he was protective of Dee, appeared to love her a lot. Which led to yet another question: if Gray was the child's father, why didn't he admit to it?

This was not the way to spend a vacation. And definitely not the way to get over the past and learn to forgive myself . . .

The pain didn't come as it usually did since Amy's death. I saw her sweet face before me, a beatific smile lighting it up in a way I'd never seen in life. It was so real, so *here*, I couldn't help but reach out to the vision. Rather than dispersing, the smile widened, the lips parting slightly to show the gap where she'd lost her upper eyetooth the week before her death.

I shook my head. It had to be the headache, the fast food, nights of disturbed sleep . . .

But the vision didn't fade. If anything, it seemed to become clearer. The brightness that surrounded her was unlike anything I'd ever seen before.

"Amy," I whispered, my hand reaching toward her face.

"Sometimes what you're most afraid of is exactly what God is wanting you to face."

It wasn't Mac's voice I heard; it was the soft voice of a child, the voice that had been silenced forever in death.

Tears streamed down my face. Was this what Dr. Hadley had been afraid of? That my guilt would send me over the edge of reality? She'd been my strength throughout my growing up, the one I leaned on when my grandmother wallowed in the grief and loss of my father. Yet, I hadn't been able to trust her after Amy's death, hadn't been able to trust myself around the other children. So, I'd run away and hid myself first in the book I was writing and then among the inhabitants of Foxxemoor.

I shook my head again, but the face remained before

me.

"Forgiveness is yours already, Lyssie. Ask, receive, and accept."

"Dear God," I cried. "If this is from You, please hold Amy within Your arms and give her the love she didn't get here on Earth. Please, please forgive me for not being able to save her. Forgive me for not coming to You and begging for Your grace."

As the vision began to vaporize, there was the hint of a hand atop Amy's head. She looked up in wonder, and as she turned away, I heard a voice I will never forget.

"Your faith is your gift to Me. Your forgiveness, My gift to you."

Chapter 12

The doctor had been and gone, leaving Diana in the gentle hands of Mrs. Rhodes. He had determined that in this, the fifth day of fever, if such excellent nursing could not pull the girl through, nothing would. It was little comfort to the man that sat silently by the girl's bed, one of her small hands cupped within his own. He cursed himself for what he had allowed to happen to Diana, especially for the incident that sent her fleeing from the great house.

Leo Craven stole a furtive glance at Mrs. Rhodes asleep on a nearby cot. She'd given him quite a set-to, as had his daughter, their words of warning urging him to see for himself the state of the little governess before him.

Diana moaned in her sleep, and Craven leaned forward to touch a hand to her brow. Was it his imagination, or did she seem cooler, less feverish than when he had first entered the room?

*It should never have happened here, he told himself harshly. But even in the telling, he knew it could not have been helped. Despite the danger and possibility of witnesses, the greater danger had lain in discovery. And **that** **was** something Leo Craven could not afford . . .*

What can you say when you've had an epiphany, a vision that you cannot discount as real or deny? I felt jubilant, lighter than the air itself. My heart sang in harmony with my soul, giving me a strength of purpose and direction. I could feel the truth of those final words, the ones spoken as the vision of Amy disappeared. I knew I'd been called for something; I just had to wait and let Him tell me what it was.

As I drove back to Foxxemoor, I nearly filled an entire side of my tape. While one part of my brain was still trying to get a handle on the experience at the park, the other part was busy adding scenes to *Craven*. The writer's block had broken at the same time my heart had been healed.

The urge to get to my laptop was strong, but there were things I needed to take care of first. I wanted to check on Dee and make sure she was all right, and Pier and I should have our talk. If she still wanted me, I would remain at Foxxemoor a while longer.

A few dark clouds began to roll in from the northwest, and as I parked before the garage, I noticed how low they seemed to hang in the sky. I switched on the radio, hoping to hear the weather, but a quick run-through of the stations yielded nothing but music. Glancing back at the sky, I sighed and shut off the car.

As I started up the walk, I realized how anxious I

was to talk with Pier. There were so many things I wanted to tell her, to ask her about. I wished I could share my vision but knew she wouldn't be receptive.

I ran up to my suite, and as I tossed my purse and package onto the love seat, noticed a letter propped against the lamp on the end table. I instantly recognized the handwriting, and opening the envelope, sat on the edge of the sofa to read the letter.

"I tried to phone a couple of times," Dr. Hadley wrote, "then decided that a letter would do just as well. Though, if you would use your email, you would have gotten this information sooner."

The letter was short and to the point, but I read it through twice just to make certain I had not misunderstood what it said. The pages slipped from my hands and onto the floor as my eyes blurred, all the joy inside me crushed and forgotten. I'd been tricked, the pawn of an elaborate ruse.

Pier phoned Langston shortly after Amy's death, looking for me. The doctor had remembered her unusual name, and thought nothing of telling her where I was. It wasn't until a few days later that Dr. Hadley began to suspect there was more to Pier's call than the simple request for information.

"You know how the call reporting is sent to me," Dr. Hadley continued. "I noticed Margaret Foxxe's name and number with a request for possible assistance. When I called, Mrs. Foxxe told me her granddaughter was having a difficult time accepting her mother's death. She asked if I might recommend someone who would be willing to come to Foxxemoor and help Deidre through this rough period. When she suggested you, I adamantly advised against it. She seemed very gracious, took down the names of the people I suggested, and thanked me. You can imagine, therefore, my surprise to hear you were at Foxxemoor. Under the circumstances, dear, do you really think that's wise . . ."

I continued to stare in front of me while events of the last few weeks played and replayed in my mind. I'd thought Pier was my friend, that *we* were friends. Now, my questions about her mysterious attitude at Tan-Tar-A suddenly made sense. She'd always known how to manipulate me, offering Foxxemoor to help with my writing had been her ace in the hole. No wonder she hadn't tried harder to find time for us to be together. All she'd cared about was that I was comfortable enough to want to stay. The longer I stayed, the more chance there would be for a relationship with Dee.

But she'd been angry last evening when I'd chosen Dee over her. That hadn't been faked.

It didn't matter. Everything that had happened since my arrival at Foxxemoor took on a new light. Doubt about my own feelings, my interest in Gray, Ryan's attraction to me, and, especially, Pier's statement of life-long friendship were all in question. Was any of it based in reality, or had it all been a part of the ruse?

Dee. I thought about our hard-won friendship and how much it seemed to mean to her. She wouldn't have known of her family's duplicity, was as much a pawn in this mess as I was—more so. Whatever happened, *that child must not be hurt.*

I didn't understand. If they'd wanted my help with Dee, why hadn't they just asked? Why had they gone to such elaborate lengths to deceive me?

Ok. Right. It was there in front of me all along. The honest approach could have led to my refusal, and probably would have. By inviting me here, there was a good chance that I would grow fond of Dee and offer my assistance, which would have made it unnecessary for them to reveal the original deception.

I got up and paced the length of the room, my mind racing, causing my head to spin.

Control. I had to maintain control. Anger was dangerous, damaging. Think, Lyssie, analyze. The single driving force behind this was their concern for Dee. While this made their deception easier to understand, it also made the betrayal more painful.

I buoyed myself for the upcoming confrontation, took a deep breath, and strode out into the hall. At Pier's suite, I tightened my hand into a fist and pounded upon the door, my knuckles aching with the force of the blow. I knocked several times, and when she failed to answer, I stood there a moment without direction.

Breathe, think.

I started toward the staircase, then changed directions and headed for Dee's rooms. I found Sarah Williams vacuuming the sitting room, and waited impatiently for her to notice me and turn off the sweeper.

"Dee was able to convince Edna she was well enough to get up." Sarah's round face broke into a beautiful smile. "If you're looking for her, she was told not to go beyond the garden. Of course, that doesn't mean she'll be easy to find. The little devil can find more places to hide!"

"Not the flu, then?" I tried hard to keep my anger from showing in my voice.

"Doesn't look like it, which is a good thing. That child hates being down, and with this nice weather, it would have been nearly impossible to keep her in bed."

I thanked her for the information and continued on my mission. At this point, I wasn't certain which had the upper hand, the anger or my bruised ego. I felt tears threatening to fall, and willed them back. I wasn't about to give into them, into the weakness. I was glad Dee hadn't been around. I would've hated for her to see me like this, so out of control. The thought helped me regain some semblance of the poise I usually possessed.

Nearing the living room, I heard Margaret and Pier's voices echoing down the hallway. I drew in a deep breath and walked into the room.

It had been two days since I'd last seen Margaret, and I was instantly aware of the toll her illness had on her. It lent a fragility to her aristocratic good looks that had not been there before but had not erased the cool dignity with which she held herself. Even the dark smudges beneath the pale blue eyes did not detract from the woman she was. Raising her eyes to mine, I recognized the strength and conviction that radiated from them.

"Ah, Lysette, did you have a nice day in town?" She smiled, indicating that I should join them.

I glanced over to where Pier sat, her chair pulled close to Margaret's, a notebook in her hands. She grinned up at me as she closed the book, her eyes still bloodshot. Neither woman was at her peak, and had it been anything else, I would have waited. As it was, I felt the time for watching whose toes I might tread on was past. It was time for honesty, and I'd have it even if I had to drag it out of them.

I refused the offer of a seat and stood there, looking from one to the other of them. The words of condemnation didn't come. Anger had turned to frustration, and I found myself at a loss, impatient with my lack of action.

"I just finished a letter from Dr. Hadley," my voice shook, but the import of the statement was crystal clear—at least from Pier's reaction. I met her gasp with coldness. "I see there's no reason to elaborate what she wrote." I folded my arms across my chest, regarding the women before me. "I believe, however, that I'm entitled to an explanation."

Pier shrank back into her chair and lowered her bloodshot eyes. Her hands clutched at the book in her lap, the knuckles whitening with the increased pressure.

"Of course you're entitled, my dear." Margaret's clear voice echoed strangely in the quiet room. "Why don't you come have a seat, and we'll talk about it." She smiled again, an obvious attempt to win me over.

"Thank you, I'd rather stand." I mentally dug my heels into the carpet, refusing to allow myself to be coerced into accepting what they'd done. I felt indignant that she even tried.

"I'm sure once you have heard our side of it, you will understand why we felt our, uh, little arrangement was necessary." Margaret smiled again, eased herself out of her chair, and walked to within a few steps of me.

"Arrangement?" I glanced from one to the other of them. "I would hardly call it an arrangement, Mrs. Foxxe. That would imply some agreement reached by both parties." My voice steadied, the tone icy. "Try deception, blatant duplicity, but hardly an arrangement." I stared pointedly into the older woman's eyes. "Perhaps you could enlighten me, tell me why it was necessary to create such an elaborate ruse. If you'd wanted my help with Dee, why didn't you just ask?" My question was aimed at Pier, but Margaret chose to intercept it.

"Originally, that was our intention. When we discovered the reason you'd left Langston, however, we thought there might be some resistance."

My laugh was dry, without humor. "You think?"

Margaret Courtney Foxxe raised an impressive eyebrow. "Precisely the attitude we'd feared. We had no wish to scare you off. The alternative approach was deemed best."

"So, you tricked me. You offered your home as a kind of writer's paradise. That should have been my clue. A paradise always includes a snake." I swallowed hard. "I suppose you hoped I'd become so fond of Dee I'd offer to stick around for her sake." An inclination of Margaret's head was all I needed to know my assumption was correct. I looked at Pier to find she'd sunk even further into her chair. The bitterness I now felt was a gorge in my throat.

"I would think," Margaret was saying, "that after your recent experience, you would appreciate our quick attention in this matter."

There it was, the moment I'd dreaded, the reference to Amy Webster's tragic death. In spite of the beautiful vision I'd had at the park, this was not a topic I wanted to discuss, especially with these people. I felt the blood rush into my face as my fury deepened. A small sound came from Pier, and I flashed cold eyes in her direction.

"After my 'recent experience,' Mrs. Foxxe, it's a wonder you wanted me at all."

"Don't be absurd. We knew what happened was no

fault of yours. It was a horrible tragedy, but you were never to blame, Lysette. You're acting as if we deliberately set out to hurt you."

My eyes flew to her face. "Wouldn't you feel hurt if you suddenly discovered you'd been played for a fool?" I turned my attention back to Pier. "And you, how could *you*, Pier? I trusted you!" She still refused to look at me.

I threw my hands up in despair, walked past Margaret, and stood over my old friend. "All that talk about life-long friendship, sounding me out and pouring your heart out to me, what was that? A game, Pier? Were you after sympathy and compassion, or were you trying to see how far I would fall for one of your schemes?"

Pier's bloodshot eyes finally met mine, the grey-green orbs hard and cold. "I didn't want to do it! Why do you think I acted as I did at Tan-Tar-A? Yes, seeing you took me back to our carefree days in college, reminded me of all the fun we'd had. *That's* what I concentrated on, Lyssie. *That's* how I convinced myself that it was all right to invite you to come home with me." She shook her head, the desperation in her voice finally reaching me. "I knew I had to get you to come to Foxxemoor, *she* gave me no choice. I wasn't about to mention Dee's problems and risk you saying no."

She shoved herself up out of the chair and cast a hateful look in Margaret's direction. "You've no idea what it'd been like around here, the pain, the bitterness, *everyone dying*! When they agreed to let me go on vacation, I jumped at the chance to get away! I was stretched so tight, I thought I would die too. The price to pay for a little freedom was to get you to come back here to check out Dee, to deceive you if necessary." She threw the notebook she'd been holding across the room. "They never told me about that little girl until after I'd gotten back here. If I'd known, I'd never have gone along with them. You've got to believe me, Lyssie."

Our eyes met and locked. I could see the torment behind hers. No matter what Pier had done, I believed her now.

"You lied to me." I said weakly, unable to recognize my own voice.

"You were invited here with the most honorable intentions." Margaret's cool voice came to me from across the room. Looking up, I found she had moved to stand before the windows.

"Honorable?"

"Lyssie," Pier took me by the shoulders and shook me. "I didn't lie, not really. Once we started talking, I knew I needed you to come back here *for me*. The bond between us was still there. I wanted that, needed your sane and comfortable presence in this house. For me as much as for Dee."

This hadn't gone at all like it was supposed to. But then, how was it supposed to have gone?

"I understand your feeling of betrayal," Margaret said slowly. "And I'm sorry you found out as you did. You have to understand our position. Dylan's walking out on Deidre could damage the child permanently. It was imperative to keep that from happening."

"Then why haven't you sought professional help for her? Why me? I haven't any real training."

Margaret gripped the back of a nearby chair. "I have very little use for the so-called professionals, Lysette." Her voice was hard, tight. "Years of therapy never made a difference in Dylan, why should I feel it would help my granddaughter? No, that was not the solution." She made an impatient movement with her hand. "Then I remembered the story Pier told us about your background, your personal tragedy in the deaths of your parents. Your history and work with troubled children made you the ideal candidate. You could come and live with the family with no further disruption to Deidre's life."

The tears that had threatened to fall could no longer be held in check. They spilled from my eyes, running onto my cheeks in a torrent. All the righteous indignation in the world could not overturn the reasons for their deception. It had all been for Dee, and I felt like an ungrateful fool.

I turned and ran from the room, down the hallway, and directly into Ryan, who was just entering the front door. He held me at arm's length, steadying me and staring into my tear-drenched face. He reached out, brushing the tears from one cheek.

"I suppose this means the jig is up." He said lightly. "Why don't you come over here, and we'll talk about it?"

I knew he was trying to help, but I'd had enough talking for the moment and wasn't up for any more. I pulled away and ran out the door, off the porch, and just kept running. My mind was reeling, so out of control there was no way to stop it. I hated being deceived, hated them for luring me, using my writing as bait. I had to stop, had to understand, had to accept their reason behind their actions.

Dee. Her bright little face filled with trust as she shared the secret of her mother's 'visit.' How many times had I felt she needed attention, someone to care for her and love her? I knew she needed help coping with everything that had happened in her short life. Why had they been so determined to have *me* help her instead of a qualified professional?

Because you're non-threatening, Lysette, my subconscious answered me. *You're Pier's old friend, a non-professional who has worked with children with similar problems. And you've been there; you're a survivor. What could be more perfect?*

But the lies? I'd always prided myself on my honesty, deliberately avoided people who found it difficult to live the same way. How could I accept it now from someone I'd thought I could trust?

As I exited the oak-lined lane to the stables, I ran headlong into Gray. Just as Ryan had done back at the house, Gray reached out to steady me. Taking one look at my face, he led me into the stable office. Easing me into a chair, he knelt before me, his dark eyes filled with tenderness and concern.

"You've finally discovered why Pier brought you here." He concluded, drawing some tissues from his pocket and handing them to me. "I'm sure they tried to make it sound reasonable."

I took the tissues and mopped my face. "I-I was so angry. I h-hate being lied to." A new set of spasms wracked my body.

"Of course you do," he soothed, putting his strong arms about my shoulders and hugging me.

I felt the heat of his body through his lightweight cotton shirt, and the sound of his heart became my lifeline. I allowed myself the comfort of his arms as the sobs continued to shake my body. His hand went to my head, and he smoothed back my hair as whispered words I could not understand attempted to calm me.

"I was against this from the first," he told me. "I tried to warn you but didn't want to hurt you in the process."

I pulled slightly away, gazing up at him. "Y-you said I shouldn't take things at face value, or s-something like that. Why didn't you just come out—"

A gentle finger caught a tear as it rolled down my cheek. He regarded it for a moment, then looked into my eyes. "I was going to, Lyssie. Then I got to know you." He pulled abruptly away and stood. His hands slipped into the pockets of his jeans as he stared at me. "I thought you should be warned but didn't think it was my place to do it."

"Why? Didn't you think I had a right to know?"

He turned his back on me, and I felt he was trying to shut me out. "You started to make some headway with Dee, and you didn't even realize it. All of us saw it. You two had found one another naturally, why do something to spoil it?"

"Because I had a right to know!"

He faced me once more. "So you could be hurt and confused like you are right now? So you could leave here?" He came over to me and pulled me roughly out of the chair. "Is that what you want, Lysette? To leave?" He crushed me in his arms, his mouth coming down hard on mine. I resisted—but only for a moment.

My arms went around Gray's neck, and I melted against him. My mouth sought his with an urgency I'd not known I possessed, and the call was answered with a passion that seemed to come from the very core of his being. I felt myself relax in his arms, the anger draining from me and leaving me weak. I could have stayed that way forever had it not been for my nagging subconscious, which made me question the sincerity of the man in my arms.

I pushed myself away, stumbling back from him.

"Lyssie—" His voice sounded tortured as he spoke my name.

"You, you don't understand. I-I left Langston because I didn't think I could d-do it anymore. There, there was this little girl . . . Amy. I failed her." My stomach cramped as the thought of failing Dee entered my mind.

"It's all right, Lyssie. Everything's ok." He advanced toward me, imploring me to accept something I wasn't certain I could.

"I-I have to think, to decide what to do."

"What's there to decide?" His hands caught my arms, and he tried to pull me back to him.

"No, I can't think clearly when you're holding me. It becomes all jumbled up." I backed away until I was on the other side of the room. "Nothing seems clear anymore."

"I want you to stay, isn't that clear?" He asked gruffly.

"For you, or for Dee?" My voice shook as I studied him for the answer.

"For both of us!" He smashed his fist into the wall behind him, the wallboard crumbling from the impact. "I'm sorry you had to find out about Margaret's stupid plan, sorry you've been hurt. But isn't the good you've done, the time you've spent here worth it? Aren't *we* worth it?" His dark blue eyes were like smoldering coals as they burned into mine.

"We? Do *we* exist, Gray, or is that just another part of the game to convince me to stay?" I knew it was the wrong thing to say the moment it left my mouth. The fury in his eyes blazed even brighter as he glared at me.

"*That's* what you think? Fine. Believe whatever you want." He turned and headed for the door into the stable.

"Gray, wait. I'm sorry. I-I don't know what I'm saying, what to do." I started forward, but the expression on his face stopped me.

"Either stay or go, it's your decision. Make it on your own." He slammed out of the office, leaving me there to stare after him.

I looked about me in dismay, realizing that my desperate flight from the house hadn't gotten me any closer to a solution to the mess I was in. I'd come running blindly down here, down to the man I believed I loved, and was in and out of his arms so quickly it made my head spin. What had happened? Had I rejected him or the other way around?

I couldn't stay there, couldn't risk his possible rebuff and anger. As twisted as Margaret's plan had been, it was nothing compared to the hole I was digging for myself.

I left the stable office and walked out into an afternoon that had become prematurely dark. Heavy black clouds threatened overhead, adding to my sense of disquiet. I walked without thought, realizing too late that I had gone past the main path to the house. Rather than backtrack, I decided to use Dee's shortcut through the evergreens. I wasn't more than a few steps within the trees when I discovered the mistake I'd made.

I must have wandered past the area Dee had taken

me because I was now in the middle of tightly packed trees and undergrowth that made the going very difficult. I thought about turning back, but the trees were so dense that I was afraid I might lose my way. Instead, I proceeded in the direction I'd been heading, picking my way along the rough ground with caution.

I heard the wind pick up, and high above me, the towering pines swayed, their heavy branches producing a mournful sound that echoed eerily around me. The enclosure was alive with sounds, indistinguishable in origin, and oddly threatening in nature. My overactive imagination succeeded in getting the better of me, and as the massive evergreens shut out the remainder of light, I felt alone and trapped in a world of semi-darkness where shadows took on ominous shapes.

I stumbled over some roots, putting my hands out to break my fall. As I landed against the hard ground, my hands were skinned and the knees of my jeans ripped. My hands and knees stung from the blow, and pine needles stabbed at the tender flesh. I tried to check my injuries, but the light was too dim to make anything out.

Dragging myself off the ground with the aid of a nearby tree, I continued my forward progression. I no longer wanted to be alone, was tired and spent from the anger. I wanted, *needed*, the light and safety of Foxxemoor.

My eyes ached from crying, and trying to pierce the dim light made them even more painful. A sudden movement in the dark shadows in front of me caught my attention, and I called out for help. There was nothing but the echo of my voice in response.

Again the movement of shadows and what appeared to be the outline of a human being. My mad impetus led me to the spot in a matter of seconds, but there was no sign of anyone or anything in the darkening shadows. I looked about me, confused about the direction I was now facing. Could I have gotten turned around? Was I going deeper into the grove of trees or heading toward Foxxemoor?

As I attempted to rationalize, to calm myself, I saw the movement again, off into the shadows on my left.

I didn't call out this time, just started to run, sobbing for breath.

"Please, Father, please help me. Guide me, Lord." I prayed as my lungs seemed to tighten within this confined space. Claustrophobia had never been a fear of mine, but here in this dark green world of whispers and shadows, the fear washed over me, clutching at my chest. I stumbled again, caught my balance, and blundered on after the elusive figure that seemed to beckon from beneath the shadows of the giant evergreens.

CRACK!

The sound exploded in the air all around me. There was a muffled cry somewhere beyond the elusive shadow.

I lunged forward, crashing through the undergrowth and struggling over protruding roots, fallen limbs, bramble bushes, and downed trees. I broke through the tangled mess in a sudden rush and found myself on the main path within a few feet of Dee's lone maple. Another small cry, and I was running toward the tree, my heart catching in my throat.

Dee lay sprawled at the base of the tree, her favorite branch beneath her small body.

"No, Father, no!" I cried as I raced to her still form.

"I'm here, I'm here. I know now that You brought me here, Father. Don't let me lose another child!"

My hands moved gently over her, searching for broken bones and visible injuries.

"Dee?" Tears fell and splashed upon her ashen face. When she opened her beautiful, dark eyes, I cried out in joy.

"I was waitin' for you," her voice was little more than a whisper. "I was sittin' up there, an', an' then I heard this noise, an' I was fallin'." Her small hands reached for me, and I took them within my own.

"It's all right, honey," I reassured her as I leaned down and kissed her on the forehead. "Are—are you hurting any pla—"

Dee struggled to pull herself into a sitting position. "My bottom hurts a little, and so does my back." A crack of thunder threw her into my arms. "I don't like it in here no more, Lyssie. Can we go home now?"

I drew the child closer, hugging her to me and thanking God she was alive. Another flash of lightning was followed by a crash of thunder. I stood with the child in my arms and ran toward the house.

Dee snuggled into the crook of my arms. Her arms stole up around my neck and she hugged me tightly to her.

"I-I heard you guys fightin'," she told me. "I saw you run out of the house an' decided to follow you. By the time I left my hidin' place, you were already gone. I was sure you went this way, so I thought I'd wait for you to come back."

"It's all right, Dee." I held her close, slowing my steps as exhaustion overcame me.

"I'm sorry they lied and tricked you, Lyssie. I mean,

no one likes being lied to, but—but–” She put her little face next to mine. *“Please don't leave me,”* she whispered. “Everybody goes away, everybody I love. Both my grandpas are gone, an’ Mamma. I don’t want you to go too.” As tears rolled down the child’s grimy cheeks, I felt mine threatening to join hers.

“Dee—”

“Puh—lease, Lyssie.”

“I’ll stay for now,” I told her. We emerged from the oak-lined pathway just as the first raindrops began to fall.

Dee urged me to release her, and hand in hand, we ran to the shelter of the porch. Ryan was on the swing and struggled to his feet as we climbed the steps. His dark eyes surveyed our disheveled state and narrowed in concern.

“What—”

“It’s a long story,” I began.

“I fell out of my tree.” Dee let go of me and wrapped her arms carefully around his legs. “I hurt my back an’ bottom, Uncle Ryan.”

He patted her on the head, looking to me for an explanation.

“I didn’t see her fall, but I heard the crack of the branch and Dee cry out. She was on the ground by the time I got to her.”

“Perhaps you could carry her into the house?”

“I can walk,” Dee told him. “I’m ok, see?” Her small face rose to his. “Don’t let Lyssie leave,” she whispered, stealing an anxious glance in my direction.

Ryan met my gaze. “I don’t think we need to worry about that right now, sweetheart.” He turned her around in the direction of the screen door. “We’d better get you inside and call Dr. Kimberly, so he can check you out."

I followed them to the living room. Pier was no longer there, but Margaret sat on one of the window seats, pouring over the notebook Pier had thrown a little while ago. I noticed that it was labeled 'Household Accounts' and wondered what she'd found so interesting.

I was so exhausted that I was finding it difficult to stand. I sank onto the 'man-eating' sofa where Dee joined me, laying her little head against my shoulder. Ryan told his stepmother what happened, and she was soon on the phone to the doctor. Her clear, authoritative voice summoned the man out to Foxxemoor as soon as possible—more proof of the power this family held. Had the request come from anyone else in the valley, I doubted the man would have been so willing to comply.

The call made, Margaret came over and knelt before the sofa, taking Dee in her arms. With things under control, I pulled myself up and headed for the door. Dee called after me, and I turned to give her a weak smile.

"I'm just going upstairs, honey. That's all." I told her.

"Promise?" The frown on her face tore at my heart.

"I promise."

Ryan followed me out into the hallway, taking hold of my arm and leading me across the hall into the den. I was aware of dark paneling and rows of books, my exhaustion making me too tired to notice anything else about the room.

"You all right?" Ryan cupped one of my cheeks in his hand. I had no will left to pull away, just stood there and allowed him to enfold me in his free arm. "I'm sorry, Lyssie," he said against my hair. "Sorry this has hurt you so much."

Without warning, the tears came again. Ryan's arm tightened around me, his voice soothing. I found comfort in the sound of his voice, and within a few minutes, my sobs finally subsided.

He set me from him, brushed the remaining tears from my cheeks, and smiled. "I should go see about Dee. But first I want to make sure you're really ok."

"I'm fine. Worried about Dee, but other than that . . ." I moved away from him and advanced further into the room. Feigning interest in the rows of books before me, I plucked one from the shelf.

"I'm here for you if you want to talk, Lyssie. Please, don't shut me out."

I gave him a tremulous smile. "I appreciate that. Right now, I'm too tired to think." With the book in my hands, I started past him. I was conscious of his closeness as I went through the doorway but was still surprised when he caught hold of my arm to stop me.

We were in the hallway between the living room and den, and as I gazed up at him, his dark eyes filled with tenderness, it seemed natural to go into his arms. He kissed me on the forehead before releasing me. Turning toward the staircase, I was startled to find Gray standing just a few feet away, the fury in his eyes more than apparent.

I felt naked, exposed, and glancing back at Ryan, the triumphant look on his face made me also feel used.

My breath caught painfully in my throat, my legs shook as I reached out to the wall to steady myself. The closed-in feeling I'd had in the evergreens returned, and I suddenly felt as if the walls were caving in. I was aware of the two men, but unable to do or say anything;

it was all I could do to maintain consciousness.

Gray was the first to move. He stormed past me, pain and betrayal etched across his face. I heard the sound of Ryan's advancement, the dull tap, tap of his cane against the floor tiles sending a crazy fear through me.

I didn't turn, couldn't bear the thought of seeing or facing either man. I drew in a deep breath, released my hold on the wall, and walked quickly down the hallway.

And I didn't slow my pace until I was safely inside my suite.

Chapter 13

Diana felt her strength slowly flow back into her body. It had been three days since she had awakened, free from fever at last. Mrs. Rhodes and Ashleigh Craven's tender nursing had done so much to restore her body but little to help the fear she continued to feel.

Now, as she faced Leo Craven, his hard eyes regarding her with tightly checked fury, she realized she had survived one danger just to face another.

"But surely, sir," she spoke with hesitance. "Surely nothing could justify such a heinous act as murder . . ."

While Dr. Kimberly examined Dee's little body, I was in the process of painfully extracting broken pine needles and thorns from my knees and hands. As Kimberly told the family how lucky they were, and patted Dee on her bruised back, I watched as peroxide boiled dirt and germs from my wounds. When the doctor had gone and Mrs. Merrick seated Dee at the dinner table for her favorite meal of hot dogs and macaroni and cheese, I finished bandaging my wounds and sat curled up on the loveseat, wondering how I could ever face the family again.

It seemed like weeks ago, and not just that morning, that I'd talked with Mac, that Gray kissed me for the first time. The memories were hazy, wrapped in a fog as though from a time long ago. I tugged at them, trying to hold onto them as tangible evidence of my sanity, but they were elusive, evaporating the same way as the specter within the grove of evergreens.

Pulling my legs onto the sofa, I hugged them to me, trying to gain some comfort in the action. It offered little, if any, and my nerves propelled me into action. I paced the length of the room, trying to expend the energy, my weary body wishing the same for my overactive brain cells. I'd promised Dee I would stay, and somehow, I would keep that promise. The child had lost so much, and the thought of hurting her further was unbearable.

I'd find a way to avoid the twins. Surely, in this big house and on an estate of this size, that wouldn't prove difficult. An understanding could be reached between Margaret and me, with an agreement that there would be no further deceptions, no lies. If the woman wanted me to stay, she would have to meet my terms. As for Pier . . .

I recalled the pain in her eyes when she'd looked at me and was certain she'd been telling me the truth. Mac said much the same thing that morning, about her needing me, and I'd no reason to doubt his sincerity. I wondered how Margaret had forced Pier to go along with her, what secret she held over my old friend.

My mind ran with the thought, following different tangents and eventually returning to the obvious: the notebook labeled 'Household Accounts.' From the little I'd gleaned from Pier in the last few weeks, there was no indication she had anything to do with the running of the house, or anything else for that matter. Other than the duties she'd had in regard to Dee, and the time she spent assisting Ryan, Pier seemed to be a free agent. Yet, she and Margaret had been head to head, discussing the contents of the book when I'd interrupted them. Whatever was going on, from their expressions, it was extremely important.

A knock on my door brought me back to the present, and taking in a deep breath, I steeled myself for what might prove an uncomfortable encounter.

I greeted Mrs. Merrick with a sigh of relief and smiled my thanks as she set a dinner tray upon the coffee table.

"I didn't think you'd be up to dinner with the family." She gave me an apologetic smile. "I want you to know I'm glad you'll be staying on for Dee. She gave us the news a little bit ago. Henry and I think it's wonderful. She's become fond of you in this short time, and it would've broken her heart if you'd gone." Her cheeks flushed, and she lowered her eyes. "Mrs. Foxxe is always telling me I'm impertinent, speaking my mind as I do. If I've offended you—"

"No offense taken," I assured her. "You've been very kind to me, Mrs. Merrick, and I really appreciate all you've done."

The blush deepened and spread down her neck. "It's

a pleasure, Miss Daniels. Ah, I've been wanting the chance to talk to you, if you've a moment."

I indicated for her to have a seat and joined her on the small sofa. She sat on the edge, her back straight, knees rigid. Her eyes darted across the room, then lit upon my face.

She laughed, clearly self-conscious. "I'm not sure how to say this, so I'll just say it straight." She smoothed out her apron, her expression serious. "Things have been going on around here that aren't quite, well, normal. With all that's happened in the last year, that's not surprising, but . . . " She shifted her position on the loveseat. "This is a large household, so there's no keeping track of food and such. Someone's always getting hungry and raiding the icebox or digging for snack items. It's a chore to make certain we have things on hand. Cook says it's been just a bit more than usual, but I wonder." She shook her head. "That's only part of it, though. Dee's always talked about her mother in the present tense, like she's still around. We're used to that, but lately, it's been different. Tonight, while she was eating supper, she told me something that disturbed me."

"That she'd seen her mother?"

Mrs. Merrick nodded. "Good, she told you. I thought she might. I don't know, Miss Daniels, things just don't seem quite right. Not with Dee, or the rest. Maybe it's the missing money—"

"Money?"

She looked up, startled, and I got the impression Mrs. Merrick had said more than she'd meant to.

"Oh, well, uh." She dug into the pocket of her apron and pulled something out. "As I was saying, ordinarily I wouldn't have thought anything about it, but then Cook reminded me about Dee's swing, and how it might be nice if Henry put up another one—the ropes had rotted, and it broke just before you came," she explained. "Anyway, I'd always thought that was a bit queer, the ropes, I mean. Henry was always checking to make sure the swing was safe for her, so when it broke, we were pretty surprised. Heavens, I'm going on and on!" She opened her hand and unfolded the piece of napkin within it. In the midst of a brown stain lay a small piece of orange plastic. "When you mentioned Dee's milk tasting funny, I got to thinking. That child is just never sick and had been so ill all morning. I, um, well, I drained what was left in the glass through a strainer, and this little piece of plastic-like stuff was all that didn't pass through."

I took the napkin from her and looked at the item carefully. The thing was so tiny; it was hard to determine what it might be.

"Did you ask Dee about it?"

The housekeeper shook her head. "You're the only one I've told. If Mrs. Foxxe had any idea, well, I'm afraid Dee would be in a lot of trouble."

"You know what it is?" My curiosity was piqued as I looked from the tiny piece of orange then back to Edna Merrick's face.

"Dee's such a good kid, Miss Daniels, just curious, that's all. I'd thought she was beyond the age when you had to worry so much about her getting into things like this. But when they're all around you like they are, I guess I shouldn't be surprised. The medication Ryan and Mrs. Foxxe have alone would fill a pharmacy. If you combined that with whatever Pier might have, or

Gray, even Henry and myself, well . . ."

"You think Dee found some medicine and put it in her milk?" I couldn't keep the edge of terror from my voice.

"I'd hate to think so, but it makes a strange kind of sense when you think about it. I mean, what would plastic be doing in her milk? I've tried to think of another explanation but haven't been able to come up with anything. I was going to tell Mrs. Foxxe, as I said, but things became rather hectic today, and I didn't think of it again until Dee started talking about her mother." Edna Merrick rose and brushed the wrinkles from her apron. "When she said you'd be staying and taking care of her, I thought I could just as easily tell you as anyone. I'm sure you can talk to her about it, let her know in just the right way that she mustn't touch the medicines or take them unless an adult gives it to her."

I swallowed hard, the sudden smell of the food turning my stomach. I tried to cover my feelings, patted Mrs. Merrick on the arm, and assured her that Dee and I would talk about it. After she'd gone, I removed the food tray from the coffee table and placed it in the bedroom until I felt better able to handle it.

I recalled Dee's pale face and how horribly sick she'd been that morning, her conviction that it had been the milk that made her ill. If she'd taken medication from someone in the family—the implication was obvious, or was it? If Mrs. Merrick was right about that bit of orange she'd discovered in the bottom of the glass, then either Dee had taken the medicine on the sly, or someone in the family had given it to her. Neither scenario was acceptable.

Without warning, I heard Dr. Hadley's voice

reading the results of Amy Webster's autopsy, and the contents of my stomach rushed into my mouth. I ran for the bathroom, making it just in time, my mind reeling.

Someone in this house was playing a deadly game with Dee, pretending to be her mother, wandering about the house frightening Pier—for I'd seen her afraid on several occasions—and coming into my bedroom to hover over me as I slept. Could that someone have gone a step further in their nasty little game, giving the child medicine that made her ill? And if that were the case, what would have happened if Dee finished the milk?

I sat there on the rich blue tiles of the bathroom floor, my head in my hands, willing my mind and body to relax. It was then I realized God had given me the answer. I'd asked Him to lead me, to guide me to where I needed to be. He'd sent Mac to remind me that what I was most afraid of was where God may need me the most. He called it a "twist of faith."

Tears filled my eyes as I raised my head in prayer. I'd been so afraid of failing another child that I left the only job I'd ever had. I'd run from my fear straight into the trap the Foxxe's set for me. What they didn't realize was that it was right where God wanted me to be all along.

Dee found me still on the bathroom floor an hour later. She treated me as if I were the child and she the adult, helping me to my feet and into the bedroom. She made me lie down while she covered me with the quilt. With her little hand on my forehead, she pronounced I didn't have a fever.

"You have what I had this mornin'," she told me solemnly. "Best thing for you, young lady, is to be in bed. Least, that's what Ole Edna said." She watched me with concern. "Are you feelin' better, Lyssie, or do you want me to go get someone? Uncle Gray's just down—"

I caught hold of her hand and pulled her gently onto the side of the bed. "I'm ok, honey. I've just had a rough day. Even grown-ups get sick sometimes when they overdo."

She grinned. "You eat too much in Bristol this mornin'?"

"Something like that," I agreed. It took a few minutes, but I managed to work the conversation around to the subject of her milk. She told me again how she'd awakened early in the morning feeling a little hungry and had taken a couple swallows of the milk. Since it hadn't tasted very good, she'd put it back on the night table and went back to bed.

"I think I went to sleep, but I'm not sure. I just remember feelin' really sick." She shrugged. "An', I was."

I couldn't help but smile at her matter-of-fact statement and attitude. "Dee, this may sound funny, but I want you to think very hard before you answer me."

She nodded her little head, her pale hair falling over her eyes. Brushing it back, she gave me her full attention.

"Honey, did you put anything, anything at all in your milk?"

"Huh? I don't know what you mean, Lyssie. The chocolate was there, and my straw—"

"What color was the straw, do you remember?"

There was a blank look on her face that suddenly brightened. "It was blue an' white. Striped! I stirred the milk with it. Is that ok?"

I patted her hands. "Perfect. Now, I'm going to ask you something else, ok? And you need to tell me the truth."

"I wouldn't lie to you," she said with sincerity.

"Ok. Have you ever gotten into any of the family's medicine without permission?"

Dee shook her head. "Mamma told me I wasn't s'posed to, ever. She said it would make me sick, maybe make me so bad I'd have to go to the hospital. She was real worried 'cause she had it around all the time. We talked about it when I was little, an' she made me promise to stay out of it."

"Good. That's very good. Your mother was right, Dee, and I don't want you to ever forget what she said. Taking medicine that isn't yours can hurt you, might even kill you. And it's just as important that you remember to let an adult get you any medicine you need to take."

"That's what Dr. Kimberly always says too." She wrinkled her nose. "I don't know why everybody's so worried, though, 'cause the pills you have to take always stick in your throat an' make you gag. Even the liquid stuff they tell you isn't goin' to taste bad always does. Yuck!" She made a horrible face and put her hands around her neck as if she were choking. "I hate takin' medicine even when I'm sick. I'd never take it if I wasn't!"

With that settled, we decided some fresh air might do me good. Dee led me down the back staircase which was hidden down the corridor, separating my suite from the next one on this side of the south wing. We came out onto the patio from a side door and took a walk in the garden.

It had stopped raining some time ago, and the area smelled clean and refreshing. Dee showed me some of her favorite hiding places, swearing me to secrecy, then asked if I'd like to sit in the gazebo for a while. I was a little reluctant at first, but seeing no one else around, relented.

When asked, she told me about the swing Mrs. Merrick mentioned.

"It broke right under me! But I was holdin' the ropes real tight, Lyssie, so I didn't fall or nothin'." She smiled, obviously proud of herself. "I miss the swing, but I can always find somethin' to do. But I don't think I wanna climb any trees for awhile. That was real scary."

I found the story about the swing a little curious, especially after her fall this afternoon. I decided that I would check out the branch first thing in the morning. If there was even the slightest indication it had been tampered with, I would take the information to her grandmother at once.

I tried to laugh off my fears. After all, I did have a penchant for the dramatic. But it didn't work. While I had no idea why anyone would want to harm Dee—the thought seemed ridiculous—yet, after what had happened, I wasn't about to take any chances.

We'd been in the gazebo about fifteen minutes, Dee entertaining me with various animal imitations and general silliness, when our attention was drawn to a quarrel taking place on the patio. Pier and Ryan appeared to be in a face-off.

I held Dee back to keep her from alerting them to our presence. I couldn't see their faces from this distance, but from the tone of their voices, I knew they wouldn't welcome an intrusion. In the quiet garden, their words echoed out to where we sat.

"I'm sick to death of your clinging!" Ryan pushed Pier away from him, moving from her to the opposite side of the patio. She said something I couldn't make out, before going toward him. She halted when he swore at her.

Dee tugged at my arm until I turned to her. "We're doing that eaves thing," she whispered, a question in her voice.

I put a finger to my lips and nodded. "I'll explain why later. Ok?" She snuggled up next to me on the padded seat, our attention drawn, once again, by the angry words coming from the patio.

"See, see what I mean?" Ryan shouted at his sister. "You can't leave me alone even when I ask. You're always there, pushing, coddling, hovering. Constantly at my elbow! Well, I've had enough of it, enough of *you*!"

He said something else I was unable to make out, thrust his sister out of his way, and then headed for the door to the south wing. Pier jumped at the slamming of the door but stood where she was for a few minutes. A hand went to her cheeks in a motion that suggested she was wiping away tears. Suddenly, she shoved at some deck chairs, knocking them over. In a flash, she ran in through the main entrance of the house. With all that happened between us this afternoon, I figured she could use someone to talk to. I was still hurt by what she'd done, but under the circumstances . . .

I'd never been one to hold onto anger or keep a grudge. Perhaps it was my Langston background, but after that first flare, I'd realize it was a silly waste of time and energy. That's how I felt now, ridiculous for having made such a big deal out of something I easily understood. Besides, Pier was my friend, and I didn't want to lose her.

I was able to convince Dee that we should go in, and while she went off in search of a snack, I continued up the main hallway, determined to seek Pier out. As I neared the front door, I heard the sound of squealing tires and the resultant spray of gravel coming from the drive. I ran out the screen door just in time to see Pier's fiery red Mustang speeding out of sight down the lane.

"I suppose we have you to thank for that show of temper." The sound of the voice startled me. I recognized the flippant tone as Gray's.

He was stretched out upon the porch swing, one leg dangling on the floor. His cocky expression mirrored his voice, and I faced him coolly, my shoulders back, head high.

"Sorry to disappoint you. The culprit happens to be your brother. Dee and I just heard part of their argument."

"Ah, so you've taken up Dee's habit of eavesdropping." His mouth twisted in a wry smile. "An admirable quality to impart to the young. But as I recall, something you were doing when you first arrived here."

A sudden fury burned within me, and I felt the fire upon my cheeks. I opened my mouth to give a retort, thought better of it, and headed toward the door. But he was already there in front of me. He caught hold of my arm, and I tried to shake him off. My effort ended with him grasping both of my wrists at once.

"What happened to your hands?" There was little kindness in the tone, more curiosity than anything else.

I struggled to no avail. "I fell!" I told him, trying to regain possession of my hands.

He jerked me roughly against him, his eyes cold fire as they stared down at me. "You weren't in this big a hurry to get away from my brother awhile ago. What's the rush now? We are, after all, twins." He released me so abruptly I almost fell backwards. Righting myself, I brought up a hand to strike him for the hateful words. He caught my wrist inches from his cheek.

He held me in a vise-like grip, his face as cold and hard as steel. "Never lash out in violence unless you're prepared to receive some of the same." He said between tightly clenched teeth.

I yanked my arm from his grasp, and we stood there, regarding one another in stony silence.

I heard Dee beckon me from somewhere inside the house, and with a final look of contempt mixed with confusion, I turned my back on Gray Foxxe. As I opened the screen door, I heard him gruffly clear his throat.

"You're staying then?"

"For now." I said coldly, turning my back on him. I headed into the house in search of Dee.

Chapter 14

She wanted to believe him, to trust him once again, but everything inside Diana told her that he was lying. Why else would the door to her room continue to be locked, with trays of food brought to her as if she were a prisoner?

For perhaps the dozenth time that afternoon, Diana turned the knob on the door, pressing her shoulder against it in the hopes it would budge. But her efforts continued to no avail. She sank down upon the cold floor and wept, recalling the warnings she had been given many months ago when she had been engaged as governess for Ashleigh Craven. Few people had anything good to say about the master of Craven; the norm was tales of his peculiar nature and frequent rages. Leo Craven had been a spoiled, selfish boy who had become a maniacal, self-centered man intent on satisfying his own desires no matter who may be hurt in the process.

A wracking sob wrenched through Diana's soul. In spite of it all, she had found herself helplessly, hopelessly, falling in love with the master of Craven. . .

We snacked on wheat crackers and orange juice in Dee's room as I tried to forget the nasty scene on the porch. After we'd finished our snack, Dee helped me put the nightlights in the south wing hallway. They emitted a comforting amber glow, and spaced as they were, approximately three to four feet apart down the corridor, it would be virtually impossible for anyone to remain unrecognizable.

The remaining lights were parceled out in my sitting room and bedroom, with the last one placed in Dee's room near the spot where she thought she'd seen her mother. She thought the lights were part of a great game and was disappointed when we plugged the last one in.

It was getting late for Dee. When she started becoming petulant and cross, I convinced her it was time for bed. She was adamant about not sleeping in her own room. So, armed with sleeping bag, pillows, and a variety of dolls and stuffed animals, I got her settled on the floor near my bed. She was beginning to feel the aches and pains of her fall, and before I read her a bedtime story, I retrieved some children's Tylenol from Mrs. Merrick, administering the medicine to Dee's dislike.

Making a face, followed by a line of complaints, she took the pills, chewing them with a good deal of grumbling. Afterward, she lay back upon the pile of pillows and listened attentively as I read her the story of

Sleeping Beauty, falling asleep long before the end of the book.

Her slow, even breathing continued for some time before I managed to pull myself up from the floor and make preparations for my own bedtime. A hot bath left my knees and hands stinging, and after replacing the bandages, I dug around in my purse until I found some of my own pain killers. Two extra-strength Tylenol, and an attempt to work on *Craven*, lessened the pain a little but did nothing to rid me of the excess energy I felt. Picking up the book I'd taken from the den earlier, I laughed aloud when I saw the title: *Jane Eyre*. How ironically appropriate!

Deciding there was no way I could settle down long enough to read, I pulled a pair of jeans over my pajamas and slipped into a lightweight summer sweater. With Dee sleeping peacefully, and apt to remain so, I eased out into the hallway, pulling the door closed behind me.

The nightlights still burned in their appointed places, giving me an added sense of comfort in the darkened corridor. I walked silently down the staircase and continued through the downstairs hall and out onto the patio without spotting a soul.

A cool breeze rustled the leaves of the trees and bushes, and the melancholy sound of crickets added music to the night. Someone had righted the chairs Pier pushed over, and I pulled one up and sat down to enjoy the relaxing quiet.

Things seemed to be coming to a head at Foxxemoor, the tempers of the family colliding toward that final combustion I'd described to Gray. I wondered about Pier, hoped that she'd gone in search of Mac and was finding comfort and understanding in his arms. She deserved that.

The gentle whisper of the wind as it played in the leaves and branches of the trees did more than anything else to relax the tensions of the day. I felt the slow process of unwinding in the relaxation of my neck and shoulder muscles first, then graduating throughout the rest of my body. I settled back in the chair, content. Nothing could shake me now or disturb my hard won peace.

The night sky was filled with glistening stars that appeared like tiny diamonds sprinkled across a cloth of black velvet. Their soft light rivaled the quarter moon, and with the glow of the garden lamps, added a mystical quality to the night.

The day's memories were overridden by thoughts of *Craven* and the mournful cry of a girl trapped within the house of a murderer. Diana's peril filled me, and I wished I'd had the foresight to bring my tape recorder with me. The temptation to return to my suite was brief, and I drifted along with the visions in my brain. I allowed the action to play out, closing my eyes and letting my fictional creations take on dimension. I became lost in imagination, mindless of the passing time and late hour as the gentle breeze continued to wash over me.

I've no idea how long I sat like that. It was the sound of muffled crying that caught my attention, made me open my eyes. At first I believed it to have come from inside my own head, Diana crying out for help. Then, it came once more. My eyes swept across the garden, looking beyond where the lamps cast their halo of light and into the darkness beyond. Nothing. The silence of the night was almost eerie—even the crickets had ceased their song.

I sat up in my chair and stretched, deciding it was time to go in to bed. It had been a long hard day filled with revelations of all kinds. The end hadn't been nearly as satisfying as the beginning, but I knew that somehow, it would all work together for good.

The cry came again, piercing the stillness.

What was it about the sound that was an eerie reminder of my experience in the evergreens? I shivered in apprehension, convincing myself it came from an animal in the woods. But as the soft whimper came once more, curiosity succeeded in getting the better of me.

With as little noise as possible, I got out of the chair and edged my way across the patio and onto the walkway. I moved quietly, my bare feet an advantage. I continued out into the halo of the garden lamps and beyond the gazebo where darkness reached out before me. I stood, listening, waiting for the sound to once again float to me on the breeze, holding my breath in a kind of wondrous suspense.

"Ahhhh."

It came from somewhere behind me in the direction of the south wing.

I whirled around, surprised to find Gray coming toward me on the walkway. From where I stood, outside the boundary of light, he couldn't see me, and I was able to watch him unobserved.

He was limping badly, far worse than I'd ever seen before. The frown on his face seemed to deepen with every step he took. He was studying something in his hands, and I squinted to see if I could make out what he held.

As the cry drifted across the garden on the breeze, Gray's head snapped up as suddenly as if he'd heard a cannon shot.

"You hear it, too." His eyes flew in my direction, a look of alarm on his face. I realized how it must have seemed, a disembodied voice coming at him out of the darkness. I quickly made my way down the path and into the glow of the lamps, flashing him a weak, apologetic smile.

"I've been trying to figure out where it's coming from. Each time I think I've got its location, it seems to change on me."

Gray's frown deepened as he stuffed whatever he'd held into the pocket of his jeans.

"What are you talking about?" His voice was gruff, without warmth.

"The sound of crying. You did hear it, didn't you?" I looked at him in confusion. I could have sworn that's what he'd reacted to a moment before.

"Don't be absurd." He proceeded to walk past me, but I couldn't let him go like that. I regretted our angry words and wanted to explain to him about what he'd witnessed between Ryan and me. I didn't want things to end like this, with misunderstandings and angry words.

"Gray?" I called after him. He stopped on the walkway but didn't turn around. "I—I just wanted to say I'm sorry for earlier. Things have been so mixed up all day long. I didn't mean to hurt you down at the stable. And later, in the hallway with Ryan—he was trying to comfort me. I was so upset—I—"

"Don't worry about it. We'll discuss it tomorrow after we've had a good night's sleep."

He continued to walk away, hadn't even turned

around when he'd spoken. Maybe I should have left it alone, but I couldn't help myself, couldn't help the way I felt about him.

"Please." I followed him into the darkness, careful to stay on the walkway. "Please, Gray."

I was a couple of steps from him when he finally stopped. He turned to me, his face hidden by the night shadows. His figure seemed to waver in the dim light, reminding me of the silhouette I'd sworn had been in the evergreens.

Reaching out, I felt the soft cotton of his shirt and knew this wasn't my imagination; he was real.

His hand clutched my wrist, and within seconds, I was in his arms. He crushed me against him as his mouth sought and found mine. It was over as quickly as it happened. He set me from him, and without a word, continued on his way.

My hand flew to my lips, my fingers seeking the answer to a question that burned into my brain. I shook my head in an attempt to dislodge the idea that clung stubbornly on.

No, it wasn't possible, yet . . .

The cry came again, the plaintive sound echoing through the night. This time I was sure; it was coming from the south wing.

I flung off my ridiculous thoughts and ran to the house in search of the owner of the mournful cry. By the time I reached the staircase, I'd convinced myself of my mistake. After all, it was late, and my mind was far from clear.

Of course it had been Gray in the garden; it was foolish to think otherwise. The kiss had been different because he'd been in a hurry. He'd placated me, so he could continue to wherever he'd been going.

The last of the lights in the house had been switched off, the exception was the low wattage bulb used in the hall leading to Dee's suite. This made the nightlights she and I put out earlier the only other lights on. I wasn't familiar enough with the location of the wall switches, so I allowed time for my eyes to adjust and then proceeded up the stairs.

The tiny nightlights still lit the south corridor with their soft yellow glow, and I made it to my suite without a problem. The door from the hall into the sitting room was open. Certain I'd closed it, I proceeded with caution.

My first thought was for Dee, asleep on the floor of the bedroom, and terror gripped my heart. Though I was leery about what I might find, I knew I had to get to the child.

I rushed through the connecting door, switching on a lamp as I passed by. Dee's makeshift bed was empty. I checked the bathroom, then grabbing the flashlight from the nightstand, I ran from the room, turning it on as I went down the hall.

With the aid of the flashlight, I entered Dee's suite and found the wall switches. Bathing the rooms in a reassuring glow, I did a fast, but thorough search of her rooms.

Calm down, I ordered myself as the knot in my chest grew larger. Think. Think!

All right. Dee must have awakened while I was in the garden, and finding herself alone, gone off in search of company. Or, maybe she'd been so uncomfortable, she'd gone downstairs to Mrs. Merrick to get more medicine.

The last scenario I quickly discarded, recalling how much she disliked taking medicine even when it was necessary.

Then what?

Margaret, perhaps, maybe Pier? I looked at my watch, surprised to find it after two. I'd been out in the garden for more than three hours! It was far too late to disturb anyone, and it was logical to assume Dee was with one of them. She was fine. Exhaustion was muddling my mind, causing hallucinations.

But once in the south wing hallway, I knew it was not an hallucination that the nightlights, which had been working just minutes before, were now out. Nor was it my imagination that the little flashlight would no longer work. I flipped the switch two or three times, but the bulb stayed dark—and so was the corridor before me.

I edged my way down the hall, my hand touching the wall to lead me past the drop in the floor entering the south wing, then beyond to Pier's suite.

I'd left the door to my rooms open, the lights on. The door was as I'd left it, but all the lights were off. I reached around the corner of the doorway for the wall switch, and took my hand away, astonished. The switch was in the up position: on!

Nothing made sense. I was in a nightmare from which I could not awaken! Events of the day flashed before me, joy and calm turned to confusion and betrayal, clashes of personality and temper . . . and most of all, fear.

Something akin to a moan reached my ears, and I spun around and back into the dark hallway. The dim light coming through my sitting room windows cast shadows on the area of the corridor where I stood.

There, in the deepening shadows in the hall beyond, was a faint movement.

I took a deep breath, closed my eyes, and then opened them again. The dark form I had imagined I'd seen was still there, and just like in the evergreens, it seemed to beckon for me to follow it. Shoving the flashlight into my pocket, I answered the call.

How much was my imagination and how much a trick of the dark shadows? I was inexplicably drawn down the hall, deeper and deeper into the blackness till I reached the end of the hallway.

My hands, stretched out in front of me, encountered nothing but the far wall, and turning about in the darkness, there was a sense of loss and disorientation. My ears were attuned to the night, the immense vastness of the sounds of silence overwhelming my senses. I wanted to go back, return to my room, lie on my bed, and wait for the nightmare to pass.

Father help me.

My silent prayer was met with a kind of shuffling sound off to my left. I followed it, finding a door near the end of the hall. I sought the knob and struggled to open the door. I pushed at it with my shoulder, then, kicking it, heard the sound once more.

Dee.

I called her name, my voice hollow as it bounced off the walls. I shoved the door with all my might and found myself flying through it and into a small room.

Light from the single window helped me locate Dee where she sat huddled against one of the walls. I touched her shoulder and her head turned toward me.

"Lyssie?" Her small voice sounded odd, like she'd only just awakened. "Lyssie, where are we?"

"I'm not sure, honey." I took her into my arms, hugging her tightly to me. I drew in a deep breath and carried her out into the hall.

I stared before me in surprise, a cry of alarm squeezing its way out of my aching throat.

Each of the nightlights glowed brightly along the corridor.

And as I looked down, the flashlight in my pocket flickered on.

Chapter 15

Ashleigh had been and gone, leaving her governess in a dreadful state of confusion. Diana knew the child still liked and trusted her, but the loyalty she felt toward her father refused to waver. If Leo Craven said Miss Diana was to be kept within the locked room, then that was how it must be.

Diana wrung her hands while her mind sought a plan to out-fox Craven. Somehow, she must find a way to escape. She could not allow her feelings for the child, or those secret ones for the father, to deter her. She had no choice but to seek justice for the murdered man. If she did anything less, neither God, nor her conscience would forgive her.

Leo Craven had gone too far this time. If there was no one else strong enough to oppose him, how much farther would this man go? For that reason alone, Diana must see to it that Craven was punished. Even if it cost her life in the end, she must not fail . . .

The rest of the night was spent peacefully, as though nothing of consequence had happened. I settled Dee back upon her makeshift bed and shut and locked the door leading into the hall, doing the same to the connecting door between the sitting room and bedroom. I sat on sentry duty for some time, mind and body aching for sleep, but refusing to give in. Sometime after three-thirty, I was left with no other choice than to lie down. It had been a long, eventful day and night, the resulting exhaustion carrying me well into the next morning.

I awoke a little after ten, stiff and sore from my fall and the awkward position I'd slept in. Sunlight filtered in through the curtains, bringing with it a sense of added security. As I gloried in the morning light, snuggling deep in the comfort of the bed, I wished there was some way to explain away the events of the night before. Perhaps my exhaustion had caused a strange aberration of the mind, causing my overactive imagination to misinterpret what happened. I'd been stressed to the breaking point, tugged and pulled in too many directions. Maybe . . .

Just as surely as I knew it was the sun that lit the morning sky, I knew I hadn't hallucinated last night's events. While I may not be able to explain what occurred, it didn't mean that something out of the ordinary hadn't taken place. I refused to believe in ghosts and goblins or specters that beckoned from beyond the darkened shadows of the mind. I didn't know the why or the how, or even understand; God had the answers and He would guide me.

I drew in a deep breath, chewing over my own

explanations. A loss of power in this part of the house—logical. Margaret and Pier had spoken about Dee 'wandering around' at night. Maybe the 'wandering' was really sleepwalking episodes—also logical. As for the door to the room I'd found the child in, it had stuck just as mine had done several nights before. There it was, conclusions made with logic, all tied up nice and neat. Done.

Dee was no longer in residence; her makeshift bed had been pushed against a wall with her dolls and stuffed animals arranged neatly on top. Both doors were closed, the locks no longer in place. The room appeared normal, undisturbed by the night's activities. I was anxious to begin my day, determined that despite my lingering fear of caring for another child, and the underhanded way I was brought into the family, I would stay here as long as Dee needed me. Or, as long as the Foxxe's allowed me to remain.

I decided to begin a notebook of specific problems I felt Dee needed to have addressed by a professional. The journal would also include some of the strange occurrences here at Foxxemoor, including Dee's broken swing, her insistence of having seen her mother, the suspect plastic-like material found in her milk glass, and last night's sleepwalking excursion. After I examined the maple branch, I would determine whether or not that should be included as well. Perhaps someone like Dr. Hadley would find these bits of information useful. In the meantime, I'd be on hand to observe and be the companion Dee so obviously needed.

As I finished dressing, the phone rang, and I was surprised to find Gail Morris on the line.

"I know it's late to be asking for today, but an old

friend showed up with her little girl. She and Dee were classmates last year, and I thought it would be a nice opportunity for them to play. Besides," she added with a laugh. "Linda's something of a writer herself, and she's dying to meet you."

Her enthusiasm made me smile. "It sounds wonderful. I haven't seen Dee yet this morning, though, so I'm not sure how to answer you."

There was a pause on the other end of the line. "Tell you what, you call if you can't come. If I don't hear from you, I'll see you for lunch at twelve-thirty. Sound ok with you?"

I told her it did, she gave me her number, and I signed off. The prospect of getting Dee away from the house for a few hours sounded like an excellent idea to me. I wasn't looking forward to the repercussions that might follow the wake of yesterday's revelations, and the longer they could be put off, the better.

The quickest way to find Dee was likely through Mrs. Merrick. I dialed the number for the kitchen and was in luck: Dee was there having a mid-morning snack.

Everything went smoothly from there. Mrs. Merrick wasn't aware of any plans involving Dee for the day and agreed with me about Gail Morris's invitation.

"The family's gone now, anyway," Mrs. Merrick told me when I went to the kitchen to collect Dee. "I don't expect any of them back before late this afternoon." She grinned over at Dee. "I'll bet she's talking about your friend Cap."

"Yes!" Dee jumped up and hugged the housekeeper and then me. "She's my bestest friend ever!" As she ran out of the kitchen she called out, "Be back in a minute."

The cook, Mrs. Merrick, and I burst out laughing. "I hope it's the little girl you mentioned," I said, thrilled to see how excited she was.

"Oh, I'm sure it is. The moment you mentioned 'Linda,' I couldn't think who else it could be. The Ayres' used to have one of the outlying farms on the estate. When they moved, Dee was heartbroken. She and Cap were in preschool and kindergarten together."

When Dee returned, I asked how she was feeling. She assured me nothing hurt other than her bottom. She had no idea what I was talking about when I asked about her sleepwalking. She just looked at me in wonder, shrugged, and begged to leave for the Morris farm right away.

Laughing, I said, "We're not expected for a while, kiddo. Why don't we take a walk to kill some time?"

I didn't forewarn her of my intention to check out the maple tree, but I received no complaints as I led us onto the stable path. Nearing her tree, Dee became less animated and caught hold of my hand. She didn't say anything when I went over to the tree, just continued to grasp my hand tightly.

"Are you afraid?" Looking into her little face, I searched for clues to her behavior.

Dee shrugged her narrow shoulders. "I think that's the worsest thing that's ever happened to me. It was really scary, 'specially after you told me it could happen."

"After I—" I nodded, remembering the warning I'd given her as she swung upside down on the branch. "But you weren't swinging, were you?"

She shook her head. "Nope, just sittin'."

I convinced her to release my hand and then went

over to examine the area where the branch had been attached. The trunk was scarred by the breakage, large splinters of wood protruded from the spot, but I could see no telltale sign that it had been tampered with. There were no wood shavings on the ground—though they could have been washed away by the rain. I looked where the branch had been and was surprised to find it missing.

"Do you know what happened to the branch?"

Dee shook her head, backing up a little. At first, I thought she was afraid, then I realized she was scoping out the area around the tree, hunting for the limb. We looked for a while, giving up when Dee started to become antsy.

Even without the branch, I determined it had really been an accident. Dee's frequent use of the limb as a swing would have weakened it. At least this wasn't another thing to be added to the list of mysteries surrounding the child, and I could rest a little easier.

When we got back to the house, it was nearing the time we should start for the Morris's. I took Dee up to her room, got her cleaned up, then helped pick out a clean outfit to wear. She allowed me to brush out her long, silky hair, and within moments it was shining and neat. To keep it that way, I braided it and moussed her long bangs back from her eyes.

She ate up the attention, making it clear that it had been a while since anyone spent this much time exclusively on her. She pranced and preened in front of the full-length mirror on my bathroom door, smiling at me through the glass.

"I wish everyone could see me now," she told me as we made our way down the staircase. "I ain't looked this good since Mamma took care of me!"

"Haven't," I corrected. "Haven't looked this good."

She wrinkled her nose. "Ok, Lyssie. I *haven't* looked this good. Either way, it's the truth!"

She led the way out into the kitchen where Mrs. Merrick and the cook gave her glowing compliments. Her face beamed with excitement as she thanked them. It felt wonderful to be responsible for bringing that light and happiness into her eyes.

Mrs. Merrick gave me the directions to the Morris farm, and we were on our way. It took about a half hour to reach it, and the moment we pulled in the drive, I knew this had been the right thing to do. Dee jumped up and down in anticipation, her entire body vibrating with joy.

Gail Morris had a picnic set up on their patio. After introductions to Linda Ayres and her daughter Caprina—Cap for short—the girls and the Morris's two boys went off to play on a large jungle gym.

The humidity had gone back up, and the breeze we'd been enjoying the last several days had ceased. We sat beneath the patio awning, sticky and uncomfortable in the rising heat, commiserating with one another about the change in weather.

Any other time I might have felt overcome with shyness as we sought subjects we each had in common. But there was something about Gail Morris that put me at ease.

"Gail tells me you're a writer." I smiled at our hostess, receiving a wink in return.

Linda Ayres blushed. "Oh, nothing like writing a novel," she said nervously. "I do the correspondent reporting for our little town newspaper."

"That sounds interesting." The other woman made a face and laughed. "Really," I said.

"Thanks for saying so. That's sweet." Linda Ayres looked to her hostess, received an encouraging nod, then turned back to me. "A while back, I started a manuscript of my own. It's not a murder mystery or anything dramatic, but I think it might have an audience."

Dee called out for me to see her hanging upside down on the jungle gym. I swallowed back the warning that I wanted to give, and waved instead. Keeping my eyes on Dee to assure myself she was ok, I spoke to Linda Ayres. "So, what's it about?"

Turning back to them, I noticed the look of triumph the two women exchanged. This was obviously the opening they were hoping for.

Linda embarked on a description of the manuscript, the story of a compulsive gambler and the trouble he got into because of his addiction.

"You see, I've rather an extensive amount of research gathered. Then, of course, I've my own experience to draw on." Linda finished her narrative with another grin for her friend. "I know there are a lot of self-help books out there, so I thought I'd do mine a bit differently. It's a fictional self-help!"

I nodded, searching for something to say. "You mentioned drawing on your own experience?"

The question seemed to embarrass Linda. She appeared to blush from head to toe.

"Oh, go on, Linda," Gail urged. "You've come this far."

Linda Ayres poured herself a glass of lemonade and took a sip. "It shouldn't be so hard, I know. I've said it often enough." She drew back her shoulders and stared me directly in the face. "I'm a compulsive gambler, or rather, a recovering one. I went through a program a few years back and haven't gambled since. There aren't many Gambler's Anonymous support groups around here or where I live now, so I occasionally attend the AA meetings—you know, like Gray Foxxe."

Before, I'd been listening out of consideration; now she had my full attention. I was about to say something when Gail broke in.

"Not Gray, Linda. Ryan." Gail corrected. "Ryan went through the program the same time you and Dylan did."

I was totally confused. "Are you saying Gray's an alcoholic, and Ryan's a compulsive gambler?" A memory flashed through my mind, and I heard Gray stating that he didn't drink.

Gail shook her head. "Uh, oh." I could tell she was upset about what she'd revealed. As she searched for a way out of the situation, her friend chimed in.

"I know all about Ryan and Dylan, Gail. It's Gray I'm talking about." She smiled at me. "I don't know if he's an alcoholic; he's never spoken up at the meetings, from what I understand."

Gail tried to hush her friend but to no avail.

"You have to remember, Lyssie, Bristol's not a metropolis, and a family as important as the Foxxe's gets talked about. It may say it's anonymous, but when you're somebody, it doesn't stay that way."

"That's true," Gail agreed, the reluctance to join the conversation obvious. "You kids be careful," she called out, causing all of us to turn our attention to the children.

"You know," Linda Ayres continued, "it was all over town in a matter of days when I started attending meetings. I didn't think I'd ever hold my head up again. Then the talk went around about Dylan Courtney and Ryan Foxxe, and everyone forgot about me."

"It was really just Dylan," Gail said quickly. "She and Ryan were engaged at the time. I'm sure he just went along to keep her on track."

"And to better understand the disease," Linda contributed.

While I was still trying to assimilate these new scraps of information, the children came over, demanding to be fed. We had a typical picnic: grilled hamburgers, potato salad, baked beans, and chips for the kids. As the children laughed and stuffed their faces with food, Linda questioned me about how to contact agents and editors. Neither woman seemed to believe that I wasn't an expert in the field and continued to ply me for information. By the time Dee and I left a little after four, I'd exhausted the little I knew about the writing profession.

Dee napped on the way back to Foxxemoor, completely worn out by her romp with the other children. Though she refused to admit it, I felt the activity may have been too much after her fall. Her little face was pinched in pain as she slept, and I decided it would be an early night for her. Watching her from the corner of my eye, I came to another decision as well: I would arrange to have Dee moved into my room for the time being. Until I could be certain the pranks were over, or the perpetrator exposed, I'd feel better having her with me.

True, I seemed to be a victim of the prankster as

well, but I was determined to no longer be such an easy target. From now on, my doors would be locked, and the one into the hall would be barred with a chair. If I had to, I'd get more nightlights and put them in every available outlet in the house. This might seem drastic but, after last night's experience, warranted.

I decided something else, too. Though I'd wanted to tell Pier and Gray about my experiences and Dee's 'visitation' from her mother, I wouldn't now. If one of them were involved, it would simply put them on their guard, forcing them to find another way to . . .

To what? Where was all this leading? What was more, how had I even come up with all these crazy ideas?

Yes, I had an active imagination, but there was no denying that odd things were happening at Foxxemoor.

But aren't you becoming a little over-dramatic? The voice in my head taunted.

I pulled onto the Foxxemoor lane and, as the house came into view, I again felt that sudden surge of inspiration I'd experienced on my first day. The house, the very atmosphere of the place, lent itself to flights of fancy; it was no wonder I got carried away. Pier had been right about the aura of Foxxemoor helping with my creativity. I just had to stop letting my tendency toward the dramatic color reality. I was a sensible, down-to-earth individual with both feet planted solidly on the ground. I'd keep it that way.

You're also a hopeless romantic.

And I needed to find a way to quiet that voice!

I gently woke Dee, and after giving her time to orient herself, we started for the house. We were just a little past the fountain when Gray and Pier came out onto the porch. Despite the anger in their voices, Dee left my side, running to join them. Not in a hurry to face either of them, I followed with a bit more decorum, slowing my pace to give them a minute to calm down.

Though Dee called out to them, they appeared not to hear her. I could tell from the rigid set of Gray's shoulders that he was upset, and recalling the blaze in his eyes yesterday, didn't envy Pier's position. As Pier headed for the porch steps, Gray yanked her around, glaring down at her.

"What is it with the two of you?" She demanded, rounding on him with her fists in front of her. "Is it open season on me this week?"

"Just tell me what you did with those papers and I'll leave you alone."

Pier pulled from his grasp, put her small hands against his chest, and shoved. Gray staggered slightly, acted as if he would retaliate, then stood his ground.

"Well?"

"I don't know what you're talking about. And even if I did, what makes you think I'd tell you anything after this caveman act? It's not impressive, brother dear. You need to remember that I'm not easily frightened. Not like Dylan." She returned his glare, her face triumphant at the sting of her words.

"Why you—"

"Hello up there!" I shouted. I'd seen the expression on Dee's face when her mother's name was mentioned. This wasn't a scene she needed to witness.

My voice caught their attention as I'd hoped it would. As Dee climbed the steps to the porch, she launched into a description of her day. By the time I reached them, both Pier and Gray were doing their best to concentrate on what she was saying. I could tell from the looks they exchanged that their discussion was far from over. Once this distraction was past, they would be at one another's throats again.

Neither of them so much as glanced my way; I might as well have been invisible. I tried not to let it bother me. I'd been prepared for something like this and stood near the screen door, waiting for Dee to finish.

Dee rambled on for several more minutes. Gray finally cast a silent plea in my direction. His eyes were hard and cold when they met mine, but the meaning was clear: he wanted to get back to his argument with Pier and expected me to get Dee out of the way. I consoled myself with the knowledge that he *had* been aware of my presence after all, even if it had been cursory in nature.

I quickly averted my eyes, wondering if he'd seen the involuntary tremor he'd sent coursing through my body.

"I think we should let Mrs. Merrick know we're back, Dee." I held my hand out to her. She smiled at Pier and Gray then came over to me.

"Lyssie's takin' care of me now," she told them proudly.

Pier gave me a quick glance, refusing to meet my eyes, and smiled at her niece. "Maybe you can take care of one another." Her taut voice was filled with emotion. I had the sudden urge to let her know it was all right, that I understood what she'd done and why. Something held me back.

After Dee told the two goodbye, we went on into the house. Just as the screen door was closing, I heard

Gray start his attack once again.

"Just tell me where you put Dylan's papers," was the last thing I heard.

After letting Mrs. Merrick know we were back, I asked if they had a rollaway available, so Dee could be moved into my rooms. While Dee went off with the housekeeper to look for the bed, I went up to my suite. Sarah Williams was in the rooms, closing the windows and doing some general tidying up. She gave me a big smile when she saw me, nodding toward a folder on the desk.

"Mary sent that out for you. She said to tell you that she hoped it was what you were looking for." She wiped her hands on her dust cloth then pointed to the windows. "Finally got those air-conditioners working this afternoon. It'll take a while, but, by tonight, you should be pretty comfortable."

"I'm sure everyone's relieved it's fixed. And thanks very much for playing messenger. How much do I owe your cousin?"

"She put the amount and her address inside the cover. She said you shouldn't worry about getting it to her right away. She trusts you." Sarah turned her back and continued with her housekeeping duties.

I picked up the folder, scanned through the pages, and decided to leave it until tonight. I placed it back on the file containing my handwritten notes from *Craven*. Then, changing my mind, I put it inside my canvas tote that lay nearby. I turned to find Sarah watching me. She nodded in approval.

"I'm sure that's for the best," she told me, her eyes darting toward the open door into the hallway. "I'm not sure the family'd be too happy to know you're doing some research on them. A lot of the stuff Mary copied for you doesn't shed a kindly light on the Foxxe's, or the Courtney's, for that matter. Keeping that stuff out of sight is likely the right thing to do, considering." She gave me a hesitant smile. "Don't get me wrong, I like working for them. They're not all that difficult—with the help, anyway. It's just some of their goings on, well . . . I'll leave you to form your own opinion."

A couple more swipes of the dust cloth, and Sarah disappeared out into the hall. I sat for a few minutes, contemplating what she'd said. Shrugging my shoulders, I went on to the task of figuring out where to put Dee.

It wasn't long before the child came leading Henry Merrick into the suite. She was talking a mile a minute, with Mr. Merrick taking it all in stride. As he rolled the bed in, he winked at me, made a comment on Dee's story, and followed us into the bedroom.

My idea about the best location for the bed was quickly vetoed as Dee showed me the spot she preferred—the same area her small bed occupied when she and her mother shared these rooms. I'd forgotten about that, and the gentle reminder from the child sent a shiver up my spine. I shook it off, telling myself I was being too sensitive.

After the bed was put in place and Mr. Merrick had gone, I set about making up the cot with the sheets and cases Dee brought with her. When the bed was made and decorated with dolls and stuffed animals to her satisfaction, Dee plopped into the middle of it, sighing in contentment.

'I'm glad you wanted my company, Lyssie. I've really missed this room."

I searched her face for any sign of melancholy, but all I found was the same kind of happiness and excitement she'd possessed all day. I returned her smile, asking if there was anything she wanted to do.

I was at a loss, uncertain what was expected of me. My job at Langston had never been truly defined, the position something Dr. Hadley had invented instead of one with clear parameters. I'd been available as a friend and confidante to the children, the basis comparative to that of a glorified babysitter. I watched and listened for danger signs and trouble points the children may have hidden during their sessions with the therapists. Eventually, they would open up to me in a way they were unlikely to do with the doctors. But I was no spy. I made it clear to the professionals at Langston that I would not break the confidences of the children. I assisted them, showing them the direction to take in their sessions and never, ever, betrayed the trust the kids put in me.

As I looked across at Dee, I saw no sign of the troubled little girl I'd witnessed when I first came to Foxxemoor. She displayed no fits of temper, her good humor following the distress of hearing I might leave and the trauma of her accident showed a resiliency I hadn't thought I'd see. Had I been wrong? Had her family?

Thoughts of her revelations regarding her mother intruded, skewing the picture I was seeing. Deep down, Dee was still a very confused little girl.

Right now, the child seemed lost in thought. Her bright little face appeared reflective beneath the pale, unruly bangs that finally won out over the mousse.

"Wanna see one of me an' Mamma's favorite

places?" Dee's eyes lit up at the idea. She jumped off the bed and came over to me.

"Why not?" Once again I allowed her eagerness to propel me, and I soon found myself trailing after her down the south corridor.

Despite the dim daylight that filtered in, and the soft amber of the nightlights reflecting off the walls, the hallway retained that eerie quality that I remembered so well from the night before. I had to force myself to continue following her, concentrating on her voice and the joy she exuded.

"It's called a 'window's walk,' an' me an' Mamma would go up there and sit for hours and hours. Last summer, we had chairs just inside the attic door so that we could sit an' read or lay in the sun. That's what Mamma liked to do, you know, to get a suntan."

I felt a catch in my throat as Dee stopped before the door to the room where I'd discovered her last night. As she placed her hand on the knob, I looked about me, taking in the area that I'd only seen in darkness.

The door was nearly at the end of the corridor, just a few feet from the back wall and far removed from the other suites in this wing. Because of its location, the area was shrouded in a strange half-light, and the incongruity of its position, after the measured lengths from one suite to the next, made it appear odd and out of place.

Dee didn't have any trouble getting the door to open, and as it swung inward, light from the room's window revealed a small storeroom. Half the area was filled nearly to the ceiling with boxes and crates.

"Mamma's stuff." Dee flung over her shoulder, a slight crack in her voice.

My eyes swept the piles of items: books, clothing, and other personal things that appeared to have been hastily discarded. A couple of the boxes looked as if they may have been rifled through, their contents strewn carelessly about on the floor around them. I was certain there hadn't been such disorder last night—there hadn't been any obstacles to go around. I'd been able to come straight into the room and over to the far wall where Dee huddled. I would have noticed if things had been set so far out in the room. Today, it wasn't as easy to maneuver.

Dee began piling things back into the empty boxes, and I bent down to help her. She handled each item with tenderness, pausing now and again over something that caught her eye. She lingered longest over a blue silk scarf that she held to her face for a few minutes. After she folded it and put it atop one of the fuller boxes, she gazed up at me. I fully expected to see her dark eyes filled with tears. Instead, she had a soft, secret kind of smile on her lips, and the hand that she held out to me did not waver.

"It's this way." She opened what I had believed to be a closet door to reveal a flight of stairs leading upward. She flipped on the light switch and started to ascend the staircase.

It struck me then, her talk of a 'window's walk' finally making sense. Dee was taking me to the roof of Foxxemoor.

"A widow's walk." I hoped the tightness of my voice didn't show. I didn't want to dampen her excitement by my uncontrollable urge to run.

Face your fears, Lyssie. You can't expect to conquer them if you don't.

It looked as if now would be as good a time as any to give it a try.

I followed Dee up the stairs, the beat of my heart increasing in tempo with every step I took. When she stopped for a moment, I thought she might have changed her mind; then I realized she was unlocking a trap door just above her head. Once unlocked, she pushed it upward, and daylight rushed in along with the heady smell of the outdoors.

We were on the roof within seconds, and as Dee walked out across what seemed a great expanse, I maintained my position close to the wall of the third floor that rose up behind me.

"See that," she pointed to a door next to me. "It goes into the attic. I don't like to go that way; it's full of icky spiders." She made a face and went to try the door. "It's locked." She pressed her face against the window in the upper part of the door. "That's where we used to keep our chairs, just inside the door so we didn't have to go where all the spiders are. I have a little chair just my size. Like my pony!"

She danced out across the open space, and I called to her to be careful. She regarded me with a strange expression, and I realized that I was the only one who was afraid. In an effort to tame the fear, I closed my eyes, took a long, deep breath, and releasing it, opened my eyes with the determination not to spoil this for Dee.

I looked up into the hazy blue sky where the first signs of evening were beginning to show. I watched as birds flew far above me to distant treetops to sing their evening song. Staring out across the roof, I saw the grove of evergreens, the oak-lined path to the stables and, way off in the distance, the hill and meadow where Gray, Dee, and I had our picnic.

The peace and tranquility took me out of myself, and I found I was less afraid. I walked over to where Dee stood near the center of the widow's walk and drew in another deep breath. You could see the roof of the stables just visible through the trees, then beyond to the pasture where the horses grazed. The scene was breathtaking, and I understood why Dee and her mother liked it up here.

Dee grinned at me over her shoulder, then walked over to the edge where a black wrought-iron fence edged the roof. As her small hands clutched the fence, I swore it swayed under her weight. Once again, terror gripped my heart.

"Dee, come back from the edge, honey. I think the railing's loose." I kept my voice calm while my insides churned in fear.

"It's ok; I do this all the time." She put her weight on the fence as she leaned forward and looked straight down. This time I was certain the railing moved.

I was across the roof, pulling her away from the edge within seconds, and setting her back out of harm's way. But in saving Dee from the fate I feared, I'd made a dreadful mistake: I'd looked down.

Foxxemoor had been built in an era of high ceilings, which made the distance between each floor greater than in modern houses. Although we were little more than two stories up, for an acrophobic like me, this was like standing on the edge of the world. I stood there, frozen in terror, afraid to move, unable to do anything but look down into the abyss.

"Lyssie?" Dee's voice came to me over a vast

distance. I tried to answer her, tried to force my eyes from the ground below, but I was lost, helpless.

Time seemed to stand still as I remained perched near the edge of that rooftop. Every pulse in my body beat frantically, making my entire being vibrate under their pressure.

"Lyssie, Lysette?" A calm voice behind me tried to break through the fog in my brain. "Lysette, do you think you could turn around and look at me?"

How could I tell him I was unable to do as he asked when I couldn't even find my voice?

"Lysette, I'm going to grab you and bring you back from the edge. I don't want you to be frightened. Just stay calm and don't move."

If I could have done so, I'd have laughed. Move? I'd been cemented to that spot so long I doubted anyone would be able to budge me!

Something was thrown over my head, arms came around me, and while a gentle voice urged my legs into action, my feet, amazingly, propelled me along. I was still unable to focus my mind, was only aware of the soothing tones and the feeling of floating within a void.

Slowly, my senses returned, and I found myself back in the storeroom, which seemed to be filled with people.

It was Mac's arm that was around me, supporting my weight as I leaned against him. Pier held my hands, talking nonstop, repeating over and over again that I was all right.

Memory returned and panic seized me as I frantically searched for Dee. I sighed in relief when I spotted her in the doorway, following Gray into the room. The fire in his eyes as he caught sight of Mac was answered by the tightening of Mac's grip on me. The tension in the air was palpable even in my diminished state. I shrunk from it against Mac's protective arm.

"What are you doing here?" Gray rushed into the room past Dee and stood threateningly before us.

"He saved me." I heard the wonder in my voice as I attempted to penetrate the fog that began to descend around Gray.

"Lyssie!" The note of alarm in his tone sent a strange thrill of happiness through me. Just before the darkness closed in around me, I reached out to Gray and felt him lift me into his arms.

Chapter 16

After careful observation of everyone who came and went from the room, Diana discerned Mrs. Rhodes as the easiest mark. The housekeeper did not watch her as the others did, which made it impossible to fool them. Mrs. Rhodes' faith in Diana outweighed the need for caution, and the girl was determined to use it to her advantage.

Now, as Diana pulled the small piece of paper from the door catch, she regretted the confidence she had been forced to break. God willing, Mrs. Rhodes would forgive her.

When the house was dark and quiet, everyone long in bed, Diana replaced her house slippers with sturdy shoes and pulled on her heaviest cloak. This time she would not leave without being prepared.

She stole silently down the darkened corridors, paused at the top of the staircase to listen, then descended the stairs as fast as her legs would carry her. When she got to the door of Craven's office, she put her ear against it and held her breath. Hearing nothing, she slipped carefully inside. The gun rack was to the right of the desk, visible in the soft moonlight. She knew where he kept the key and just which pistol she wanted to take . . .

When I came to, Pier was at my bedside, a pinched and strained expression upon her face. The stress of the last few days showed in the bags beneath her normally clear, gray-green eyes, and there were lines etched on either side of her mouth. I wondered when she'd last gotten a good night's rest and if she was aware of the disturbances I'd been experiencing.

Now, as she gazed at me with concern, I detected an air of distraction.

The sudden memory of Gray's stony face when he'd spotted Mac in the storeroom urged me to action. As I attempted to rise from the bed, a wave of dizziness overtook me, forcing me back upon the pillows.

Pier reached out to ease me down. "You'd better give yourself a few minutes. You fainted." Her voice was taut with emotion.

"Mac?" I asked, my voice hoarse, my tongue so thick it felt twice its normal size.

"Downstairs somewhere," she fidgeted in her chair. "When you're feeling well enough, I need to see what's going on. I don't like the idea of leaving him alone."

"Why don't you go now," I told her, wincing at the memory of Gray's slugging him. "I—I don't think it's wise for them to be alone, either."

It was all the encouragement she needed. Flashing me a weak smile, Pier stood. "I'll check on you later."

She was out the door in a matter of seconds.

I took my time, allowing my body the chance to reacclimate itself before I attempted to get up. Although I'd have liked to thank Mac for my rescue, I didn't feel up to another scene. I just hoped Pier was in time to keep Gray in line.

I sat on the window seat in the bedroom and looked out at the garden. There was no activity, except for the scores of birds taking advantage of the bird baths and feeders, its tranquility helping to reduce my inner turmoil. I'd always known my fear of heights was great but had never reacted quite so strongly as I had today. After this experience, it would be a very long time before I tried such a thing again. I didn't like to think of myself as a coward, but I wasn't all that brave, either.

About an hour after I'd regained consciousness, Dee and Mrs. Merrick brought up a dinner tray. After the housekeeper left, Dee came over and shyly kissed my cheek. She didn't say anything—she didn't need to; her dark eyes told me how glad she was that I was all right.

While Dee and I ate a leisurely dinner, she related how she'd run in search of help when I froze near the railing on the widow's walk. She'd found Pier and Mac on the porch and sent them up to me. Seeing Gray down by the garage, she'd dashed off to let him know what was going on.

"The moment I told Uncle Gray where you were, he stopped what he was doin' to Pier's car an' came runnin'. He was awful worried, Lyssie. I tried to tell him that Pier an' her boyfriend already went to help you, but he just kept mutterin' somethin' to himself an' ran to the storage room. When you fainted, he swore all the way to your rooms!" She giggled, blushing. "I think he likes you."

Her honest appraisal of the situation made *me* blush. "Thank you for such quick thinking." I tried to change the subject. "I want you to do me a favor and promise not to go up on the widow's walk for a while. At least not until you can get someone else to go with you and they've had the chance to fix that railing."

"Ah—h," she sighed. Finally agreeing, she returned to tackling her dessert, a milk chocolate cake with creamy white frosting. As good as it looked, when she asked if I was going to eat my slice, I passed it over to her, my stomach still a little shaky.

Midway through the second piece of cake, Dee looked up at me. "You know them papers Pier an' Gray were talkin' about when we got home? Um, I think *I* know where they are."

It took me a moment to realize what she was referring to. I saw again the scene on the porch, the angry words between brother and sister ringing out loud and clear.

"Did you tell either of them?"

Dee shook her head. "Mamma gave them to me to put in a safe place." She took another bite of her cake. "I'm not sure I should tell them, Lyssie. Mamma told me to keep them for her. She said it was 'portant *no one* should know I had them."

The emphasis on the words 'no one' disturbed me for some reason I couldn't quite put a finger on. "Then why did you tell me, Dee?"

She refused to look at me, concentrated, instead, on what was left of her dessert. " 'Cause you're—safe."

Before I had the chance to question her about what she meant, she jumped up and told me she was going 'visiting.' She wanted to tell the rest of the household about her day at the Morris's. It was obvious she didn't want to discuss anything else, the sudden change in her behavior telling me not to force the issue. As she went out the door, I said I'd see her later. She didn't respond, and with a sigh, I watched her go.

I thought about starting the articles Mary Dean copied for me but switched on the TV instead. I ran through the channels a couple of times and finding nothing of interest, shut it off. As I pulled the articles out of my tote, the phone rang. From the tone of the ring, I could tell someone in the house was calling, and I hesitated before answering.

"Ryan here. I just heard what happened on the roof. Are you all right?" His rich, deep voice was filled with concern.

"Fine, thanks." As I related what happened, I heard his quick intake of breath.

"What possessed you to go up there if you knew that could happen?"

"I didn't know. Not really. I mean, of course I knew about my acrophobia, but I figured I'd stay as far away from the edge as possible. Besides, I didn't want to upset Dee."

"That's crazy, Lyssie. You risked yourself to placate a kid?"

I was taken aback by the anger in his voice. As I was about to speak, he continued.

"I'm sorry. I shouldn't have shouted. I'm just concerned. You know, Dee's a smart kid, she knows what it's like to be afraid of something. She'd have understood. And if you were planning to stay back where you felt safe, why were you at the railing when

Mac and Pier found you?"

"Dee was leaning over, and I saw it move. I didn't think, just reacted. All I knew was that I had to get her away from that thing as fast as possible. I pulled her back, then—" I saw myself perched on the roof, unable to take my eyes from the ground below, and once again the overwhelming fear held me within its grasp. "I f-froze."

"Well, from now on, stay off the widow's walk! And don't allow Dee to go up until we've had the chance to get the rail fixed."

I assured him that neither of us would be returning to the area—me, never again, and Dee only if she found another adult to take her. He asked if I felt up for a walk in the garden, but I told him that as soon as Dee came in for bed, I intended to follow suit. He sounded disappointed but took it well.

I wondered if Gray would show the same consideration as his brother and call or stop by my rooms. Dee said he'd been afraid for me, and recalling her words that he liked me, reminded me of the feeling I'd had as I collapsed into his arms. Perhaps he wasn't so mad at me after all. Maybe he'd accepted the apology last night in the garden . . .

I shook myself mentally. I needed to stop all these romantic notions before I got into even more trouble than I already had.

The urge to call Dr. Hadley struck from out of the blue, and I dialed her home number before I had the chance to think about what I was doing. As her phone rang, I wondered what I would say if she answered. She would be against my remaining at Foxxemoor, that much I knew. Telling her my reasons behind the decision were not likely to lessen the concern she was bound to have.

Her answering machine kicked in, and taking a deep breath, I left a brief message, telling her not to worry; I was fine and would call back later.

With that taken care of, I breathed a little easier until I thought about Mac, and I wondered why there had been no further word from Pier. I contented myself with the 'no news is good news' idea and settled on the loveseat with the folder of articles.

Dee came in just as I was starting to glance through the papers. I tucked them back inside the tote when she asked if we could watch some TV before bed. She didn't say anything more about her mother's mysterious papers, and I didn't ask. She was acting more like herself, and I didn't want to risk upsetting her.

By nine o'clock she was out and wasn't even disturbed when I carried her to the cot we'd set up earlier. Removing her sneakers, I covered her with the lightweight blanket she'd brought in from her bedroom and tucked a few of her stuffed animals around the bed with her. I smiled down at the sleeping child. She'd had a big day, and I was proud of the way she'd managed to keep her head when I'd lost mine.

With the room quiet, I pulled out the articles and started to read. Mary Dean had outdone herself. There were pieces from the *Bristol Gazette*, *Kansas City Star*, a couple of the national tabloids, as well as from *The Midwest Review*, a more localized tabloid. The reports varied, a few of them favorable, but most giving a bleak, judgmental account of the troubled last three years.

The picture painted by the tabloids was one filled

with sensationalized 'faction,' giving accounts of a family mired in scandal and mystery. Nothing was as it appeared to be on the surface, they screamed, and proceeded to inform their readers of the downfall and destruction of another All-American dream.

Despite documented reports stating that Miranda Kelly Foxxe's death had been from cancer, innuendo and speculation hinted otherwise. None of this seemed of interest until after Phillip Courtney's heart attack and death. The marriage of Edward Foxxe and Margaret had followed so closely on the demise of her husband, that the gossipmongers suggested they were in some way to blame for their spouse's deaths.

A mock-up of a financial statement showed how the marriage of the surviving partners was beneficial to both parties, particularly to Margaret and Dylan, who would now own a great deal more of the stock—a marriage settlement by the smitten Edward Foxxe.

There were statements from stockholders expressing their distress and distaste and a prediction of hard times to come for FoxCo as well as the entire Foxxe holdings. Within the stories ran an undercurrent hinting at the irrevocable damage done when the families joined. Mention was made of Edward Foxxe's inability to control his children, with Gray and Ryan cited as being "hot-tempered, hard drinking, and fast living." Pier was depicted as a "moody, egotistical individual who had failed to inherit her mother's beauty or consideration for the community at large." Perhaps the most scathing reports were of Dylan Courtney. It was pointed out that her erratic behavior and misconduct had caused her to be expelled from so many colleges and universities that not even the family money could get her into another one. Furthermore, story after story agreed that Dylan's single saving grace was the beauty that launched the famous doll, something that, the tabloids appeared happy to point out, would not last.

In sharp contrast, the *Bristol Gazette* treated the families with sympathy and dignity. They mourned the losses, praised those that died, and lauded the union of the Foxxe and Courtney families. While much of what appeared was support for the favorite sons of the community, it was obvious there'd also been an attempt to put down the raging gossip.

Flipping through the pages, I found an old report of Pier's accident on Mull's Hill, an obscure piece from the *Gazette* about a "fray" in a local bar involving Gray and Ryan, and another story offering details about the latter event. An assault charge had been settled in favor of the two brothers, stating that the "scuffle had begun after an irreverent remark was made about Ryan Foxxe's fiancé, Dylan Courtney."

I was growing tired and started scanning through the articles when I came upon a headline that caught my attention. "Edward Foxxe to Resign as Chairman at FoxCo." The story stated that Foxxe had been little more than a figurehead at Foxxe Industries for the last five years. The sudden decision to resign was met with speculation and suspicion.

"It had been evident years ago that Gray was being groomed as the eventual replacement for his father; then Ryan appeared to usurp his brother's position. However, in light of recent events, neither of Foxxe's sons appears to possess the elder's business acumen, making it doubtful the board will elect either.

Furthermore, this reporter has it on good authority that Foxxe's attorney, Noah Garrett, has drawn up a new will for the mogul that will change the face of Foxxe Industries as we now know it."

Doubts and aspersions were cast on both brothers' characters, concluding with the comment that "with rumors of dissention within the Foxxe family, is it any wonder Edward Foxxe would wish to safeguard his empire from children who seem bent on destroying it . . ."

I looked for further mention of the mysterious will and or "safeguards" but didn't see anything until after the report on Ryan and Edward's car accident. As Pier said, there had been brake trouble, the initial suspicion that the line may have been deliberately cut. The report intimated that the motive lay behind Edward's upcoming resignation. When nothing turned up to substantiate the claim of foul play, the verdict of accidental death was accepted and filed.

Interspersed with the story of the accident was news of Dylan's disappearance. The information that she was last seen leaving FoxCo just days before the crash that killed her stepfather seemed of particular importance. The article was more concerned about the arson of Noah Garrett's law office and his connection to the Foxxe's than in anything else. While it spoke of Dylan being a "person of interest" to investigators in both cases, the allegation of Edward Foxxe's "missing will" and Ryan's struggle to recover received top billing. Little was mentioned regarding the search for the missing woman. More than two weeks had gone by before authorities picked up the ball on Dylan's disappearance, and then it appeared they had done so more because they wished to question her than out of concern for her whereabouts. Now I understood Gray's bitterness.

It was after midnight when I closed the folder and shut off the light. As I lay down and pulled the sheet over me, I prayed for an uneventful night. I looked over to the window where light from the garden spilled gently into the room. In spite of the heat, I wished the air-conditioner wasn't on. I longed for the reassuring sound of crickets and the whisper of the wind as it made the curtains dance in its wake. Despite my exhaustion, I was unable to settle down as the articles replayed in my mind.

Different words and phrases kept popping up: arson, allegations of foul play, Ryan and Gray's drinking and gambling, Pier's selfishness, and the depiction of Margaret as a money-grabbing fortune hunter out to further line her pockets. Then there was Dylan's often unsettling behavior which managed to get her ignored at a time when she most needed help. It all blended in with the idea that the families were nothing but trouble. Even the softer words from the *Gazette* didn't lessen the overall sense of foreboding I'd felt while reading the stories. It made me question the intelligence of allowing Dee to remain in such a household.

I watched the minutes pass by on my clock, my ears pricked for sounds out of the ordinary. I realized I'd forgotten to lock the doors, lay there for several minutes contemplating it, and eventually fell asleep without getting it done.

I awoke to the sound of mumbling coming from the sitting room, and rolling over, noticed Dee's bed was empty. At first, I didn't think much about it, just figured she was talking to a member of the household. But when the door into the hallway opened, and I truly *opened* my eyes, I realized it was barely dawn. A look at the clock confirmed this, making me curious about what was going on.

I drug my lightweight robe from the closet and, as I put it on, headed into the corridor. Dee was barely visible at the far end, just entering the north wing. I could still hear her voice but was unable to see who she was speaking to. I thought she might be with Gray since his was the only occupied suite in that wing. As she disappeared around the corner that led to the back stairs, I ran to catch up.

By the time I'd reached the staircase, Dee was no longer within seeing or hearing distance. I cautiously made my way down the darkened stairs, past the entrance to the kitchen, and through the hallway to the door that opened onto the patio. A slight sound behind me revealed I was being followed, but I didn't turn to check who it might be. I'd seen the patio door spring shut, knew that Dee was outside, and desperately wanted to know who she was talking to.

When I opened the door and stepped out into the heavy morning air, I'd no idea what to expect, but it certainly wasn't what I found.

Dee stood just a few feet in front of me, her small head thrown back, her arms flung out at her sides. Hearing my step, she turned and grinned at me, then danced wildly around in circles.

I stared, my mouth agape, unable to believe what I was seeing. Unlike Dee, when I heard the door behind me, I did not turn to see who it was; I was too entranced by the scene before me.

Hundreds of butterflies filled the morning air with dazzling colors of blue, yellow, orange, black, and white. There were Monarchs, Swallowtails of all kinds, Painted Ladies, White Peacocks, and dozens more I didn't have names for. They seemed to occupy every available space of the garden.

And within the very midst of them danced the fairy child, laughing happily.

Chapter 17

The night was unusually cold, and as Diana pulled her cloak tightly about her, she stole into the courtyard. The full moon made it easy to see—too easy. Should anyone be at a window, they would have no difficulty recognizing her. Therefore, she kept within the shadows of the great house to conceal herself, slowing her steps to maintain the silence.

At the far end of the courtyard, she saw a sudden movement which was followed by a cry of pain. Fear burned within her breast as two figures came into view, pummeling a third. A knot formed in the pit of her stomach as she recalled the other time, and she was determined that her cowardice would not be repeated.

She pulled the pistol from within the fold of her cape and clutched it firmly in her hand. Drawing in a deep breath, she stepped out into the open . . .

A gasp and cry from behind made me turn from the incredible scene before me. Margaret brought one hand to her mouth as she sought the back of a chair with the other. Gray was slightly in front of her, his attention as wrapped up in the sight of the child and butterflies as mine had been. As I watched their reactions, Pier came through the door from the north wing. Her mouth flew open the moment she saw the extraordinary scene we'd been drawn to. Her face was deathly pale as she advanced onto the patio. When she grasped Gray's arm, he pulled her against him and she began to weep.

"What kind of sick joke is this?" Ryan's angry voice broke the barrier of silence. Unlike the rest of us who seemed to have followed Dee out of the house, he'd come through the main entrance.

Pier must have noticed, as I did, that Ryan did not have his cane, and she rushed to his side. Offering him her shoulder to lean on, Ryan accepted without comment.

"Who did this?" He demanded again. The only thing that answered him was the gentle sound of the butterflies' wings.

Gray was at my elbow, a firm hand clutching the sleeve of my robe.

"Get her into the house. *Now!*"

I looked to find his eyes hard and dark, the tone of his voice making it clear he expected to be obeyed.

I couldn't imagine why they were all reacting this way. True, this was not a sight one might expect, but the beauty and magic of it was so amazing that I saw no reason for such distress. Yes, I knew the significance, that the butterfly had been a special symbol of Dylan's, but failed to understand why *these* creatures should

upset them so much. Dylan was no longer here to bring them to the garden for luck, nor could she have managed such a spectacular showing as what was now before us. It was obvious from the sheer number that the creatures had found their own way here, and Dee . .
.

The child's soft voice as it drifted to me from the sitting room was suddenly etched across my mind. She'd sounded like she was talking to someone, as if she was following them . . .

"*Now*, Lyssie, before all hell breaks loose."

I snapped to attention, and after a glance at Gray, went to retrieve Dee from the middle of a swarm of butterflies. Her eyes were glazed when I took hold of her hand, and she looked at me with confusion. At first, I thought she would rebel, refuse to come with me, but she came placidly without saying a word. Passing Ryan, he flashed a menacing look in Dee's direction. He seemed about to say something to her when a large tiger Swallowtail flew into his face.

Pier watched as we made our way to the house, her tear-drenched face white and pinched. Gray moved to support Margaret, and as Dee and I went through the main entrance, I noticed that the four of them appeared to be drawing together.

I ushered Dee inside and up the stairs to my suite, worried since the child still hadn't spoken. The hand I held was cold as ice, and she moved like an automaton, without apparent cognition of what was happening around her. I spoke to her in soft tones, reassuring her that everything was all right, and coaxing her to share what had caused her to get up so early and go to the garden. Still she said nothing, her small face blank, emotionless.

When we got to the suite, I lifted her and carried her to the bed. Her eyes remained glazed, and I became more frightened for her by the minute.

"Dee?" I called to her. "Dee, if you can hear me, honey, please look at me."

Her head turned toward me; she blinked several times, gave me a wry smile, then closed her eyes. She seemed to deflate like a balloon as she collapsed onto the bed, her head almost thudding against the pillow. I lifted her small wrist, seeking her pulse and found it strong and rhythmic. I sat by the side of the bed for a long time, noticed it was nearing six-thirty, and lay my head on the pillow next to hers. Her soft breath against my hair was comforting, but my hand on her back, feeling the rise and fall of her chest, had a more calming effect on me.

I must have dozed, for the next thing I knew it was after eight. Dee was no longer in the bed, and a note was propped next to me on the pillow.

"At bracfast," it said in a childish scrawl, making me smile.

I dressed as fast as I could and, remembering the morning humidity, braided my hair as I trotted down the staircase. I was too curious about the butterfly incident to think twice about the undercurrents within the family. Besides, like Dee, I needed some breakfast.

There wasn't anyone in the dining room, so, grabbing a piece of toast and a glass of orange juice, I went out onto the patio. Very few of the butterflies remained in the garden. I noted some blue Swallowtails and more White Peacocks than might be ordinary, but other than that, they seemed to have disappeared as magically as they arrived.

No one came out to join me, and I finished my breakfast alone. The air was still heavy from the humidity and a slight fog lingered near the tops of the trees, dimming the sunlight. In the short time I'd been outside, perspiration had already formed on my brow and ran in rivulets down the back of my neck.

I picked up my dirty dishes and deposited them in the tub on the sideboard in the dining room. I still hadn't seen anyone and had this eerie feeling that I'd been left alone in this rambling old house with all its secrets and mysteries to surround and taunt me. I shrugged off the feeling and decided to take a walk. I had no idea which direction to take, just knew that I needed to be out in the open air, no matter how oppressing the heat was outside.

Passing the living room, I caught a glimpse of Margaret deeply engrossed in a large book spread upon her lap. Her melancholy expression drew me to her, and as I entered the room, I cleared my throat to announce my presence.

She didn't look up immediately, but when she did, I was taken aback at the difference in the woman before me. Her mouth drooped at the corners, there were dark circles beneath her eyes, and the hand that held the book on her lap was shaking. Margaret stared at me vacantly, giving me the impression she failed to recognize me. Her pale blue eyes met mine with hesitation, and after a while, she gave me a vague kind of smile and indicated that I should pull up a nearby chair. As I did so, I realized the book she held was a photograph album. Looking over her shoulder, I saw pictures of a small girl with pale blond hair and an engaging smile.

"She was so lovely," her tremulous voice sounded distant, unattached to the woman beside me. "From the beginning we knew she was a special gift." She caressed the photos and moved the book to the arm of the chair so I had a clearer view.

From the tone and past tense, I thought she must be speaking of Dylan, but the pictures were of a child with long, pale blond hair and smiling, dark blue eyes.

"Dee?" I asked, confused.

Margaret shook her head. "They do look remarkably alike, don't they?" She patted my arm. "No, dear, that's Dylan." She smiled again. "She was always such a live-wire, constantly into something. I could never keep up. Phillip said not to worry, we'd have a nanny. It was just as well, I'd never been around children and didn't know the first thing about taking care of one. It was all so frightening." The look she gave me had a kind of desperation about it. "That sounds horrible, doesn't it, not knowing how to manage your own child? Then, of course," she continued, not waiting for my answer, "My whole world had always revolved around my husband."

Margaret Courtney Foxxe pulled the album back onto her lap. She turned the page, and from where I sat, I was able to see the picture that now held her attention, an informal family portrait. Again, the towheaded child smiled engagingly at the camera, her small fingers interlaced in those of the handsome man next to her.

"He was an artist, you know. Always wanted to be a painter." Her fingers traced the outline of the man in the photo. "But he knew he had a responsibility to FoxCo, and a second generation partnership was nothing to scoff at. Phillip understood his place in the scheme of things, and he handled himself with pride." A wistful expression came over her face. "And my place was by his side."

I eased back in my chair and let her voice carry me into the past.

"He was ten years my senior," she went on, "but the moment I met him, I knew we'd be married. Those were truly happy times, exciting and free. When I became pregnant, we celebrated, knowing it would add to our happiness," she released a girlish giggle. "We prepared for the birth of our child as you would for a royal heir.

"Dylan was so beautiful, so perfect. She became Phillip's inspiration. Before she was a week old, he had the design for the doll. And Edward, always ready for a gamble, ran with the whole thing before either of us were able to assimilate what was happening." A wan smile played about her lips. "Edward insisted on using Dylan's name. Our protests were dismissed with Edward's insistence that it would make the doll more marketable. The one concession was the hair color."

As she turned the page of the album, I peered over at the next grouping of photographs. Half the page was filled with a blond Dylan Courtney; the other half held the image I was used to: rich black hair and those bewitching, dark blue eyes.

"We started the tours when she was four, a promotional thing, you understand. As successful as it was, people kept commenting on her pale hair like it was a disappointment. So, I decided, why not?" She put a hand to her head and ran her fingers through her own short, dark hair. "Mine was a few shades darker than yours," she said. "But the comments . . . I just wanted everything to be perfect. All it took was a little time at the salon and *voila*! Mother and daughter came out with hair as dark as a raven's wing. Edward applauded what I'd done but Phillip . . ." She shook her head. "No one could argue about the success of the tours after that. Here was the live version of the doll that was sweeping the nation, second in popularity to Barbie. I loved the excitement and publicity, felt as if I were in my element. I'm afraid Dylan didn't fare as well."

She continued to describe the past in wistful tones, and looking at her, I tried to find the woman I'd come to know in the sad and broken individual before me. Her shoulders, once so erect and proud, were hunched and drawn, and the smooth, aristocratic voice had been replaced by a rapid, almost slurred speech. Where was the regal bearing, the cool dignity? Could the incident this morning have caused this change?

Despite the occasional disjointed sentences and straying thoughts, a story began to emerge that held me fascinated.

As the success of the Dylan Doll skyrocketed, the child became increasingly remote and difficult to handle. The Courtney's were replacing nannies and traveling companions more and more often, Dylan's mood swings becoming too much for anyone to manage for any length of time. The more Margaret spoke of the problems, the more certain I was that Dylan had suffered from a form of hyperactivity. But there had been no formal diagnosis—there could have been stigma attached to that. Instead, they began using sedatives to control her during the tours.

My heart ached for the girl that became more of a

commodity than the child she was. Tales of her rebellion made it clear she'd been screaming for help, but no one seemed to hear her.

"She became so difficult we were finally forced to take her to the doctor. He suggested a psychiatrist." Margaret drew in a sharp breath. "It was horrible, embarrassing to have that cheeky little man tell us how we'd failed her. His nerve, accusing us of stealing her identity. Her identity indeed!" She pushed her shoulders back in a show of defiance. "We never took from Dylan, only gave. Gave until it hurt. But that never mattered, didn't make any difference."

As her teen years progressed, so did the signs of Dylan's mental disorder. Still, the Courtney's and Foxxe's refused to believe there was anything seriously wrong with the girl. It wasn't until she'd gone away to college that they were finally forced to face the unacceptable.

"She was expelled from three universities. Three! Not even our generous donations could get her back in." Margaret's hands shook as she turned another page in the album. She was no longer looking at the pictures; her eyes focused on the past.

"The last time she was expelled, she disappeared. When she finally returned home, there was no explanation. Nothing. Soon, it became a habit. Irrational periods of weeping were followed by wild behavior that might end in her leaving for days. We finally had no choice, we had to find answers." Margaret's eyes pleaded with me for understanding. "When they diagnosed her with manic depression they acted like we should have known. But how could we have known? We'd been to so many doctors, I'd lost track of them. We'd tried to get her help. How could they blame us?"

I put a hand on her arm to offer comfort. It was all coming into focus, everything I'd heard about Dylan. How she must have suffered! Now I understood why they had gone to such lengths to procure my help with Dee—why Margaret held such contempt for professional therapists.

"By the time she was diagnosed, a pattern had already been set. She drank, did drugs, flirted with danger and with men. You name the vice, my daughter likely had it. No one was safe from her." She sighed deeply. "The Lithium helped, but even on medication Dylan was erratic. After Deidre was born, Dylan seemed a different person. She was happy, *really happy*. The engagement to Ryan was a godsend. But she messed that up and turned to Gray." She shook her head. "Then she was gone. Gone!" Margaret slumped back into her chair, and the photo album slid from her lap onto the floor before I could catch it.

I knelt on the floor, carefully picked up the album, and closing it, put it on the coffee table. As I returned to my chair, Margaret put a hand on my arm, her fingers digging into the soft under flesh.

"Gray was right; I have no idea how to care for Deidre. I don't want to make the same mistakes with her that I did with her mother. You believe that, don't you, Lysette?"

I gently removed her hand from my arm. "Of course I do." I told her as she groped toward me. I took her hand and gave it a squeeze. "Mrs. Foxxe, Margaret, it's all right. Really. I've decided to stay, just like you've asked. Dee just needs a little guidance and a lot of understanding. She's had so much happen around her in such a short time that she's confused. I'm sure—"

Margaret's nails bit into my palm. "*She won't let me!*" The whispered words sent a chill down my spine.

I tried to pry her nails from my hand where droplets of blood had already appeared. "Dee loves you very much. Perhaps if you could—"

Margaret removed her hand from mine, shaking her head vigorously. "Not *Dee*. *Dylan*!" Her breath came in short, sharp gasps. I tried to calm her, to keep her from hyperventilating. She shook me off and reached over to the end table next to her.

Margaret lifted a brown prescription bottle, opened it, and removed an orange capsule from inside. I gasped, remembering the small bit of orange Mrs. Merrick had found inside Dee's milk glass.

"Look," Margaret slowly opened the capsule and turned both halves upside down in her hand. Nothing came out. "This is my medication, or rather, it *was* my medication. Now, all that's left is the outer casing." She poured the rest of the capsules out into her hand. "She's done this before when she's trying to get back at me for something. I always knew who was responsible but never told. I'd cover it up, say I'd forgotten. But it was a lie."

"There must be another explan—"

"No," she said. "This is just the thing she would do. Like the butterflies this morning." A look of fear came over her face. "*She's come back.*"

She was becoming hysterical, and knowing she'd been unable to take her medicine, I knew she needed to remain calm to avoid a seizure. I tried to talk to her, said what I thought would be reassurances, but she was already too keyed up, too agitated.

"She's furious, you know. We didn't start looking for her right away, didn't make it all about her. Edward, darling Edward was dead, Ryan was in the hospital, and they were trying to say it wasn't an accident, that someone had deliberately cut the brake lines. We were frantic, and dealing with one of Dylan's tricks or outbursts was not on our list of priorities." She got up and began pacing about the room, wringing her hands and muttering to herself.

No longer confident I could do anything to help her, I ran out of the room in search of someone better equipped to handle the woman. A noise from across the hall led me to the den. I pounded on the closed door, and not waiting for an answer, rushed into the room. Gray was at the desk, bent over the notebook of household accounts that I'd seen Pier and Margaret studying a few days before. He looked up at me, a scowl on his face.

"What is it? Has something else happened?" He asked with impatience, shoving the notebook inside a drawer and locking it.

I gave him a synopsized version of what Margaret told me about her medicine. "She thinks Dylan did it, that she's here."

His face was shuttered when he looked at me. "Where's she now?"

"The living ro—" Before I'd finished the sentence he'd jumped up from the desk. With a couple of strides from his long legs, he was in the living room with me following closely behind. Margaret, however, was nowhere in sight.

"We've got to find her before she hurts herself," he

told me.

"Just tell me what to do."

With complete composure, he sent me to look in the garden, saying he would get the Merricks and Sarah to help him with the house. She hadn't much of a head start and, with luck, should be easy to find.

I ran out into the garden, searched the gazebo and several of the areas Dee had shown me where someone could hide, but Margaret was nowhere to be found. Dee came in through the side of the garden, her hands clutching a package which she quickly placed behind her back.

"Whacha doin'?"

"I'm looking for your grandmother," I told her, trying to keep the panic from my voice.

"I just seen her, Lyssie. She looked kinda funny." Dee followed me back onto the patio.

Swallowing hard, I knelt before her. "Where did you see her, honey?"

The child's keen sense of recognizing underlying emotions was apparent in her face. "She was goin' to the swimmin' pool."

Thanking her, I ran to the main entrance of the house with Dee's final words echoing in my ears.

"Grandmother can't swim."

Throwing open the door, I yelled Gray's name as I headed down the hallway. We met before the marble staircase.

"What?" He clutched my shoulders as he gazed down at me.

"The pool." I said, breathless. "Dee saw her heading there."

He was out the door and across the front lawn

before I'd descended the porch steps. I trailed after him, wanting to be there to offer my support.

Ryan was coming out of the garage as I started by. He asked what the rush was about, and nearly out of breath, I stopped long enough to fill him in. A shadow fell over his handsome features.

"Go, hurry," he urged. "Stop her, stop *him*."

I didn't understand what he meant, just knew I had to get to the pool. I continued my journey, running until I thought I would collapse.

Just as Dee said, Margaret was at the pool, her gaze shifting between Gray and the twelve feet of water before her. For every step Gray took toward Margaret, she inched closer to the water's edge, a look of determination on her face. I watched from the opposite side, praying and ready to dive in after her should it prove necessary.

"She used us all," Margaret was saying. "She never cared, never wanted anything she had, except for Dee." Her wild eyes flew about the area, coming to rest on me. "I wonder if she approves of you. If not, you'll know soon enough."

A prickling went up my spine as I recalled my mysterious night visitor. I shrugged it off, concentrating on what was happening in front of me.

"If she's back," Gray said calmly, "then we'll deal with it as we've always done. You can't let her win, Margaret."

"Can't I? What's to stop her from destroying the rest of us? Phillip and Edward are gone. They were the only ones to ever get her to listen to reason. And that didn't always work."

There seemed to be a struggle going on inside of

Margaret, and I watched in both alarm and fascination as the distinct changes took place in the woman before me. One moment, it appeared as if the aura of calm assurance she usually possessed had returned, and in the blink of an eye, the facade collapsed, replaced by a frightened and desperate individual.

"We should never have encouraged the twins," she mumbled, shaking her head. "Neither had the strength to oppose her, were more likely to fall prey to her tricks and conniving. Ryan was the stronger one, but she turned him against her. And Gray—" another step forward and she was balanced on the brink. "I don't know. Don't know!"

"It's over now." Gray's tautly drawn features belied the calm voice.

Margaret threw him a look filled with suspicion. "If only I could believe that!" The seizure began with tiny tremors that soon had her entire body shaking uncontrollably.

Gray moved like quicksilver, running over to her and lifting her into his arms before she teetered off the edge. His dark gaze fell on me as he ordered me back to the house to tell Mrs. Merrick that Margaret had gone into seizure.

I did as I was told, then waited in the foyer for Gray's return. Instead of bringing Margaret back to the house, however, Edna Merrick met him at the garage. Ryan, who'd come to stand beside me, said they were taking her to see Dr. Kimberly at Bristol Community Hospital.

As usual, the calm, imperturbable quality of Ryan's voice and attitude helped set me at ease.

"Try to relax, Lyssie, things will turn out all right."

He reached out and traced the curve of my jaw with a gentle finger. "In the meantime, put it out of your mind before those worry lines etch themselves permanently into your pretty face." He leaned down and kissed me lightly on the mouth.

"Do you think Dylan's back?" I asked, moving out of his embrace.

He shrugged. "That's one explanation. I'm sure there are others." A mask fell over his face as his voice hardened. "If she's alive, this is the one place she'd return to, isn't it?"

I wondered what he meant but didn't have time to ask; Sarah interrupted us, bringing me a phone. Taking it, I walked down the hall and into the empty living room.

"Got your message and decided to call," Dr. Angela Hadley said in a rush. "I haven't much time, dear, I've a meeting in a few minutes, but I wanted to ask what you're still doing there?"

"The situation isn't as clear as you might think. And if you're in a hurry, this isn't the time to try to explain."

"You know your own mind, I suppose. But I doubt you know just how messed up that family is."

"I'm beginning to," I answered dryly.

"Watch yourself, Lysette. I mean it. I did some checking, and from what I've learned, there might be a maniac down there killing people."

"If you're referring to the brakes on Edward Foxxe's car, that was disproven—"

"Not disproven, hushed up. Money can do that, you know. And the disappearance of that woman, the child's mother, that's fishy as well. The point is, if you have anything tangible, we could get a court order to pull the child—"

"No!" I told her sternly. "I realize things are a little odd, but they truly care about Dee. That was the whole reason for getting me here, as you know. I'm going to stick around, try to help if I can. Right now, I think it's best for Dee to stay at home. If things change, I'll try to convince them to send her to Langston or some place similar."

"I'm not sure I agree with you, but—Look, dear, I have to run. If you need anything, don't hesitate to call."

I promised I would and signed off. The call had upset me more than I wanted to admit. If Dr. Hadley had been checking the family out, her sources would have been impeccable. This meant if they smelled something fishy, there was something to it. Following this line of thinking, that would mean it was likely the brakes on Edward Foxxe's car had been tampered with. But if they had been cut, why would the police drop an investigation if it spelled murder? Surely money, even the combined assets of the Courtney and Foxxe empire, couldn't buy them off? Could it? And if it had, that would mean . . .

I put my head in my hands, rubbing my face in an attempt to wipe away the disturbing thoughts. But nothing could erase the doubts and questions in my mind. Perhaps Margaret was right, maybe Dylan was back. She could be the source of the pranks being played on the family and on me. If she was, sooner or later she would slip up, give herself away, and be forced out into the open. It just didn't make any sense. Why would she do this? What possible motive could she, or anyone, have for terrorizing this family? Or endangering a small child?

Of all the questions, this last one frightened me most.

Chapter 18

"You heard what I said." Diana didn't recognize *the two men before her, or the third that lay crumpled in a heap at their feet. Since she'd surprised them, only she had spoken, the night remaining silent but for the occasional cry of anguish from the injured man. Even that was barely audible above the moan of the wind.*

"If you leave now," she continued, "I'll not raise the alarm, and you can make good your escape. But mark my words, gentlemen, if you try anything, my screams will bring the wrath of this household down around your ears."

"She ain't nothin' but a girl." One of the ruffians spat out. "We can take 'er."

"Don't let my gender fool you, sir. I'm a dead shot." She leveled the gun with a steady hand, aiming at the larger man's heart. "One step toward him, or me, and I won't hesitate to fire." She pulled the

hammer back, and the click as it notched into position rang out in the quiet courtyard.

A moment's indecision, then the two men ran off into the darkness beyond. It wasn't long before Diana heard the sound of horses beating a hasty retreat.

She ran to the side of the downed man. "It's all right now. I'm a friend," she reassured him as she struggled to help him to his feet.

The bruised and bloodied face rose to meet hers and Diana gasped in surprise: it was Leo Craven . . .

The incident of the butterflies had a profound effect on every member of the household. Tempers, which were barely held in check, were now even closer to the surface, ready to blow at a look or a word. I'd compared the family to a powder keg, awaiting the fire that would result in detonation. Those beautiful creatures in the garden this morning had supplied a spark to light the fuse. It was only a matter of time before the final explosion.

Shortly after Margaret's return from the doctor, arrangements were made with her sister in St. Louis for her to go there until things settled down at Foxxemoor. The Merrick's agreed to provide transportation, packing was completed in record time, and before three that afternoon, they were on their way.

Ryan, always so calm and charming, tried hard to maintain control, but his words had an added edge to them. Under pretense of wanting my company, he'd sought me out only to question me about the possibility of Dee's involvement with the butterflies. I did my best to convince him of her innocence, to tell him that the sheer number of the creatures was proof that it had been a natural occurrence.

"Natural?" The glint in his eyes and his cynical tone said he didn't believe a word I said.

"There's no way—" My protest was brushed away with a flick of his hand.

"You really have *no* idea what's going on here," he said as he turned to leave the living room. At the entrance, he glanced back at me. "Don't underestimate her, Lyssie. She *is* Dylan's daughter, after all." The statement was punctuated by the tap, tap, tap of his cane as he went down the hallway.

I saw Pier in the dining room and attempted to talk to her about Mac. She pleaded a headache, grabbed a sandwich from the sideboard, and was gone before I knew what was happening. I tried to find Dee, but no matter how hard I searched, she remained elusive. Hidden, no doubt, in one of her many secret places.

After his return from town, Gray, who was rarely at the house, seemed to lurk around every corner. His dark eyes darted to and fro like he was waiting for something else to happen. He thanked me for my help with Margaret, his voice emotionless. I desperately wanted to talk to him, but he refused to meet my eyes. While he remained cordial, there was nothing about him that encouraged conversation. We couldn't even sit in companionable silence. Like the other members of his family, he was too keyed up to remain still for long. He paced across the living room, went out into the hallway, and returned a few minutes later to begin the process all over again.

His eyes were never still, constantly darting here and there, lighting for a mere second then active once more. He was tensed, aware of every sight, every sound, like some hungry lion ready to pounce at a moment's notice.

My nerves, already stretched taut, were pushed beyond reason—and his nervous behavior didn't help. I looked for diversion in the multitude of magazines available, but none could hold my attention. I found myself watching Gray in anticipation of his next move.

Even Sarah Williams, who did not 'live-in' at Foxxemoor, seemed significantly affected by the incident. Her eyes moved anxiously about the living room as she dusted, the smallest sound making her start. She seemed particularly watchful of the twins. I caught her observing them from beneath lowered lashes.

As Sarah continued to straighten things in the room, Gray approached her.

"Would you consider staying over a few nights till the Merricks get back?" He asked as the woman fidgeted like a bug beneath a microscope.

"My family's expecting me home by five-thirty, Mr. Foxxe. With tomorrow a holiday, it's especially inconvenient."

"Holi—" Gray started, then shook his head. "The fourth. I'd totally forgotten."

July fourth. I'd been at Foxxemoor a month yesterday and hadn't even realized it. In many ways it seemed like so much longer.

"It's a day the whole family gets together," Sarah was saying. "It just wouldn't be fair to my husband or the kids." Sarah looked in my direction, her hands running up and down the feathers on her duster.

Gray sighed, his frustration obvious. "I understand, Sarah, but couldn't you reconsider—at least for tonight?" His voice was harsh despite visible efforts of trying to control it.

"I'm truly sorry, but the best I can do is stick around and help Cook clear up after dinner. That's an hour and a half extra—longer than I should stay with all I have to do at home."

Gray finally relented to the compromise, and Sarah scooted out of the room. I could tell she didn't want to give in at all, saw that Gray was far from satisfied, and wondered about everything that appeared to be unspoken between them.

Dee saved me a little while later with a request to go swimming. We asked Gray if he'd like to come along, but he refused with a look of apology for Dee. I was thankful for the distraction, and even though the pool reminded me of Margaret's sad and desperate act that morning, I found the water and Dee's company a wonderful diversion.

We splashed about in the pool, playing catch with her beach ball. We laughed and joked, enjoying one another's company, but I sensed a strain beneath it all. There was so much I wanted to ask her about: what led her outside this morning; what did she think about the butterfly incident; and what was in the package that she'd tried to hide from me. Instead, I made a point of coaxing her out of whatever doldrums lurked beneath the surface. I needed to show her that she could count on me no matter what.

"Lyssie, look!" Dee paddled over to me barely holding onto her swim ring, her expression triumphant.

"Wow!" When she reached me, her little arms came around my neck as she giggled.

"Did you see me? Did you, Lyssie? I was

swimmin'!"

"Yes, you were. That was very good."

She nodded, grinning. "But I won't do it yet without my ring, 'kay? That'd be too scary." She separated from me and kicked her way through the water to the steps. Sitting on one of the upper ones, she laughed as her legs drifted up to the surface. "Know what?"

"What?" I asked, delighted to see her so happy despite the tension in the house.

"I've got a loose tooth." She opened her mouth wide and took hold of a lower front tooth, wiggling it back and forth. "Ouch! I guess it's not as loose as I thought."

"Have you lost a tooth yet?" I waded over and sat next to her.

Dee shook her head. "But I will. Mamma said it happens in first grade, an' I'm gonna be in first grade when school starts." She smiled as she looked up at me. "Know what else?"

I returned her smile and waited for her to go on.

"I know all about butterflies. Mamma told me."

I held my breath for a moment, gathered my thoughts, and said, "And what's that, sweetheart?"

Dee placed her elbows on her knees, putting her head in her hands as she turned slightly toward me. "They're like Jesus," she said with complete reverence.

"Oh?"

She nodded. "See, they start out all fuzzy, a caterpillar. They're that way for awhile, then they go into a cocoon and, just when you think they died, they come out a butterfly. Mamma says it metamorsis."

"Metamorphosis."

"Uh huh."

"So how's that like Jesus."

Dee's dark eyes lit up. "Well, they were mean to Jesus and He died, Lyssie. Then they came around and put Him in a cave and everyone thought He was gone forever. But He was just in there changin', like the butterfly. 'Cause He came out. He was alive again so that He could save us when we're bad. A butterfly can't do that, though."

The solemnity in her eyes and simplicity of the story put tears in my eyes. To keep her from seeing them, I gave her a hug. Every time I thought I had Dylan pegged, some new revelation showed yet another side and complexity to the woman. The faith Dylan imparted to her child was dichotomous to the vindictive woman feared by her mother.

The humidity continued to rise and become even more oppressive. Sitting out of the water like this, perspiration quickly beaded across our foreheads and necks. The haze in the air reminded me of mornings in the mountains, only this one seemed to be trapping in the heat and making it difficult to breathe. Not even the coolness of the water offered relief, so we decided it was time to return to the comfort of the air-conditioned house.

On the path, the shade from the poplars failed to bring relief from the heat. We trudged along the lane in silence, too hot to carry on a conversation. We were behind the garage when voices floated to us on the still air. Once again, Dee and I were unwilling witnesses to another heated family argument.

"What *is* this?" Pier's furious tone echoed hollowly in the stillness. "And *you*, Ryan, didn't you just tell me the other day to leave you alone?"

"You know what I meant." There was a quiet fury to Ryan's voice that startled me. As Dee and I were about to leave the shelter of the trees, I held her back.

"Oh, I know what you meant, all right, so why don't you just let me go? You don't need me around to help you, you spelled that out clearly enough. Now leave *me* alone!" A sharp cry from Pier made me burst from our cover.

"I'll let you go when you've told me where those papers are," Ryan seethed. "I'm not playing with you, Pier."

We rounded the corner of the garage in time to see Ryan looming over his sister, Pier's arm held tightly in his free hand. The sound of a breaking twig underfoot brought them both to attention. With his grasp on her loosened, Pier pulled away from her brother and ran to her car.

"If you and Gray want those stupid papers so much, find them yourselves. I'm sick of playing mediator, sick of your quarrels and ranting! As far as I'm concerned, the two of you are on your own." She climbed in her car and quickly locked the doors against him. Rolling down the passenger window a little, she called me over to her.

"Remember how I said it was wonderful you were attracted to my brothers? Forget I ever said it. Neither of them is worth the time or effort."

From the corner of my eye, I saw Ryan start for the car, but before he got very far, Pier had already pulled out of the drive and was heading down the lane. Ryan's profile was of clenched jaws and hard, fiery eyes that spoke of the same bent toward violence that I'd seen in his brother. Not wishing to expose Dee to a further outburst, I scooted her up the path and quickly into the house.

Dinner was very strange that evening. Dee and I ate alone in the dining room, the huge, empty space offering cold comfort after a day that seemed to last forever. It began raining while we ate, a slow, steady patter that sounded forlorn in the too silent mansion. Sarah and Cook let us know when they were leaving, Sarah informing us that the phones had been placed on an 'all call' to ring throughout the house. She gave us a rueful smile, then left us to our own devices.

We attempted to fill the evening with games and books, but neither of us was able to relax enough to get into them. Dee complained that her back and bottom still hurt from her fall, and I went off in search of the children's Tylenol for her. I felt more than a little odd foraging around in the kitchen cabinets and was relieved when I found the medicine.

The house was too quiet for my taste, the only sounds coming from the increased frenzy of the storm. Lights had been left blazing in most of the downstairs rooms because Henry Merrick wasn't around to see they were properly shut off. I took the time to turn them off, locked the back and front doors, and decided to leave the foyer and hall lights on for Pier and the twins so they wouldn't come home to a dark house. I assumed they all had their own keys, and after checking the downstairs a final time, went back up to Dee.

While I'd been gone, she'd finished bathing, put on her pajamas, and climbed into bed. She took the Tylenol with a minimum amount of grumbling—after a gentle reminder that she'd requested it in the first place. When she was finally settled down, I listened to her prayers. She refused the offer of another story, asking, instead, if I would just sit with her till she fell asleep.

" 'Member those papers of my mamma's I told you about? I, uh," she lowered her dark eyes and toyed with the top sheet. "I know where they are."

"That's what you said before." I spoke gently, afraid to say or do anything that might change her mind about sharing this confidence.

"I don't like them bein' mad at Pier, Lyssie, but I don't know what to do." Her eyes appealed to me for a solution. "Mamma didn't want anyone to have her papers. She made me promise to keep them for her. But, but—" Tears rolled down her cheeks. Dee reached out to me, and I took her into my arms and held her close.

"Do you know what's in the papers, honey? Why Gray and Ryan want them so much?"

She shook her head as she withdrew from my arms. "She didn't tell me. Just said to put them in a safe place where no one could find them. It was right afore—afore s-she went away, an' I did what she said. I forgot all about them until Uncle Gray was yellin' at Pier. Then I got worried 'cause I hate when they're mad. An' now Uncle Ryan's mad too. I don't know what to do. I—I tried to ask her this mornin' but—"

I put my hand beneath her chin and raised her face so our eyes met. "Dee, did you see your mother this morning?"

Her eyes were a little wild. She pushed my hand away, pulled back, and turned to the side so she didn't have to look at me.

"I—I think—" she began feebly. "She—she wouldn't talk to me." Tears came in torrents, the sobs wracking her small shoulders. "Was it just a dream, Lyssie?" She begged for an answer as she turned back to me. "If it wasn't, why does she keep goin' away?"

I took her back into my arms, trying to soothe her while attempting to calm my rapidly beating heart. Had Dylan been here or was it the dream Dee feared it to be? Had Ryan and Margaret been right in pointing a finger at Dylan for the butterfly incident? Logic was on my side, that there had been far too many of the beautiful creatures to think anyone could have simply brought them here. Yet . . .

My reassurances continued, words of comfort to ease the broken heart and confusion of this child who had lost so much. I told her not to worry about the papers, said that it was unlikely they were what the twins were looking for. I wanted to believe this as much as I wanted her to, and as I continued to rock her, I felt indignation grow inside of me.

Dee mumbled something through her tears. Lowering my head, I asked her to repeat it.

"I gave 'em to you, Lyssie. Now you can be in charge." She nestled into the curve of my arm, and I resumed the gentle rocking motion that seemed to soothe her. I puzzled over her words, deciding an explanation could wait until morning.

How dare Dylan Courtney play these terrible tricks on her daughter! And the torment she was causing her mother and the rest of the family was unconscionable.

Again I was caught between the insensitivity of the woman and the faith in God she had imparted to Dee.

Flawed. Both Ryan and Gray said Dylan was flawed. Was her cruelty part of her illness, from the loss of her childhood in the name of promoting the doll? I couldn't understand the depths of indifference and malice that it would take to devise and play such hateful pranks. Or could I?

Elizabeth Webster was such a person. Hadn't she been Amy's torment, the ultimate cause of the little girl's death?

With Dee's tears spent, her body relaxed in my arms. When her breathing became slow and rhythmic, I lay her back upon her pillows, asleep. Kissing her softly on the forehead, I vowed that neither Dylan nor anyone else would be allowed to destroy this precious child. Dr. Hadley was there to help if necessary—and above all, God would guide me, show me how to help and protect Dee. All I needed to do was listen.

The rain continued to beat hollowly against Foxxemoor. I leaned my head against the cool pane of glass before the window seat, gazing out at the rain sodden garden. The sheets of rain left little visible; even the garden lamps failed to cut through the blackness of the night.

To keep from brooding, I switched on my laptop. As I sat with my fingers poised over the keyboard, I did the unexpected, logged into my ISP and checked my email. I was surprised to see a message from Dr. Hadley marked with an 'urgent' symbol. Opening the message, I was confused to find no personal note. Instead, she had cut and pasted reports from her various law enforcement connections into the body of the email.

I scanned the notes and saw that most of the contents contained the same information I'd read in the articles Mary Dean copied for me. As I was about to delete the email, I spotted the name of Dr. Hadley's FBI friend in Kansas City.

"Angela, it would be best if you could convince your young friend to leave that household as soon as possible. I don't want to alarm you, but while local law enforcement insists everything is under control, they are also aware of the Bureau's continued interest in everything related to this family's activities. Edward Foxxe's death, the arson of his lawyer's office, and the disappearance of Dylan Courtney are only a very small part of the whole. I cannot divulge our interest, can only advise that your girl may find herself caught up in a situation she's ill-equipped to handle."

With a clap of thunder, the lights winked, and before the electricity could be affected again, I had the laptop off and unplugged. Lightning streaked across the sky—one, two, thr—thunder boomed once again; the storm was directly overhead.

I needed something to take my mind off the dire warning in the email. Picking up *Jane Eyre*, I decided to go down to the den and exchange it for something lighter.

I was glad I'd had the foresight to leave the hall and foyer lights on, their welcome glow eliminated any chance of someone hiding within the darkened shadows. I was midway down the staircase when a sudden thought struck me; locked doors would not keep Dylan Courtney out. Not when she was sure to have her own key to the house.

I proceeded with caution, alert to anything out of the ordinary, uneasy that Dee and I had been left alone in this huge house. A crash of thunder shook the mansion, and I clutched at the banister. Lightning flashed somewhere near the front of the house as rain changed to hail.

Please, God, don't let us lose power.

At the entrance to the den, I reached inside seeking the light switch as I watched both ends of the hallway. The light came on, not an overhead but a lamp on the corner of the desk, and after giving the room a once-over, I went in to exchange my book.

The lamp barely reached the outer corners of the room, keeping most of the bookshelves in the dark. The area around the antique office desk was bathed in golden light that was reflected off the oak paneling behind. The desk held a newer computer with a large monitor. Chairs were placed throughout the room giving it the look of a miniature library. Switching on another table lamp, I replaced *Jane Eyre* and browsed among well-worn, hardbound volumes as well as newer, less used editions. As I searched the shelves, I put the worries and distractions of Foxxemoor behind me and lost myself in authors and titles. I was about to select a recent James Patterson suspense when I spied an old favorite by Phyllis A. Whitney lying on a nearby table. Since there didn't appear to be a bookmark in it, I chose it instead.

Grabbing my book, I switched off the table lamp and, looking out across the room one last time, noticed the desk drawer Gray had locked earlier was ajar. Closer inspection showed evidence that it had been pried open with a sharp object. There were splinters of wood and larger, broken pieces around the keyhole. Whatever was used scratched and broke the top outer edge of the drawer as well. It sat askew, off its track and at an odd angle. Without thinking, I pulled it out, adjusted it, then pushed it back in. The drawer still refused to close properly. I took it out again, set it on the desk chair, and peered inside the empty hole.

Something had fallen or been shoved along the back wall of the desk, and I reached in to pull it out. My fingers snagged the article, and I tugged lightly, hearing a slight ripping as paper tore. Kneeling before the desk to gain a better angle, I saw the brown edge of a notebook and sheets of white paper. Once more, I thrust my hand into the space and this time obtained a better hold. Out came the notebook, cover and pages bent and torn, the label of 'Household Accounts' smudged but still visible.

My hands trembled as I replaced the drawer then sat at the desk with the notebook in front of me. Any other time there would have been no question in my mind what to do; I was not a snoop. But this was no more a usual circumstance than the day I'd joined Dee in the puddle. Biting my lip nervously, I opened the book.

A log of expenses lay before me, recorded in a neat and precise hand. Items bought and used—food, appliances, household necessities, and bills, everything was recorded and balances tallied beneath each transaction. Every week a new balance, termed 'allowance,' was recorded and subsequent expenses deducted. Discrepancies were noted in red when the balance in the book did not tally with the bank reconciliation. Red question marks and notations to ask various members of the staff and household for explanations were interspersed in the margins. It made little sense to me, but as I flipped through the pages, one thing stood out clearly; money had been disappearing from the account off and on for nearly a year—the amounts growing as the weeks went by.

The last page was dated over a month ago, and from the ragged edges of paper remaining in the spiral, I knew the more recent entries had been torn out. I scanned the few remaining blank pages and discovered a strange list of objects recorded on the next to last page. Written in pencil, I got the impression this list was not expected to be reviewed, and for that very reason, my curiosity was piqued.

The list contained the name of a room followed by an object with a question mark next to it. The living room was listed most frequently with things like antique vase, crystal, depression glass, etcetera, after it. Paintings, books—for I assumed 'den 1ˢᵗ ed.' stood for a book—diamond earrings, cufflinks, necklaces, and scores of other things filled the lines. It was an odd kind of list, and I couldn't help but wonder what it was all about. One thing was obvious, Margaret and Pier were aware that someone was pilfering from the house and the account.

An unexpected sound of footsteps in the hall made me jump. I quickly put the notebook inside the drawer, closed it, and grabbed up my book. I was to the edge of the desk when Gray stopped before the doorway and peered inside.

"Don't move," his husky voice stopped me. "With that light behind you, and your hair over your shoulders, you look like an angel."

He came into the room and stood before me. His dark hair glistened from the rain and his damp clothing clung to his body. Reaching out, he lifted a lock of my hair and let it slip through his fingers.

"It's like silk, so golden and shining. Soft." His cool, clammy hand went to my face, gently tracing the curve of my jaw. "You should wear your hair down more often, Lyssie, it makes you even more appealing."

"I—" A finger brushed my lips, and I felt the fire in his touch.

"Sh," he smiled and pulled me against him, his mouth closing over mine. His hands burned through the thin cotton of my shirt, and I felt myself yielding as the pressure of his mouth on mine signaled his increasing passion.

The book dropped from my hands as my arms encircled his neck. I tangled my fingers in his wet hair, drawing his head closer to mine. When he uttered a little laugh and pushed me back against the desk I stiffened, withdrawing my arms to place my hands firmly against his chest. Gray pulled back, his dark eyes smoldering as they gazed down at me.

"Second thoughts, darling?" He flashed a wicked smile. "What is it, Lyssie? Do you suddenly have doubts who you're with?" His laughter mocked me. "Who am I, Gray or Ryan? Huh?"

I *did* have doubts, but that wasn't the reason I'd stopped the advance. I searched his face for the signs I'd felt would always distinguish the twins but emotion clouded my vision. My eyes flew to his right arm, but it was covered by a long-sleeved shirt.

"Uh, uh, darling, that's cheating," he taunted me. "You've been in both of our arms, kissed us. Surely you can tell the difference."

I yanked back and stumbled into the desk chair. I didn't understand the game he was playing. The passion and fire in his eyes had been replaced by a wild, dangerous look that frightened me. I no longer found him intriguing or desirable, and I desperately wanted to escape. But I'd backed myself into a corner, and the only exit was blocked by this man that had become a stranger.

"Please—" My voice sounded small and weak.

"Afraid, Lyssie? A moment ago we were kissing. You were ready to give yourself to me. How can you be afraid?" He loomed over me, placing a hand on either side of the chair to further block me in.

"Why are you doing this?" Tears burned in my eyes, my throat tightened. "I—I don't understand."

"Don't you? I think you understand perfectly. You've been toying with us from the moment you arrived."

"No!"

"Oh yes you were. Do you think we didn't know what you were up to? Do you think we're fools?"

I was really crying now. I tried to stop, tried to push back the emotion and find the strength to shove the man away, but I was helpless, unable to do either.

Please, Father, I prayed.

I felt ashamed, ridiculous for allowing myself to fall in love with Gray, to have cared for either of the twins. I wanted to run and hide like Dee, so that I didn't have to face him—or myself.

He shoved angrily at the chair, raised his hands in the air and shouted an obscenity. He turned away from me, walking toward the door with a barely perceptible limp which still didn't reveal his identity.

"I'm sorry," he said without turning. "I didn't mean to frighten you." He sighed deeply, a sound that seemed to come from his very soul. "It's been another long, hard day. Go to bed, Lyssie." He went into the hall, and I listened to the sound of his footsteps as they continued into the foyer—Gray?

When I heard the opening and closing of the front door, I ran from the room as if it were on fire. I took the stairs two at a time, dashed down the corridor and through the open door of my suite, locking the door behind me. I yanked a heavy occasional chair across the room, wedged it beneath the knob, then collapsed on the floor where I stood.

My body trembled uncontrollably, and I curled up in a ball, hugging my knees against my chest. I felt frightened, humiliated, and furious.

Tears flowed again, and as I lay there on the floor, I swore that I'd never again be used in such a way.

Chapter 19

Diana helped Craven into the house, his occasional hesitations and deep intakes of breath evidence of how badly he'd been injured. She eased him onto a sofa in the drawing room where a weak fire still burned in the hearth. After throwing on a few more logs and stirring up the embers, she went in search of medicine and bandages.

When she returned, Craven was where she had left him, his face pale and drawn. As she began to gently bathe away the blood covering his face, his dark eyes flew open to stare at her in surprise. A strong hand reached out and took hold of hers as she began to mop his brow.

"Thank you, Diana." Their eyes met and locked. Before Diana knew what was happening, she was within his embrace, crushed against his chest, his mouth hungrily seeking hers. For a moment she gave in to the ecstasy, but then she pulled sharply back.

"If you please, sir," she said, indignant. "I tend you only to make you well for your hanging."

His laugh was gruff as he drew the slight girl back into his arms. "You tend me because, in spite of yourself, you love me . . ."

The ringing of the phone followed me as I struggled upward from sleep. I awoke to find myself still on the floor of the sitting room, the predawn light filtering weakly through the windows. The air seemed colder than it should be, and I hugged myself in an effort to warm my body.

The phone rang again, and by the time I managed to lift myself off the floor, Dee came out of the bedroom rubbing the sleep from her eyes.

"There's some man on the phone askin' for you," she yawned. "Why are you in here?"

I gave her a weak excuse that she appeared to accept, then went to answer the phone. I was surprised to hear Mac's voice.

"Lyssie, thank you, Father. I was afraid I'd get one of the twins." His voice shook slightly. "Now, don't panic—Pier's been in an accident. She's in the hospital, but she's all right."

"How—"

"Please, just listen, ok?" He paused and drew in a deep breath. "She's been so agitated the last couple of hours that not even the sedatives are working. She insists she needs to talk to you right away."

"Dee and I will leave as soon as we're dressed," I promised, shivering as much from apprehension as from the chill in the air.

I got directions to the hospital and, hanging up the

phone, gently broke the news to a still groggy Dee. She watched through half-closed eyes as I pulled on jeans and a T-shirt and then followed me in a daze down to her room. After she was dressed, she was adamant that we couldn't leave until she had her 'favorite sweater,' a bright yellow cable knit that made her pale skin appear even paler. As Dee pulled the sweater on over arms covered with gooseflesh, she asked the same question that had been running through my mind: Why was it so cold?

While I retrieved my purse from the suite, Dee ran back to hers and returned with her Baby Dylan doll, clutching it tightly as if a safeguard against further unpleasant developments. I tried to put her mind at ease, attempted to entice her with a promise of breakfast at McDonalds, but the offer was received with little enthusiasm; the child was too worried and exhausted to care about anything other than her aunt.

We reached the bottom of the staircase as Sarah Williams came in the front door. She started at the sight of us.

"Cook's sick, so I thought I'd help out for a couple hours," she told us, pulling her key from the lock. "What are you two doing up so early? It's not even six yet."

"Pier's been in an accident. We're on our way to the hospital." Dee yawned again, and I flashed an entreaty at Sarah. "There doesn't seem to be anyone else around, so I had to get Dee ready to go with me. Now you're here—"

"I'll be happy to watch her," she assured me, holding a hand out to Dee. "Just one thing, Miss Daniels. I'd like to be out of here by ten, with the holiday and all. I only came because the Merricks are gone. I thought I'd fix breakfast and put together a casserole for your dinner."

"No problem." I kissed Dee on the forehead and tousled her hair. "You go ahead with Sarah, sweetheart, and she'll get you something to eat. Maybe afterward you could take a little nap. Ok?"

"What about Pier?" Dee's lower lip quivered.

"I'll give her your love." She nodded and took hold of Sarah's outstretched hand. "You might have one of the twins check the air-conditioning, Sarah. It's freezing in here."

Sarah Williams rolled her eyes. "Something's always wrong with those units. They're so old; they should be replaced. Oh well, I'll pass along the info. Let me know if there's anything Pier needs."

I thanked her again, asked if she'd tell the twins about the accident, then hurried out the door and down to the garage.

The sky still looked threatening, grey and overcast with a promise of more rain and storms to come—not a very nice day to celebrate July 4th. Water continued to drip from the trees, a sign the rain hadn't stopped long ago, and the north wind brought a drop in the humidity making the air cooler than it had been in days. Small puddles had formed on the hood and trunk of my car, and as I opened the door, a spray of rainwater drenched my arm as it drained from the car roof.

I drove into Bristol with the radio blasting, not wanting to give into disquieting thoughts. As I followed Mac's directions to the hospital, my insides felt like jelly, keyed up and anxious. No matter what had happened between us in the last few days, Pier Foxxe was still one of the best friends I'd ever had. The thought was rather sobering and made me wonder why I'd never realized it before. The years spent apart could not erase all the things we'd shared during those four years at college. Yes, she could be difficult, impossible at times, but she'd always been there for me. It was surprising to realize I'd been able to count on her, even trust her, in a way I'd never done with anyone else—not even Dr. Hadley.

Please, Father, surround Pier with your love and your healing.

Pier would be all right. She had to be.

The hospital was a modern structure built with several wings jutting out from a central hub. It was quiet inside with no one at the information counter to offer assistance. I kept to Mac's instructions and found my way to the small lounge outside the cluster of rooms where they'd placed Pier.

Mac's face was tightly drawn, the grey eyes behind the photo-ray glasses strained and tense. He held out his arms, and I took his hands and squeezed them. I got the feeling from his expression that he was attempting to restore his strength before tackling an explanation.

"She came to my office at the college yesterday all shook up, ranting and not making a bit of sense," he finally said. "I hated leaving her but had some late classes and didn't have a choice. I gave her the key to my apartment and told her to go there and try to relax. By the time I got home, she seemed a lot better. I mean," he raked a hand through his hair. "*She asked me to pray with her*. That's never happened before. We were both in tears when we were finished. I was jubilant."

As he brushed at the tears in his eyes, I noticed his rumpled demeanor. "That's a start," I said, offering him a smile of encouragement.

Mac nodded. "Yeah, it is. But then I made a mistake by taking her out to dinner. We ran into her brothers, one right after the other, and the arguments . . . Pier went off in a huff, and by the time I got back to my apartment, she was already half drunk." He paced the length of the room, his tall, lanky body bent under the strain.

"I tried to calm her, to get her to tell me what was going on. She just talked in circles. There was something about her father's will not being the only thing missing from Foxxemoor, that his crash wasn't an accident. Those were the most coherent statements I got from her." His eyes appealed to me for understanding. "The more I questioned her, the more agitated she became." Again, his hand raked through his hair. "I thought I'd hidden her keys so she wouldn't find them, but I was wrong. She tore out in the middle of the storm. Next thing I know, it's three-thirty and the sheriff's at my door telling me she's been brought here in an ambulance. Pier asked them to contact me instead of her family, then clammed up until I arrived." He swallowed hard. "Her car's totaled, and from what they said, it's a miracle she's alive."

The fear that had been building as he spoke clutched at my chest, and I had to force my voice up through a raw throat. "D-did they say what happened?"

He shook his head. "No, but Pier insists she didn't have any brakes." He stopped to look at me when a small sound escaped me, a question in his eyes. "What's wrong, Lyssie?"

"It's just . . . that's what happened to Ryan and their father." I moved away from him, my mind racing. Both twins had been down at the garage in the last twenty-four hours, and Dee had told me that Gray had been 'doing something' to Pier's car. Coincidence? A dreadful feeling told me it wasn't.

I turned to find Mac watching me suspiciously, and I faltered under his gaze.

"Lyssie—" At the sound of a door opening behind me, his attention was drawn away. "Marjory, wait." He touched my arm. "I'll be right back."

He joined the nurse outside the closed door to the room I assumed Pier occupied. I watched as they conferred, my mind whirling.

Two accidents in the same family, both caused by faulty brakes. Initial investigation of the first accident had shown a possibility of foul play. The case had been dropped, but was it because of Margaret's interference rather than from a lack of sufficient evidence? Had it been pursued, as Dr. Hadley's sources suggested it should have been, would the authorities have found that Edward Foxxe's death was a planned and deliberate act of murder? And was the same perpetrator now after the rest of the family?

My chest felt constricted, my breath coming in short, halting gasps. Noticing a water fountain nearby, I went to get a drink, determined to calm down. I wouldn't give in to my fears or let on that I knew more than Mac had told me. Not yet, not until I had something more substantial on which to base my suspicions. All I had was supposition and conjecture, and speaking prematurely would just cause more problems.

Calm. Calm.

Father, help me to have ears to hear, eyes to see, and a mind to discern the truth.

Pier had been drunk, upset, and could've imagined brake failure simply because she'd been too impaired to apply them. With the roads slick from the rain and her penchant for fast driving, anything was possible. It didn't mean that someone had tried to kill her.

Mac returned to my side, his kind eyes filled with concern.

"She's still fighting the sedatives. Fighting the staff, period. Marjory is giving you ten minutes with her. I pray to God you can calm her down."

He accompanied me to the door of the room, opened it, and as I passed him, I saw the anxious glance he gave the figure in the bed.

"I'll be right out here if you need me." He gave me a weak smile before closing the door behind me.

I didn't like hospitals, their cold sterility made me shrink up inside with the memory of watching helplessly as my father lay dying. Now, as I looked about the plain little room and at Pier's small form in the bed, a cold shiver ran along the base of my spine.

Focus, I told myself sharply. Forget the past and concentrate on the present.

I touched Pier's hand, and her eyes flew open. They were rimmed with red, their normally bright color pale and washed out. She clutched my hand and drew me onto the bed next to her.

"S-sorry f-for," her speech was slurred and tears streamed from her eyes and down her cheeks. "D-didn't want to hurt you," she sighed heavily. "Th-they gave me some—thing, and I can't think str-straight. Please listen."

"It's all right, Pier. Don't worry—"

She shook her head. "Must—talk. Must. Mar'gret knew about money, sus-suspected the rest. She, she said she'd g-go to authorities unless I helped her." She swallowed hard and reached for the glass of water on the bed table. I got it for her, and after she'd taken some through a straw, she pushed it away.

"Sh-she wanted you for Dee," she struggled to continue, her eyes rolling to the back of her head. "I prom-promised to take care of both. Got you, but he wouldn't listen, didn't care. Just laughed." She gave me a ghost of a smile.

Putting my hand on her arm, I tried to tell her it was all right, but it was obvious there was more on her mind than an apology. I could see she was working hard to keep unconsciousness at bay.

"Brakes-not-there." She said in one breath. "He-he's scared, angry because I found out." Her eyes closed, and her head moved, revealing the large bandage that covered the left side of her face. An angry purple bruise spread from beneath it down to her chin.

"Who's scared, Pier?" I asked, my voice far steadier than I felt. "Who are you talking about?"

She didn't answer and after a few minutes, I tried to release my hand from her grasp. Her fingers closed even more tightly around mine.

"No! D-don't go, must understand. D-daddy," her eyes fluttered open and filled with tears. "He found out, m-made a new will. They needed him gone. He— Dylan. Some-something to do with company, with money—lost too much. They wanted it back." She rolled her head from side to side, her anger at being unable to express her thoughts properly was obvious. "Guessed. Money, gam-gambling. S-said would help, wouldn't tell," she gulped back a sob. "Furious, didn't trust me," she drew in a deep breath. "Should've stayed, should've told. Knew he was des-desperate. Didn't think, didn't believe he would, would—"

"Who Pier?" My heart thudded against my ribs, every intake of breath getting shorter and shorter. Thoughts tumbled over one another in an avalanche of confusion. I wasn't certain if she'd heard me, so I shook her arm in an effort to rouse her. "You have to tell me who you're talking about, Pier, or I can't help you."

Pier's grip tightened, her nails digging into my hand, her eyes suddenly wild. "Dee? Where?" Panic rose in her, and as she attempted to rise, I eased her back onto the pillows.

"It's all right. Sarah's with her till I get back." I could tell this didn't reassure her. "Pier, who are you so afraid of?"

"He—money bad enough, but then Daddy—" she sobbed, struggling to keep her eyes open and maintain the consciousness that seemed to be ebbing away. "Will do anything—needs papers to protect himself from *her*. Oh dear God, *please*." She pulled me down until my head was next to hers. "Dylan is making him sc-scared, more desperate. *Don't let him hurt anyone else*." So much energy was expended by this last statement that she had no strength left. Pier closed her eyes, and within seconds her breathing slowed as her body finally accepted the soothing release the sedatives offered.

That one of the twins was gambling and stealing from the company came through clearly. Pier implied that her father's discovery of this information resulted in his death. And having confronted the guilty party, Pier now lay in the hospital, lucky to be alive and terrified what her brother might do next. I could go to the authorities, but she hadn't given me his identity . . .

I refused to accept the likely candidate, recoiled from the thought that either of the twins could be guilty of such heinous acts.

But I had seen the penchant for violence, felt the cold fire in his eyes, the power of his grasp.

"Needs papers to protect himself from her." Pier's words resounded in my brain.

Dee had those papers.

I flew off the bed and ran from the room. Mac tried to hold me and calm me down. I shook him off, told him to stay with Pier, then sprinted down the corridor and out of the hospital as fast as I could.

Confusion and disbelief drove me through Bristol, past the town square where sodden July 4th decorations hung drooping from last night's storm, and beyond to the blacktop that led to Foxxemoor Lane. Scenery flew by, colors mixing into a blur as my eyes remained on the road before me. Fear and caution were thrown aside as my foot pressed the accelerator, pushing the car to speeds that were far from safe for that narrow, country road. Up a hill and around a bend and I slammed the brake pedal to the floor as I spotted a tractor and baler just a few feet in front of me. The car skidded, fish-tailing on the still wet pavement, and my brain reacted automatically, turning into the skid and then coming to a dead stop in the middle of the road.

My heart beat a staccato within my chest as I eased the car back into motion. It wouldn't help anyone if I got into an accident. I had to regain control of myself.

Besides, Sarah Williams had agreed to remain with Dee until I returned. It was a little past eight-thirty, so she'd not be in a hurry to leave. She'd be there. She *had* to be.

The final approach to Foxxemoor seemed to take forever. In my present state, a minute seemed like an hour with every second agonizingly slow. I managed to get myself under control, a necessity if I was to successfully take hold of the situation. If what Pier intimated was true, and one of the twins was responsible for their father's death, then I needed to devise a plan to get Dee out of harm's way. With Margaret, Pier, and the Merricks away, I didn't think it would be wise for the child and me to remain under the same roof as the twins.

I pulled in front of the garage, threw the car into park, and was heading toward the house in the blink of an eye. Nearing the fountain, a movement from the roof of the south wing caught my attention. A bright yellow object was hooked over the broken railing of the widow's walk, which was now suspended precariously in the air. The object flapped in the wind, its vivid color in stark comparison to the overcast morning: Dee's sweater!

I sprinted into the house, calling for Sarah as I raced through the front door. I took the stairs two at a time and, reaching the top, was panting so hard I was forced to rest for a moment. Again, I yelled for Sarah, my voice more of a gasp than anything substantial as I continued to stumble through the entrance to the south wing. A hand on the wall guided my steps and helped me remain upright.

That couldn't be Dee's sweater; she'd promised not to go up there. She'd *promised.*

I hadn't thought to check the area beneath the widow's walk; some instinct had propelled me without thought. Now, stumbling down the hallway, I hoped, prayed that if it *was* Dee's sweater on the railing, she'd managed to pull back from the edge in time, that she was waiting up there alone and frightened, hoping someone would come for her.

The door to my suite was open, and as I started past, I glanced in to see one of the twins standing over the desk, going through the drawers. Seeing me, his expression was like that of a small boy with his hand caught in a cookie jar. He shoved the drawer shut, and seemed about to speak when I blurted out, "Dee's on the widow's walk. The rail is broken—"

He rushed by me—Gray?—a blur of red shirt and blue jeans and ran down the hallway. I followed in his wake, my breath coming a little easier so that I no longer needed the wall for support. He was already up the stairs by the time I reached them, and I climbed quickly upward. I was on the top step when his cry came to me.

"No, my dear God, no!"

My heart felt as if it had been ripped from my chest. "W-what?" My stomach backed up into my throat as the unthinkable suddenly became a possibility.

"No, no, it can't be." His anguished moans brought me out onto the widow's walk, my fear of heights no longer an issue.

Terrified, tears filling my eyes, I moved a step closer to where he knelt at the edge of the roof.

"Please—"

He stood slowly and turned to me, a forlorn expression upon his face. His outstretched hands clutched Dee's sweater. I met his eyes, their darkness bright with unshed tears. I shook my head, unable to believe or accept what he was telling me.

"Lyssie," he pleaded.

Father, please . . . I prayed as I went to him, and he took me in his arms. I leaned into him, needing the strength and comfort we could give one another. Instead of tenderness, I found myself in an iron grip, held as in a vise. Confused, I struggled to get away. His hold on me tightened, and as he spoke, his mouth against my ear, a shudder of terror raced throughout my body.

"Did you have a good visit with Pier, darling? Did you find it enlightening?"

An involuntary gasp signaled I had some idea what he was referring to, and he swung me roughly around until my back was against his chest. My arms, pinned behind me, were jerked up painfully.

"Now, sweetheart, we're going to talk." The voice in my ear was cold and hard.

"I don't—"

One of his hands grabbed hold of my hair and shoved my head forward, forcing me to look over the edge. I closed my eyes, refusing to look down, more terrified of what I might see below me than of the height.

"Dee and I had a brief discussion awhile ago, and she informed me that she'd given you her mother's papers. Unfortunately, we were interrupted before I could get her to tell me where they were. She took advantage of the situation and ran off." He kissed my cheek and laughed, a venomous sound that had nothing to do with mirth. "All you have to do is tell me where they are, and I'll let you go."

Could I believe him about Dee? Was she really all right?

He twisted my arm again, and I cried out in pain. "Come on, Lyssie, let's get on with it. I'm getting impatient and I'm not at my best that way."

"I don't have them!" I screamed. "S-she didn't—"

"I'm not in the mood for games, Lysette. Dee may not be much, but she's not a liar. Perhaps you need a little more persuasion." He drug me over to where the broken railing hung suspended above the ground and forced me to kneel before it. I kept my eyes closed, commanding myself not to panic.

"I realize this may seem excessive to you, but after Pier's betrayal, you can understand that I have no other choice. I need Dylan's things, Lysette. Now, before my dear sister has the chance to spread any more of her malicious slander."

"Please, I don't—"

"It would be so easy to let you fall. All I'd have to do is let go." His voice was silken, the laugh maniacal. "The first time is always the hardest. My father, then . . ." Another laugh as he bent down, his mouth against my ear. "By now I'm a pro, Lyssie, so don't tempt me." I was shoved forward on my knees and felt when they left the safety of the roof. "*Now where in hell are those papers!*"

"Are these what you're looking for?" A voice came from behind us, and I was brought roughly to my feet and swung around to face the other twin.

I searched his face, but the man in the tan cotton shirt and jeans opposite us gave me no clue to his identity. His handsome face was as hard as granite, and the hand that held a wad of folded papers in his fist was equally as threatening.

"Do you propose a trade?" The twin behind me mocked.

Thunder rumbled in the distance, an ominous sound that made me tremble. The twin across from us retracted the outstretched arm. He raised an expressive eyebrow.

"Makes sense, doesn't it? I've something you want—"

"And I've something *you* want." We maneuvered away from the edge and toward the center of the widow's walk. "You think I don't know what's been going on between you two? Come, brother dear, don't play me for a fool. You tried that with Dylan, remember?"

"As I recall, we both got burned."

A laugh filled with sarcasm. "If only you knew! No, bro, you were burned, I was only slightly singed. How could it be any other way with our lovely Dylan? Now, Lyssie here, is another matter." He whirled me around, kissed me, then shoved me away from him so abruptly I fell, skinning my hands and tearing the knees of my jeans on the rough surface.

I gulped back a sob and turned to find the twins squaring off. The twin in the tan shirt folded the papers and stuffed them into his back pocket.

"You knew it wouldn't be that easy, didn't you? You've been awaiting a moment like this all our lives," the red twin said.

They circled one another as a distant roar of thunder echoed through the valley, muffling the wail of a siren somewhere in the distance.

"Payback? That's your game, not mine. I'm through with the competing, the fighting. I've known what you were doing, the gambling and petty thievery. And like Father, was even willing to look the other way when you juggled the books—until it was no longer petty. Embezzlement's a different matter. And when the implication points in my direction—"

"You can't prove a thing. You or Pier." Red advanced and Tan dodged to within a few feet of me.

I backed out of their way, my eyes never leaving their faces, still trying to distinguish one from the other. I huddled against the wall to the third floor, ready to dash for the open trap door.

"Dylan could prove it, though, couldn't she?" Tan taunted. "And Father. That's why he drew up the new will—"

"What 'new' will? Only one I know about is the one Margaret delivered to probate."

"Which one of you set fire to the law office? I'll bet it was Dylan. She liked to watch things burn. But the brakes on the Caddy—"

Red flew at his brother, and the twins were in a huddle, fists flying. One of them slipped and took both of them down to roll about on the roof as they pummeled one another with their fists. The twin in red landed a blow to his brother's chin, the sound of knuckles meeting jawbone making my own jaw clench in pain. The force of the hit stunned Tan, and seeing his chance, the aggressor spun around and sat astride his brother. He held back Tan's arms by pinning them against the roof with knees and hands, laughing maniacally as he stared down into his captive's face.

"You were never good at wrestling, bro, took too

much pride in fairness."

"Take the papers and go!" The other twin spat out, blood from a cut lip trickling down his chin.

"Oh, I'll go. I've no choice, after all." A fist came up and slugged the helpless man in the face. "I owed you that for all the years of having your 'perfection' thrown in my face." The sarcastic laughter was accompanied by a sneer that reflected an all consuming hatred. "Perfect? Far from it! Not perfect enough to hold on to Dylan or father her child. But I was. You and that self-righteous, sanctimonious father who thought he could just write me out of his life—but the old man got his. And Dylan," Red laughed as he smashed his fist into his brother's face. "Dylan thought she could hold Dee and the kid's inheritance over my head, thought it gave her some kind of leverage. But I showed her, and now it's your turn." Confident of his power, he released his hold to go for the papers and was flipped over onto his back. As Tan attempted to right himself, wiping blood from his eyes, Red regained his feet and charged. Contact propelled the two dangerously close to the area where the railing had broken away. They landed on their knees, skidding to a stop, both clutching at the other's throat.

"Dee's down there, brother, all broken and mangled. She fell through—"

"Don't believe him!" I shouted, sure he was lying. "He was furious because she ran off and hid."

The twin in red chuckled. "And if you believe that, I have some property—"

Hands grasped at throats, gouged at eyes as they both stumbled to their feet and attempted to retain their holds. They were covered with blood and sweat, their shirts torn, with abrasions visible on backs and arms. Fighting and violence was always frightening, but watching these men who where mirror images of one another, a true part of the other, was a travesty, a freak show that made no sense.

I heard shouting and realized with a start that it was coming from me, the words repeated over and over again until I was hoarse. "Stop! Dear God, make them stop!"

Red's sardonic laughter rang in time with a roll of thunder and the sirens that were steadily drawing nearer. Amid the blood, a smile touched his lips.

"Our girlfriend is worried about us. How about we call a truce, you give me the papers nice and easy, and I make like Dylan and disappear?"

"Mamma?" Dee's voice called out.

I saw Red's eyes grow large, a look of astonishment and disbelief on his face as he released the hold on his brother.

"Mamma?"

The word seemed to hover in the air around us. Tan, sensing his freedom, backed away from Red, away from the perilous position near the broken railing. The other twin didn't move, seemed to barely breathe, his eyes fastened on the door to the third floor that was behind me.

"It's not possible," Red's voice quavered with a palpable fear. He shook his head and thrust a hand out before him.

I heard what I thought was the sound of a bolt lock being drawn back, and the door behind me creaked.

We saw it at the same time, Tan and I, Red's backing away, the look of terror in his eyes. I tried to jump to my feet and run to him, but I was frozen to the spot, unable to even turn my head to see who was at the door. My heart broke as I witnessed the failed effort of one twin to save the other. The remaining twin groped uselessly at the empty air where his brother had stood a moment before. Time seemed to stand still as the helpless cry echoed hollowly across the valley and was followed by a sickening thud as the body hit the ground.

"No!" Tan cried, peering over the ledge, his fist pounding against rough shingles and making his knuckles bleed anew. He rolled over onto his back and cursed the heavens as a clap of thunder sounded from directly overhead.

"Mamma!" Dee's plaintive voice echoed from below, and realization spurred me into action.

I scrambled to my feet, turning around to face the attic door and backing away as quickly as possible. A gust of wind pushed at the door, and it creaked open a little further. My eyes were riveted to the spot, to the window that had been just above my head. Thick, black, impenetrable darkness was all that was visible beyond, and nothing, no one stood in the partially opened doorway.

My hand flew to my mouth, and I cried out as I was touched from behind. I tried to pull away, but a firm, gentle hand held me. Turning around, I faced the remaining twin.

Blood and bruises covered his face, but I found recognition in the dark blue eyes. But how could I trust senses that had repeatedly betrayed me?

Gentle fingers touched my face, and eyes brimming with tears stared down into mine. "Are you all right?"

The words were scratchy as they came from his bruised throat, but the fear and concern for me were crystal clear.

I nodded, taking hold of the hand that caressed my face. "Is he—"

He looked away, a shudder coursing through his body. "I'm pretty sure. We should go—"

The wail of sirens as they headed down the lane toward the house reverberated in the air around us.

"How—"

"Lyssie?" Dee, clutching her Baby Dylan in one hand and a bound packet of papers in the other, emerged on the top step below the trap door. She looked from one of us to the other, then scanned the widow's walk with her dark eyes.

"Why are you all bloody?" She demanded. Then, without waiting for an answer, her face fell, and she asked plaintively, "Uncle Gray, have you seen my mamma?"

Chapter 20

When an envoy from London arrived with a special dispatch, everything Craven had told her suddenly became a reality. It had been difficult for Diana to believe he had been working undercover for the military—a double agent sworn to secrecy! Who could have imagined anyone as self-serving as Leo Craven involved in an elaborate plan to protect the coast from a possible invasion by Boney's forces? But then, who else but Craven could take the locals' fear and turn it to his advantage?

Somehow, spies within the organization had broken his cover—Diana had witnessed the murder of one of them. Now, released from his commission, Craven was at loose ends. Furious at this turn of events, he roamed about the great house and estate glowering at everyone. No matter what Diana and Mrs. Rhodes did, Craven refused to stay down long enough for his injuries to heal. Leo Craven had plans, and until they were carried out, he would not be still.

As the days and weeks went by, Diana soon became aware of what Craven had in mind. With rumors abounding, the diabolical master of Craven decided to turn a new leaf and show his benevolence to the people. The man's sudden change of heart was looked upon with suspicion, and then taken at face value with news of the upcoming nuptials.

Now, as Diana lost herself within the loving embrace of her new husband, a sigh of contentment emitted from the master of Craven. His lips hungrily sought hers as he pulled her firmly against his chest. As they gave themselves to the ecstasy, Diana knew with certainty that life with him would never fail to be exciting.

What seemed a continuous roar of thunder was now accompanied by fat raindrops that exploded on impact with the roof. We clung to each another, Gray, Dee, and I, as we made our way through the trap door and into the storeroom below. Dee's question still echoed in our ears, her constant chatter as we continued on to my suite adding to the confusion and horror of what had just transpired. Nothing seemed capable of penetrating the fog in my brain or erasing the terror I'd seen in Ryan's eyes just before he fell. The vision of his broken body lying out in the storm was far more important than the possibility that Dylan might be somewhere in the house. But there was something in Dee's words that soon had me hanging on every syllable. And when she related how she thought she'd seen Dylan going up the stairs to the third floor, even Gray's head snapped to attention.

"It was right afore I told Uncle Gray to find you, Lyssie, how I knew where you were." Dee told me with pride. But as much as she'd wanted to see her mother, the child could not bring herself to follow her.

"You know how I hate the dark *and* the spiders," she said, her nose wrinkling with characteristic disgust. "I called for Mamma to wait, but I guess she didn't hear me." Her narrow shoulders sagged as a new thought struck home. "She wouldn't just go away again, would she?"

Dee stopped on the threshold of the sitting room and held us there with a silent plea in her eyes.

As tears formed and threatened to fall, Gray knelt before the child and took her gently into his arms. "If she's here, honey, if it wasn't just wishful thinking, she'll stay." The look we exchanged over the top of Dee's head revealed the same confusion I felt.

Had the sight of Dylan in the doorway to the widow's walk caused Ryan's fall?

Words that had been meant as reassurance failed to hit their mark, and the child's inner turmoil surfaced with an abrupt withdrawal from Gray's arms. Tears streamed down her face as she stared up at him with a silent accusation. He reached out to her, but she pulled back, flinging her arms out before her.

"I seen her shadow," Dee sputtered, gulping back a sob. "It was there in the hallway with the butterfly. It was how I knowed Lyssie was on the window's walk and needed you." She stood there, blinded by tears, just wanting us to believe her. Refusing to be comforted, Dee threw herself upon the sofa and poured out her anguish in muffled sobs.

Gray's eyes appealed to me for assistance, his

scratched and bloodied face displaying his own raw emotions. It was clear how torn he was, but no matter how badly we felt for Dee, there was a far more pressing matter before us.

I gathered the child in my arms and offered soothing words to calm her. She allowed me to hold her as she clung tightly to her doll, but the packet of papers she still held was flung toward Gray. He picked it up from the floor, threw me a look of apology, and left the room.

Thunder roared and the wind whipped mercilessly at the trees outside my windows, rattling the screens and howling eerily through the cracks and crevices of the house. The sirens were now just outside, and within moments, the door chimes added to the cacophony of sounds.

Gradually, Dee recovered enough to relate how Ryan accosted her shortly after I'd left that morning. Somehow, she'd managed to wriggle free and run in search of Sarah—Ryan in hot pursuit. During the confrontation between the two adults, Dee had made her escape, fleeing to my rooms and hiding in the back of the closet.

"Mamma told me once that God talks to you sometimes if you're real quiet. I was prayin' in my head so's Ryan wouldn't know where I was," she told me, gulping back her sobs.

From her vantage point, she'd heard Ryan tearing apart the suite, his ranting about her mother, and my terrified cry of "Dee is up on the widow's walk."

"I wanted to tell you I was ok, but, but I was scared." She lowered her eyes at the memory. "And then I heard Him, Lyssie, saying to help save Mamma."

"Him?"

Dee's dark blue eyes sparkled as she nodded. "Uh huh. God. He said to wait 'til I couldn't hear your footsteps. Then, I came outta the closet to get someone to help you. That's when I seen Mamma's shadow and the butterfly." She swiped at her tears with the back of her hand. "I don't know how my sweater got up on the window's walk," she said fervently, her large eyes meeting mine. "Honest I don't. Last time I saw it was when I was eatin' breakfast in the kitchen. I didn't go up there, Lyssie. I kept my promise."

"Of course you did." I hugged her to me. "You did the right thing, honey, going to get Gray. I'm very proud of you." I was about to ask her about her mother and the reference she kept making about a butterfly, when she tugged anxiously at my arm.

"What's the sirens for, Lyssie? And why is Uncle Gray all bloody?"

"I'll explain later, ok? Right now, I want you to do me a big favor and stay here so I can go downstairs and help your uncle."

Her dark eyes, still bright with tears, regarded me solemnly. With a deep sigh, she agreed to stay put, and I left her in the safety of my suite.

Mac was in the living room, pacing nervously from the door to the rear window and back again. Seeing me, he rushed to my side and took my hands in his as he studied me gravely.

"Is Dee all right? Are you hurt?" He noticed my torn jeans and bleeding knees and bent to check them out.

"It's ok, Mac, really. Dee's upstairs. She doesn't know what's happened." I stared down to where he still knelt before me. "How, how did you know to—"

"Bring the cavalry? After you stormed out of the hospital, I got to thinking about Pier's rantings, and it was like a light going on. She was out, didn't need me, but you might. I couldn't sit there knowing you and Dee were alone with a man who'd attempted to kill his sister—and had likely caused the death of his own father." He rose and led me over to the sofa, easing me onto it as if I were seriously injured. "I arrived at the sheriff's office within minutes of their getting the report on Pier's car." He nodded. "The bleeder screws had been loosened, just like the Cadillac's had been. My disjointed story might not have carried much weight if Sarah Williams hadn't called to report that Ryan had gone off the deep end. He ordered her out of the house, threatened to fire her for coming between him and Dee when he was trying to discipline her. Craziness." Mac shook his head. "My biggest fear was not getting here in time."

Just then, Gray and the sheriff entered the room. Mac and I looked up to find the two men shaking hands.

"It looks like Miss Courtney had enough to put him away for a long time. From what we have here, I'd say your brother was involved with some heavy duty characters, most likely mob related. We'll be working in conjunction with the Bristol PD, do some more digging. We'll be in touch."

A deputy came into the room, drew the sheriff aside and conferred with him. I took the opportunity to go to Gray and offer my support. As I slipped my hand into his cold, damp one, he gave me a weak smile.

"His neck," he choked out the words, tears filling

his eyes.

"I'm sorry." I put my arms around him and held him close. He clung to me in much the same way Dee had a few minutes earlier.

"He called me perfect," he said in my ear. "*Me*, the flawed twin. I had no idea, no idea he felt that way."

"Um, excuse me, Mr. Foxxe. We checked out the attic, and there's nothing there. As a matter of fact, from the dust on the floor, my men are able to definitively state that there hasn't been anyone up there for quite some time—no marks on the floor, nothing. Seems the bolt on the door to the widow's walk is broken. My guess is the wind must have forced the door open." The sheriff spread his hands in apology. "As for the little girl seeing her mother, I'd have to say it's her imagination working overtime. There's no one else in the house." The sheriff held his hand back out to Gray. "I'm really sorry about your brother, Mr. Foxxe."

Gray took the proffered hand. "Yeah, me too." His voice broke on the words.

I walked the sheriff to the door and thanked him for his assistance. As I closed the door behind him, a scraping on the stairs caught my attention, and I looked up to see Dee sitting on the top step. When our eyes met, she turned quickly away, rose, and ran down the hallway to the south wing. I started up the staircase after her when the events of the past few hours and days hit me with such force that I sank to my knees.

Ryan was dead, a confessed murderer and more. Ryan, who had always been so kind and gentle to me, solicitous of my feelings, and quick to declare his love for me. Had he cared as he'd claimed, or had it been part of the game he was playing? It was difficult to associate that loving man to the one who had ruthlessly dragged me to the edge of the widow's walk and threatened to shove me off.

And what about Pier's fear for Dee? Had it been founded in reality? Were the incidents involving her swing and favorite tree not the accidents we thought them to be, but a deliberate act by a desperate man, a man out to get his child's inheritance?

My breath came raggedly as I recalled the tiny piece of orange material Mrs. Merrick had discovered in the child's milk, Dee's comments that it had tasted funny, and her illness after having just a little of it. Could it have been the remnants of medication as the housekeeper suspected? And if it was, that would mean that Ryan had tried—

Some things did not bear thinking. Besides, the answers had likely died with Ryan.

I looked up to the head of the staircase, indecisive, all energy drained from my body. The beauty and opulence of the house struck me as strongly as it had on my first day here, but it could no longer claim the peace and tranquility it once offered.

Foxxemoor, the 'bird of prey.' In the last three years, these walls had witnessed more heartache and despair than in its previous hundred. Pier had told me once that her ancestors were not the type to linger after death to haunt future generations. Perhaps that had been true before, but what about now?

With my hand on the banister, I pulled myself up, still uncertain of direction.

Déjà vu. That ever mysterious sense of having been in the exact same place before hit me with overwhelming force. Standing there, the tempo of my heart picked up as a memory flooded back to me.

I had stood here with uncertainty that day, unable to decide if I should go back to work on *Craven* or go to the stables for my first ride. I'd hesitated, facing neither up nor down, when Ryan had come into the hallway below. He'd been in a hurry, but had given me one of his engaging smiles and urged me to "Opt for playtime."

Tears burned in the corners of my eyes, tears for the waste of a life, tears for those he'd hurt, and for those he'd left behind to pick up the pieces. Foxxemoor may not have been haunted in the past, but I believed that was no longer true. There were memories around every corner, fresh and startlingly alive. Surely that was a form of haunting.

"I still don't get it," Mac's voice floated up from the hallway below. "How could he chance being in the car with your father that night? He could have been killed as well, unless—"

"That's the million dollar question, isn't it? His gambling losses, embezzlement, involvement with the mob, even torching the law office can be accepted as part of his desperation. But how could he be certain he'd survive the accident? How much of his injuries were real?" Gray cleared his throat, and as he came into view, he was limping badly. "They never found a reason for his inability to walk—it was vague and based on the pain Ryan said he was in. The whole accident report was based on what he told everyone." Gray sighed.

"It doesn't make sense."

"Maybe that was the point, *he* was in the car, *I* wasn't. If there was any suspicion, it would be directed at me. Anyway, we'll never be sure where the truth ended and the lies began."

Gray shook his head. Spotting me on the stairs, concern etched across his face. "Dee all right?"

"I, I'm not sure. She was on the steps when the sheriff left. When I caught her eye, she got up and ran down the hallway. Perhaps you, we, should go talk with her."

"Look, I've got to get back to the hospital before Pier wakes up. If I'm not there, she'll worry." Mac held out his hand.

"Take care of her." Gray clasped the other man's hand. "Tell her, no, *give* her my love."

"You got it."

The two men regarded one another for a moment. Whatever silent exchange was made, it was clear they had reached an understanding. With a smile and a nod, Mac left.

Gray took the stairs two at a time and reaching me, enfolded me in a quick embrace.

"Will you help me tell her about Ryan—" His voice broke, and he turned slightly away.

I put my arms around him and drew him back against me. "I'm here for you."

He held me tightly for a moment, and then in a hoarse voice said, "We need to see about Dee."

Hand in hand, we climbed the remaining stairs. As we turned into the south wing, I thought about all the pain and confusion Dee had been through during the last year. If I found it overwhelming, it was unimaginable what Dee must feel. She would need counseling, patience, and a lot of love and understanding, and I'd see that she got them. I clutched his hand tighter, and he gave mine a reassuring squeeze.

The door to the suite was still open, and we went in to find Dee standing in the bedroom doorway. She was so still it appeared as though she wasn't breathing. Afraid she'd gone into the same kind of catatonic state as on the morning of the butterflies, I placed a finger to my lips and motioned for Gray to quietly follow me. Under no circumstances should she be startled.

We tiptoed across the carpeting, though it was unnecessary since the carpet was so thick it absorbed every footfall. Still, our efforts had been in vain—Dee either heard or sensed our presence.

"Sh–look." Instead of her usual stage whisper, she'd managed a real one.

She didn't need to point or tell us where to look; it was immediately apparent what had captured her attention. A beautiful, majestic Monarch was on my pillow, its rich orange and black markings made even more dramatic against the white cotton case. Its delicate, laced wings fanned slowly up and down, its antenna moving in time.

Gray's hand turned cold and damp, and as he made a move forward, I tugged on his hand to hold him back.

I saw it happen as if in slow motion. The doll Dee was holding fell from her arms, bounced once on the thick carpeting, then landed against the door jamb. As the porcelain head of Baby Dylan shattered, the Monarch lifted gracefully from my pillow. It danced into the air above our heads and seemed to disappear as a flash of lightning lit the dim room.

Dee turned to face us, her large eyes luminous. She reached out, took one of Gray's hands and one of mine, joining them before her like some small minister presiding over a marriage ceremony.

"God says I need a daddy *and* a mommy." She grinned impishly, unconcerned with the smashed doll at her feet.

As Gray wrapped us both in his loving embrace, I felt a chill pass over me. It was there for a second, like a shadow passing before the sun, and then it was gone.

The butterfly reappeared above Dee's head, hovered for a moment, suspended in time and space, and in an instant, vanished before my eyes.

Bristol Gazette — September 12, 1998

Positive identification has been made on the remains of a young woman discovered by authorities early last month in the Lake of the Ozarks region. Police received confirmation on dental x-rays yesterday and have released information to the family of the deceased.

Dylan Courtney of Bristol, Missouri, had been missing since early January. Daughter of the late Phillip Courtney and Margaret Courtney Foxxe, she is survived by a six-year-old daughter. Miss Courtney is best remembered as the model and inspiration of FoxCo Toys' Dylan Doll series.

Although cause of death has not yet been released, individuals close to the department have stated the possibility of foul play . . .

ABOUT THE AUTHOR

Bio: 2010 ACFW Carol Award winning author, Alice K. Arenz, aka A.K. Arenz, has been writing since she was a child. Her earliest publication was in the small, family-owned newspaper where her articles, essays, and poems were frequently included. *The Case of the Mystified M.D.*, the second book in the Bouncing Grandma Mystery Series, was won the 2010 American Christian Fiction Writers Carol Award in Mystery. The first book in the series, *The Case of the Bouncing Grandma*, was a finalist in the 2009 Carol Awards contest. Both books were cozy mysteries. Her more serious mystery/suspense *Mirrored Image* was a 2011 finalist for the Carol Award in mystery.

Website: www.akawriter.com